Chaff Upon the Wind

Born in Gainsborough, Lincolnshire, Margaret Dickinson moved to the coast at the age of seven and so began her love for the sea and the Lincolnshire landscape. Her ambition to be a writer began early and she had her first novel published at the age of twenty-five. This was followed by many further titles including *Plough the Furrow*, *Sow the Seed* and *Reap the Harvest*, which make up her Lincolnshire Fleethaven Trilogy. She is also the author of *Welcome Home*, *The Buffer Girls* and *Daughters of Courage*. Margaret is a *Sunday Times* Top Ten bestseller.

Margaret Dickinson

Chaff Upon the Wind

PAN BOOKS

First published 1998 by Pan Books

This edition published 2017 by Pan Books
an imprint of Pan Macmillan
20 New Wharf Road, London N1 9RR
Associated companies throughout the world
www.panmacmillan.com

ISBN 978-1-5098-3915-5

1 3 5 7 9 8 6 4 2

A CIP catalogue record for this book is available from the British Library.

Typeset by SetSystems Ltd, Saffron Walden, Essex
Printed and bound by CPI Group (UK) Ltd, Croydon, CR0 4YY

Visit **www.panmacmillan.com** to read more about all our books
and to buy them. You will also find features, author interviews and
news of any author events, and you can sign up for e-newsletters
so that you're always first to hear about our new releases.

For Una and David

Acknowledgements

My very grateful thanks to all my friends at the Museum of Lincolnshire Life in Lincoln for their wonderful technical help and encouragement always and also for their kind permission to use *Sylvie*, the 1913 Ruston Proctor general purpose traction engine No. 46596, whose home is at the museum, as the model for Jack Thorndyke's threshing engine.

The Manor House in this novel has been inspired by the beautiful Manor House Museum at Alford, Lincolnshire, owned by the Alford and District Civic Trust Ltd. My thanks to John Needham for his kind interest and guidance.

My very special thanks to John Winter of Heapham, Lincolnshire, for the loan of papers and books and his patience in answering all my questions.

My love and thanks to all my family and friends who are a constant source of practical help and encouragement.

One

'Now get back into this kitchen, Kitty Clegg, before I take me a copper stick to ya backside.'

'I'm just off across to the wash-house, Mrs Grundy.' The girl paused in the back doorway. She tilted her head to one side and glanced up coyly from beneath her long, black eyelashes yet she failed to hide the mischief dancing in her brown eyes. 'I thought I'd just hang them wet sheets out while there's a good drying wind blowing and get these in to soak.' She nodded towards the bundle of washing she was carrying in her arms. 'You know Master Edward needs a clean nightshirt and sheets every day while he's so poorly.'

The cook's expression softened. 'Aye, poor little scrap,' she murmured. 'I heard him coughing and wheezing half the night, I did.' The round face, flecked with tiny red broken veins, sagged sorrowfully. 'He'll not make old bones . . .' She dabbed away a sudden tear with the corner of her white apron. 'You're a good lass to Master Edward, doing extra bits for him along with your own work and sitting with him in your own time when he wants a bit of company, I'll grant you.' She sniffed, then eyed the girl shrewdly. 'But just you remember, young Kitty, I aren't so green as I'm cabbage-looking and to my way of thinking it's not Master Edward on your mind at this very minute.' The chins wobbled as Mrs Grundy nodded her head and wagged her pudgy finger at the girl. 'I know what's going

1

on in that scheming little head of yours. The minute that threshing set arrives in the stackyard do you start wearing a track between me back door and yon wash-house. It was the same last year and I know what you're up to. Chasing that young feller, Jack What's-'is-name, that's what. And him as fickle as the weather vane on yon barn roof.' Mrs Grundy sucked her teeth in a tut of disapproval. 'Well, don't say I didn't warn you, when it all ends in tears.' She shook her head again. 'I don't know what'll become of you, Kitty Clegg, really I don't.'

Kitty's dark eyes sparkled and, as she smiled, the two dimples in her cheeks deepened so disarmingly that Mrs Grundy, small and plump and jolly, chuckled and flapped her hand towards her. 'Oh go on with you then, ya little minx. But don't let the master catch you, else ya'll be dismissed without a reference and I'll get me knuckles rapped, an' all.'

'Ta, Mrs Grundy,' the young girl trilled. 'I'll give you a kiss at Christmas.'

'Cheeky young wench.'

But Kitty had skipped out of earshot and was dancing on light, dainty feet across the yard, the bundle of washing tucked under one arm, but her whole attention directed towards the stackyard.

Above the wall at the end of the long garden that stretched from the back of the Manor House to the farm-yard and buildings beyond, Kitty could just see the chimney of the traction engine as it moved majestically into the yard puffing little clouds of black smoke lazily into the blue August sky. Behind it rattled the red threshing drum, like a huge square box on wheels. The noise filled the air and Kitty felt a sudden fluttering somewhere in her chest and her knees trembled.

He was here. Jack was here, and, if she was quick, she

could run the length of the straight path through the back garden, slip through the door in the wall at the end and maybe, just maybe, he would speak to her.

The girl scurried towards the wash-house and plunged the dirty linen into a deep tub of cold water. Then she picked up the basket, heavy with wet sheets, pillow cases and long white nightshirts, and carried it out into the yard. Shaking out one of the sheets, she stretched up to throw it over the line strung across the small paved area, then pegged it firmly in place, but her glance darted again towards the stackyard. Even above the noise of the engine she could hear the shouts of the other men, gathered to witness its arrival, as Jack Thorndyke coaxed the unwieldy machinery into position.

Kitty pushed the last clothes-peg into place and glanced over her shoulder at the house towering behind her, her sharp eyes scanning each of the windows in turn. No one was watching, not madam or any of the household; not even Mrs Grundy had appeared in the back doorway. But the garden path was too risky, so easily seen from the house. Kitty bit her lip and then, picking up her long skirt, she ran silently towards the corner of the house, ducking low as she passed the window of the master's study that looked out on to a courtyard. Through a side gate in the wall, she stood a moment on the broad drive in the cool shadow of the tall trees. She was out of sight from the house now, but she still glanced to right and left, making sure there was no one about. Then past the stables and the garage where the master's new motor car stood in shining splendour, round the corner and into the stackyard.

Kitty caught her breath as she saw him. He was standing on the footplate of the gleaming engine, his strong hands turning the wheel with ease as he brought the great lumbering machine to a halt in the centre of the yard.

'That'll do, Jack,' his workmate shouted and waved his arms.

The noise spluttered and died and Jack Thorndyke was climbing down.

Kitty edged forward. 'You're here again then?'

He turned and looked over his shoulder. Then, seeing who it was, he turned fully round and came towards her, wiping his grimy hands on a piece of rag.

'Aye. Looks like it, dun't it?' The sun gleamed on his black hair and his arms, tanned and thick with muscle, glistened with sweat. He wore workaday clothes: an open-necked, striped shirt with the sleeves rolled up, a dark waistcoat and trousers with string tied beneath the knees, and heavy, solid boots. Smut blackened his broad forehead and square jawline, but his blue eyes glinted, challenging her. Kitty caught her breath, wishing that she was dressed in something – anything – a little more becoming than the plain skirt, white cotton blouse and copious apron of a kitchen maid. Even her pretty black curls were hidden beneath the triangular cloth tied tightly around her head.

Nervously, she smoothed her hands, suddenly hot, down the sides of her apron, her gaze drinking in the sight of him. His broad shoulders and wide chest narrowed suddenly to a surprisingly slim waist. His strong hands were huge, so big and powerful that Kitty could imagine them spanning her own tiny waist in their grip. He stood with his arms akimbo, knuckles resting on his hips, his feet planted apart. Kitty felt the colour creeping into her face as his bold gaze rested unblinkingly upon her. She looked up at him. He was so tall that the top of her head only came up to his shoulder.

'You're early this year, ain't ya?'

'That's right. We'd nowt else on, so we've come to help with the last of the harvest.'

There were only the two of them who came with the threshing set: Jack, who owned it, and the man who worked for him, Ben Holden. They travelled the county to find work and the additional labour required was provided by each farmer who hired them. Four or five men who worked on the Manor Farm lands stood about, intrigued to see the huge machinery filling their stackyard.

'You – you'll be here for a while then?' Kitty asked Jack.

'Only for a few days.'

Kitty knew she could not stop the disappointment from showing on her face. 'But the threshing? When will you start threshing?'

'Not yet. There's Nunsthorpe Hall Farm and Home Farm needin' help with their harvest after we finish here and then . . .' He reeled off a list of farmers in the district where he and Ben would find work in the coming weeks. Ben Holden was a skilled thatcher and Kitty knew that soon after the end of harvest the now almost empty stack-yard would be filled with neatly thatched stacks.

'We'll maybe do a day or so's threshing here about the end of October,' Jack was saying, 'but it depends how much Mester Franklin wants and when. Mebbe he'll want us every few weeks.' He paused and his mischievous eyes teased her. 'Then again, he may not want us back till after Christmas to thresh him out.'

Christmas! That seemed an age away to Kitty.

'But . . .' Jack was saying, 'I'll be leaving me threshing tackle here at the Manor for a week or two, so just you mind you keep an eye on my *Sylvie* for me, won't you?' For a moment, he laid a possessive hand upon the side of his engine and then he was moving towards Kitty. With the tip of his forefinger, he traced the line of her cheek. Down, down and round under her chin with a surprisingly gentle, featherlight, touch.

'You're even prettier than I'd remembered,' he said softly, with a low cavernous chuckle that began somewhere deep in his chest. Then he was turning away, back to his engine.

'Oh, so you remember my name then?' she said pertly, tilting her head to one side.

'Course I do. I remember all the girls' names.' He paused and then added deliberately, 'The pretty ones, that is.'

She felt a blush begin to creep up her neck, but to hide her nervousness she said saucily, 'So I've been told.'

His deep laughter echoed around the yard so that one or two of the other men looked up and grinned. Kitty saw them nodding towards her and Jack and then one, shouting across to the others, said, 'He dun't waste much time, does he?'

'Naw, not Threshing Jack,' came the prompt reply.

Kitty felt the flush of embarrassment deepening and spreading up into her face. She turned away, but at Jack's 'Hey, wait a minute,' she hesitated.

She stood very still, not daring to turn back to look at him as she heard him step towards her. She felt him close to her, could smell the manly sweat of him mixed with the smoke from his engine that clung to his clothes and never, however much he washed, seemed quite to leave him. She closed her eyes and swayed. Oh how she remembered the smell of him, how she'd longed to feel his hands on her waist, the touch of his lips on hers.

'You're only a kid,' he'd teased her a year ago. 'Wait till you're older.'

And now, this year, she was sixteen. Now, she was a woman. Maybe this year . . .?

He was bending down towards her, his mouth close to her ear so that she could feel the waft of his breath upon her cheek. 'Meet me later, pretty Kitty. Up in the woods yonder.'

Her heart seemed to stand still and then began to thump so loudly that she thought he must surely hear it. She tossed her head and, feigning lack of interest, said, 'I might. Then again, I might not.' But as she pretended to flounce away, holding her head high in the haughty manner of her betters, she heard his deep chuckle following her.

Two

'Come on, girl,' came Mrs Grundy's voice as Kitty stepped across the threshold. 'Look sharp, else you'll have me in trouble an' all, and I can see you're heading for it already. Never mind what I say, you'll take no notice . . .' The older woman shook her head, looking for all the world as if she didn't quite know whether to laugh or cry. 'Eh, Kitty, we've all been young once, but just mind yourself with 'im. You know what they all say about Jack Thorndyke, now don't you? And besides, he's too old for you. Why, he must be twenty-five or six, if he's a day.'

Kitty opened her mouth to make a retort, but at that moment one of the bells in the row above the pantry door bounced on its spring and tinkled. They both looked up towards the sound.

'That's Master Edward. Go an' see what he wants, Kitty.'

'I can't go upstairs in this, Mrs G.' She pointed to the hessian apron she wore over her white cotton pinafore to protect it from the dirty jobs in the kitchen. Since, for a kitchen maid, such tasks formed the bulk of her daily work, it seemed to Kitty that she hardly ever divested herself of the rough apron. She put her hands behind her back and struggled to untie the knot in the strings. The bell sounded again, more urgently this time.

'Go on with ya. Quick. Mebbe he's havin' one of his wheezy attacks.'

'But what if I meet the mistress or – or . . .' Her eyes widened as she added in a whisper, 'What if the master comes back?'

Mrs Grundy laughed. 'She'll not bite ya, Kitty. Anything you do for that lad of hers, you do for her.'

'But what about the master?' Although Kitty would never admit to being frightened of anyone, she could not help being a little in awe of the big, blustering figure of Mr Franklin, whose roars of rage when he lost his temper could be heard in the kitchen.

'Oh I grant you he shouts a bit now an' then. But as the gentry go, the Franklins aren't so bad. An' I should know 'cos I've worked for some snobby beggars in me time, let me tell you . . .'

Kitty hid her grin. Get Mrs Grundy launched into her stories of the places she'd worked as a young girl and the people she'd served and they'd both be here till the next morning.

Mrs Grundy had been in service from the age of twelve, starting as a kitchen maid and working her way up through several different jobs until she had come to the Manor to take up the much respected position of cook. She had never been married and the 'Mrs' added to her name was a courtesy title befitting her position within the household, yet she was a motherly soul and genuinely fond of the young girls who came and went under her charge. To Kitty she seemed old, yet the woman was only just fifty. Maybe the roundness of her body, the florid complexion and the grey hair pulled tightly back under the white frilled cap she always wore did nothing to dispel the image of advancing years. At the end of a long and tiring day, she would sit with her feet on the warm bricks bordering the huge fireplace, a glass of sherry from the dregs of a bottle sent back from the dining room in her hand, and launch into her childhood memories.

'My dad was in the Crimea, y'know,' she would begin proudly. 'He fought for our dear old Queen, he did, God rest her.' Here Mrs Grundy would dab her eyes with the corner of her apron. 'Wounded, he was, in the leg and she gave him a medal . . .' And on she would go, the sherry loosening her tongue even more than normal and making her reminiscences maudlin until the tears were trickling down her red cheeks.

Kitty would listen with half an ear. She had heard the stories so often now, she could almost recite them herself, yet she truly liked Mrs Grundy and would do nothing to hurt her feelings.

The bell rang yet again and Mrs Grundy flapped her hand at Kitty. 'Go on with ya, girl. The lad must want summat.'

'But . . .' Kitty, poised on her toes, tried one more protest. 'Where's Lucy? Surely she ought to go? Or even Sarah. Not me.'

Mrs Grundy sucked her tongue against her teeth. 'Oh that one! That Sarah's an idle creature. Taken to 'er bed today with a cold, so she ses.' Mrs Grundy sniffed her disapproval of housemaids who dared to be ill. 'And Miss Miriam keeps young Lucy on the run. No, there's no one else today, Kitty. You'll have to go. It'll be all right.'

Kitty had managed to untie the strings and remove the sack-like covering. Now she smoothed her hands down her white apron and tucked a stray black curl back beneath her cap.

'Go on, girl,' Mrs Grundy urged and Kitty pushed open the door and went down the three steps into the main hallway of the house. She stood listening for a moment. Mrs Franklin would be upstairs in her sitting room which adjoined her bedroom, reading her mail, writing letters or planning the day's menus. Soon, Mrs Grundy would be summoned by the bell from that room to discuss the various dishes with the mistress.

Even though she had heard the master leave the house just after breakfast, Kitty was still nervous that the front door might suddenly be thrown open and he would stride into the hall. She ran swiftly up the servants' staircase, the old, uneven floorboards creaking under her light weight. Turning to the left, she hurried along the passageway leading to the west wing, past the main staircase which the servants were not allowed to use and to the door of Master Edward's bedroom. She paused a moment and glanced over her shoulder as she heard the sound of Miss Miriam Franklin's voice, high-pitched and petulant, coming from behind the closed door opposite.

'Useless! You're a great, useless lump, Lucy. Get out – get *out* . . .'

There was a startled cry and the door flew open. Cap awry and hair coming loose from its pins, Lucy, who was personal maid to both Mrs Franklin and her daughter, pushed past Kitty. 'That does it!' Kitty heard her mutter through clenched teeth. 'I'm leaving. I won't stay another minute in this house. That girl's not right in the head . . .'

Kitty stood gaping, and then through the open door of the bedroom she caught sight of Miriam, scantily clad in her underwear, sitting at her dressing table, a glass jar of cream balanced in her hand as if she were poised to launch it.

Their glances met and held.

'What are you staring at, girl? Get on with your work.'

Keeping her voice deliberately level and calm, Kitty stepped forward. 'Shall I close the door for you, miss? You don't want to catch cold sitting there like that.'

Without waiting for Miriam to reply, Kitty pulled it shut. As the sneck clicked, there was a thud against the opposite side of the panelling and the sound of shattering glass.

Kitty jumped and then she smiled as she turned towards Master Edward's bedroom. Miss Miriam was certainly in one of her tantrums this morning, she thought as she knocked on his door.

'Come in.' The voice was faint and breathless.

In the huge bed, lost among a mountain of white pillows, lay Master Edward Franklin. His blue eyes, large in his pale face, widened as he saw her. Only two years separated their ages, yet frequent illness made him seem even younger. Boys of fourteen, Kitty thought, ought to be out tramping the fields and getting into mischief, not shut up alone in a sickroom.

'Kitty,' he said huskily and tried to pull himself up, but the effort brought on a spasm of coughing.

She hurried to the bedside. 'Lie still, Master Edward, you'll make yarsen worse.'

The boy smiled and, for a moment, some of the suffering left his face. 'If I was much worse, I'd be dead.'

'Master Edward!' Kitty, her lips twitching, pretended to be shocked. 'You shouldn't say such things.'

The grin widened, stretching across his thin face. 'Oh Kitty, it does me good to see you. Why don't you come up more often?'

Kitty chuckled. 'You know I can't when I'm working. Not me, Master Edward, I'm only a kitchen maid. I shouldn't be here now really. It should be Lucy or Sarah.'

Sarah Maybury was the housemaid, the only other 'upstairs servant' at the Manor besides Lucy.

'Lucy has her hands full with my sister.' Edward tried to laugh, but the laugh turned into a cough again.

'See, you'll have me in trouble for making you worse,' Kitty teased gently, straightening the bedclothes and leaning across to plump up his pillows.

Edward caught hold of her arm. 'Stay and talk to me.'

Only inches apart, her soft, brown gaze looked into his fever-bright eyes. 'Please, Kitty,' he pleaded softly.

'I wish I could,' she said gently, moved by the young boy's loneliness. 'But I daresunt.'

'It'll be all right. My mother . . .' he began.

Straightening up, Kitty said firmly, 'Aye, your mother. If she catches me in here when I'm not supposed to be, I'll be fer the sack.'

'I wouldn't let her dismiss . . .' he began and then, altering his words to suit her way of talking, said, 'sack you.'

Kitty giggled and they smiled at each other, his gaze holding hers. He sank back and sighed. 'Oh Kitty, how I wish I had your strength, your vigour.'

She gave a wry snort of laughter. 'Good job I am strong an' all, with the hours I have to work . . . Oh heck!' She stopped and clapped her hand to her runaway mouth. 'I'm sorry, Master Edward, I didn't mean nothing.'

But he was still smiling, his face showing more colour than it had when she had entered the room. 'I know you didn't, Kitty. And stop apologizing. You can say anything you like to me, you know. I would never tell.'

A door banged somewhere along the landing and Kitty jumped. 'Oh heck, what am I thinking of, dawdlin' about here. Mrs Grundy'll 'ave me guts fer garters. What was it you wanted, Master Edward? Why did you ring?'

'Can't remember now. But I'll think of something. I'll ring more often if you're going to answer it.'

'Oh, now . . .'

He gave a wheezy laugh. 'It's all right, Kitty, I'm only

13

teasing. But you're a refreshing change from Lucy's tearful face. Or Miss Starchy Knickers . . .'

Kitty gave a little squeal of delight at his saucy name for the housemaid. 'Master Edward!' she said, pretending to be shocked yet the description was apt. Sarah Maybury fancied herself above the rest of the servants at the Manor. 'Gives hersen airs and graces, that one,' Mrs Grundy would sniff. 'What with 'er and her stuck up ways and Lucy always in tears, thank goodness I've got you, Kitty.'

'What was all the commotion just now?' Edward was saying.

'I don't know yet, but I'll no doubt hear all about it when I get back downstairs.'

'Do tell me later, won't you?' he pleaded. Kitty nodded, feeling a stab of pity for the young boy who had so little in his life that his sister's tempers were the only exciting event in his day.

He was sighing now. 'My sister really is the end, you know. Six maids in three years have come and gone and it's all Miriam's fault, not Mother's. Now it sounds as if Lucy'll be the seventh to leave. No one can handle my dear sister's tantrums, at least not since Nanny got too old and retired.'

Absentmindedly, Kitty straightened the already smooth counterpane. 'Can't they indeed?' she murmured and then felt his gaze upon her.

'Kitty,' Edward began warningly, 'what are you up to?'

Kitty widened her eyes, feigning innocence. 'Me, Master Edward? Now what could I, a lowly kitchen maid, possibly be "up to"?'

He wagged his finger at her. 'I know you, Kitty Clegg,

there's something going on in that pretty little head of yours. Now, you just—'

Another door banged, closer this time, and Kitty jumped. 'I've gotta go, Master Edward. Just tell me quick what you wanted. Please!'

He sighed, his ploy to keep her with him failing by the minute. His voice flat, he said, 'Just close the window, will you? There's a draught.'

Kitty crossed the room and reached to push up the top part of the sash window.

'Oh!' Her arms suspended in midair, a surprised gasp escaped her lips.

'What is it? What can you see?' Edward was sitting up in bed again.

'I never realized,' the girl murmured, pushing the window up slowly until it was closed, 'that you can see right into the stackyard from your window.'

Her whole attention was gone now from the boy in the bed as she watched the tall, burly figure of Jack Thorndyke polishing his engine with loving care until the dark green paintwork and the brass fittings and copper pipes gleamed in the sunlight and the name *Sylvie*, picked out in gold lettering on the front of the smokebox door, shone.

'Oh,' Edward said and dropped back again, pushing into the pillows as if he would bury himself in them. 'Oh yes. I can see everything that goes on down there, Kitty.' His voice dropped to a whisper. 'Everything.'

She heard his words with only half an ear and their underlying meaning escaped her. 'I'll have to go down,' she said, though whether she meant back to her duties in the kitchen or out again to the stackyard, neither she nor the boy really knew.

'Yes, you do that, Kitty. You go down.'

She hurried across the room towards the door, two bright spots of colour in her cheeks.

As she closed the door softly behind her and sped along the passage towards the stairs, she could not see the boy in the bed turn his face into the pillows, or hear his muffled groan of anguish.

Three

As Kitty pushed open the kitchen door, the sound of wild crying met her.

Lucy Jones was sitting at the kitchen table, mopping at her tear-streaked face. Mrs Grundy, standing beside her, looked up as Kitty came in.

'There you are. Thank goodness you've come. P'raps you can talk a bit of sense into this silly girl, Kitty. She's threatening to give notice.'

'I'm not threatening,' Lucy wailed. 'I mean it. She – she attacked me. I'm sure she's not right in the head.'

Mrs Grundy leaned closer. 'Now, you listen to me, me girl. Don't you go saying such dreadful things about the young mistress. You hear me?'

Lucy snivelled miserably, but said no more.

Kitty stood on the opposite side of the wide, scrubbed table and leaned on her hands, regarding Lucy thoughtfully. The girl did look a sight and no mistake. Her face was blotchy with the storm of her weeping and her hair was ruffled and pulled from its plait. The pretty frilled cap that Kitty secretly envied so much was held only by one hairpin and hung down over her left ear. The delicate lace bib of her white apron had been torn away, leaving a triangular rip in the black fabric of her maid's dress.

'What happened, Lucy?' Kitty asked. 'What did Miss Miriam do?'

At the offer of sympathy from someone closer to her

17

own age than the cook, fresh tears welled in Lucy's eyes. 'She pulled my hair, Kitty, and tore my dress. Just look!'

'I can see that,' Kitty said tartly. 'But what happened? What caused it?'

Turning away, back towards her range, Mrs Grundy said, ''Spect you deserved it.'

'How would you know?' In her self-centred misery, a sneer twisted Lucy's mouth. 'You've never worked above stairs. You've never been a lady's maid. How would you know?'

Despite her bulk, Mrs Grundy whipped round with surprising agility. She raised her arm and began to wag her finger at the girl, but before she could speak, Kitty broke in, 'Now don't you go upsetting Mrs Grundy.' She laughed, her eyes twinkling at the older woman, whose face was red with anger. 'She's already threatened me with her copper stick once today.'

Kitty caught the glance of the cook who glared at her for a moment and then, with a grunt, turned away. Thwarted in giving vent to her rage, she banged a huge cooking pan on to the range as if wishing Lucy's head was beneath it. The smile faded from Kitty's mouth as she turned back to the weeping maid. She didn't particularly like the girl in front of her, never had. She was a whining, sour-faced creature who complained from morning until night about anything and everything. But Kitty had a real affection for Mrs Grundy, whose rough and ready manner hid a soft heart.

'Come on, out with it. What did happen?'

Lucy sniffed again. 'I told you,' she muttered. 'She attacked me.'

'But *why*? We all know Miss Miriam's got a quick temper, but there's got to be summat that set it off.'

Lucy sniffed again. 'How should I know? She's vicious.'

18

'Now don't you start that again,' came Mrs Grundy's warning voice, 'else . . .' But as Kitty held up her hand, palm outwards, the older woman subsided, though she could still be heard muttering darkly to herself.

'What *happened*?' Kitty persisted, determined to get at the truth.

'It was her new riding habit,' Lucy began reluctantly. 'You know, the one with the white ruff at the neckline. Well, last time she went out riding she tore the lace. I mended it but – but I'm not very good at sewing and she said – she said I'd made a pig's ear of it. Oh she's got such a mouth on her when she starts. Lady, my eye. *She*'s no lady.'

Now Mrs Grundy turned and came back to the table. 'No wonder she was mad. A lady's maid that can't sew. I never heard the like. What do you expect, girl?'

Lucy stood, drawing herself up to her full height so that she towered over the short, dumpy figure of the cook. 'In my previous position,' she said, with deliberate condescension, 'they employed a seamstress to do all the sewing and mending jobs. Not like here, where they can't afford a proper complement of servants.'

'Then why, pray,' Mrs Grundy asked, hands on her hips and her head wagging from side to side, 'didn't you stay in your previous fancy position instead of lowering yarsen to come and work with the likes of us, eh?'

Lucy sniffed. '*My* young lady went away. To finishing school. And if you ask me, that's exactly where she . . .' she jerked her thumb towards the door leading to the upstairs, 'ought to go too. Might teach her some manners.'

'Now just you look here—' Mrs Grundy began again.

Kitty, forestalling another argument, said, 'Let 'er go, Mrs Grundy. She ain't happy here, that's obvious. There's plenty more girls'd like 'er job. Ladies' maids are two a penny.'

Lucy turned her pale grey eyes upon Kitty, looking down her long nose. 'I expect you think you could do the job, don't you? Well, you're welcome to it. See how you like having your hair torn from its roots.'

The girl turned away and missed seeing the gleam in Kitty's brown eyes. It did not, however, escape Mrs Grundy's notice. 'Kitty,' she began warningly. But Kitty, too, turned away to hide the smile that twitched at the corner of her mouth, trying to still the sudden swift excited beating of her heart.

Why not? she asked herself. Why shouldn't I be a lady's maid? I've worked in this kitchen for three years, she reminded herself, remembering the day her mother had brought her to the Manor.

They had stood on the pavement looking up at the impressive old house that stood on a road leading out of the market town of Tresford. No one knew exactly when the house had been built. Some said that the central part had been built in the sixteenth century, originally a mud and stud structure that had been encased in brick walls at a much later date and probably added to by various owners down the centuries. Inside, the rooms led from one to another in a maze of passages and stairs and creaking boards and there was a strange feeling that the rough-hewn timbers held the secrets of long ago and the walls still enveloped the ghosts of the generations who had lived there.

Kitty had arrived on a bright, warm morning in May and as she stood in front of the house, her gaze roamed over the pale mauve flowers of the wistaria that wound its way around the front door and crept over the brickwork, threatening to engulf the sash windows above. She loved the grey mottled thatch of the roof, the three sets of chimney stacks, so symmetrically placed. Prickly, vari-egated holly bushes guarded the front gate and a tiny blue butterfly hovered over the flowers on one of them. Kitty had made a step towards the gate to take a closer look but her mother had grasped her shoulder and propelled her further along the road and into the wide driveway at the side of the house.

'Servants by the back door. Always know your place, Kitty.' It was her mother's maxim and she had drilled it into her eldest daughter for as long as the girl could remember. 'When you go into service, Kitty, you give your life to those who put the food in your mouth and give you shelter. They deserve your devotion and your undying loyalty always – no matter what it costs.' Her voice dropped almost to a whisper as she repeated the words, 'No matter what it costs you.'

At the side of the house, the wide driveway circled a clump of trees – hollies with dark green leaves, a sycamore, a yew tree and pines that stretched tall and straight to the sky. The drive opened out before the stables which were built at right angles to the house and against the wall enclosing the garden at the rear of the house. And beyond the driveway, more trees bordered the beck that ran along the edge of the Manor House grounds and then curved away, meandering through the flat farmland.

'Oh Mam, look, just look at that huge tree. Look at its big roots,' the excited young girl had exclaimed. 'It must be hundreds of years old. Why, it's higher than the house.'

'Yes, yes, Kitty, come along.' Her mother was impatient now, pulling her past the towering copper beech and through the gate in the wall at the side of the stables. Gripping Kitty's hand, Betsy Clegg had scurried past the ground floor windows of the house, keeping her head averted until they came to the back door. Then she had seemed to breathe more easily.

Puzzled by her mother's obvious agitation, Kitty had said, 'What's the matter, Mam?'

'Nothing – nothing, child. I just didn't want to be seen by—' She broke off and then added swiftly, 'Be seen from the house, that's all.'

'Why?' Kitty had questioned innocently. 'Aren't we supposed to be here?'

'*You* are,' her mother had said, 'but I'm not so sure that I . . .' Again she altered what she had been about to say and instead said impatiently, 'Oh do stop asking questions, Kitty, and let's get inside.'

Her mother had almost pushed her through the back door and into the kitchen.

'Well, here she is, Mrs Grundy.' Sitting down at the large table, Betsy accepted the cup of tea the cook placed in front of her. The thirteen-year-old Kitty stood awkwardly, gawping at her mother's familiarity with the cook in this big, awesome house.

''Ow've ya been, then, Betsy? By, but it seems a long time since you worked here. I still miss you. We allus got on well together, didn't we?'

Kitty, her sharp ears missing nothing of the conversation passing between the two women, looked about her. This kitchen was immense. Under the window was a deep white sink with proper taps, Kitty noticed, rather than the pump handle at the side like the sink they had at home. That would make her life a little easier, she thought. Directly opposite the window, an enormous brick fireplace dominated the wall, but into its recess had been fitted a more modern black cooking range. On the wall alongside it, copper pans hung in neat rows, battered with constant use, yet they still shone and sparkled in the light. Kitty could imagine the work that had gone into cleaning them and her arm ached at the thought. Suspended from hooks in the ceiling were huge hams, wrapped in cloth, and at one end of the kitchen stood a dresser, its shelves lined with willow-patterned plates, cups and saucers. Kitty bit her lip, realizing she would have to get used to handling such fine china.

In the corner near the dresser, a door opened on to a flight of steeply twisting stone steps that led both upwards into a dairy and a pantry beyond and also downwards into a cellar where rows and rows of the master's wine lay in racks. Above this door a row of tiny brass bells bounced on curved springs and in the same corner was the door leading into the front hall of the house. But much of the upper part of the house, Kitty knew, would remain a mystery to her and she turned her attention back to the place that would, from now on, be her home.

She was still standing beside the large table in the centre of the kitchen. Its wooden surface was worn into gentle, undulating hollows by the constant scrubbing it received to bring it almost to whiteness.

'We did.' Kitty's mother was nodding agreement to Mrs Grundy's reminiscence. 'And we had some good times, as well as . . .' Her voice faded away and the cook cut in as if to cover an awkwardness.

'Let's see, 'ow long is it since you left?'

Kitty saw her mother's glance flicker towards her and then fall away. 'About seventeen years,' she murmured.

'And you've got a lovely family, ain't you? You bin all right with John Clegg, then?'

'He's a good man. A good husband and father. But I – I fear he's never been happy with his job on the railway.'

'Well, he ought to be, Betsy. Stationmaster now, ain't he? And you've always had a railway house. A nice house, too, much nicer than a farm labourer's cottage.' She sniffed. 'Some men are never satisfied, if you ask me.'

'Well . . .' Betsy twisted her fingers together. 'He always loved his job with the horses, you know, but after . . .' Again a swift glance at Kitty. 'After he left the Manor, the only jobs going round here at that time were on the railway. It was the wrong time of year for a farm worker's job, you see.'

'I remember,' Mrs Grundy said softly. Then, as if trying to reassure her old friend, she added brightly, 'But that's men for you. Always wanting what they haven't got. He'd never've had the position he's got in the town now if he'd stayed with horses, now would he?'

Betsy shrugged but made no reply.

'Well, he wouldn't.' The cook answered her own question. 'Besides,' she added as a fresh thought struck her, 'if he 'ad stayed here, he wouldn't be with horses now anyway.'

For a moment Kitty's mother looked puzzled as Mrs Grundy leaned forward. 'He'd have been driving that there motey car.' She gave a cackle of laughter. 'But poor old Bemmy's got the job instead. *And* he hates it, I can tell you.' She leaned back in her chair and nodded wisely. 'Your John Clegg's done all right for himself if only he'd think so. So don't you go on blaming yarsen for the rest of your life, Betsy, that he lost his job wi' horses because of you.'

Kitty's mother smiled weakly, but looked unconvinced, even by the stout-hearted Mrs Grundy.

At this point Kitty had butted in. 'Did you work here, then, Mam? At the Manor? You never said.'

The two women had looked up at her then, almost as if they had forgotten she was there, but it was the cook, not her mother, who said sternly, 'Well, one thing you'll have to learn here, m'girl, is to speak when you're spoken to and not 'afore.'

Kitty had clamped her mouth shut, feeling a stab of dismay. She had hoped the cook would be a kindly soul and yet already she was telling her off. Then Kitty had seen Mrs Grundy wink at her mother and at once the young girl had sensed that the reprimand had been merely to let a cheeky kitchen maid know her place from the outset. It did not herald a life of misery for her under a bad-tempered superior.

Betsy Clegg had risen to her feet. 'I'd best be getting back. The bairns'll be shouting for their tea.'

''Ow many you got then, Betsy?'

Her mother had nodded towards Kitty. 'She's me eldest, then there's two lads and three more girls. The youngest, Robert, is only eight months old.'

Mrs Grundy shook her head slowly. 'Well, I can see now why you want young Kitty 'ere placed.' Their attention had turned to Kitty, still standing by the table.

Betsy had sighed. 'Well, I hope you can do summat with her, 'cos she's a wild one, I don't mind admitting. But she's got her good points, I'll say that for her, even though she's me own. She's a worker. Set her owt to do, an' she'll do it. Anything from scrubbing to sewing. Neatest little stiches you ever did see, she can do.'

'Well, she'll have no energy left for her wild ways once she gets working here, and there'll be more of the scrubbing than the fancy stitching.' Mrs Grundy's mouth had been a firm, resolute line, but still the young girl had seen the twinkle in the cook's eyes.

That moment had set the tone of their relationship. Mrs Grundy was strict and worked Kitty hard, but she was always fair and had a rough, but kindly concern for the little kitchen maid in her charge.

On that first day and for several weeks afterwards, Kitty had seen little more of the Manor beyond the kitchen, the backyard and its wash-house, and the way up the back stairs to her attic bedroom under the thatch.

But now, three years later, thought Kitty Clegg with growing excitement, now there was a chance for her to better herself. Ever since that first day, she'd been little more than a skivvy, with chapped and calloused hands and wearing rough, scullery maid's clothes. But not any more, she told herself. Come hell or high water, she was going to be Miss Miriam's new lady's maid. You just see if I'm not, she said to Mrs Grundy.

But the challenge was only in her mind and not a word passed her lips.

Four

Nervously Kitty smoothed the palms of her hands down her clean apron, patted the cap enveloping her unruly black hair, licked her lips and knocked boldly on the door of Mrs Franklin's sitting room on the first floor.

A gentle, cultured voice called 'Come in' and Kitty pushed open the door. Even though, on this warm August day, bright sunlight streamed in through the long windows to her right, Mrs Franklin was seated to one side of the fireplace where a fire burned in the grate. Her head was bent over a frame of petit point, her nimble fingers threading the needle through the canvas, one hand above the work, one beneath it. Kitty closed the door quietly behind her and tiptoed into the room to stand a short distance from Mrs Franklin. Fascinated by the brightly coloured wool speeding in and out of the canvas, the neat stitches forming the picture before her eyes, Kitty spoke without thinking. 'Oh how clever you are, madam.' The words, perhaps somewhat presumptuous from a lowly kitchen maid, were nonetheless genuine.

Mrs Franklin raised her head and Kitty's gaze met hers. The mistress of the Manor House was nearing her fortieth birthday, but her luxuriant blonde hair showed only a trace of silver here and there in its abundance. It was beautifully dressed, high on her head with neat curls framing her forehead. Her face was serene, her complexion smooth with only the merest hint of tiny lines around her hazel eyes. Her gentle mouth curved into a welcoming smile. Every time Kitty saw her mistress she marvelled again at her beauty and wondered afresh how she had come to marry a man like the master.

'Why, thank you, Kitty.' Mrs Franklin waited a moment but since the girl did not speak, she prompted softly, 'What can I do for you, my dear? Nothing wrong in the kitchen, I hope?'

'Oh no, madam,' Kitty said swiftly. 'I'm very happy working here . . .' She bit her lip, holding her breath as a sudden twinge of uncertainty gripped her.

But Mrs Franklin was smiling. 'Do I hear a "but" in there somewhere, Kitty?'

'Oh no,' Kitty said again. 'Well, not really.' She pulled in a deep breath and the words came out in a rush. 'I've come to ask you – to see you – about Lucy.'

'Ah yes,' Mrs Franklin sighed deeply and there was a sadness in her fine eyes. 'Poor Lucy,' she murmured. 'She's given me her resignation. I don't want to take it, but she – she seems adamant.' She sighed again and murmured, more to herself than to the girl, 'I don't know what we're going to do. Really, I don't.'

Eagerly, Kitty took a step forward, bending towards her employer in her excitement. 'Please, would you consider me for the position of your lady's maid? For you and Miss Miriam, I mean. I can sew . . .' With her chapped, kitchen maid's hand, she gestured towards Mrs Franklin's embroidery. 'Not as good as you, madam, of course, but me mam taught me and she – she . . .' She just stopped herself from blurting out who her mother had been and the position she had once held in this very house. That had been before the present Mrs Franklin had lived here, before she had become mistress of the Manor and perhaps mention of it at this time would do young Kitty no favours.

But to Kitty's surprise the kindly eyes were regarding her steadily. 'Oh yes. I know about your mother.' The words were spoken softly and there was a fleeting, rather strange look in the lady's eyes, yet it was gone in an instant, so swiftly that Kitty thought she must have imagined it.

Mrs Franklin concentrated once more on her embroidery and for a moment there was silence in the room, save for the heavy ticking of the grandfather clock in the corner and the gentle rasping sound of the wool being pulled through the tiny holes in the canvas.

Mrs Franklin looked up at Kitty. 'Do you really think you could cope? I mean . . .' Her voice trailed away and mistress and maid stared at each other, both knowing the meaning behind the unspoken words.

Can you cope with Miss Miriam's tantrums, her quicksilver moods and her treatment of every one of the stream of maids who have come and gone during the last three years? This was the question in Mrs Franklin's eyes. Slowly Kitty nodded. 'I'd really like to try, madam.'

A small smile quirked at the older woman's mouth. 'Well,' she murmured softly as if, once more, thinking aloud. 'At least you know what to expect.' She paused, appearing to consider. 'What about Mrs Grundy? Does she know you've come to see me?'

'Not exactly,' Kitty said truthfully. 'But I think . . .' Now the smile that had twitched at the girl's lips spread itself across her mouth. 'I think she knows I'm "up to summat".'

Mrs Franklin laughed. 'Well, Kitty, I will think about it. But I must speak to Mrs Grundy, you understand, because it would leave her without a kitchen maid.'

Kitty's heart sank. She was not a conceited girl, but she knew that Mrs Grundy would not want to let her go. The cook had trained young Kitty to her own ways and hated change. But all she could say now was, 'Yes, madam,' and

'Thank you, madam,' give a small curtsy and leave the room, her heart not quite as hopeful as when she had entered it.

'Would you walk out with me if I were a lady's maid and not a scruffy kitchen maid then?'

She sat on top of the five-barred gate looking down at Jack Thorndyke, who squinted up at her against the setting sun, a straw hanging out of the corner of his mouth. 'Mebbe. Mebbe not.' Casually, he removed the chewed end and prodded it towards her. 'Who said I wouldn't walk out with a kitchen maid, then?'

She shrugged. 'No one. But I 'eard as how you walked out with Evie Miller on Sir Peter Rowell's estate. An' she's Lady Rowell's personal maid.'

'So? What of it?' He moved away from her, stepping into the cornfield, the wheat rustling around his long legs.

'Are you still keeping company with her then?'

Jack bent down and, with his knife, cut several ears of the corn. Straightening up, he turned and came back towards her. Laughing his deep, rumbling laugh, he said, 'Mebbe.' And then, irritatingly, added, 'Mebbe not.'

'Oh you,' Kitty said and jumped down from the gate, her skirts flying. 'You're a right Jack-the-Lad, aren't ya?' she accused. 'Good name your mam give you. After all the girls. I don't know why I bother with you, Jack Thorndyke.'

There was a brief frown on his face, his thick dark eyebrows drawn together as if a cloud had suddenly passed across the sun, but the next moment he reached out and caught the back of her neck with his strong hand. He pulled her towards him and although she resisted at first, she was no match for the strength of this man, not even against the one arm with which he held her. He pulled her to him and bent his head, laughing now into her eyes, his breath on her face, his lips only inches from her mouth. 'You bother, young Kitty Clegg, 'cos you've waited a whole year to see me again. You've waited to see what it would be like to lie with a man like me.'

Kitty gasped and her eyes widened at his boldness, at his presumption. But she could not speak. There was nothing she could say, because what Jack Thorndyke said was true. Every word of it. And he knew it. The realization that he could read her thoughts and her girlish desires so plainly made the colour creep up her neck and suffuse her face.

Chuckling softly, as if enjoying her embarrassment, he released her and stepped away from her. Leaning his back against the gate and holding the long stems of wheat just below the ears, he counted, ' . . . Seven, eight, nine,' and then began to plait them together.

Kitty swallowed and, trying to marshal her whirling thoughts, made herself concentrate on what he was doing. She marvelled that such broad hands, so used to working the huge engine, could nevertheless plait the fine stems so nimbly.

'What are you making?'

'You'll see,' he murmured, his eyes never lifting now from his intricate work.

Fascinated, she watched as a shape began to appear. 'You're making a corn dolly.'

'Where I come from, we call it a corn maiden, but yes, that's right.'

Kitty clasped her hands in delight. 'I've seen 'em, of course, but I've never seen one being made.' She paused, watching, then eager to know, demanded, 'Is that the head with the ears of corn for the hair?'

31

The plaiting was being fashioned into a tiny spherical shape that curved in and then sharply out again.

'Uh-huh. And now the shoulders, see? And in for the waist,' he murmured. 'Tiny waist, she's got, Kitty. Just like yours.'

Then his clever fingers widened the diameter of the rounds to form a bell-shaped skirt.

'But she's got no arms.'

'Those are worked separately. Now, take my knife and you go and cut two lots of five straws. Cut the ears off. I don't need them this time.'

She did as he told her, handing them to him. He set the finished body on top of the gate post while he cut the stems she had brought to the length he wanted. Two tiny arms, as if dressed in billowing sleeves, were fastened to the main body, the hands formed by the cut-off ends of the stems and tied together in the front.

'Now, young Kitty. What's missing?'

She blinked at him. 'I dunno. What is missing?'

'If she's a corn maiden she should be carrying a sheaf of corn. But as she's so tiny, we'll use just the ears. About six we need.' He held out the knife towards her again. 'You cut them for me, Kitty.'

She took his knife and stepped into the corn once more.

'Leave about a couple of inches of stalk below the ears,' he called and she nodded, bending to cut half a dozen ears as he instructed.

She turned and held them out towards him. 'All right?'

'Perfect,' he smiled. 'I can see you're wasted in the kitchen. I should have you out here with me in the fields.'

Kitty said nothing, but waded her way back through the corn to stand beside him. With the stalks slotted through the tied hands, it now looked as if the maiden were carrying a sheaf of corn in her arms.

32

'There.' He held it out to her, balancing it on the palm of his hand. 'That's for you.'

As Kitty reached out with fingers that trembled a little to take the maiden, he stepped closer and touched her chin with the tips of his fingers. 'Will you be my Harvest Nell this year, Kitty Clegg?' he asked her softly.

'Oh Jack.' It was a great compliment he was paying her. Not only was he giving her a countryman's favour in the shape of this corn maiden, but he was asking her to be the Harvest Queen and ride on the last load from the field. It was every bit as good as being Queen of the May or Carnival Queen.

'We'll make a bigger one of these,' he nodded towards the doll she held gently in the palm of her hand, 'from a whole sheaf of the last corn we cut. It'll ride with you on the final load to the barn.'

Kitty's eyes shone. 'Oh thank you, Jack, thank you. I'd love to be your Harvest Nell.'

Five

'Mrs Grundy tells me that your mother was personal maid to my husband's mother.'

Kitty was standing once more on the turkey red and blue carpet in Mrs Franklin's sitting room facing her employer. The fire crackled in the grate, the clock ticked in the corner and all around were Mrs Franklin's personal pieces of furniture. This room, more than any other in the whole house, seemed to reflect the mistress's personality. It was a tranquil room and tastefully furnished. A small, leather-topped writing desk stood against one wall and beside it was a beautiful chiffonier, black with hand-painted pictures on its doors and drawer fronts. Delicate porcelain figurines stood on top. In the far corner stood a piano which, Kitty knew, Mrs Franklin played sometimes, but only for her own amusement and never in front of anyone else. Pictures lined the walls. A likeness of the old Queen Victoria hung among oil paintings of the Manor House and there was a companion landscape of Nunsthorpe Hall.

But at this precise moment Kitty was seeing none of these things for her full attention was on her mistress.

'Yes, madam,' she said huskily.

'I knew, of course,' Mrs Franklin went on, 'that your mother had worked for the family before I came – my husband made that perfectly clear when he wanted you engaged as kitchen maid here – but I hadn't realized that

she . . .' There was the slightest of pauses. ' . . . had been
employed in that capacity.'

Kitty was silent though her quick mind was tumbling
over itself with surprise, scarcely hearing now what Mrs
Franklin was saying. The master? Why had he concerned
himself with the engaging of a lowly kitchen maid? That
sort of thing was always handled by the mistress. So
why . . .? She could tell nothing from Mrs Franklin's tone
of voice or from her expression. Today she was sitting on
the wide window seat, her back to the light, her face in
shadow and she had the advantage of the young girl
standing in the full light from the window.

To Kitty's surprise, Mrs Franklin suddenly patted the
cushion beside her. 'Come and sit down, Kitty, and we'll
have a little chat.'

'Madam?'

There was surprise in her voice, but then she heard Mrs
Franklin laugh softly. 'Come along, my dear, it's quite all
right.'

Still Kitty hesitated. It was not that she was a timid girl
– far from it. 'Bold as brass and cheeky with it,' was often
Mrs Grundy's view of her kitchen maid. But Kitty knew
her place within this household, had had it instilled in her
by her mother long before she ever came into service and
that place was not sitting beside her mistress on the soft
cushions of the window seat in her private sitting room.

Nervously, Kitty perched on the edge of the seat.

'Why did you not tell me about your mother having
served as a lady's maid? She must have been good because
my late mother-in-law . . .' a smile twitched her mouth,
'was not an easy lady to please.'

The woman's kindness brought a rush of words from
Kitty's lips. 'I thought you might think I was trying to

use that. I thought it wasn't – well – quite honest. And besides . . .' She faltered.

'And?' Mrs Franklin prompted.

Kitty felt her cheeks grow warm. 'I – I'm not sure why me mother left here. I mean . . .'

Mrs Franklin's hazel eyes were regarding her gently, almost with a look of pity. 'No, my dear, I don't suppose you do.' Softly, she added, 'I suppose there are many things children don't know about their parents' lives.'

Again there was silence while Kitty waited. Surprisingly, Mrs Franklin said, 'Tell me about your family, Kitty.'

'My – my family, madam?'

'Mm. Your father, for instance. Does he still work on the railway?'

Kitty's eyes widened. 'How . . .?' she began but then, realizing her question might be thought impertinent, she stopped.

'He worked as my father-in-law's groom,' Mrs Franklin was explaining. 'But he left here – well – about the time he and your mother were married and I understood that he got a job as a porter.'

'He's the stationmaster now, madam. I suppose that's how me mam and dad met, then? When they both worked here, I mean.'

Mrs Franklin's gaze dropped away. 'I suppose so, Kitty. Your mother had gone by – by the time I married Mr Franklin and came to live at the Manor, although your father was still here then. But yes, I suppose they must have met . . .' Her voice trailed away and there was a long pause before she said, 'And you have brothers and sisters?'

Kitty grinned. 'Oh yes, madam, the house fair bursts at the seams with all us lot. I'm the eldest, then there's George and Timothy. Then there's our Milly, she's nearly thirteen, then Grace and Jane and the youngest, he's called Robert.

At least, that's his proper name but he's such a little chap, we all call him Bobbie.'

'What a lovely big family,' Mrs Franklin murmured and Kitty thought she detected a note of envy. 'And are they all – healthy?'

Kitty felt a pang of sympathy for her employer, knowing that the gentle, loving mother was thinking of her own delicate son who was not expected to 'make old bones', as Mrs Grundy put it.

'Mostly, madam, yes, but Timothy, he gets the wheezes like Master Edward.'

Mrs Franklin's face was full of compassion. 'So that explains why you're so patient with Edward.' Her glance held Kitty's own. 'Don't think I don't know about you spending some of your own time with my son, Kitty. It doesn't go unnoticed and it does you credit, my dear.'

Kitty blushed and stammered. 'Th-thank you, madam.'

'Well then,' Mrs Franklin went on more briskly. 'I have spoken to Mrs Grundy and while she is loth to lose you as her kitchen maid . . .' she leaned closer, as if sharing a secret, 'she said you were the best kitchen maid she'd ever had.'

Kitty's eyes sparkled. 'Did she? Did she really?'

'Yes, really.' The woman's face sobered. 'But you do know, Kitty, don't you, that although you'll be my maid, you'll also have to act as Miss Miriam's personal maid and – well . . .' she sighed. 'It's no secret, is it, that my daughter can be . . . a little difficult to work for?'

Kitty almost gasped aloud. She could hardly believe that she was sitting here being spoken to by Mrs Franklin almost as an equal, that her employer was taking her into her confidence in such a way. She felt honoured to be so trusted. Kitty squared her shoulders and said seriously, 'Yes, madam. I do know.'

'And you still think you could cope?'

Kitty's brown eyes stared straight into the troubled eyes of the older woman. 'Yes, madam,' she said firmly. And although she did not say the words aloud, in her mind Kitty added, Miss Miriam just needs someone who will stand up to her and not allow herself to be bullied. But she could not voice these thoughts, not to the girl's mother of all people.

She heard Mrs Franklin give a gentle sigh. 'Well, Kitty, I'm willing to let you try. But I wouldn't want you to leave because of my daughter's behaviour. You're a good, trustworthy girl, my dear, hardworking and honest, according to Mrs Grundy, and I wouldn't want to lose you.'

Feeling as if she was bursting with pride, Kitty left the room, running down the stairs and into the kitchen.

'Mrs Grundy, oh Mrs Grundy, you old *darling*, you.' She caught hold of the cook's rotund little body and tried to whirl her around the table.

''Ere, 'ere, steady on,' Mrs Grundy gasped, clinging to Kitty. 'You'll 'ave me over, ya daft 'aporth.'

Kitty stopped her whirling. 'Fancy you saying such nice things about me to the mistress. Oh Mrs G., she's given me the job. I'm going to be her personal maid and wear a smart black dress and pretty frilled apron and cap. Oh Mrs Grundy, thank you, thank you.'

The older woman shook her head. 'Don't thank me yet, child. I ain't so sure I've done you a kindness, 'cos you'll be maid to Miss Miriam an' all.'

Kitty laughed, carried away on a wave of euphoria by her success. 'I know, but don't you worry, Mrs G., I'll handle her.'

Mrs Grundy still looked none too sure. 'I hope, for your sake, ya do.' Then she gave a wry smile. 'I'm pleased for you, lass, if it's what you really want. But I certainly haven't done mesen any favours. You're a good girl and I'm going to have a job replacing you.'

Kitty was still a moment. 'Well, er, about that, Mrs Grundy . . .' she began.

The cook looked at her sharply. 'You know of someone? Out with it then, girl.'

'My sister Milly. She's coming up to thirteen. Would you consider her?'

Mrs Grundy was beaming. 'Consider her? I'll do more than that, lass, if she's another of Betsy Clegg's daughters. When can she start?'

Suddenly, the kitchen was filled with the sound of their laughter.

Six

The two sisters stood facing each other in the attic bedroom they were to share.

'Now, you just mind your p's and q's, our Milly, 'cos you're here on my say-so, so don't you go letting me down.'

'Ooh no, Kitty. I won't, really I won't.' Pale grey eyes, wide and filled with apprehension, stared back at her. There was no likeness between the sisters, indeed it was difficult to imagine that they were so closely related. Milly was a nervous creature, pallid and thin, with lank mouse-coloured hair. She had none of Kitty's pert prettiness, nor the hint of mischief and daring that so often sparked in the older sister's eyes. 'And just you do everything Mrs Grundy tells you and don't go listening to what anyone else ses, see? Specially not that Sarah Maybury. Lead you into bad ways, she will, with her toffee-nosed manners.' Although Kitty had not lived at home for the past three years, she remembered that her younger sister could be easily led by others. 'You hear me, Milly?'

'I'll work ever so hard, Kitty, honest I will. And make you and Mam proud of me.' Tears welled in the young girl's eyes and Kitty threw her arms about her and hugged her hard. 'It's lovely to have you here, our Milly. I have missed everyone since I came into service. But now I've got you here, me own sister.' She released her and stood back, but kept her hands resting lightly on Milly's shoulders. 'We won't get a lot of time off together, but when we do, we'll have such fun. You'll be all right, Milly,' Kitty reassured her now, feeling a little guilty for having been rather sharp with the girl who, despite having reached thirteen, the age at which most girls were expected to start work, nevertheless looked at this moment like a forlorn little child. 'Just do what Mrs Grundy tells you and you'll not go far wrong.'

'She's a bit – fierce, ain't she?' Milly's voice quavered.

Kitty laughed. 'Not really, when you get to know her. Her bark's worse than her bite, as they say. She's a kindly old stick, really.'

'She likes you,' Milly murmured. 'And her and our mam seem very friendly.'

'Well, it seems they knew each other years ago when our mam worked here.'

Milly's eyes widened. 'Mam worked here? In this big house? When?'

'Before she was married to our dad. Seems he was the groom here then an' all.'

'Oh,' Milly said, pondering this information which was quite new to her. 'Oh Kitty, how romantic. Can you imagine our mam and dad meeting in secret?' She giggled. 'Maybe in the hayloft, eh?' Then she was eyeing her older sister speculatively. She put her head on one side and, much to Kitty's surprise, there was a hint of slyness in her tone as she added, 'Are there any nice grooms here now then?'

Kitty stared at her, then laughed. 'I really haven't noticed.'

'I bet!' Milly scoffed and some of her nervousness seemed to disappear.

Kitty shrugged. 'I've got me eye on someone far better than a groom.'

41

'Who? Do tell?'

But Kitty tapped the side of her nose and said, 'That's for me to know and you to find out, young Milly, so there. And besides, you're far too young to be knowing about such things.' At this moment the three years that separated them seemed far greater. Kitty felt herself to be a young woman, whereas she still thought of Milly as a schoolgirl. She was forgetting completely that at Milly's age she, too, had been embarking upon her first job and had thought herself very grown up.

'Now,' Kitty said. 'Let's have a look at you before we go downstairs.' Her expert glance ran over Milly's grey dress and apron and the triangular cloth that covered her hair, the type of attire that Kitty herself had so recently discarded with such glee. 'Yes, you'll do. But let me give you a word of warning. Always keep a clean apron handy and mind you wear the sack apron over this when you're doing mucky jobs. Mrs Grundy hates to see her kitchen maid with either a dirty apron or dirty hands. It throws her into a right old paddy so keep yer hands clean and your nails scrubbed and,' she added, grasping one of Milly's hands and holding it up for inspection, 'you'd better stop biting ya nails an' all.'

Milly nodded, only half-listening as her envious gaze took in her elder sister's appearance. 'You look ever so smart, our Kitty.'

Kitty preened before the mirror, proud of her new uniform. Black dress, stockings and shoes and a snowy white apron with a frill of delicate lace round the bib. Gone was the unbecoming headgear that hid all her raven hair and on top of her curls there now perched a dainty cap. She had scrubbed her hands and Mrs Grundy had given her some cream to rub into them each night.

'Now that you'll be handling madam's silks and satins,

you can't have rough, chapped hands like that, lass,' the cook had said.

Kitty whirled around from the mirror and reaching for her sister's hand, smiled and said, 'Come on, our Milly, it's time we went and started our new jobs.'

Kitty ducked quickly as the glass jar flew towards her and shattered against the oak door, splintering into a thousand tiny shards.

'A kitchen maid. I won't have a dirty kitchen maid touching *me*!'

Kitty's heart beat faster, thumping so loudly inside her chest that she was sure Miss Miriam could hear it. But she stood and faced her new young mistress. The girl was quite beautiful; there was no denying the fact. Quietly, but with a new-found strength in her tone that surprised even her, Kitty said, 'You'll have none of them pretty glass jars left, miss, if you keep chucking them at the door. Besides, I aren't a kitchen maid, now. I'm your personal maid. Your mother appointed me herself to be her maid – and yours.'

Miriam sprang up from the dressing stool and moved towards her. 'I aren't? I *aren't*? Why, you can't even speak properly.'

'Mind the glass, miss. Ya've nothing on ya feet.'

'Dun't ya dare tell me what to do,' she began, cruelly mimicking Kitty's strong accent. 'Ya scruffy little . . . Ouch!' Her words ended in a howl of pain as she hopped on one foot.

'I told you so,' Kitty said and stepped towards her, the glass crunching beneath her stout-soled shoes. She grasped the girl's arm firmly and propelled her back towards the bed and away from the glass.

'Sit up there and let's 'ave a look at ya foot.'

'Let go of me.' Miriam twisted her arm out of Kitty's grasp, but she did hoist herself up on to the high bed and lift up her foot, thrusting it towards the maid for inspection.

'Ya've got a bit of glass in ya foot,' Kitty said, bending over it. 'Hold still now and I can get it out – there, that's it.' Triumphantly she held up the splinter of glass, the end coloured red with the girl's blood.

'Oh! It's bleeding,' Miriam cried, petulantly.

''Course it is, but it's nowt. I'll bathe it.'

'Oh no you won't!' Suddenly Miriam reached out and Kitty found the pretty lace cap being torn from her head, the hairpins securing it tugging at her hair. Then Miriam dug her strong fingers deep into Kitty's curls and grasped a handful. Kitty gave a cry of pain, but Miriam only twisted the hair even more, pulling the maid's head towards her.

Their faces only inches apart, Kitty stared into the girl's green eyes that were glittering with spitefulness. 'You are not going to be my maid.'

Kitty reached up for the tangled mane of thick auburn hair. Digging her fingers into its depths, she, in turn, grasped Miriam's hair and was gratified to see the look of astonishment in the girl's eyes. 'Oh yes I am,' Kitty muttered through clenched teeth with an outward show of calmness she certainly did not feel inside. 'Your mother—'

'My mother,' the girl spat out the words so that Kitty felt the shower of spittle on her face. 'Just wait till my mother hears about this. She'll dismiss you at once and without a reference.' It was the ultimate threat, for to find work among the gentry without a good reference from a previous employer was virtually impossible.

'I don't think so,' Kitty said slowly and deliberately. 'I reckon that ya mam is only too pleased – relieved, even –

to have found someone who's prepared to take you on. And someone who already knows what they *are* taking on.'

That's it, Kitty thought, I've really gone too far this time. I'll be out on my ear for this, sure as eggs is eggs.

'You insolent little baggage . . .' Miriam began but then, suddenly, Kitty saw a shadow of uncertainty flit across the girl's face and knew her words had struck home. Miss Miriam might be spoilt, petulant and quick tempered with more than a little spitefulness in her nature, but she was also beautiful and very clever. She excelled at her lessons, could draw and paint skilfully and her embroidery already adorned the walls of the dining room. No, Miss Miriam was no fool. She knew herself exactly what she was like; she knew only too well.

Then Kitty saw a calculating, devious gleam come into the girl's beautiful green eyes which were still so close to her own. Miriam's grip on Kitty's hair tightened, making the young maid bite her lip to stop herself from crying out in pain.

'Well, you might think you can go running to my mother with your tales, but my father, Kitty Clegg, my dear father who dotes on me will be absolutely horrified when I tell him what you've done.'

Seven

Kitty hardly slept that night, knowing that, with the morning, the summons would come from the mistress – or, worse still, from the master – and by lunchtime she would probably be on her way home with her bags packed and without a job.

Downstairs even earlier than normal, she was heavy-eyed and clumsy with nervousness.

'Whatever's got into you, Kitty. This new job gone to your head already, has it?' Mrs Grundy grumbled as Kitty dropped a cup, the china pieces skittering across the tiled floor in a hundred fragments. 'You're not setting a very good example to your sister, now are you?'

'I'm sorry, Mrs G. It's just that ... Oh!' She jumped and looked up at the clanging bell above the door.

'By heck, Kitty, you look as if you've been summoned to the torture chamber.' Mrs Grundy leaned towards her and asked, shrewdly, 'Not getting trouble from that little madam already, are ya?'

'Yes, no, well ...'

'Mek up ya mind then, lass.' She too glanced up at the bell. 'That's the mistress anyway, so I should run along and see what she wants.'

I know what she wants, Kitty thought, trying to swallow the fear that rose in her throat. That's why I don't want to go up. But there was no escape as the cook said again, 'Go on, Kitty. Don't keep her waiting.'

*

'There you are, Kitty. I thought this morning I'd teach you how to do my hair,' Mrs Franklin greeted her. 'I've an hour to spare and you can practise putting it up in this style for me. It'll help you to understand how to do Miriam's as well. Now, I've laid out all the pins and combs, so let's begin, shall we?'

Kitty moved forward to stand behind her mistress who was seated in front of her dressing table. The next hour was pleasantly spent and, for a while, Kitty even managed to forget the cloud hanging over her.

'There,' Mrs Franklin said at last. 'You've done very well, Kitty, for your first attempts. Now, run along and see if Miss Miriam needs you.' She smiled. 'I expect she's probably gone riding and left her bedroom looking as if a whirlwind has passed through it.'

'Yes, madam.'

Closing Mrs Franklin's bedroom door behind her, Kitty took a deep breath, straightened her shoulders and marched across the landing to the opposite wing and knocked on Miss Miriam's door. When there was no answer, she opened the door and stepped into the room. Glancing around, she saw at once that Mrs Franklin was quite right. Miriam had left her room looking as if it had indeed been hit by a tornado. The bedclothes were pushed back into an untidy heap and clothes were strewn around the room. The wardrobe door was open and two drawers in the dressing table were pulled out, their contents tossed on the floor as if she had been searching for something in frantic haste. Face powder was littered on the carpet and the glass stopper of a perfume bottle lay in the middle of it. Handkerchiefs, combs and hairpins were scattered everywhere.

Surveying the chaos, Kitty shook her head and made a little noise of disapproval. Miss Miriam certainly knew how to test her maid's patience one way or another. Then she smiled wryly, pushed her sleeves up above her elbows and set to work. After all, Kitty reminded herself, this was what she was being paid to do.

An hour later, the bedroom was restored to order. As Kitty was laying clean underwear in the huge chest of drawers, the door opened and Miriam, dressed for riding, poked her head round it. 'There you are. I've just been to see Teddy and he's asking for you.'

Kitty turned and stared at the girl. 'But I—'

Miriam, obviously thinking Kitty was about to make an excuse that she had too much work to do, waved her hand airily. 'Oh leave all that. You can do that any time. Go and spend half an hour with Teddy. He gets so fed up being on his own.'

To Kitty's surprise, the girl glanced down and fiddled with the whip she held in her hands. 'I know I ought to spend more time with him, but I can't.' She bit her lip and added, 'I – I tried to stay with him just now, but it upsets me to see him suffering so. He's bad this morning.'

For a brief moment, the selfish pout to Miriam's mouth softened and a look of sadness flitted across her bright eyes. She turned away swiftly and Kitty was left staring at the closed door.

So, she thought with amazement, Miss Miriam has a soft spot for her sickly younger brother. For the first time, Kitty's heart warmed towards her new young mistress. If she was kind to him, even if to no one else, then Kitty could forgive her a great deal.

*

Edward was sitting up in bed against a mountain of pillows, his lips parted as he fought to pull in the next breath.

'Oh Master Edward, can I get you anything? Shall I fetch your mother?'

He shook his head and gasped his reply in short, staccato phrases, pulling in a rasping breath between each one. 'No – it's all right. It's just an asthma attack.'

It was very frightening to watch the young boy fight for each breath, his skin shining with sweat, his lips tinged with blue, yet Kitty was not afraid. Before she had come into service, she had often sat through the night with her younger brother, Timothy, while her mother had a few hours' rest.

'My mother says – you're her new – maid. And Miriam's too.'

Kitty avoided a direct answer by saying, 'I don't think you ought to try to talk, Master Edward. Lie quietly. Shall I come back when you're feeling better?'

'No . . .' His voice was high-pitched. 'Don't leave me. Please – stay. I – don't want to be alone.' His hands plucked at the edge of the bedclothes covering him.

She moved to the side of the bed and hitched herself up to sit on the edge. 'My brother Timothy gets asthma. Me mam always tells him to lie ever so still and try to let himself go limp all over. Ya know, like this.' Kitty slumped her shoulders, dropped her head and let her arms and hands relax completely. 'And try to breathe gently. Don't try to take in deep breaths, just little ones.'

The boy let out a breath and his hands lay still. He closed his eyes and for a moment there was no sound in the room. Kitty watched him. Now he wasn't breathing at all.

'Ya've got to breathe a bit, though, Master Edward.'

A small smile twitched the corner of his mouth and his eyes opened. He tried to taking a gentle, shallow breath and then pushed it out again, wheezing as he did so.

He followed her instructions for several minutes, not saying anything, while Kitty sat beside him, just watching.

'It's a horrid feeling,' he said at last. 'As if someone's sitting on your chest.'

Kitty smiled. 'Timothy always ses it's like being buried in a haystack.'

'I know – what he means.' He paused for another few moments, concentrating on his shallow breathing and trying to lie still. Then he said, 'Talk to me Kitty. Tell me about your family.'

'Why should you want to know about my family? We're not anybody interesting.'

'You are to me, Kitty Clegg,' he murmured, so softly that she scarcely caught his words.

Kitty shrugged. Maybe, she thought with sudden intuition, any conversation was preferable to the lonely hours he spent shut away in his sickroom.

'Well, now,' she said settling herself more comfortably on the bed beside him. 'There's me mam and dad and us eight kids.'

'Eight? Heavens!'

'Lie still, Master Edward, and don't talk, else I won't stay.'

'Please, Kitty. Go on. I won't say another word.'

'Promise?'

The boy pressed his lips together and nodded.

'Me dad's the stationmaster and we live in one of the station houses. Me mam cleans the waiting room and the offices, an' that.' She paused and then added, 'I didn't know until I came to work here three years ago that me mam used to work for your grandmother.'

The boy's eyes widened and he opened his mouth, but remembering his promise just in time he closed it again, giving a slight shrug with his thin shoulders as a negative reply.

Kitty nodded, as if understanding what he had been going to say. 'No, you'll not remember it, 'cos it was before I was born, before me man and dad were married. Anyway,' she went on, 'I'm the eldest at sixteen, then there's our George who works on the land. Then there's Timothy, he's the one who has asthma, then Milly, she's thirteen and she's just come to work here to take my place as kitchen maid. After her, there's Grace, Jane and the little one, Bobbie.'

Silently, Edward held up seven fingers and looked at her questioningly.

'Oh yes,' Kitty murmured and a note of sadness crept into her voice. 'There was eight of us. Little Connie died not long after I started working here. She – she got whooping cough. Connie, Gracie and Timothy all got it, but she was so bad . . .' Her voice faltered, still remembering the dreadful day when Mrs Grundy had sat her down on a kitchen chair and broken the awful news to her that her little sister had died. 'The mistress is giving you a week off to go home and help ya mam,' the cook had said. 'Isn't that kind of her, now?'

Kitty felt again the lump in her throat that she had felt then. It had been her first direct experience of her mistress's thoughtfulness.

Now Edward did speak, the painful rasp of his breathing already easier. 'I had whooping cough too, three years ago. That's when this asthma started. Maybe Timothy too?'

Kitty nodded. 'Yeah. Me mam said it left him with a weakness. Maybe you're right, maybe . . .'

Heavy footsteps sounded on the landing and the bedroom door flew open.

Kitty twisted round and her heart thumped as the booming voice of Mr Franklin filled the room with anger. 'What on earth are you doing in this room, girl? Out, at once.'

Kitty slid down from the bed and scuttled out of the room, but not before she had heard Edward's breathing once again become harsh and agonizing.

Eight

'I thought I told you that girl was never to work above stairs?'

Kitty, on her way down to the kitchen, her arms full of Miss Miriam's laundry, paused outside the drawing-room door at the sound of the master's voice raised in anger and knew instinctively that she was the subject of their discussion. She held her breath. Now it would come. Now she would hear the master telling his wife what Miriam must, by this time, have told him about their battle.

But Mrs Franklin was speaking calmly. 'I didn't think you would object.' She was quite unruffled by her husband's temper, adding, with mysterious but deliberate intention, 'In the circumstances.'

Mr Franklin grunted. 'It's one thing to employ the girl, quite another for her to have free run of the house where I might encounter her.'

'Henry, the girl cannot help being who she is. She's a good child and she has already shown that she can handle Miriam.'

Kitty winced as she continued to eavesdrop. Surely now, it was going to come out what had happened between her and Miss Miriam!

To her surprise, Mrs Franklin was saying instead, 'I am thankful to have her here. I never thought I'd hear myself say it, but I am. She has always been a good little kitchen

53

maid, and now she's worthy of something better. And she's so good with poor Edward too.'

' "Poor Edward", be damned! The boy's a milksop, a mother's boy. He'll never amount to anything worthwhile if you continue to mollycoddle him.'

'Edward will be a fine young man,' Mrs Franklin said in a voice so quiet now that Kitty scarcely heard her words, 'if he lives long enough.'

'Stuff and nonsense,' Mr Franklin boomed. 'There's nothing wrong with the boy that a day's riding in the fresh air wouldn't cure. Thank God for Miriam, I say. Now that girl's got spirit. Takes after me . . .'

Kitty had never imagined that the mistress – that lovely, gentle creature – could be so authoritative and towards, of all people in the world, her husband, but now, there was silence as Mrs Franklin made no reply.

'Clegg. Clegg! Where are you?' Miriam's voice echoed shrilly from the first-floor landing and Kitty nearly dropped the tea tray she was carrying down the stairs from Mrs Franklin's sitting room.

'Coming, miss.'

She hurried up the steps into the kitchen and banged the tray down on to the kitchen table. 'Wash them pots for us, our Milly. Miss Miriam's shouting for me and she don't 'alf sound in a temper. I'd best go straight up.'

'But I've got all these taties to peel for Mrs Grundy. I can't—'

But Kitty was gone, through the door and up the stairs two at a time.

Miriam was sitting at her dressing table, her long auburn hair cascading down her back in a wild tangle of curls.

'And about time. I want you to brush my hair and put it up. I suppose you do know how to put hair up, don't you?' The girl eyed Kitty sceptically through the mirror.

Silently thanking Mrs Franklin for the hour's instruction, Kitty said, 'I'll do my best, miss.'

'Get on with it then,' Miriam said, tossing the hairbrush towards her.

As Kitty stood behind her young mistress and brushed the long shining hair with easy, rhythmic strokes of the hairbrush, Miriam said softly, 'So, neither of us went telling tales, then?'

'Evidently not, miss.'

Miriam's eyebrows rose fractionally and she pulled her mouth down at the corners and repeated mockingly, ' "Evidently not." Such big words for a kitchen maid.'

Kitty, without pausing in her task, took a deep breath. It was time to take a firm stand. 'Am I? Is that what I am, then, Miss Miriam? Just a kitchen maid?'

She could see the girl struggling with an inner conflict, could see Miriam debating with herself, realizing that, despite the disadvantages, it was better to have Kitty Clegg as her maid then no maid at all.

In the girl's green eyes there was a sudden glint of mischief, which Kitty saw at once and understood.

'Well,' Miriam drawled, 'if you are so determined to be my maid, then you'd better learn to speak properly. No more "I aren't" or "ya mam".'

Kitty bridled. 'I aren't ashamed of the way I talk,' she began, but then, with the same spark of devilment, she mimicked the speech and mannerisms of her betters. 'But I can, if I so wish, talk like the gentry, m'lady.' She waved her hand in the air in an affected gesture.

Miriam's eyes widened as she stared at Kitty in the mirror. Then suddenly she threw back her head and laughed. 'Do you know, Kitty Clegg, I think, after all, that we might do very well together.'

There was no fear that Kitty could not have time off to be Jack's Harvest Nell, for it was the custom at the Manor Farm that when nearly all the corn had been cut, a small circle of uncut wheat was always left in the centre of the last field. On the Saturday of Harvest Festival weekend, this would be cut and the thresherman would fashion a sheaf-high corn maiden from it. In triumph the last load would be carried to the farm's stackyard amid much shouting and laughter and merrymaking, with the Harvest Queen sitting on top. On the Sunday, the Franklin family and all their servants, including the threshermen, would attend the Harvest Festival service in the church in the centre of town.

'I'd like you to come to the church with me today, Kitty,' Mrs Franklin told her on the Thursday morning before the weekend of the festivities. 'Bemmy will drive us and carry everything in for us.'

'You mean I'm to help you decorate the church, madam, for Sunday?'

When Mrs Franklin nodded, Kitty bit her lip. 'What about Miss Miriam? She wants me to cut her hair this morning and . . .'

Mrs Franklin waved her hand. 'That will have to wait, Kitty. We must decorate the church. All the ladies will be there this morning. We must not be late.'

'Yes, madam – I mean, no, madam.'

'Run along and get ready then, Kitty. We'll be leaving in ten minutes.'

Kitty ran lightly up the back stairs to her bedroom to

fetch the short cape she wore over her maid's uniform when walking into the town.

'Clegg, where the hell are you?' She heard Miriam's angry shriek as she came down the stairs from her bedroom under the sloping thatch to the floor where the family's bedrooms were.

Pushing open the door to Miriam's room she began, 'I'm sorry, miss, but—'

'Oh there you are. Come along, I want you to wash my hair for me and then trim the ends with these scissors.' She turned on the stool to face Kitty. 'Well, what are you standing there for, dithering in the doorway? Come along. I've been waiting long enough.'

'I'm sorry, miss,' Kitty began again, 'but ya mam – your mother – wants me to go with her to the church to help—'

Miriam sprang up from the stool and launched herself across the room. Grasping Kitty's arm, she dragged her away from the door. Caught off balance Kitty stumbled and fell and when she had scrambled to her feet, it was to see that Miriam had slammed the door, locked it and was now holding the key in her hand and waving it towards Kitty in triumph.

'There! Now you'll have to stay and help me.'

Kitty felt righteous anger surge through her. Miriam had no thought of the trouble she was causing for Kitty, making her disobey Mrs Franklin's orders. The girl was completely and utterly selfish.

'No, I won't. Give me that key this minute.'

Miriam laughed and dropped the key down the front of her corset. 'Come and get it, if you dare.'

'Oh I dare,' Kitty said grimly and stepped towards her.

Miriam raised her hands across her bosom and grinned defiantly at the advancing Kitty, her green eyes flashing with excitement. Kitty tugged her arms away and grasped hold of the top edge of the girl's laced-up corset.

'Ow, you little bitch! That hurts,' Miriam screeched and lashed out at Kitty, catching her on the shoulder. Kitty held on, undaunted by the blow. That was one advantage of being part of a large, boisterous family, she thought, you learned to take care of yourself.

'Let go. Do you hear me?' Miriam tried being the imperious mistress, but to no avail as slowly the corset began to give under Kitty's grasp.

Suddenly, Miriam twisted away, wrenching Kitty's hands painfully so that the maid was forced to release her grip. Miriam flew across to the dressing table and picked up the scissors, holding them in her clenched hand like a dagger, ready to strike a blow.

'Now see if you're so brave, Kitty Clegg.'

Kitty stood her ground and sighed. 'You're being silly, miss,' she said, managing to keep her voice sounding far more calm than she felt inside. 'Put them scissors down afore one of us gets hurt.'

'Them scissors, *them* scissors?' Miriam mocked, her voice rising in something approaching hysteria. 'Ain't you learned nuffin' yet, you scurvy little kitchen maid?'

Kitty opened her mouth to reason once more. There was a knock on the door and, startled, both girls looked towards it.

'Miriam? Kitty?' came Edward's breathless voice. 'What's – happening? Open the door.'

'Go away, Teddy dear,' Miriam said, her tone at once gentle and so normal that Kitty could not help but marvel. My word, she thought, Miss Miriam is certainly a good actress. Though which was reality and which was the act, Kitty could not begin to guess.

But it seemed that Edward was not to be dismissed so

easily. 'Please, Miriam, do – open . . .' Clearly, even through the thick oak panels, they heard his rasping breath. 'Open the door.'

Kitty looked towards her young mistress, but now she said nothing. She was watching her intently, waiting to see what the girl would do.

Slowly, Miriam's hand was lowered and she dropped the pair of scissors on to the dressing table with a clatter. She looked up and met Kitty's gaze. Softly, in a tone that could not be heard beyond the door, she said, 'You win – for now, Kitty Clegg. But only because of Edward.' She raised her voice and called, 'It's all right, Teddy dear, I'm just coming. We – we were just having a bit of fun.' She was raising her arm to an awkward angle and trying to thrust her hand down the front of her corset. 'I can't feel it . . .' Then suddenly she was convulsed with helpless laughter. 'Come here, Kitty,' she spluttered, 'you'll have to get it for yourself after all.'

Kitty found herself laughing too and in a moment the two girls were leaning against each other until tears ran down their faces while Kitty fished the key from between Miriam's breasts.

As she retrieved it and moved towards the door, she felt Miriam grasp her arm, but not now in the vicious grip of temper. 'Don't tell Edward what happened. Please, Kitty. It – it would upset him and – and I couldn't bear to make him worse.'

Close to her, Kitty could see the genuine anguish in the girl's eyes.

Quietly and with an outward composure, even though the last few minutes had left her trembling inside, Kitty said, 'Course I won't, miss.'

As she unlocked the door, she heard the girl mutter, 'Though I expect you will tell my mother this time.'

Kitty did not look back but smiled to herself. Oh Miss Miriam, if you think that then you've still a lot to learn yet about your new lady's maid.

'Kitty, are you all right?'

'Of course, Master Edward. We were just funning. Please, go back to bed. You'll catch cold again. Look, you've nothing on your feet.' She tutted disapproval and gently took his arm and steered him towards his bedroom door.

'Can't you stay a while?' he asked, as she made him climb back into bed.

Pulling the covers straight, she said, 'I'm sorry, but your mother's waiting for me to go to help decorate the church for Sunday. I'll try to come up later.'

Flying through the kitchen, Kitty gasped, 'Where's Bemmy? Has he gone?'

'Oh aye,' Mrs Grundy said, never pausing in rolling out a huge round of pastry. 'He went ages ago. Picked madam up from the front door an' all. Oh you're in trouble, me girl . . .'

But Kitty waited to hear no more, for she was through the back door, round the corner of the house to the wide driveway and out of the front gate into the road. The mistress would dismiss her without a reference for this, she worried as she hurried along the road, and I can't tell on Miss Miriam. She sighed, for the first time wondering if she had indeed taken on more than she could handle.

Usually, Kitty loved walking into the centre of the town. Tresford was a small but very old market town, mentioned in the Domesday Book, and its name came from the three fords that crossed the brook. At the town's heart stood the church, its square tower rising above the meandering streets of prosperous houses and neat cottages. On her half day off, Kitty loved to wander through the streets, especially on market days when the busy, bustling throng clustered around the stalls and the market men shouted their wares, vying with each other to catch the attention of the shoppers. But today, she looked to neither right nor left. She didn't stop to peer in the window of the chemist's shop with all the different coloured bottles with strange sounding names, or the sweet shop with its tantalizing array of boiled sweets and pretty, white and pink sugar mice. She didn't so much as pause to look in the window of the hat shop where a new bonnet stood displayed on a hat stand. Today, Kitty was in a hurry.

She rounded the last corner and saw the church with the road curving around it. She could see the motor car parked outside the gate and Bemmy struggling up the path with a heavy box of apples. She ran the last few yards and arrived breathless and flustered as Mrs Franklin emerged from the church and came down the path towards the motor.

'Ah, there you are, Kitty. Just bring the last box in for Bembridge, would you, please?'

'Yes, madam,' Kitty said and struggled to pick up the wooden box containing an assortment of vegetables and carry it into the dim interior of the church. Her footsteps echoed on the flagstones and, panting with exertion, she set the box on the floor and then tiptoed to where Mrs Franklin was kneeling in front of the altar, carefully making a mound of the red shiny apples.

'Bring the box here, Kitty.'

Kitty tiptoed back down the length of the aisle. Softly, measuring every tread, she carried the box to Mrs Franklin.

'Where shall I put it, madam?' she whispered. She had never been so close to the altar before, never near enough to see the fine gold embroidery that decorated the silk altar cloth. She was gazing at it, standing with the heavy box still in her arms when Mrs Franklin said, 'Put it here, Kitty, beside me on the step.'

'Oh – er, yes, of course, madam. I'm sorry.' Setting the box down she added, 'I was just thinking how lovely the cloth is.'

'Why, thank you, Kitty.'

Kitty stared down at her but Mrs Franklin merely carried on placing the vegetables and fruit in an attractive display at the foot of the altar steps, the harvest festival's offering. 'You mean – you did that? Made that cloth?'

Mrs Franklin smiled. 'I worked it when I first came to live at the Manor as a young bride.'

Was there a trace of wistfulness in her tone? Kitty wondered. 'I wish I could do something like that. It's really beautiful.' Overcome in her admiration, she had even forgotten to whisper.

'I'm sure you could, Kitty, given the chance. I've been surprised at your cleverness with a needle, though of course your workmanship has been more practical than decorative.'

The girl was still gazing dreamily at the altar, at the brass cross and candlesticks set upon its surface and the stained-glass window above it. She was imagining herself kneeling here in a long white dress and a veil with the handsome Jack Thorndyke kneeling beside her.

But it was Mrs Franklin standing beside her now saying, 'Come along, Kitty, I've some flowers I'd like you to arrange in the font. Do you think you could manage that?'

Reluctantly, Kitty tore herself away from her daydreaming and followed her mistress.

One day, Jack Thorndyke, she promised herself, one day I'll get you up this aisle. You see if I don't.

Nine

'I hear that you're to be the Harvest Queen, Kitty?'

Kitty was hanging her mistress's coat in the wardrobe on their return from the church. 'Yes, madam,' she said after a pause. 'That is, if it's all right with you?'

Mrs Franklin smiled. 'Of course it is, my dear. Have you a pretty dress to wear for the occasion?'

'Only me Sunday dress, madam.'

'But that's grey. Very suitable for churchgoing, of course. But hardly festive enough for such an occasion as Queen of the Harvest, Kitty.'

'No, madam.'

Mrs Franklin sat before the mirror on her dressing table and removed the long pins from her hat. She lifted it from her head and held it out for Kitty to put back into the hatbox. Smoothing her hair into place, Mrs Franklin stood up. 'I do believe there's a dress in Miss Miriam's wardrobe that might do very well. It's a shepherdess's costume she wore to a fancy dress ball last year.' Kitty felt the woman appraising her from head to toe. 'You're a little more slender than my daughter, but I think it should fit you. Run along to her room and ask her, my dear. Tell her that I gave my permission.'

'Oh there you are, Clegg. At last!'

Kitty opened Miriam's door to see her sitting at the

dressing table, her hair straggling down her back in a long, wet tangle. She was grasping the scissors once more, but now she was holding out a length of her hair to the side and hacking at the end of the strand with impatient snips.

'Oh miss, don't. You'll spoil your lovely hair.'

The girl glared at her through the mirror. 'Well, if I do, it'll be *your* fault.'

Pursing her lips, Kitty held out her hand. 'The scissors, miss, if you please.'

Miriam handed them to her and Kitty put them safely into the pocket of her apron. Then she took up a brush and comb and began to try to untangle the hair.

'Ouch! That hurt.'

'I'm sorry, but you've got it in a right state. It's like a straw stack. Do sit still, miss, else it'll pull all the more.'

For once Miriam did as she was asked and sat meekly while Kitty struggled to comb through the unruly hair. It was over an hour before she had smoothed out every knot and clipped the ends of the hair to uniform neatness. 'There,' she said, standing back. 'Now let me just get some warm towels and I'll dry it for you.'

Miriam yawned. 'Very well. But do hurry. We're dining at Nunsthorpe Hall tonight and I want to look my best. I think I'll wear the blue satin, Kitty.'

As she began to rub the girl's long hair, Kitty said, 'Miss, you know I'm to be the Harvest Queen, don't you?'

Through the mirror their eyes met. 'No, I didn't,' Miriam answered shortly.

'Well, Jack Thorndyke's asked me to be his Harvest Nell.'

'Really? What a great honour for you.' Her tone was heavy with sarcasm, but through the glass Miriam's eyes were still watching her.

'Your mam, I mean, your mother said I should ask you if I might wear your shepherdess costume.'

The girl shrugged her shoulders feigning lack of interest, but somehow Kitty knew that it was an act. She wondered briefly if Miriam could be a little envious that she, a lowly maidservant, had been asked to be the Harvest Queen, but she dismissed the idea as ridiculous.

'I suppose so.' Then, her eyes sparkling with mischief, Miriam wagged her finger at Kitty. 'But there's one condition, if I do lend you my dress.'

'Yes, miss,' she said warily, 'what's that?'

'At the Harvest Supper, which we all attend, you'll introduce me to this Jack Thorndyke.'

Kitty laughed with relief. Was that all? Well, she couldn't see the harm in that. None at all.

'Of course I will, Miss Miriam.'

Kitty closed the back door behind her and stood for a moment listening. It was a warm, late summer night, a million stars dotting the dark velvet sky. She tiptoed up the three steps and, lifting her skirts, ran down the grass path to the wall at the bottom of the garden. Again she paused to glance back at the windows of the house. A light burned only in Edward's sickroom, for the rest of the family, Mr and Mrs Franklin and Miriam, had left to dine at Nunsthorpe Hall.

'You mark my words,' Mrs Grundy had tapped the side of her nose and nodded knowingly. 'They're trying to wed Miss Miriam off to Sir Ralph's son and heir, Guy. Mind you, she could do a lot worse for herself. He's a nice lad. He used to come here a lot when he was a youngster with his father to visit. Course, Sir Ralph is the master's landlord. He owns all the land we farm, and,' she pointed to the floor, 'even this house.'

Kitty looked up in surprise and Mrs Grundy nodded sagely. 'No, ya didn't know that, did ya?'

'I knew the mester dun't own all the land he farms, but I didn't realize he didn't own this house.'

'Well, he don't. Fall out with the Hardings and we'll all be out on our ears.'

Kitty had carried on ironing the flounces of Miriam's petticoat, listening with half an ear to the cook's ramblings, but, all the while, glancing at the mantelshelf above the range and wishing that the hands of the clock would turn faster towards nightfall when she could creep out to meet Jack.

'Mind you, Sir Ralph's such a nice feller, I can't see him ever turning anyone out of their home, no matter what. His wife died, y'know, when Master Guy was born and the old master and mistress – they were both still alive then of course – were so good to Sir Ralph. He always used to be here. Then of course when that bit of trouble happened . . .'

Kitty's head lifted. 'Trouble? What trouble?'

'Oh nowt that concerns you,' the cook flapped her hand and turned swiftly back to her original line of thought. 'Guy's a bit older than Miss Miriam, but that's no matter.' She laughed and shook her head. 'He'll 'ave his work cut out with that little madam, if he does take her on, and no mistake. Too like 'er father, that one. She'll be the lucky one 'cos he's a lovely feller, Master Guy. Just like his father.' Mrs Grundy levered her bulk out of the chair at the side of the range. 'So, we've all got the night off and I'm going to walk into town to see me sister. As for you, young Kitty, just you mind what you're up to when I'm not here to keep me beady eye on you. And mind you listen out for Master Edward, won't you?'

Now, in the darkness of the garden, Kitty was holding her breath as she pushed aside the lilac bush that half-hid the door in the wall. She lifted the latch and pushed at it, the old, rotten timbers scraping protestingly on the ground. She doubted if this door had been opened in years. She winced at the noise which seemed to echo loudly through the stillness of the night. She glanced back once more before she slipped like a wraith through the door and out of sight of the house, praying that her absence would not be discovered. Only Milly, her sister, knew she had gone out.

'Where are you going, Kitty?' the young girl had asked, her eyes large and worried in her pasty round face. 'What if Master Edward rings down again? What'll I do?'

'Go and see what he wants, of course.'

'But he'll ask for you. He – he always does. Where are you going?' she asked again.

'Just out.'

'But . . .?'

'If you don't know, you can't tell, can you?' Kitty said. 'I won't be long.'

Now as her eyes became accustomed to the blackness, Kitty moved among the dark shapes of the threshing drum and the traction engine.

'Jack?' she called softly. 'Jack, are you there?'

She listened again and then she heard his low whistle and his tall, broad shape loomed up through the darkness. She felt his hands span her waist and he was lifting her off her feet and swinging her round. She gave a little cry of surprise and delight and then the sound was stilled by the touch of his lips seeking hers. Her heartbeat quickened as she wound her arms about his neck and he was carrying her out of the stackyard. Straddling the fence, he stepped into the neighbouring meadow where the new haystacks stood. Burrowing a hollow for them and gently laying her down on the warm, sweet-smelling hay, he lay beside her, crooking his arm for her to rest her head.

'I thought you hadn't waited,' she said.

'Said I would, didn't I?'

'I couldn't get away. Master Edward kept ringing down for me.'

'Master Edward? Who's he?'

'Edward Franklin. The son.'

'Oh aye. I'd forgotten about him. I thought there was only a daughter. But now you mention it, I do remember a lad from last year.'

'Yes,' Kitty murmured. 'Poor Edward. Everyone seems to forget about him.'

His fingers touched her cheek in the darkness, then traced their way down her neck, down and down, lingering on the swell of her bosom. His mouth close to her ear, his lips brushing her hair, he murmured huskily. 'Should I be jealous of this Master Edward, who can ring down for you any time he pleases?'

Kitty giggled. 'He's a *boy*. He's only fourteen and he's sick, poor thing. He hardly ever leaves his room.'

'Boy or not, I bet he likes you though, doesn't he, pretty Kitty?'

'Not in the way you mean, Jack Thorndyke,' she teased him playfully, pushing away his hands that were becoming far too bold in their searching. 'I'm only the maid. But he's lonely . . .'

'Oh Kitty, Kitty, you're lovely,' Jack whispered. 'You stay away from him, Kitty, 'cos you're mine. All mine.' His mouth was moving against hers, stilling her words and driving away all thoughts of the lonely young boy in his sickbed.

'Milly? *Milly*? Are you asleep?'

The girl's face, heavy-eyed, appeared from beneath the covers. 'Not now, I'm not,' she muttered crossly. 'Whatever time is it, our Kitty? Where've you been?'

'Never you mind,' Kitty said sharply, her fingers touching her lips still tender from Jack's passionate kisses, her whole body tingling with excitement from his caresses. As she undressed in the darkness, a shudder that had nothing to do with the cold night air ran through her. She could hardly wait to see him again. Only a few hours and he would be striding into the kitchen, along with the other workers, for the breakfast that Mrs Grundy cooked for the harvesters every morning.

She would watch him as he flirted with the cook, winked at Milly and then his eyes would come to rest upon her . . .

'I know where you've been anyway,' Milly muttered morosely. 'You want to watch yarsen with that Jack Thorndyke, our Kitty. He's no good. Even Mrs Grundy ses so. He's Jack by name and Jack-the-Lad by nature, she ses. So you—' Her words ended in a muffled squeal as Kitty pounced on her, pulling the bedclothes over her young sister's head to stifle her scolding.

'What do you know about it, young Milly? You mind your own business and leave me to mind mine.'

Milly struggled to free herself, giving little yelps of fright. Kitty loosened her hold and the girl pushed off the covers, struggling for breath.

'Don't blame me, then,' Milly gasped, 'if ya get yarsen into trouble.'

'I won't,' Kitty muttered shortly. 'I didn't wake you up

to be given a lecture. I just wanted to know if you'd had any trouble.'

'No, I didn't. But it was no thanks to you that I didn't. You were gone hours. The master and mistress came back and I was dreading them ringing down for you.'

Kitty pulled in a startled breath. 'Oh heck. I thought they'd be a lot later than this.'

'Later than this?' Through the darkness, Kitty could hear the surprise in Milly's voice. 'It is gone midnight, you know.'

'Oh Lor'. Is it?' In Jack's arms, she had lost track of the time.

'What about Miss Miriam? Did – did she ring for me?'

'No, you're lucky. She didn't. The master shut hissen in his study and the mistress and her went straight to their rooms.'

Milly yawned and turned on her side away from her sister as Kitty climbed into bed and snuggled down beside her.

Tomorrow. She would see Jack again tomorrow and then, in just two days' time, she would be his Harvest Nell.

Ten

Saturday dawned with a morning mist that heralded a hot day.

'Perfect. Just perfect,' Kitty said, clapping her hands with glee as she stood at the bedroom window and stretched her arms. Then she leaned forward, seeing over the wall the figure of Jack Thorndyke moving around his engine.

'He's here already.'

'Mm.' Milly, still buried beneath the bedclothes, was not interested.

'Jack. He's in the yard already. Oh, I wish . . .' She was tempted to throw up the sash window and call to him, but on this day of all days, she dare not. She could not risk spoiling the excitement by inviting trouble from the moment of rising.

'Come on, our Milly, stir yasen. You'll have Mrs Grundy puffing up them stairs to see where you are if you're not careful.'

The girl gave a groan, pushed back the bedclothes and swung her feet to the floor. Seeing that Milly had at least made an effort, Kitty hurried down the stairs. First job of the day was to fetch rainwater from the butt outside the back door and heat it for Mrs Franklin and Miss Miriam to wash in.

*

'So today's the day, is it, Kitty?'

'Yes, madam.' Kitty could hardly contain her excitement and her fingers were trembling as she laced Mrs Franklin's corset. Her mistress gave a little laugh. 'Well, as long as you've completed all your tasks, you may be free after luncheon for the rest of the day. I'm sure the other staff won't mind. They'll all have time off this evening to come to the Harvest Supper in the big barn.'

'Oh thank you, madam. Thank you very much.'

Jack wanted her in the yard for three o'clock, he'd said, and that would give her ample time to dress in the lovely shepherdess's costume still hanging in Miss Miriam's room. For several days, each time she had opened the heavy door of the mahogany wardrobe, Kitty had fingered the blue and white striped cotton of the underdress and the plain blue of the overdress which bunched up on either side. At the neckline, pretty lace would ruffle around her slender throat and Milly had promised to help dress her curling hair, sweeping it up at the sides to fall in ringlets and curls at the back.

Miriam was still in bed and when Kitty set the jug of hot water on the washstand and drew back the curtains, she was greeted with a groan from the bed so like Milly's that she almost laughed aloud.

'Whatever time is it?'

'Eight o'clock, miss. Same as usual and you don't want to be late for prayers, do you?'

Every morning, promptly at eight thirty, the family and all the household servants gathered in the dining room for morning prayers after which breakfast was served to the family. 'You know how the master doesn't like anyone to be late.'

The girl gave another grunt, turned over and burrowed her head beneath the covers. Kitty waited, though this morning she was hard-pressed to be as patient as usual. It had become a ritual, acted out every morning, and Kitty had learned quickly that if she stood quietly and said no more, after a minute or two, Miriam would think better of arousing her father's anger and throw back the bedclothes. Rather like Milly when threatened with the cook's wrath, Kitty thought.

As they finished and were both ready to descend the stairs with only a minute to spare, Kitty said, 'Miss, may I come back after breakfast and take the dress to my room?' Her hand gestured towards the wardrobe.

Miriam looked back over her shoulder. 'Dress? And what dress would that be?'

She's teasing me, Kitty thought. She knows very well what dress I mean. But, putting a smile on her mouth, Kitty said, 'The shepherdess's dress you said I could wear today to be Harvest Queen.'

Miriam's left eyebrow rose. 'Oh no, Clegg. I don't think so.'

'But . . .'

Miriam held up her hand and said, 'I shall be wearing the dress today, Kitty, for I shall be Queen of the Harvest.'

Kitty's mouth fell open in a gasp and she knew that anger and disappointment flooded her face. 'Jack Thorndyke asked *me*.'

' "Jack Thorndyke asked me",' Miriam mimicked her and then leaned towards her. 'But just remember, Clegg, that Jack Thorndyke is employed by my father who would, I am sure, rather see his *daughter* feted as Harvest Queen than one of his servants.'

Despite her feisty spirit and her boldness in standing up to Miriam's tantrums, Kitty knew herself to be defeated this time. Miriam whirled around and left the room as the gong sounded to herald morning prayers, leaving Kitty to follow miserably in her wake.

Kneeling with the rest of the servants, Kitty put her hands together and closed her eyes with an expression of piety. But inside her head she was repeating, not the words of the Lord's Prayer as Mr Franklin had bidden them, but . . . *Oh please, God, let it rain this afternoon. Let the skies open and everyone get soaked to the skin. I know I'm being wicked, Lord, and very mean, but please, oh please, just let it rain . . .*

The sky remained a clear blue with only tiny puffs of white cloud floating lazily across its wide expanse. The sun shone down, mocking mercilessly, as Kitty watched Jack hold out his hand to help Miriam climb up on to the decorated cart. Her heart twisted with jealousy as she watched her young mistress laughing down into his upturned face.

She had been gratified – but only briefly – at the surprise on his face when they had appeared in the stackyard. His glance had gone from her, still dressed in her maid's black dress, white apron and frilled cap, to Miriam standing by her side dressed in the shepherdess's costume, a garland of flowers entwined in her chestnut waves. Miriam's green eyes were shining and her lips were parted in a smile of triumph and excitement.

His glance had rested once more, briefly, upon Kitty and then his shoulders had lifted in a tiny shrug of helplessness as if to say, 'Sorry, but what can I do?'

The last vestige of hope in Kitty's heart died then. She had thought that he might have objected, that he might have insisted that she, Kitty, should still be his Harvest Nell, as he called the Queen, but no, his gaze had gone back to Miriam and now he was holding out his hand to her with a courtly little bow and leading her towards the cart, festooned with ribbons of every colour. The two horses pulling it were bedecked in polished horse-brasses and ribbons too.

Jack was not in his normal workaday attire either. Although not in his Sunday best, he had shaved and his face was clean and bore no trace of the grime from his smoky engine. In the open neck of his striped shirt he wore a spotted necktie and his black hair glinted in the sunlight. Even the toes of his brown boots, Kitty noticed, were polished.

Miriam sat on a square of hay in the cart. Jack climbed up beside her and took up the reins. 'Hold on, miss,' Kitty heard him say as he flicked the reins and shouted 'Walk on' to the horses.

The rest of the field workers fell in behind the cart with whistles and drums and one man had even brought his accordion. As they paraded from the yard around the side of the house and into the road, they were joined by the wives and children of the workers too. Even Mrs Grundy, Sarah Maybury and Milly had appeared at the side gate to see them go by, but Kitty kept her eyes downcast. She could not bear to see the pity for her in the cook's eyes.

At the front door of the Manor, out of the corner of her eye, Kitty saw the mistress and now she dared to take a peep. When she saw first puzzlement and then a frown of displeasure cross Mrs Franklin's lovely face, the girl felt a slight lifting of her acute disappointment. It was obvious, by the look on her face, that the mistress had not been a party to her daughter's scheme.

'Kitty?'

Now it was her turn to be surprised as she responded to the person who had fallen into step at her side.

'Master Edward. Oh, you're feeling better. How

wonderful!' Even her despondency could not dim the pleasure of seeing the boy not only up and dressed, but well enough to be out of doors and walking beside her to join in the merrymaking.

'I came . . .' He paused to pull in a deep breath and Kitty realized at once that he was not as well as she had supposed. 'I came – to see – you – as the Harvest Queen.'

'Oh,' she said flatly. 'Oh I see.' She could think of nothing else to say.

'My sister – up to her tricks, eh?'

'Well . . .' she began and then bit her lip and said no more. Even though the day was spoilt for her, she could still not be disloyal to her young mistress. It was typical of Miriam's behaviour. As everyone had tried to warn her, she had known what she was taking on when she had begged and pleaded to become Miriam's maid.

So now she had better just put up with it.

Kitty lifted her head and plastered a smile on her face.

'Well, Master Edward, the dress does look a lot better on her than it would have done on me.'

But Edward did not smile. Instead he said softly, 'As well, maybe, but not better, Kitty. I'll not have you say that about yourself. Oh no.'

The day was not after all entirely spoilt, for as Kitty watched the men cut the final circle of corn, saw Jack bind it into a sheaf and tie on some plaits he'd made earlier in the day – much bigger plaits than those on the tiny corn maiden he'd made for her – all the time Edward was at her side.

'It's an effigy of Ceres,' he told her.

'Who's she, then?' Kitty wanted to know.

'The Goddess of Fertility. It's to ensure a good harvest next year. Look, he's putting it beside Miriam on the cart.'

Now the whole procession turned again and as the sun

sank low in the horizon, they followed the wagon from the field back towards the big barn, singing and dancing and making such a cacophony that Kitty felt sure the whole of Tresford must hear the merrymaking going on at the Manor.

'Are you staying for the Harvest Supper, Master Edward?'

'No, I think I'll go in now and up to my room. I'm a bit tired.'

'I'll bring you up a tray later, if you like.'

'No, no, Kitty, you stay and enjoy yourself.'

She pulled a face and then grinned at him. 'I'll still have plenty of time to do that. I'll bring you something. About nine o'clock all right?'

He nodded and, as he turned away, she was sure she heard him say, 'I'll look forward to it, Kitty.'

Eleven

Squares of hay had been set around the sides of the barn and down one side were trestle tables covered with white cloths. Now Kitty ran back and forth between the back door of the Manor and the barn helping Milly to bring all the food from the kitchen.

'You've been busy today.'

'Cook's had me on the run all day, Kitty. I'm dead on me feet.'

'You'll soon get ya second wind when the music and the dancing starts. You can't disappoint that young farmhand. What's his name? Tommy, is it? He'll be asking you for a dance, I don't doubt.'

'Oh go on, our Kitty. Don't tease.' But the younger girl's cheeks were faintly pink and there was renewed vigour in her step as she scuttled back to the kitchen for another load.

At eight o'clock, as all the farm workers and their families began to arrive, everything was ready and Kitty had time to run up to her bedroom and change into her one pretty cotton dress. At least I'm not going to spend all night in my uniform, she told herself, whatever Miss Miriam says.

Miriam insisted on opening the dancing with Jack. Kitty, standing in the shadows near the door, watched enviously. She should be dressed in the pretty costume and dancing in Jack's arms, proudly proclaiming to everyone present that she was his girl. He had given her the tiny corn maiden, a replica of the effigy that now stood in pride of place at the end of the barn as a symbol of a good harvest and an offering for a good one next year too. *She* was his girl, not Miss Miriam. What did she want from him? Kitty asked herself. He was from a different world to hers . . .

At that moment, her thoughts were interrupted by a movement in the doorway and she shrank back further into the shadows.

Mr and Mrs Franklin had entered the barn. As they always did, they had come to look in on the festivities. Mr Franklin would say a few words of thanks to all the workers and tell them to enjoy themselves. Lastly, Kitty thought, he would not miss the opportunity of reminding them that he expected to see them all in church the following morning and then he and his wife would leave. No one but Kitty seemed to have noticed their arrival and the music and the dancing continued with Jack and Miriam still whirling in the centre of the throng.

Mr Franklin's booming voice came to Kitty. 'What on earth is the girl thinking of? Did you know about this, Amelia?'

From the shadows, Kitty saw her mistress shake her head, and then she heard a few snatched words above the noise. 'It should have been Kitty but . . . took her place . . . Harvest Queen.'

Mr Franklin's head swivelled to look down at his wife. 'The Clegg girl, you mean?' His voice was louder and Kitty could hear every word he said. 'Well, so it should have been. I'll soon put a stop to this.' And he marched towards the centre of the barn, pushing his way through the jigging couples until he reached his daughter.

The other dancers became aware of their master and

moved quickly aside. In a moment there was only Jack and Miriam left in the centre of the floor. As the music faltered and petered out, Mr Franklin grasped his daughter's arm and said in his loud voice, 'That's enough of this nonsense. You had no right to take the Clegg girl's place as Harvest Queen.'

Miriam's face flamed at being so publicly humiliated and by her own father too. Kitty felt a stab of pity for her. After all, she was only young and wanting a little fun, and she did look so pretty in the shepherdess's costume. Even Kitty, envious as she was, had to admit the truth of that.

The master was almost dragging her from the barn, but at the door Miriam twisted herself free of his grasp. For a moment father and daughter stood staring at each other while the girl turned slowly round to face the gathering. Some looked back at her, others lowered their gaze, embarrassed by the scene.

Miriam took a step forward and, looking around her, smiled sweetly. Lifting her voice, she said, quite calmly, 'Thank you for allowing me to be your Queen of the Harvest. I've had a perfectly lovely day.' Her bold glance went to Jack Thorndyke. 'And thank you, Mr Thorndyke, for opening the dancing with me.' There was a moment's pause while Kitty saw that their glances met and held. Then Miriam was speaking again, glancing around and graciously gesturing with her hand. 'I have to go now, but, please, do enjoy the rest of the evening. Good night and once again, thank you.'

Then she turned and, with her head held high, walked proudly past her startled father without looking either to right or left.

Kitty found she had been holding her breath without realizing it and now she let it out in a long sigh of utter admiration. The little minx! You had to hand it to her, she thought, shaking her head almost in disbelief. That was the most 'queenly' speech Kitty had ever heard. It was just as if Miriam had been addressing her adoring subjects, and the little madam had turned an embarrassing situation cleverly to her advantage. Now it was her father, not her, who had been made to look foolish.

As the Franklins departed, chatter broke out on all sides and the musicians began to play again. Jack was standing before her, grinning. 'You've got to hand it to her, haven't you?' he said without preamble.

Kitty nodded. 'That's exactly what I was just thinking. She always gets her own way, does our Miss Miriam.'

'Is she like that all the time? How on earth do you put up with it?'

A wry smile touched Kitty's lips. 'I suppose it must be all that red hair. She has the temper to match it.' Then she added, though a little reluctant to admit it, 'In a funny sort of way, I admire her.'

He was looking out through the open door at the retreating figures of the Franklin family, until through the darkness they were lost to sight. But still he continued to stare after them. 'She's certainly a very beautiful girl.'

'Now listen here, Jack Thorndyke.' Kitty reached up and gripped his chin, forcing him to look down at her. 'Just you keep your eyes this way. Ya've no chance there, m'lad, not if you want to carry on working in this district.'

Jack laughed his loud, rumbling laugh and opened his arms wide to her. 'I've more sense in me head than that, Kitty Clegg. Besides, I've enough trouble with you, ain't I?' And, putting his arms about her waist, he led her into the dance.

*

'Oh, whatever time is it?'

Some time later, Kitty stopped dancing suddenly.

'Eh? Why, what's the matter? She doesn't want you running after her tonight, surely?'

'No, not Miss Miriam. Master Edward. I promised I'd take him a tray up about nine, seeing as all the staff have been given the night off.'

'Oh him.' Jack's tone was resentful. 'He didn't look so sickly to me today, walking all the way to the field and back again. With you.'

'Well, he is. He went up to bed straight after. He was tired.'

'That's just a ruse to get you up to his bedroom. You want to watch yasen there, Kitty.'

'Don't be silly, Jack. He's only a boy.'

'Oh aye?' Jack said and the two words were laced with sarcasm. 'Boys of fourteen are quite capable, y'know, and I've heard all sorts of tales about what the young master of the house likes to do to the maids.'

She pulled away from him. 'Don't be disgusting, Jack Thorndyke. Master Edward's not a bit like that.'

'It's you that's the fool, Kitty, if you think that. All men are "like that" and boy or not, young Master Edward will think of himself as a man. Specially where you're concerned.'

'It's not like that,' she said again. 'Not between me an' him. Besides, how could it be? I'm only a servant.'

He gripped her shoulders, roughly now. 'Oh, so you'd like it to be, eh?'

'No, no, of course not.' Exasperated now, she wrenched herself free. 'I'm not standing here arguing with you. Ya can please yarsen whether you believe me or not.'

As she pushed her way through the dancers towards the door, the sound of his mocking laughter followed her.

*

He was sitting cross-legged in the centre of his bed, still fully dressed. There was no light burning in the room and the only faint light came from the window where the curtains were pulled back. He was sitting facing the window, staring down the darkened garden, over the wall and into the lighted barn at the far side of the stackyard. The faint sound of music drifted in through the open casement.

Kitty set the tray down on the dressing table and went towards the window.

'Leave it open, Kitty. I want to hear the music.'

'But it's draughty, Master Edward . . .'

'Teddy,' he said gently. 'Please call me "Teddy".'

'I don't want you to catch a chill.'

'I won't.' There was a pause before he said very softly, 'I thought you'd forgotten.'

'I'm sorry if I'm late, Master . . . Teddy, but . . .'

'It's all right.' He unwound his legs and slid to the floor. 'You're here now.'

He was standing before her and holding out his arms to her. 'Dance with me, Kitty. Please?'

'Oh M— Teddy, do you think you should? I mean, won't it make your breathing worse.'

He chuckled. 'Just for once, Kitty, I'm going to risk it.'

She stepped towards him and tentatively put her hand on his shoulder. She felt his right arm slip around her waist and the hand holding hers was trembling slightly. He pulled her closer to him and they began to dance, moving in time with the faint sound of the music from the barn. They did not speak and only occasionally could she see his face in the dim light. Even then, his eyes were unfathomable depths in the shadows.

Somewhere along the landing a door banged and Kitty jumped physically and stepped backwards out of the curve of his arm. 'I – I must go. If anyone catches me here, I'll be in awful trouble.'

She could see that he was smiling faintly. 'Well, I wouldn't want to cause you any more trouble, Kitty. I reckon you've had enough disappointment for one day.'

She shrugged. 'It's all right, really. I can understand why she did it. After all, she doesn't get a lot of fun either, does she? There aren't many young people around here she's allowed to mix with.'

He sighed. 'I hope you'll always be as understanding of my sister, Kitty. Really I do. Now, off you go, and . . . thank you.'

Still holding her hand, Edward raised it and brushed it gently with his lips.

Twelve

'Kitty, you're to pack some of Miss Miriam's clothes and Bemmy will drive you to the Hall,' Mrs Grundy told her. 'She's gone to stay with the Hardings for the week and you're to go too, seeing as there's no mistress in the house to chaperone the young people.'

Kitty felt herself torn. Part of her was thrilled at the thought of spending a few days in the gracious Hall that lay about two miles off in several acres of parkland, but away from the Manor she would not see Jack. After helping with the local harvesting, Kitty had feared that Jack and Ben would move on.

'Mester Franklin dun't want any threshing doing until early November and then only for a day,' Jack had told her, a smile twitching at the corner of his mouth as he watched her face.

'So you're going?' she had said flatly.

'We-ell,' he said slowly, 'yes – and no.'

'What's that supposed to mean? Are you leaving the Manor or not?'

His grin widened. 'Like I said – yes and no.'

Kitty gave him a playful smack on his arm. 'Stop your teasing, Jack Thorndyke, else I'll—'

His hands spanned her waist and he lifted her up and swung her round.

Startled by his sudden action, she gave a little squeal. 'Put me down, Jack. What if someone sees?'

He was laughing openly now as he lowered her to the ground again. 'Let 'em see. They'll see a lot more soon.'

Kitty's eyes widened. 'Whatever do you mean?'

'I'm going to be around for a while, young Kitty, so you'll not get rid of me so easily.'

With a surge of excitement that left her breathless, Kitty put her hands on his chest and looked up into his eyes. 'I don't want to. Oh Jack, you know I don't want you to go away.'

'I'll be away in the day, o' course, while me and Ben are working on the other farms, but at night – *every* night – I'll be back here.' He paused and then added, with a note of triumph, 'Mester Franklin has given me leave to sleep in the room above the old stables, well, garage, I suppose it is now.'

'Oh,' Kitty cried. 'The little room Bemmy used to have before he moved into the attic rooms in the house? Oh Jack, that's wonderful. Wonderful . . .' And, joyfully, she had thrown her arms about him, uncaring herself now who might see.

And for the following two weeks, it had been wonderful. Every night she had crept out to meet him in the yard or in the copse across the field behind the Manor. Once she had even allowed him to take her up to the tiny loft room.

'What about Ben?' she'd asked him nervously. 'Is he sleeping here too?'

'No. His family – his wife and three kids – live about five miles from here. He goes home every night. That's why Ben likes being in this area so much. And I . . .' He had reached out for her then, pulling her towards him. 'I haven't any objection to being here either.'

'You going to stand there daydreaming all day then?' Mrs Grundy's voice pulled her back to the moment.

'You mean Miss Miriam's gone there already? I didn't know. She never said anything this morning. When did she go?'

'Apparently, Bemmy drove Mr Franklin and her there after breakfast. I don't know any more than that except that he's brought word back that she's staying and you're needed there.'

'But,' Kitty blurted out without stopping to think how it would sound, 'haven't they got servants? A maid who can look after her and chaperone her too?'

'Course they've got servants in a great house like that. Far more than we've got here.' Mrs Grundy glanced at Kitty in surprise. 'What's the matter with you? Most girls'd give their eye teeth to spend a few nights in such a place. It'll be like a holiday for you, girl. You'll only be expected to look after your own young mistress, not do any of the housework like you still have to do here.'

Kitty was silent, avoiding the cook's searching gaze.

'They're very well off, y'know, the Hardings, and with Guy being the only son, well, Miss Miriam'd be set for life if she married him.'

Kitty tried one last desperate effort. 'But what about madam? I'm her maid too.'

'Sarah will look after her. Madam won't mind. You know how good she is, and besides,' she added, turning back to stir the bubbling stockpot, 'if anyone wants that girl safely married, it's her mother.'

Kitty sighed. She had no choice but to go. She'd wanted the job, she reminded herself, and she should have realized that she would have to follow her young mistress wherever she went. If only it wasn't while Jack was still here. She'd been so thrilled when she'd learned that he'd be coming back to the Manor and now it was she who was being forced to leave. She bit her lip wondering how she could sneak out to see Jack before she was obliged to go.

'And don't forget to slip in and see Master Edward before you go. Poor little chap, he'll be so lonely with both Miss Miriam and you gone.'

'He's fourteen, for heaven's sake,' Kitty snapped. 'You talk as if he's about four years old.'

Since the night of the Harvest dance, Kitty had begun to think of Edward as a young man, though whether it was because of what Jack had said or because of how Edward himself had acted that night, even she could not be sure. She just knew that to her, now, he was no longer a little boy.

Mrs Grundy sighed. 'Aye, you're right, of course. But with him being so sick most of the time, well, you tend to forget he's the age he is.'

Kitty spread a thick blanket and sheet on the end of the kitchen table and picked up the small triangular iron heating on the range. She spat on the smooth surface and when it sizzled, she gave a small nod of satisfaction and moved to the table to smooth the delicate lace collar on Miss Miriam's morning dress. 'How old's Mr Guy then?'

Mrs Grundy cast her eyes to the ceiling. 'Now let me think. He must be twenty-two or three now. Yes, that's it, twenty-three 'cos I remember them celebrating his coming of age a couple of years ago.'

'And his mother died when he was born, you said?'

The cook's round face creased in sadness. 'It was all very sad. Poor Sir Ralph was very cut up about it. He used to spend a lot of time here then. The old master and the mistress were very kind to him and then of course when the present Mrs Franklin married the master, he used to bring young Guy over . . .'

But Kitty was only half listening to the cook's reminiscences. Her thoughts, as she carefully ironed the creases from Miriam's gown, were on her own problems.

Just how was she to get out to see Jack?

'Is she ready, then?' Norman Bembridge stood in the kitchen doorway.

Bemmy, as he was known, was small and stocky with bow legs. His white bushy eyebrows seemed permanently drawn together in a frown above a bulbous nose.

Kitty turned to smile at him. 'You can load those on, Bemmy. I've just me own bag to bring down now.' She was dressed in her maid's uniform with a cape around her shoulders. Perched up beside Bemmy on the motor, it would be cold even on a warm autumn day.

Bembridge eyed the huge trunk and the two small bags and sniffed. 'Staying a month, is she?'

Kitty laughed as she hurried through the door and ran up the stairs to fetch her own, very small bag.

'Kitty? Kitty, is that you?'

As she passed Master Edward's room, trying to make no sound, she heard him calling. She groaned inwardly, sighed and then pushed open the door, pasting a smile on to her mouth.

He was still in bed, a book propped against his knees, but his gaze was upon the door and met her eyes as soon as she entered the room. 'You weren't going without saying goodbye, were you?'

Kitty swallowed and crossed her fingers behind her back. 'Of course not, Master Edward. But I can't stay many minutes. Bemmy's loading Miss Miriam's cases into the motor now.'

The boy's head dropped back against the pillows and

his glance went towards the window and the outside world. 'What wouldn't I give for a ride in the motor?' he murmured.

Suddenly, Kitty felt ashamed of her selfish impatience and of her own robust good health. She could not imagine what it must be like to be an invalid, shut away in one room day after day. His improvement at harvest had been followed by another bad attack of asthma and he had been in bed for the last two weeks.

She moved closer to the bed. 'We'll soon be back, Master Edward.'

'When?'

She shrugged her shoulders. 'End of the week, I think.'

His face fell. 'Six whole days,' he sighed.

She walked round the bed, edging nearer the window that looked out over the garden and towards the stackyard beyond the wall at the end, but his gaze followed her, watching her every movement. Then her attention was caught by the sight of Jack beside his engine.

Kitty whirled round from the window. 'I must go, I'll see you at the weekend and . . .' She paused by the end of his bed and wagged her forefinger at him. 'When I come back, I want to see you up and dressed and sitting in a chair.'

Suddenly the boy grinned, the smile lighting up his face and bringing a tinge of colour to his pale cheeks. 'You're on, Kitty Clegg.'

'Jack! *Jack*!'

As the engine gave a few chugs and burst into life, Kitty's voice was drowned in the noise that vibrated through the stackyard. Anxiously, she glanced over her shoulder. Bemmy was standing beside the motor car, glowering at her. Kitty bit her lip and then she pushed open the gate and ran across the straw-strewn cobbles.

'Jack . . .'

As she touched his arm, he jumped and turned to face her, frowning. 'What is it?'

Standing on tiptoe so that her mouth was closer to his ear, above the noise she shouted, 'I'm going away. I've got to go. I don't want to, but Miss Miriam . . .'

He shrugged and bending close to her ear, said, 'Have a good time.'

She stared at him. 'Is that all you can say?'

'What?' he bellowed as the noise from the engine seemed to grow louder. 'I can't hear you.' Then he straightened, grinned down at her, lifted his hand in a gesture of farewell and turned away from her. His whole attention was on *Sylvie*, the engine so dear to him that he had bestowed upon her the pretty, feminine name.

With a sudden flash of insight, Kitty wondered if he thought more about his engine than he did of any of the girls that rumour said he courted everywhere he went. For at that moment, as his hand rested lovingly upon the machine, she, Kitty Clegg, might not have existed.

Angry tears stung her eyes. 'You don't want to hear me, Jack Thorndyke,' she muttered, but knew he could not hear her. She blinked back the tears, straightened her shoulders and, head held high, she marched from the stackyard.

As she pulled the gate shut behind her and walked towards the frowning Bemmy, something made her glance up at the house.

Watching her from his bedroom window, dressed only in his white nightshirt, was Edward.

Thirteen

The motor car bowled along the country lanes, the wind snatching at Kitty's bonnet and cape. Bembridge gripped the wheel until his knuckles showed white. Neither of them spoke. He was too concerned with negotiating the bends in the winding road and Kitty with clinging on to her clothing and her precarious seat beside him.

They passed through a hamlet, Bemmy not deigning to slow. Barefoot children ran into the road and alongside the motor, keeping pace for a few yards, laughing and shrieking and pointing, though above the noise of the engine Kitty could not hear what they said. Here and there women appeared in the doorways of their cottages and men working in the fields paused to watch the 'new-fangled motey car', as Bemmy scathingly called it, pass by.

Bembridge had served the Franklin family all his working life. He had started as a young stable lad for the present master's father, rising to the position of head groom until that disastrous day when Henry Franklin had sold all his horses and bought a motor car. Now he doubled as Mr Franklin's valet and chauffeur but he still left no one in any doubt as to the fact that he bemoaned the loss of his beloved horses.

'It's the transport of the future, Bembridge. You must learn to drive it. You're a chauffeur now, not a groom,' the master had boomed.

'But I *like* grooming 'osses,' Bemmy would mutter

frequently to anyone who would listen. 'I'm not cut out to be pandering after gentlemen at their toilet. He should have a man trained proper in that sort of work.'

'Can't afford it, now can he, Bemmy?' Mrs Grundy would remark reasonably. 'You know we all have to double up. What if I started grumbling that I'd only one kitchen maid to help me instead of two or three and a scullery maid, an' all? And I don't get any extra help on special occasions, but I'm still expected to cope *and* come up with a lot of fancy dishes.'

'Tweren't like that in the old master's day,' he would mutter, still determined to have the last word. 'He had a valet who did nowt else but valet.'

'Well, them days is gone now, Bemmy,' Cook would say and not without a trace of regret in her own tone at times.

So Bemmy, who was not yet quite ready to retire, had no choice but to drive the motor car and learn how to be a 'gentleman's gentleman'. Though he didn't have to like it and his reckless handling of the vehicle showed his resentment.

Mrs Grundy would shake her head. 'You'd think the master would tell him off, but he sits up there in the back being thrown about and just laughs. I reckon,' she nodded sagely, 'he eggs Bemmy on to drive like a lunatic. Well, I ain't ever getting in that there motey car with him, I can tell you.'

But Kitty had not been given the choice.

The motor sped down an incline, bucketing from side to side, scattering hens dawdling in the open gateway of a farm in a squawking, flapping flurry. Bemmy wrenched on the wheel and swung the vehicle in between two high wrought-iron gates and along a winding drive. Rounding a corner, they saw a square Georgian-style house over-looking a tree-dotted parkland, where deer raised their heads, eyes bulging with alarm, thin legs poised for flight. Passing the front of the house, Bemmy turned down the side and round to the back of the building and drew the vehicle to a halt outside the servants' entrance.

Without a word to Kitty, or any offer to help her down from the high seat, he clambered down and went to the rear of the vehicle to untie the trunk and bags. Kitty climbed down and stood on the ground, not surprised to find that her legs were shaking and her head was swimming.

As he lugged Miriam's trunk towards the back door, Bemmy said, 'Ya'll 'a' ter mind ya p's and q's here, gel. 'Tain't like the Manor, y'know.'

Sir Ralph employed more than twice as many servants as the Franklin family. A cook, two kitchen maids and a scullery maid, two housemaids and a tweeny, a butler, a footman and a chauffeur. The list seemed endless and, in addition, Kitty learned, both Sir Ralph and his son, Guy, had a valet of their own who accompanied them wherever they went. With no mistress of the house, there was no lady's maid; the housekeeper was in overall charge.

The moment she stepped across the threshold on to the red tiles of the kitchen floor, Kitty could feel the tension. She was appalled to hear the cook shouting at the scullery maid, a tiny creature who looked scarcely more than ten years old, but who must be thirteen at least.

'Haven't you got those taties peeled yet? Why, ya useless—' The tirade paused as she became aware that someone had entered her kitchen. 'What you staring at, me girl? Ah, Mr Bembridge . . .' The sudden change in the woman's attitude made Kitty's mouth drop open in surprise. The woman, tall and thin and not at all like the comforting, round little body of dear Mrs Grundy, came towards them. 'This is Miss Miriam's maid, is it?' She cast a fleeting, disapproving glance over Kitty, who held her head high and returned the look. 'Looks a bold little madam, to my mind,' she remarked to no one in particular. 'Well, girl,' she addressed Kitty. 'You'll know your place here, let me tell you. Mrs Bembridge runs this household with a rod of iron. A veritable rod of iron . . .' She turned her thin smile upon Bemmy. 'Isn't that right, Mr Bembridge?'

Bemmy laughed wryly. 'That is so, Mrs Norton. That is so.'

Kitty's surprised look was going from one to the other. 'Bembridge?' she asked. 'Mrs Bembridge. Is she . . .?'

Bemmy glanced briefly at her. 'Me sister,' he replied shortly.

Kitty understood. The 'Mrs' was merely the courtesy title for a mature woman in her position.

'You.' The cook, turned to her scullery maid, who appeared to have no name. 'Fetch Mrs Bembridge. She'll want to instruct the girl and no doubt she'd like a word with her brother.'

'Miss Miriam will tell me what I'm to do,' Kitty said.

The woman turned back slowly to look at her. 'Not in this house, she won't. She's a guest here too, and you, Miss Hoity-Toity, will know your place and do exactly what Mrs Bembridge tells you.'

Beside her, Kitty heard Bemmy's wheezing laugh. 'Telled yer, didn't I?'

Miriam's welcome was offhand, giving Kitty no indication that she was pleased to see her.

'Oh, you're here at last! I thought you weren't coming,' was Miriam's petulant greeting.

'There was all your things to pack, miss, if you're staying the whole week.'

'Well, you're here now, so you can start and make yourself useful.'

Over the next few days, Kitty was certainly obliged to 'make herself useful'. She had never worked so hard in the whole of her young life. Not only was she expected to look after her young mistress, but when not needed by her, Kitty was under Mrs Bembridge's authority.

'Breakfast for the staff is at six thirty,' the housekeeper, a tall, stately and overbearing figure with steel-grey hair wound up into a bun at the back of her head, instructed Kitty. 'During the morning you will do whatever Miss Miriam requires of you and when you have finished your duties for her, you will help the under-housemaid with the cleaning.'

So, Kitty thought with wry amusement, Mrs G. had been wrong. There was to be no idleness for her here either.

Later, as she worked alongside Ruth, Kitty asked, 'So what's your master like? Very strict, is he?'

The girl looked up in surprise. 'The master?' Her voice was a whisper and there was fear in every swift, anxious movement as if she was frantic to get through her work and yet at the same time terrified of not doing it properly. 'You – you mean Sir Ralph?'

'Yes.' Kitty paused in her sweeping of the carpet and leaned on the long handle of the brush.

Ruth's eyes widened. 'Oh, Kitty, don't stop.' She cast a frightened glance at the door. 'We can talk as we work, but please, don't stop what you're doing.'

Kitty laughed aloud. 'I don't mind helping you, 'cos you look as if you could do wi' a hand, but I aren't killing mesen. They don't pay *my* wages.'

Ruth's face was a picture as she stared up at Kitty, even pausing in her cleaning of the brass coal scuttle set at the side of the huge marble fireplace. For a fleeting moment a smile lightened the look of permanent fear on the young girl's face. 'Oh Kitty, you are—'

Whatever she had been going to say was cut short as the door opened and the housekeeper glided into the room. Immediately, Ruth's head was bent over the coal scuttle and she was polishing vigorously as if her life depended upon it.

Perhaps it did, Kitty thought, as she turned her head and met the steely stare of the housekeeper.

'And just what do you think you're doing?' Her glance raked Kitty from head to toe. 'Get on with your work.' Her gaze went to the girl kneeling on the floor. 'I heard laughter. Was that you, Ruth?'

The young housemaid's face flamed. She bit her lip but said nothing.

'No,' Kitty said at once, 'it weren't. It were me.'

The disapproving glance came back to her. 'Well, let there be no more of it. Not in this house when you've work to do.' She turned back again to her own employee. 'You're taking far too long in here, Ruth.'

'Yes, Mrs Bembridge.'

'And you,' she said, pointing a finger at Kitty. 'Don't lead my staff into your bad ways, my girl.'

Anger flooded through Kitty like a tide. With careful deliberation she leaned her broom against the wall and stood facing Mrs Bembridge. She folded her arms across her chest and shifted her weight to her left leg while she tapped the toe of her right foot on the floor. Kitty Clegg was angry.

'I dun't have to take orders from you. I'm here to look

after my young mistress, not to be another of your – your *slaves*.'

Colour blotched the older woman's face. 'Why, you little . . . I'll have you dismissed without a reference.'

'What'll you do?' Kitty asked scathingly. 'Go to the Manor? Tell tales to my mistress?'

Mrs Bembridge drew herself up to her full height and suddenly she was even more imposing. Her eyes narrowing, she said slowly, 'I shall tell my brother of your behaviour. He will no doubt inform Mrs Franklin that you have disgraced yourself in this household.'

Kitty felt a tremor of fear. Had she gone too far? Would old Bemmy really tell on her? He was a grumpy old stick, but she had never thought of him as mean and spiteful. Kitty lifted her chin. 'Then I shall tell my mistress how I was not treated with the respect Miss Miriam's personal maid deserved as a guest within this house.'

It was a bold gesture and could spell disaster. Out of the corner of her eye she was aware that even Ruth had stopped her frantic polishing and was gazing up in mesmerized awe while the two protagonists glared at each other.

'I understand,' Kitty said carefully, 'that your master and Mr and Mrs Franklin are very good friends.'

The other woman drew in breath sharply. 'Don't you allow servants' tittle-tattle to pass your lips in this house, my girl.'

Kitty blinked, nonplussed for a moment. 'I – I don't understand. The two families are friends, aren't they? I mean, isn't that why Miss Miriam is here?'

'Oh – er – oh yes.' Now it was the housekeeper's turn to seem confused. 'Yes, of course. I thought you were referring to . . .'

'What?' Kitty asked, intrigued.

But Mrs Bembridge snapped, 'Never you mind. Just get on with your work and we'll say no more about it.'

Then the housekeeper turned and left the room.

'Ooh, Kitty, you are daring, speaking to her like that.' There was fear, but a note of admiration too, in the other girl's voice.

Kitty swung round. 'Me and my mouth,' she said. 'Mrs Grundy always ses it'll get me into trouble one of these days. I think mebbe it just has.'

She picked up the broom and flashed a smile at the girl still kneeling on the hearth. 'Still, I'd better look willing, while I've still got a job.'

To her surprise, Kitty heard no more about her run-in with the housekeeper. Later that night when she lay in bed beside Ruth whose room she shared beneath the eaves, every bone in her young body aching with weariness, she said, 'You never did tell me about your master. He must be a right ogre.'

'What?' Ruth said, her voice already heavy with the sleep that was trying to claim her. 'Sir Ralph. Oh no, we hardly know him. I ain't never spoken to him. If he comes into a room when I'm cleaning I have to collect me stuff and leave at once. It's a rule.'

'There seem to be a lot of rules in this house.'

'What d'you mean? Isn't it the same everywhere? Wherever you work?'

'Well, in a way,' Kitty said reflectively. 'We have to work hard and be respectful, but here everyone seems scared to death all the time. If it's not the master, then it must be *her*. Mrs Bembridge.'

'Oh yes, it is. She rules the house. There's no mistress,

you see. And the master, well, he just leaves everything to her.'

'So,' Kitty said thoughtfully, 'do you think he doesn't really know what's going on, then? How you're all treated?'

There was a moment's silence in the darkness before Ruth said, a note of surprise in her tone, 'Maybe not. I'd never really thought about it before. But maybe you're right.'

Kitty snuggled down and closed her eyes. 'Well, if I was you, I'd make sure he did know.'

'Yes.' Ruth's voice came faintly to Kitty's ears as she drifted into an exhausted sleep. 'I expect *you* would.'

Fourteen

Kitty saw the young master of Nunsthorpe Hall, Guy
Harding, for the first time the following morning. He was
standing near the foot of the main staircase waiting for
Miriam to go riding with him. As her young mistress
descended, Kitty leaned over the banisters. Her gaze was
not on Miriam but on the tall, thin young man who waited
patiently in the hall below. As he looked up towards the
girl, Kitty saw his face. He was fair-skinned with hair that
was so blond it was almost white. She could not, from this
distance, see the colour of his eyes but imagined they must
be blue. He had a gentle expression and when he smiled
his whole face seemed to light up. As he held out his hand
to Miriam, Kitty could see at once that he had more than
a passing fancy for his young guest. She watched as Miriam
gave a coquettish toss of her head, a merry laugh and then
put her hand into his outstretched palm.

Unobserved by either of them, Kitty saw him hold open
the huge front door for Miriam, never once taking his eyes
from the lovely girl's face. As it closed with a heavy thud
behind them, cutting off the sound of their laughter, a
voice shrilled behind her.

'Clegg, what do you think you're doing?'

Kitty jumped, not in fear but at the unexpectedness of
the sound and she turned to see the housekeeper coming
towards her along the landing.

'Good morning, Mrs Bembridge,' she said as she faced

the woman squarely. 'I must just tidy Miss Miriam's room and then I'll be free to help Ruth. What would you like me to do today?' Kitty smiled, the two deep dimples in her cheeks appearing as she did so, her dark eyes dancing with mischief. But her tone was all politeness and though the housekeeper glowered at her, the woman could not openly accuse her of insolence, though Kitty guessed she would dearly have loved to do so.

She stood listening as the housekeeper ticked off a list of duties with the forefinger of one hand against the fingers of the other. ' . . . and the library must be cleaned thoroughly today. The master will be home at the weekend and he spends most of his time in that room when he's here.'

'I'll be down in about half an hour, Mrs B.,' Kitty promised and, picking up her skirts, she skipped lightly along the wide landing towards the guest room where Miriam slept.

'Mrs Bembridge to you, my girl, and walk properly!'

But Kitty Clegg took not a scrap of notice.

'Do you like Master Guy, miss?' Kitty was emboldened to ask as she brushed the long, thick auburn hair late that night.

Through the mirror, Miriam met her gaze steadily. 'I like him, yes, he's sweet but . . .'

There was a moment's silence as the girl sighed.

'But what, miss?' Kitty prompted.

'I thought when you fell in love you were supposed to feel, well, different.' Miriam clasped her hands together in front of her breast. 'You know, all excited, your heart racing at the very sight of your lover. Your mind filled with thoughts of him every minute of the day.' She sighed again. 'Or is that only in romantic novels, Kitty?'

At once the picture of Jack Thorndyke came into Kitty's mind and her heart did a funny little jump inside her chest. 'Oh no, miss,' and her voice came out in a strange, almost breathless whisper. 'It's not just in books.'

Miriam stared at her. 'Have you got a lover, Kitty Clegg?'

Kitty stared back at her, trying to tell if Miriam's question was genuine. She was surprised the girl hadn't guessed about her and Jack. All that business of the Harvest Queen, surely . . .? But then, Kitty answered herself, why should she? Servants kept their private life just that. Private. Besides, Miss Miriam was so wrapped up in her own life, her own desires, she would scarcely give a thought to her maid.

Kitty grinned mischievously. 'That'd be telling, miss, 'cos Mrs Grundy always ses we're not supposed to have "followers".'

Miriam laughed. 'But you do anyway, eh?'

Kitty just smiled, a pink tinge to her cheeks, but already Miriam's thoughts had turned back to herself. She leaned her elbows on the dressing table and cupped her chin in her hands, staring at her own reflection. 'I should like to be in love, but I don't think I am with Guy.'

'Well, I think he is with you, miss. I can see it in his eyes when he looks at you.'

Miriam flapped her hand. 'Oh well, yes, I expect he is, but I can't help it if I don't feel the same way about him, can I?'

'No, you can't make yourself fall in love with someone,' Kitty said and remembering Mrs Grundy's warnings, she thought to herself, or make yourself *not* love someone however 'unsuitable' you're told they are.

'Mm,' Miriam murmured and then, with a rare, honest insight into her own character, she sighed and added, 'but Guy's too nice for me. I need someone strong, someone who will master me, perhaps almost be a little cruel to me. Tall, dark and handsome, wouldn't you say, but a bit of a rogue too?'

Suddenly, she jumped up, flinging Kitty's ministering hands aside. 'We're going home tomorrow morning, Kitty. I'm bored here.'

Kitty's eyes widened. 'But what about Master Guy? He'll be so disappointed. I'm sure he's falling in love with you.'

'Then it would be far better for me to go now before he gets really hurt.'

'But miss, what will your mother say and – and your father?'

There was rebellion in the green eyes as the girl said, 'I don't care what they say. I'm not going to be rushed into marriage with someone I don't love. Not even to please them. And Guy will soon get over it.'

Kitty felt sorry for the kindly young man. It was a shame really. He was so right for Miriam. He would calm her and understand her moods and her tantrums, loving her all the time.

Kitty sighed. She knew exactly how he felt, for she was very much afraid that Threshing Jack did not love her as she loved him.

But she did not argue with her young mistress any more, for they were to return home two days earlier than expected and she would see Jack that much sooner.

'Have you missed me then?' she asked Jack pertly, resisting the urge to throw herself against him, wind her arms about his waist and press her face to his broad, muscular chest.

She felt his strong arms go around her and he was picking her up and swinging her round. She laughed in delight and threw her head back to look up at him. Slowly he let her down to stand on the ground, bending his head to kiss her lips as he did so. She returned his kiss, not caring who might see them in the broad light of day in the middle of the stackyard.

'Course I've missed you,' he said lightly and, with a deep-throated chuckle, added, 'You and your cheeky face. Ya little sister's not a patch on you, Kitty Clegg. She's a regular little scaredy-cat. A right misery, if ever there was one.'

Kitty leaned back against the circle of his arms to look up into his face. Playfully, she tapped his arm sharply, but she was grinning as she said, 'I hope you ain't been makin' a play for my sister. She's only thirteen.'

Jack laughed but neither denied nor confirmed her suspicion. His only answer was to kiss her again and whisper, 'Meet me tonight.'

'Oh Jack,' she murmured ecstatically, 'I can't wait.'

'D'ya – you – know, Mrs G.,' Kitty said. She was trying valiantly to iron out some of the roughness from her speech, now that she considered she was moving in better circles. Well, employed in them at least. 'I've never seen so many servants in me – my – life as they've got at the Hall. And all to look after only two men. It's us needs more help here. Why haven't we got a few more servants? It'd be a lot easier on everybody if we had.'

Mrs Grundy sniffed. 'There was more of us in the old days when old Mr and Mrs Franklin were alive. They'd turn in their graves if they could see this place now and how the master has gone through any inheritance they left him. Eh, Kitty, the tales I could tell you, if I'd half a mind . . .'

'Well, go on then, tell me. You know a secret's safe with me. I'm no gossip.'

The cook laughed. 'And just what do you suppose we'd be doing if I was to tell you, eh? Gossiping ourselves, wouldn't we?'

Kitty grinned impishly, the dimples deepening in her cheeks. 'Oh, go on, Mrs G. You sit down there and I'll make us a nice cup of tea and just for once in our lives we'll have a good old gossip.'

Moments later, when she handed Mrs Grundy a steaming cup of tea and a chocolate biscuit from the tin, Kitty asked, 'How long have you worked here, Mrs G.?'

'I started here as cook when I was about twenty-five. That was when the old master and mistress were still alive, of course,' she said, neatly avoiding giving her actual age away. 'The present master was about – let me think – about nineteen and he'd started his wild ways then.'

Kitty longed to press her further but knowing such a question as What wild ways? would make the cook clamp her lips tightly shut, she said nothing, letting Mrs Grundy drink her tea and ramble.

'The old master was a lovely old boy but the mistress, she was a tartar. They'd come up, you see, from what we'd call the labouring class to middle class and them's always the worst. Now the present mistress, *our* Mrs Franklin . . .' the cook's face beamed with genuine fondness, 'she was born into class. Came from a very genteel family, but, in a way, she married beneath her. They say her father lost all his money through no fault of his own and the family lived in very reduced circumstances.'

'Was it what they call an arranged marriage, then?' Kitty put in.

'I expect so. Master Henry was wild and there were one or two scandals . . .' She stopped suddenly, cleared her throat and hurried on, 'Anyway, they were married and came to live here too. Us servants were run off our feet in them days. It was like having two households to look after.'

'Did the old master and mistress only have the one son, then? Mr Henry?'

'No. I was told there'd been two other little boys but they'd died in childhood, always sickly little things they were, so I understand. But that was all before I came to work here.'

Kitty was silent, wondering if poor Master Edward suffered from similar delicate health to his long-dead uncles. She shuddered. She liked Master Edward, she didn't want anything to happen to him.

'It's funny, ain't it?' Mrs Grundy was saying. 'I remember the old boy dying. He was only ill for a little while and none of us even realized he was that bad. He never complained and always thanked us so politely when we waited on him and then, suddenly, we heard one morning he'd just died in his sleep.' Mrs Grundy shook her head. 'Just like that. Eh, but he were a nice old boy.'

'And when did the old lady die, then?'

'Only about five years ago. And that were very different, had us running after her from morning till night and then her bell would go in the middle of the night an' all. They hired a trained nurse, well, several actually, 'cos none of 'em stayed long.'

Kitty laughed. 'Sounds very much as if Miss Miriam takes after her.'

'Oh she does, believe you me, she does. She had a fine

107

temper, did old Mrs Franklin. Her son's got it and so has her granddaughter.' The cook looked sharply at Kitty. 'How are you getting on with her then? Are you managing?'

Kitty chuckled. 'Oh yes, I can handle Miss Miriam. I stand up to her and though she threatens to sack me and all sorts, I think underneath all that, she actually respects me for it.'

Mrs Grundy sniffed and began to lever herself up. 'Well, I'd best be getting on if they're to get any dinner tonight. Now, where's that young Milly got to? Drat the girl. She's not a patch on you, Kitty, even though she's your sister, so if Miss Miriam does ever give you the push, you can come back to me kitchen in a flash.'

Touched by the woman's brusque compliment, Kitty planted a swift kiss on her cheek. 'Ta, Mrs G, but now I've gone up in the world . . .'

'Now then,' the pudgy fingers wagged in her face. 'Don't you go getting ideas above your station, me girl. Else it'll all end in tears.'

Kitty gave her a swift hug and skipped lightly across the flagstone floor to the door leading upstairs. 'Fat chance while I work here, eh Mrs G.?'

'Why, you cheeky young . . .' the cook began, but Kitty was gone, running up the stairs. Faintly behind her she heard Mrs Grundy's laughter and Kitty smiled to herself. One day, she promised herself, I'll find out just what the master's 'scandals' were in his misspent youth.

Fifteen

'Kitty? Kitty – is that you?

She groaned aloud as Edward's voice came thinly through the closed door. Sighing, she set down the dustpan and brush she was carrying and opened his door. Her glance went immediately towards the bed but, to her surprise, it was empty. The covers were thrown back carelessly and the sheets rumpled.

Her gaze swivelled and she saw him sitting near the window overlooking the back garden. She clapped her hands in delight. 'Oh Master Edward, you're up – and dressed too. I *am* glad.'

The light from the window was behind him as he looked towards her, but as she drew closer to him, she saw that a faint flush coloured his face. He patted the seat beside him. 'Come and sit down.'

'I can't, Master Edward. I've work to do and . . .'

'Please? Just for a moment. And it's Teddy. Remember?'

She smiled weakly and sat on the edge of the seat, darting anxious glances towards the door. Since their return to the Manor House, Kitty had waited in trepidation for either Mrs Grundy or, worse, Mrs Franklin to reprimand her for her impudent behaviour while a guest at the Hall.

Not for one moment did she regret standing up to the odious housekeeper, but she did not want to lose her position as lady's maid and worse still, she did not want to be

109

sent away from the Manor while Jack Thorndyke continued to return every night to the loft above the stables.

She felt Edward's gaze upon her and she turned to look into his pale face.

'I – I missed you,' he stammered.

Now she smiled broadly at him, genuinely delighted to see him out of bed. 'How've you been?'

'Better,' his smile widened. 'I had to be up by the time you came home, didn't I? I promised.'

She nodded. 'Yes. And tomorrow – downstairs, eh?'

His face clouded. 'Oh, I don't know about that.'

'Do try,' she urged him. 'Your mother would be so pleased.'

'Yes,' he murmured. 'My *mother* would be.'

Had she imagined it, or had he put a slight accent on the word 'mother'?

'And Miss Miriam,' she tried to encourage him.

His face brightened again. 'She's come home too, then?'

When Kitty nodded, he said, 'Well, in that case, I might try. In fact, yes, I'll come down to dinner tonight.'

'That's the spirit,' Kitty said, standing up. 'Now, I really must get on, else I'll get the sack.'

She gave a start of surprise as his bony hand, white and slightly clammy to the touch, reached out suddenly and grabbed her rough, calloused fingers. They were the clean, soft hands of an invalid, not grubby like the hands of her active, healthy brothers. 'Oh Kitty,' he said softly, his blue eyes looking up into her face. 'I would never let them do that to you, not – not if I could stop it.'

Touched by his obvious feeling for her well-being, Kitty patted his hand reassuringly. 'Don't you worry. They'd have to throw me out bodily, and kicking and screamin' at that.'

Now the boy laughed and suddenly there was a flash

of what a normal, healthy boy of fourteen should look like. 'Oh Kitty, you are *wonderful*.'

Suddenly, she saw once more, as she had on the night of the harvest supper, the young man that Edward Franklin would one day be. As she left his room, Kitty was thoughtful. Her recent talk with Miss Miriam about love and how it should feel, and the realization of her own growing passion for Jack Thorndyke despite all the dire warnings, had suddenly made her aware of something that perhaps she should have seen before. Was Master Edward more than a little in love with her?

She sighed and picked up the dustpan and brush she had left outside his door. She hoped profoundly that it was nothing more than a boyish crush, for she felt deeply sorry for the delicate boy and she would not want him to be hurt.

After all, she was only a maid within the household and he, one day, would be master of the Manor House.

'What do I have to do exactly?' Kitty demanded, her arms folded across her breasts. 'I've never waited at table before. I don't know where to start.'

Mrs Grundy shrugged her plump shoulders. 'You'll have to try, Kitty, because Sarah's got this dreadful cold and if she sniffles and sneezes around the master, he'll likely fly into one of his tempers.'

'I don't mind helping her with the cleaning, you know I don't. But I don't want to have to serve them. Can't I just plonk the dishes down and tell 'em to help theirsens?'

Mrs Grundy laughed till her chins wobbled. 'You could, love, but you'd likely be out of a job by the morning.'

Kitty grinned back. 'Well, I'll do me best. Now, which

way did you say? Serve from the left and clear from the right?'

Mrs Grundy's brow creased. 'I reckon so. Or is it t'other road round? I never can remember.'

'Oh, you're a big help, Mrs G.'

'Don't you worry. The master'll soon tell you if you get it wrong.'

Kitty pulled a face at her. 'That's exactly what I'm afraid of.' But she went through to the dining room to view the table that Sarah had laid before taking herself off to bed to nurse a streaming cold.

'She spends more time up in that bed of hers than she spends out of it.' It seemed to the healthy Kitty that the housemaid, Sarah, was always going down with one ailment or another. But then, more charitably, she thought, maybe the girl can't help it. Maybe she's like poor Master Edward and catches anything going. At the thought of him, Kitty muttered, 'Maybe it's just as well it'll be me in the dining room tonight when he comes down for dinner, 'cos if he catches Sarah's cold, he'll be back in bed again before he's hardly out of it.'

Biting her tongue between her teeth in concentration, Kitty carried the huge tray bearing the roast leg of lamb from the kitchen into the dining room. The family were all seated around the long table.

At one end, his bushy eyebrows drawn together in a frown, sat Mr Franklin. As she laid the dish before him, he was thumping his fist on the table making the cutlery bounce upon the white cloth. 'High time the Government did something to stop this suffragette nonsense. I was reading in the paper this morning that some foolish woman had chained herself to the railings outside Number Ten.

Did you ever hear anything so ridiculous? Women should know their place.'

'And where is that, Father?' Miriam leaned her elbows on the table and cupped her chin in her hand. 'Sitting on a cushion and sewing a fine seam, I presume? Or scrubbing floors, like poor Kitty here and her like.'

'Eh?' The bushy eyebrows came even more closely together and the piercing eyes were suddenly near to Kitty as she leaned across him to set down the dish. She stood up quickly and stepped backwards.

'I thought I told you *that girl* is not allowed anywhere near me?'

Serenely, Mrs Franklin smiled. 'Kitty is helping out while Sarah is indisposed. The housemaid has a most dreadful cold.' She paused as if with deliberate emphasis. 'I'm sure you would not like her to be serving your meal tonight.'

Mr Franklin's only reply was a grunt as he picked up the carving knife and fork and began to slice the joint.

Standing at his elbow, waiting to pass the plates round as he served each member of the family, Kitty thought, he really is a handsome man for his age. Mr Franklin still had a good head of hair, dark chestnut and the flecks of white at the temples served only to give him an air of distinction. The thick moustache that drooped down at either corner hid his mouth, but the mirror of his moods was in his green flecked eyes. His daughter had obviously inherited his volatile temperament and his colouring too, whereas their son resembled his mother.

Mrs Franklin's low voice came now from the far end of the table. 'Only a little for Teddy, Henry my dear. His appetite is not yet quite normal.' And Kitty saw her mistress bestow a gentle, understanding look upon Edward that was like a caress.

Mr Franklin gave a snort of derision. 'Get some good red meat into you, boy. You'll never amount to anything if you pick at your food like a woman.'

'Yes – Father,' he said meekly and, to Kitty's disappointment, she could already hear the tell-tale wheeze of breathlessness as he spoke.

As she laid the plate of meat before him and picked up the vegetable dish to serve him, Kitty bent low and whispered, 'Tell me how much you can eat, Master Edward.'

Almost before the words had left her lips, a bellow of rage came from Mr Franklin and close by her, she felt Edward stiffen. 'Speak when you're spoken to, girl, and not before.' Down the length of the table between them, the master glowered at his wife. 'Don't you teach your servants how to behave, Amelia? Give him plenty of greens, girl. They're good for you, boy.'

Inwardly, Kitty seethed with anger as the colour flooded up the boy's neck and suffused his face. She could say nothing, but from the opposite side of the table came a girlish laugh. 'Stop bullying him, Father,' Miriam said. 'Take no notice of him, Teddy. You eat just what you can and leave the rest.'

Mr Franklin's fist thumped the table. 'I will not have insolence, girl.' It seemed, Kitty thought, that the master called no one, except his wife, by their proper name. Out of the corner of her eye as she continued to serve the vegetables, Kitty saw Miriam calmly return her father's glare.

'Stop shouting, Father. It makes poor Teddy worse.'

'Why, you little . . .' he thundered, and then suddenly he threw back his head and laughed, a great bellow of sound gusting down the table. '*That*'s my daughter. What a pity you weren't born the son of the family.' His laughter died as he looked towards his wife. 'A great pity. Don't

114

you think so?' There was an awkward pause as he added, his tone heavy with sarcasm, '*My dear?*'

'I wish I had been born a boy,' Miriam retorted. Kitty almost gasped aloud and glanced up. How could she be so cruel to her brother? But then she saw Miriam give a huge wink towards Edward and knew immediately that the girl was not, for once, being selfish. Indeed, she was deliberately drawing her father's attention back to herself and away from him. Kitty shook her head slightly, thinking Miriam really is extraordinary. Selfish, wilful and demanding one moment, the next, generous and warmhearted towards her younger, more fragile brother. When she saw actions like the one she had just witnessed, Kitty found it impossible to bear a grudge against Miriam for long.

'Then,' Miriam was saying with deliberate provocativeness, 'I could have the vote. As it is, I shall have to wait until we've won it for ourselves.'

'Never! Women will never have the vote.'

As she left the dining room, Kitty heard the thump of the master's fist once more on the table. Back in the kitchen, she set the silver salver on the table with a clatter. 'By heck, Mrs G, you might 'ave warned me 'ow they carry on in there.'

'Eh?' Mrs Grundy was only half paying attention to what Kitty was saying. She was busy turning out a steamed pudding and ensuring that the custard did not go lumpy. 'What are you on about, Kitty?' she said, bustling between the range and the table.

'You can cut the air with a knife in there. The master looks as if he's had a mite too much wine already, 'cos his nose is all red. And he was going on at poor Te— Master Edward.' She corrected herself just in time. 'Then Miss Miriam pipes up and I thought she was really in for it. But suddenly, the master burst out laughing.' She shook her head, wondering at it all. 'By heck,' she said again, 'the things I missed by bein' only a kitchen maid.'

'Aye, and there's summat else you'll have to learn now you're an "upstairs maid". You don't ever talk about the master, or the mistress, or any of the family for that matter, outside these four walls. You hear me?'

Kitty stared at her. 'Course I wouldn't, Mrs Grundy. You should know me better than that. After all,' she added with an impish grin, 'I'm Betsy Clegg's daughter, ain't I? Me mother's drilled me about bein' in service for as long as I can remember.'

As Kitty glanced across at the cook, she saw a strange, reflective look cross Mrs Grundy's face. 'Aye,' the older woman murmured, more to herself than to the girl, 'you're her daughter right enough . . .' She turned away abruptly but, once more, there seemed to be words that she had left unsaid.

Kitty shrugged and began to prepare to take the second course through to the dining room the moment the bell rang. She glanced just once at the white face of the kitchen clock high on the wall above the range. In another hour or so, when Mrs Grundy put her feet on the fender and dozed in the chair before the fire that burnt in the range winter and summer, and Milly had been sent up to her bed, she might be able to sneak out of the back door to meet Jack. Oh Jack, Jack. He had to be waiting for her. He just had to be there.

At once, all thoughts of the strange tensions between the members of the Franklin family were swept from her mind.

Sixteen

His kisses were becoming urgent, his fingers pulling at the buttons on the front of her dress, his weight on top of her.

'No, Jack, no. Not like this . . .' Kitty pushed at him, but beneath his bulk her strength was futile.

'You want it, ya know ya do,' he breathed against her hair, his voice husky. 'Why do you come out here night after night to meet me, if it's not for this, eh?'

Through the darkness, Kitty stared up at him. His face was only inches from her but even so, she could not see his features, could not read his expression. But she could hear the growing anger in his voice, the anger of a man's frustration.

'I love you, Jack Thorndyke. That's why I come to see you. Not 'cos I want a quick roll in the hay.' She waited, but the words she longed to hear him say did not come. In a small voice that quavered slightly, she added, 'You don't love me though, do you, Jack?'

His arms tightened around her. 'Course I do. You know I do.' But she knew that she had dragged the half-admission from him. The declaration had not come from his lips voluntarily and with true feeling.

She pushed at him again and he rolled away from her on to his back. Kitty sat up. 'You'll think I'm easy, if I – let you.'

'Course I wouldn't.' There was a pause before his deep voice came through the darkness to her. 'If you really loved me, Kitty, you'd say yes. You'd let me show you how I really love you.'

Angrily she turned on him. 'That's what me mam always warned me men say to get what they want. She told me I should get a ring on me finger first.'

His loud laughter echoed through the night air, so loud that she was suddenly afraid someone would hear. 'Your mam?' His voice was scathing with sarcasm. 'Aye an' your mam should know, if anybody does, if what I've heard is true.' He laughed again.

Kitty scrambled up to kneel beside him. Roughly she grasped his shoulder and shook him, but he just lay there laughing on the deep bed of hay. 'What d'you mean? What have you heard?'

He sat up then and she could see him straining to look at her through the darkness. 'You mean you really don't know?'

'Know what?' Kitty demanded.

He lay back down again and put his hands behind his head and stretched. 'Well, I aren't going to be the one to tell you, Kitty Clegg, else I might find mesen thrown off this land and there's a good bit of money coming my way for the work here. I ain't about to lose it.'

'Tell me, Jack, please. I won't say anything to anyone. I swear it. Only, tell me what it is you've heard.'

'Don't worry about it, young Kitty. It's likely only tittle-tattle anyway.'

'But what did you mean about me mam and – and me?' She was almost crying with tears of frustration now.

'It's only that by all accounts she didn't exactly practise in her young days what she's preaching now to you.'

'Oh.' Kitty sat back on her haunches, shocked. Though she still did not know the full story, she was sharp enough to understand the implication in Jack's words. There were people still working for Mr Franklin who must have known her mother and father when they had both worked here. Small communities have long memories and no doubt someone had been gossiping. Kitty said no more to Jack, knowing that however much she wheedled she would get nothing more out of him.

Tomorrow, she promised herself silently, I shall ask Mrs Grundy.

Jack was hauling himself up and dusting the hay from his trousers. 'I'll say goodnight then, Kitty. I've an early start in the morning. Looks like being a fine day.'

'Jack, please, don't go like this. Don't you understand?' She scrambled up and caught hold of his arm, feeling the hard muscles rippling beneath her touch.

There was a bitter edge to his tone as he said, 'Oh I understand, Kitty Clegg. You say you love me, but it's all talk with you. Just a young girl's talk. You still ain't woman enough to prove your love for me, are you?' With that cruel parting shot, he pulled himself free of her grasp and walked away into the night.

Kitty gulped and a sob escaped her lips. She pressed her hand over her mouth to still the sound and sank to her knees on the hay. Burying her face in her hands, Kitty wept.

'By heck, girl. You look a mess!' was Mrs Grundy's greeting the following morning. 'Have you come down with Sarah's cold then?'

Kitty shook her head, trying desperately to blink back the tears that welled all too readily. As she avoided the cook's shrewd, penetrating gaze, Kitty was angry with herself too. Angry that anyone, any man, could cause her to be so silly. She had never been a crybaby and yet at the very thought of Jack's mockery, she wanted to burst into fresh tears.

'Are you in trouble, Kitty? I want the truth now.'

Kitty gasped. 'No, no. I'm not.'

'Hm.' Mrs Grundy still looked as if she did not entirely believe her, adding only, 'But I expect it's that young feller . . .' she nodded towards the stackyard beyond the garden wall, 'that's causing all this.' And she gestured towards Kitty's blotchy, swollen face. 'Well, I did warn you, Kitty. You can't say I didn't.' She turned away and reached up to the shelf to lift down a heavy copper saucepan.

'Mrs Grundy,' Kitty blurted out suddenly. 'Was my mother – did she *have* to get married?'

The saucepan clattered to the floor, the noise resounding through the kitchen. Mrs Grundy gasped but surprisingly her attention was not on the saucepan, but on Kitty's face. 'Who's been talking? Was it him? What's he told you?'

Kitty bit her lip. 'Just – just . . .' She was in danger of giving away the fact that Jack was pressing her to give herself to him. But there was no one else she could ask. She could certainly not ask her own mother. Betsy Clegg would soon give her a clip round her ear and tell her it was none of her business. 'He – he said that in her young days me mam hadn't practised what she's preaching now.'

'Eh?' Mrs Grundy looked puzzled, then her expression cleared but only to be replaced by a look of anxiety for the girl herself. 'Oh, been asking you for that, 'as he?'

Kitty said nothing but could not prevent the colour rising in her face and giving Mrs Grundy her answer.

The older woman sighed heavily. 'Kitty, love, do be careful. I'm ever so fond of you, you know I am. I would hate to see you get yarsen into trouble.'

'Did my mother get into trouble?' Kitty asked quietly.

Mrs Grundy turned away flustered and flapping her hand towards the girl as if fending her off. 'Don't ask me that, Kitty. 'Tain't none of my business, nor yourn neither.'

'But—'

'No, Kitty. No more questions, 'cos I aren't answering 'em.' Picking up the saucepan from the floor, Mrs Grundy banged it into the deep sink and turned the tap full on, every movement quick with anger.

Kitty sighed. However much she pleaded, cajoled, begged, she knew there would be no budging Mrs Grundy in this mood. She would learn nothing more from her.

Then who? she pondered. Who would tell her the truth? One day, she promised herself, I will find out, somehow. But for the moment, her mind was filled with the handsome Jack Thorndyke and the dilemma he had put her in. She loved him so much and yet what he was asking her to do was against everything her mother had taught her.

Even so, her rebellious, nubile body longed to succumb to his desire.

For three nights Kitty waited in the draughty darkness of the stackyard in vain. Jack did not appear. Had he gone away, left the district without telling her? she anguished. The threshing set was long gone from the stackyard at the Manor as Jack trundled it from farm to farm. But until now, he had always returned here to sleep – and to see her. At least, that was what Kitty had believed.

By the fourth day even the self-centred Miriam noticed that there was something wrong with her maid. 'You're a real misery these days, Kitty. Whatever's the matter with you? I didn't think you were the weepy kind.' She sniffed derisively. 'I suppose you'll be handing in your notice because you can't stand me.'

A spark of anger made Kitty's chin rise and rashly she said, 'It isn't you, miss. I can handle you all right.'

'Oh really?' An amused smile twitched at the girl's mouth. 'Well, I'll have to see what I can do about that.' There was a light note in her voice and Kitty knew she was only teasing, but her words at least made a smile come to Kitty's lips.

'That's better,' Miriam remarked. There was a pause before she asked, with surprising concern, 'You've not had bad news about your family, have you?'

'No, miss.' Kitty bit her lip. Miss Miriam's probing was getting a little too deep.

'I expect it's some man then, is it?' Miriam said airily. When Kitty did not answer, she added, 'Ah – I see I have hit the nail on the head.'

Kitty turned away from her, busying herself folding Miriam's discarded garments which she dropped wherever she took them off.

With an unexpected note of understanding in her voice, Miriam said, 'You can talk to me about it, Kitty, if you want. *I* certainly don't mind you having a young man and I won't tell Mama. In fact,' she giggled, 'in my boring life, I'd find it quite diverting.'

Kitty wasn't sure she liked the idea of her love life being a 'diversion' for Miriam, but she merely said, 'That's just it, miss, there isn't much to tell.'

Still, she didn't want to risk telling her about Jack. She wasn't sure how safe her secrets would be with Miriam, who had such a careless disregard for the feelings of others. She couldn't risk word reaching the master's ears and Jack losing his contract at the Manor Farm.

'Oh.' Miriam stared at her for a moment and then said, 'Oh, I see. Poor Kitty.' Then losing interest, she said,

'Can you lay out my riding habit? I may ride over to the Hall this afternoon. I think Guy will be home.'

Without stopping to think and with a note of resentment in her tone, Kitty said, 'I think your love life is far more exciting than mine, miss.' Then added quickly, 'If you'll pardon me saying so.'

Miriam only laughed. 'Maybe,' she murmured, her eyes sparkling. 'Maybe so, Kitty.'

'But where is he?' Kitty shouted above the noise of the throbbing traction engine. It was November and the team had arrived back at the Manor House to do the promised threshing for Mr Franklin.

Jack's workmate, Ben Holden, shrugged his broad shoulders. 'Ah dun't know, me love. He disappears every afternoon now for an hour or so.' He glanced at her and Kitty had the impression that the man was a little embarrassed. He kept glancing at her and then looking away as if there was something he would like to say, something he would like to tell her, and yet he did not know quite how to do it. He jerked his thumb over his shoulder in the direction of the copse two fields away. 'I saw him walking across yonder . . .' He stopped and then added, 'Of course, he might be going to other farms to check if they're ready for us when we finish here.'

'You – you're not staying long, then?'

Ben shook his head. 'The mester only wants a couple of days this time.' He reached out and touched her shoulder gently. 'I'm sorry, lass, but – but I'll have to go. Meks it harder work when he goes off on one of his jaunts.'

He seemed, Kitty thought, to be apologizing for more than just being unable to stand and talk to her.

'I'm surprised at him leaving you short-handed,' she said.

The big man laughed. 'Oh we're used to him and his ways and there's not a lot we can do about it, seein' as he's the boss, now is there?'

Mutely, Kitty shook her head.

'D'ya want me to give him a message for you, love?' The man, a little older than Jack and happily married with children, smiled kindly at her.

She swallowed and shook her head. 'No, it's all right.' She turned away, sick at heart, and walked back past the stables to the back door of the house so that she could not be seen from the windows.

'Master Edward's asking for you, Kitty,' Mrs Grundy greeted her. 'Go and see what he wants, will you?'

'Why do I always have to go?' she grumbled, her thoughts still on Jack. 'Why can't Sarah or even Milly?'

'Sarah's with the mistress and I aren't letting young Milly above stairs yet. She's not half trained. Go on with you, girl. Miss Miriam's out, so you've nowt else to do. Go and keep the poor lad company a while.'

Sighing, Kitty made her way upstairs.

He was fully dressed and sitting by the window. As Kitty entered the room, Edward turned to see who it was and a smile lit his pale face and sparked briefly in his eyes.

'Kitty!' he said. 'Come and sit down.'

Still nervous of being found chatting to the boy during working hours – or at any time if it came to that – Kitty stood awkwardly near the window. Below her, the back garden stretched to the wall and beyond it she could see the stackyard. Even through the closed window she could hear the chug-chug-chug of the traction engine and see the dust and chaff misting the air.

'I love threshing time, don't you?' Edward said softly.

Kitty kept her face turned away from him, concentrating on looking out of the window, though the scene blurred as her eyes filled with tears. She swallowed the lump in her throat. I used to love threshing time too, she wanted to tell him. I used to count the days to when I would see Jack again. And now . . .

Edward's voice came gently, almost soothingly. 'I see an awful lot from this window, Kitty. People think that because I'm young and sick, I don't know what's going on. But I do. Inside the house and outside of it too.' He paused and then sighed. 'Miriam's gone riding . . .' he waved his pale hand indicating the way across the fields to the far distance, 'again. I just hope *she* knows what she's doing.'

Startled now into forgetting, for a moment, her own misery, Kitty turned to face him. 'Why? What do you mean? She's ridden over to the Hall.' As she saw the doubt on Edward's face, Kitty added, uncertainty in her own tone now, 'Hasn't she?'

Steadily, Edward's gaze met hers. 'Well, yes, maybe she has.' His young face was troubled and, fleetingly, he seemed much older than his fourteen years. 'But she shouldn't be going out alone, even to the Hall, unchaperoned.'

Kitty was silent. It was not her place to probe into the lives of her betters. It was her duty only to serve them and to give them her loyalty. But it seemed as if Edward had other ideas. 'Kitty, couldn't you speak to her? She might listen to you.'

Appalled, Kitty's eyes widened. 'Me, Master Edward?'

'Teddy,' he reminded her.

'Oh I couldn't – Teddy. Besides . . .' A small smile twitched her mouth at the thought of her strong-willed young mistress. 'I don't think she'd take a scrap of notice of me anyway.'

Edward sighed. 'No, you're probably right. But will you just promise me one thing, Kitty?'

'I will – if I can.'

'That whatever happens, you'll stick by her. You'll not – not turn against her.'

Kitty searched the boy's face. Deep in his eyes she could read the anxiety. 'You really do think she's doing something she shouldn't, don't you?'

Slowly, he nodded. 'I'm very much afraid she is, yes. I know my sister. She's bored with life in the country. She's searching for excitement. But if she's not careful she'll find more drama than she bargained for.'

Now Kitty did lean closer to him. 'But Master Guy loves her. He wouldn't – wouldn't do anything to hurt her.'

For a moment, there was a strange look on Edward's face as he stared into Kitty's. He tried to smile and reached out and touched her hand briefly, but it was more as if he were trying to reassure himself rather than her. 'No, you're right, of course. Guy Harding is a gentleman and, as you say, he loves Miriam and would never do anything to harm her.'

Suddenly his attention was caught by some movement beyond the window, in the far distance across the fields. Following the line of his gaze, Kitty saw a tiny figure emerging from the trees. Even from here, the broad-shouldered figure of Jack Thorndyke was unmistakable.

Kitty's lips parted in a gasp and she sprang to her feet, Edward forgotten. So, was that what Ben Holden had been trying to tell her, but had not known how to put it into words? Jack was slipping away to the copse to meet some girl, some trollop from the town, no doubt, or a maid from the Hall, which, across the fields, was only a mile away. Well, she wasn't going to stand by and let some other girl get her claws into him. Jack Thorndyke belonged to her and no one else was going to have him.

'I've got to go,' Kitty muttered and, whirling round, she ran across the room, dragged open the door and fled down the stairs, out of the back door and down the long straight pathway towards the door in the garden wall leading into the stackyard, not caring who saw her now.

'Kitty, no, don't . . .' he began, but she was gone.

From his window Edward watched her go, his young heart breaking.

Seventeen

Kitty was running pell-mell across the field towards him, mindless of the rough stubble beneath her thin shoes. She trod awkwardly and her ankle gave way, twisting painfully, and she fell, the sharp spikes of the short-cut crop digging into her hands and knees. Breathlessly, she sobbed, but more from the pain in her heart than the physical injury.

He was bending over her then and picking her up. Kitty struggled against him, hitting him with her clenched fists. 'I hate you, Jack Thorndyke. I never want to see you again as long as I live.'

Hardly seeming to notice her blows, he hoisted her into his arms and carried her. 'Now, now, young Kitty. What's this all about, eh?'

Giving way to the misery that had engulfed her for the past few days, Kitty buried her face against his neck and wept.

'Hey, what's all this?' Gently, he set her down on the ground but he kept one arm around her and with the other he cupped her chin in his strong fingers, tipping back her head and forcing her to look up at him. 'I never had you as the weepy kind, Kitty. Now, what's the matter?'

'You,' she sniffed and added belligerently, 'you are. You're what's the matter.'

'Me? Why me? I ain't done nothing.'

'Oh no? You've got another girl, ain't ya? You've been meeting some trollop from the town. Up in them trees . . .'

Wildly, she flung her arm out towards the copse two fields away. 'And don't try to deny it, 'cos I saw you come out o' there just now.'

Jack Thorndyke threw back his head and laughed. 'Why, Kitty Clegg, I do believe you're jealous. With those huge brown eyes, I never took you for a little wildcat. Come here.' He tried to pull her closer, but she held herself stiffly away from him.

'Where have you been then, if not to meet a girl?'

'Not that it's any business of yours where I've been, but I went to the next farm to see what needs doing when we leave here tomorrow. I'm not going a hundred miles away, Kitty,' he said softly. 'We're only going to Home Farm on Sir Ralph's estate. I can easy come back – at night. You know you've only to say the word.'

Kitty bit her lip. 'I – I thought you were meeting someone else, 'cos I've waited the last three nights and you never came.'

He hugged her to him. 'Oh Kitty, you've a lot to learn about men. I'm a healthy, lusty male and if I keep meeting you every night, I'll – well, I'll forget mesen.' His eyes darkened. 'I want you, Kitty. I want you so badly that I can't trust mesen to be near you.'

'Oh Jack,' Kitty breathed and she felt the tingle of excitement low in her groin. He did love her, she thought ecstatically. He loved her so much, wanted her so much, that he had kept away from her out of respect because he knew she didn't want to give herself to him. But if he loved her so much, she told herself, then it couldn't really be so very wrong, could it?

Suddenly shy, she whispered, 'Meet me tonight, Jack. Please. It'll be different – I – I promise.' The last words were said so low, that she wondered if he had heard,

129

yet the passion that flared in his eyes told her that he understood.

Suddenly, he bent down and, putting one arm around her shoulders and the other under her knees, he swung her once more into his arms and carried her across the uneven ground towards the stackyard. Close to her ear he whispered, 'I'll not hurt you, Kitty, I swear it.'

As they neared the gateway leading into the yard and to the stables, they heard the thud of a horse's hooves behind them and Jack, still carrying Kitty, stepped to one side to allow the young mistress to pass through the gate before them.

Fearfully, Kitty glanced up at Miriam but the girl rode straight past them without even glancing down. It was almost as if they did not exist, Kitty thought.

'There's no other place I know,' Jack murmured, resting his arms along the top of the five-bar gate, 'that has sunsets like that. Just look at that sky, Kitty. Dun't it fair catch ya breath.'

She tucked her hand through his arm and leaned her cheek against his shoulder, feeling beneath the rough texture of his shirt the hardness of his muscles.

Before them the sky was ablaze with colour, red-gold and pink suffusing into the dark blue of the deepening night sky as the sun sank lower and lower behind the horizon.

'Beautiful,' she murmured, smuggling up, smelling the sweat of him, feeling the warmth emanating from his body. He removed one arm from the gate and put it about her shoulders so that she nestled closer, burying her head against his chest. Against her cheek she could feel the gentle thud, thud of his heart.

Jack turned towards her and she saw the gold of the setting sun mirrored in his dark eyes. Putting his arm about her waist, he led her towards the looming shape of a stack. Burrowing a nest in the warm straw, he gently pressed her down and now she made no protest as he bent over her . . .

He was surprisingly gentle, knowing that, for her, it was the first time. He caressed her and whispered words of love until she was quivering with delighted anticipation and willing him to take her. She had expected pain, but there was none and she was surprised and a little shocked at herself as she found she was clinging to him and arching herself against him, giving little cries of ecstasy until even he shushed her lest someone should hear them.

When it was over, she lay against him, her head on his chest listening to the pounding of his heart as, steadily, it grew calmer.

'Oh Jack, I do love you so.'

He stirred and sat up. 'You'd better go in. It's late.'

'No. I don't want to go yet.' Her mouth searched for his, her hunger growing again and with a low groan he returned her kiss with equal ardour.

'You ought to, Kitty,' he murmured against her lips. 'What if Miriam calls for you?'

A vague unease slipped into her mind. There was something odd about the way he had said Miriam's name. It sounded far too familiar coming from the mouth of a man who was employed by her father.

'Jack . . .?' she began, but his lips were seeking hers again and she was lost once more, the thought erased from her mind before it had scarcely taken shape.

At last he pulled away from her and made to stand up, but she caught his arm. 'Jack, when shall we be getting married, then?'

Under her hand, she felt his muscles tense and then he wrenched himself away from her as if, suddenly, her touch was burning him. 'Married? Who said owt about getting married?'

Kitty gasped. 'But we must get married. Now. And you gave me the corn dolly. That must have meant something. I thought – I thought it meant that I was your girl.'

He gave a harsh laugh. 'I've told you afore, Kitty, I'm not the marrying kind. I thought you knew that.'

A surge of anger flooded through her and she scrambled to her feet. Slowly, buttoning his trousers, he stood up too.

'You've used me, Jack Thorndyke, just like you use all the girls. I've given you everything – *everything* . . .'

'Kitty, Kitty . . .' He spread his arms wide. 'I know you have. And it was wonderful. *You're* wonderful. But don't go all possessive on me.' He shook his head slowly. 'I'm the way I am, Kitty. You know the kind of life I have to lead – like to lead. Always on the move, never settled in one place. I can't change, Kitty, I don't *want* to change.'

Tears of anger welled in her eyes, but she brushed them away impatiently and stepped closer to him again, placing her palms flat against the breadth of his chest, running them down towards his narrow waist and then over his hips, caressing him with a daring she had not possessed before tonight. 'But I love you, Jack,' she said huskily, so persuasively that the man groaned and his arms went about her almost of their own volition.

'Kitty, oh Kitty, do you women know what power you have over us poor fellers?' he murmured, closing his eyes and burying his face in her black curls.

In the darkness that engulfed them completely now that the sun had sunk below the far horizon, he drew her down again deep into the straw, his body heavy upon her. He kissed her neck and his hands roamed all over her body, awaking her senses yet again until she shivered with longing. With a last moment of rational thought before passion overwhelmed her once more, Kitty whispered close to his ear, 'I'll follow you, Jack Thorndyke, wherever you go. You won't get rid of me so easy.'

Eighteen

'Married? To Threshing Jack?' Mrs Grundy's face was a picture. 'You're having me on, girl. He'll never marry no one.'

'Oh yes, he will.' Kitty skipped around the kitchen table and clapped her hands. 'He doesn't know it yet, but he will.'

'Has he asked ya?'

'No, but he gave me the corn dolly. And that means . . .'

Before she had finished, Mrs Grundy cut in, 'Is that all? And how many other girls d'ya reckon have got a corn dolly from Jack Thorndyke tucked away in their keepsake box, eh?'

Kitty's dancing was stilled and she stared at Mrs Grundy, a moment's doubt seeping into her happiness.

'Aw, Kitty.' The older woman was reaching out towards the girl. 'I don't want to see you, of all people, hurt by the likes of him. I'm very fond of you, you know. You and all ya family. Why, I had to stand by and watch when ya mam . . .' Abruptly Mrs Grundy stopped. 'Eh dearie me, there I go, letting me tongue run away with me.'

'Mrs Grundy, just what . . .?' Kitty began, but the cook's hand flapped at her.

'Don't start that again, Kitty. Don't ask questions 'cos I aren't going to answer 'em.'

Kitty sighed, but the mysteries of the past were soon

blotted out by the problems of the moment. 'Well, I don't care what you say about Jack. I love him and I know he loves me.'

Mrs Grundy was shaking her head. 'I just hope you don't get yarsen into real trouble, lass. 'Cos he's not the type to marry anyone, not even if he gets 'em in the family way.'

Kitty's lips parted in a gasp and she stood motionless with shock, staring at the round, waddling figure of the cook who turned away from her still shaking her head sadly and muttering, 'Well, I've done all I can. It's up to you, lass. But I can see tears ahead for ya and a lot of heartache. That I can.'

In the weeks leading up to Christmas, Kitty was happy. Miss Miriam spent much of her time riding to the Hall to see Master Guy, returning with glowing cheeks and a sparkle in her eyes. Kitty smiled to herself. Miss Miriam was in love with Master Guy, just like she was with Jack.

Then the family at the Manor and its servants were plunged into the turmoil of preparations for Christmas and Kitty was so busy she had little time to see Jack. But after Christmas, she promised herself, he'll be here to complete all the threshing work for the master. Then I'll see him every day. She hugged the thought to herself and sang as she skipped through her work.

In the middle of January, she heard the chug-chug of *Sylvie*'s engine as it turned into the driveway at the side of the house and moved triumphantly into the stackyard.

'He's here, oh he's here again,' Kitty murmured, pressing her nose to the window pane of Edward's room. She felt the familiar flutter of excitement. This time Jack would be here for several days, until all the threshing work was done.

Behind her, the boy in the bed, suffering a bad bout of bronchitis, said nothing.

Every morning the threshermen came to the kitchen for their breakfast and every evening, when the noise in the yard died away, Kitty would sneak out to meet Jack.

But on the second night after their arrival, he said, 'Sorry, Kitty. I've to work on me engine.'

'Well, I can be with you, can't I?'

He shook his head. 'It's a mucky job. No place for a pretty little thing like you in your white apron and lacy cap, now is it?'

'All right then. I'll see you later?'

He shrugged. 'Mebbe. But it'll be a long job.'

Close to midnight, Kitty crept into the dark and deserted yard. There was no sound save the wind whistling through the tall trees in the driveway, no light except from a fitful moon behind scudding clouds.

'Jack,' Kitty called softly. 'Jack, where are you?' There was no sound. She smiled and gave a little skip. He'd finished early. He'd be waiting for her in his little loft room . . . But when she pushed open the door, it was to see the bed ruffled and unmade since morning, his working clothes in a heap on the floor and a bowl of soapy water on the table where he had washed hurriedly, leaving a ring of grime around the rim.

Of Jack, there was no sign. Gone drinking with his pals, she thought, instead of waiting for me.

'Where were you?' she challenged him the following morning. 'We could have had the whole night together, because Miss Miriam went to the Hall and didn't come back until real late and she said before she went that I needn't wait up for her. So you see,' she punched his chest, half in play, half in accusation, 'you missed out there, Jack Thorndyke, didn't you?'

'Mebbe I did, Kitty,' was all he said. 'Mebbe I did.'

On the day they finished working at the Manor, Jack said bluntly, 'I've got lodgings at the farm where we'll be working next, Kitty.'

'But you'll come back to see me, Jack?'

'When I can,' he said shortly and turned away to climb up on to the footplate of his engine.

He came back that night and they walked together through the copse across the field behind the Manor, the frost crunching beneath their feet.

'Let's go back to the loft room,' said Kitty, snuggling closer to him.

'We can't. Not now I've left the Manor.'

'Whyever not?' Kitty stopped and stared at him, trying, through the black night, to see his features.

'It wouldn't be right.'

There was a pause before Kitty's laugh rang through the night air, echoing among the trees. 'I never thought I'd see the day. Jack Thorndyke with a conscience . . .'

He pulled her to him and silenced her teasing with his mouth.

His visits became more infrequent, the intervals stretching to two, even three, nights in a row when he did not come to the Manor after his day's work. And it always seemed to happen, Kitty thought crossly, just when she could have spent extra time with him, when Miriam was out visiting Guy or had just said, 'I'm going to bed early, Kitty, I shan't need you later.'

On each occasion, Kitty waited alone in the dark and the cold of the yard, but Jack did not appear.

Kitty began to get angry. 'Just where were you last night – and the night before that?'

The excuses were varied. 'The engine was playing up. I had repairs to do through the night. I'm sorry, Kitty, but you know me work has to come first. It's me livin'. And Ben's. He's a wife and three kids to support.'

Grudgingly, she said, 'Well, all right then. But I'm beginning to think you love *Sylvie* better than you love me.'

He'd put his arms about her and nuzzled his face into her long hair. 'But she doesn't smell half as good as you, my sweet Kitty.'

He pulled in deep breaths as if revelling in the smell of her skin and her hair. 'You're lovely, Kitty.'

And all further reproaches had been forgotten.

Now, this morning, after another long and futile wait in the cold and draughty stackyard the previous night, the tiredness was beginning to undermine even Kitty's strength. 'I wonder what excuse he'll come up with this time,' she muttered as she tied her apron strings behind her back and hurried down the stairs to the kitchen.

As she passed Miriam's door, she heard a strange sound from inside the room. She gave a soft tap, anxious not to wake the rest of the household at this early hour, and quietly opened the door.

In the pale light that filtered in through the curtains, Kitty could see the outline of Miriam's figure, still in her nightgown, bending over the marble-topped washstand in the corner of her bedroom, her head over the blue and white washbowl. She was retching, making an awful noise, as if she would bring up the very depths of her insides.

Kitty closed the door behind her and hurried across the room. 'What is it, miss? What's the matter?'

She drew back the curtains to give more light and turned to look at the girl as Miriam lifted her head from the bowl and groaned. 'I feel ghastly. It must be something I've eaten.'

Her face was grey and spittle ran from the corner of her mouth down her chin. Kitty picked up a towel and gently wiped it away. 'There, there, miss. Come back to bed. You're shivering.'

Miriam's forehead was clammy beneath Kitty's fingers. 'It'll be a bilious attack, miss. Ya mam'll get the doctor later.'

'I'll be all right, Kitty.' She climbed into the bed and lay back against the pillows, looking very like her sickly brother at this moment.

'You lie there. I'll go down to the kitchen and get you a nice drink of . . .'

'Just water, Kitty. Nothing else, just water,' Miriam murmured, her eyes closed.

Kitty bit her lip and scurried from the room. She had never known Miriam to have a day's illness in all the time she had been at the Manor. It had always seemed to her that poor Edward had enough sickness for the whole of the family and that the rest were spared. But now Miriam was poorly.

Returning with the water, Kitty was surprised to find her sitting up in bed, the colour returning to her cheeks. Taking the glass from Kitty's hand, she said, 'I feel better already. I think I'll go riding before breakfast. A bit of fresh air will blow the cobwebs away.'

'I don't think you should . . .'

'When I want you to tell me what I should or should not do, Clegg, I'll tell you.' She flung back the covers and swung her bare feet to the floor. 'Meanwhile, lay out my riding habit – *if* you please.'

For a moment Kitty glared at her, tempted to argue. Then she shrugged her shoulders and turned away to do as she had been asked.

Half an hour later she watched as Miriam, her long auburn hair flying in the wind, cantered across the fields towards the copse. Surely, Kitty thought, she's not going to the Hall this early in the morning.

'You feeling all right now, miss?' As she helped to serve the breakfast to the family, Kitty bent over to whisper in Miriam's ear. She knew she was taking a grave risk in even speaking.

'Of course I am. Don't fuss, Clegg,' Miriam hissed.

'Sorry, I'm sure. I only thought . . .'

'Well, don't think. Maids aren't paid to think.'

'What? What's going on?' Mr Franklin's newspaper rattled furiously and his glowering eyes appeared over the top of it. 'Can't we have a bit of peace in a morning? Maids, like children, should be seen, not heard.' His irate glance swivelled from his daughter and her maid to his wife sitting at the opposite end of the table. 'And what is *she* doing serving breakfast, may I ask? Where's the other girl?'

'Sarah has a cold . . .'

'Another one? If the girl keeps being ill like this, send her packing.'

He shook the paper to straighten it out and lowered his eyes again to read. 'Just look at this. These wretched suffragettes. Will they never learn?'

Kitty held her breath, waiting for Miss Miriam to make some retort. Over the past few months, the more Mr Franklin had ranted on about the Votes for

Women movement, the more his daughter had goaded him.

But this morning, Miriam's eyes were downcast as she pushed scrambled egg about the plate with her fork, clearly uninterested in eating.

It seemed she had not even heard what her father had said.

Mrs Franklin reached across the corner of the table and touched her daughter's hand. 'Are you all right, dear? You look pale this morning . . .'

'I'm all *right*,' Miriam snapped, standing up and pushing her chair back with such a sudden, violent movement that it fell backwards on to the floor with a crash.

'What on earth . . .?' The newspaper was lowered again but before he could utter another word, the girl cried, 'Oh, why can't everyone just leave me alone . . .' And she whirled about and rushed from the room, leaving Mr and Mrs Franklin staring at each other down the length of the table.

Later, Mrs Franklin quizzed Kitty.

'All I know, madam, is that she must have eaten something that disagreed with her because I found her being sick first thing this morning.'

Mrs Franklin was staring at her. 'Sick? F-first thing this morning?'

'Yes, madam. I 'spect it was something she ate yesterday, but I darsunt tell Cook. You know how upset she gets if anyone ses summat – something's – upset them.'

'Yes,' Mrs Franklin said vaguely, seeming to be only half-listening.

Kitty paused and then said, 'Anything wrong, madam?'

'Mm?' Her gaze met Kitty's but the eyes seemed hardly focused, as if her thoughts were miles away. 'Oh – er – no, at least . . . No, no,' she added more strongly. 'No, of course not.'

But when Kitty left the room, her mistress was still sitting in front of her dressing table staring into the mirror, deep in thought.

Nineteen

It was a week later when, thinking her young mistress was out riding before breakfast as she had so often seemed to do of late, Kitty opened Miriam's bedroom door and walked in without knocking. She stood a moment, shocked by the sight that met her eyes.

The girl was sitting up in bed, her face as white as the nightdress she was still wearing. There were dark shadows beneath her eyes and her hair was flying loose about her shoulders. She was holding her stomach and moaning, her eyes closed.

'Oh miss . . .' Kitty began and hurried towards the bed. Then suddenly she stopped. The way Miss Miriam looked at this moment reminded Kitty of someone and as she realized when she had last seen a woman looking so white and ill first thing every morning, she gave a little gasp and her hand flew to cover her mouth.

Kitty was remembering when she had still lived at home, a few months before her youngest brother was born. She had taken her mother a cup of weak tea and a slice of dry toast up to her bedroom every morning for several weeks. Then, she had not understood what had been wrong and there had been the nagging fear that her mother was seriously ill and would not tell her. It was only months later that the anxiety had given way to relief when her mother's stomach swelled and she explained to her

143

daughter that she would soon have another baby brother or sister.

Now, looking at Miss Miriam, she remembered how her mother had looked in those early days of her pregnancy.

'Oh no. No!'

She did not realize she had spoken aloud until Miriam's eyes opened and she stared at Kitty. 'What?'

'Oh – er – nothing, miss. I'm sorry. Can I get you anything?'

The very thought was outrageous. Miss Miriam wouldn't . . . Mr Guy wouldn't . . . Oh no, no, it couldn't be true. It mustn't be true. But the longer she watched the girl, the more she remembered her mother and the more the terrible fear grew.

Now, she could almost wish it was an illness. Anything but what she was thinking. Anything.

Unwittingly confirming Kitty's worst fears, Miriam said, 'Just a piece of dry toast. Bring it up here. I can't face breakfast.' At the mere thought of the cooked breakfast of bacon, egg, sausage and fried bread that was served each morning in the dining room, Miriam retched.

Kitty did not move from the side of the bed. She swallowed. 'Miss – you ought to see the doctor.'

'No.'

'Why not, miss?' Kitty asked quietly.

'Because . . . That's why not,' the girl snapped. 'It'll pass. It always does. It must be something I'm eating that doesn't agree with me.'

'Do you want to know what I think, miss?' Kitty said resolutely.

'Not particularly,' Miriam said morosely, 'but I expect I'm going to anyway.'

'I think – and I'm sorry for thinking it if I'm wrong, miss – but I think you're going to have a baby.'

'How dare you!' The girl lashed out swiping her arm in a wide arc, but Kitty stepped back quickly and Miriam's lunge almost precipitated her off the edge of the bed. Kitty stepped forward again and steadied her.

'How dare you suggest such a thing? I'll have you . . .' But Miriam said no more. Instead, she burst into a loud storm of weeping and threw herself against a startled Kitty, wrapping her arms about her and clinging to her. 'Oh Kitty, Kitty. What am I going to do? Please help me. I know I can be difficult, but please, don't desert me.'

'It's all right, miss. Of course I won't desert you.' She held the girl until the wild crying subsided to a miserable hiccuping.

'I'm ruined. Disgraced. Oh Kitty, I've been such a fool.' Miriam paused and seemed, now, to be speaking to herself more than to her maid. 'I thought he loved me. I thought I was different. No matter what everyone says about him I thought that with me, he would be different . . .' The voice trailed away in a whisper of hopelessness.

Kitty swallowed. 'Mr Guy, you mean, miss? But he does love you, I'm sure of it.'

The girl was shaking her head wildly against the pillow. 'No, not Guy. Of course, he loves me. I know that!' Her voice was almost scathing. 'He's like a devoted puppy.'

Then tears welled again and she rolled from side to side as a paroxysm of anguish gripped her afresh. 'Oh why, why was I so stupid? I've ruined everything . . . everything.'

A small frown creased Kitty's forehead. She couldn't understand Miss Miriam. If Mr Guy loved her, then he would marry her and the sooner the better to Kitty's way of thinking. So why . . .? The ridiculous thought forced its way into her mind that Mr Guy might not be the father, but she immediately dismissed it as foolish and, anyway, quite impossible. It had to be him. There was no one else, no other man in Miriam's life, who could possibly . . .

The girl's weeping was becoming hysterical and Kitty pushed her own thoughts aside and sat down on the bed. Instinctively, she gathered the girl into her arms again and held her close, rocking her. 'Hush, hush now.' At that moment, she felt much older than the girl she was trying to comfort. 'You must see the doctor.'

The girl shook her head. 'How can I? He'd be sure to tell Mother.'

Kitty hesitated, unsure of the confidentiality that doctors were supposed to give their patients. Yet in this case it would be difficult. The local doctor was a close friend of Mr Franklin and Miriam was under twenty-one. 'Maybe if you asked him not to, at least not yet. I mean, they'll have to know.' She gulped, sympathizing with Miriam to such an extent now that she almost felt the guilt to be hers. 'Sooner or later.'

'My father will kill me,' Miriam wailed. 'You know what his temper's like.'

Yes, thought Kitty shrewdly, like your own, Miss Miriam. But she said nothing. Mr Franklin idolized his daughter and there was no knowing what the shock of such a disgrace would do to him – or cause him to do to her.

'Your mother, then. Maybe your mother can help.'

'No, no, I don't want anyone to know.' She gripped Kitty's arm. 'I'll go away. You can come with me and I'll have the baby and give it away and no one will ever know.' She was wild in her thinking, desperately seeking any solution. But Kitty, though badly shaken, was still able to think rationally.

'We could go away, and yes, I'd go with you . . .' Fleetingly she thought of being parted from Jack for several weeks, months even, but she buried the desires of her own heart. Despite her volatile temper and her selfish ways, Kitty was very fond of Miss Miriam and ingrained into the young maid's soul was the code of loyalty to her mistress. She would, she knew without having to make a conscious decision, set aside her own feelings to help Miss Miriam in her desperate need.

'But,' Kitty went on now, 'I do think your mother will have to know. I'm sure she'll stand by you. I'm sure she'll help us.' Already Kitty, almost without realizing it, was shouldering the burden alongside her young mistress. 'You must tell her.'

'Oh Kitty, Kitty. I can't.'

'You must. I'll – I'll come with you, if you like.'

Miriam raised her tear-streaked face. 'Would you, Kitty?'

Now the realization of what she was promising, of the responsibility she was taking upon herself, filtered into Kitty's conscious mind. Yet without a moment's hesitation, she nodded and said quietly but firmly, 'Yes, miss. I'll be with you.'

They stood, side by side, mistress and maid, facing Mrs Franklin. Smiling, the older woman laid aside her embroidery. 'Well, this is a nice surprise,' she began and then seeing Miriam's troubled face, still blotchy and swollen from weeping, Mrs Franklin's smile faded and a flicker of something akin to fear was in her gentle eyes. She reached out towards her daughter. 'Why, my dear child, whatever is the matter? Come and sit down. You too, Kitty.'

Miriam gave a little cry and covered the space between herself and her mother, flinging herself dramatically to her knees and burying her face in Mrs Franklin's lap. Tenderly, Mrs Franklin stroked her daughter's hair but her gaze came slowly up to meet Kitty's troubled eyes. 'Do you know what this is all about, Kitty?'

The girl swallowed painfully and nodded. 'Yes, madam,' she said, her voice a hoarse whisper.

'Well?'

Kitty's glance went to the girl's trembling shoulders and she waited for Miriam to speak. 'Tell her, Kitty,' came Miriam's muffled voice. 'You tell her. I – I can't.'

'Madam, I . . .' The words were so hard, so very hard, to say. 'Madam, Miss Miriam is in trouble.'

For a moment Mrs Franklin closed her eyes and swayed a little. 'Oh no, no,' she whispered. It was a plea, a prayer from the heart, but it was a prayer which could not now be answered. When she opened her eyes, Kitty saw a deep sadness in their gentle depths. She felt so sorry for her. This kind, sweet-natured woman would be subjected to the most appalling wrath from her husband should he ever find out. Now, as much as for Mrs Franklin as for Miriam, Kitty vowed to help keep this dreadful secret from the master.

Mrs Franklin's hand, still resting on her daughter's hair, trembled, but then she was lifting Miriam up and into her embrace and wrapping her arms around her and, just like Kitty had done earlier, she rocked her. 'Oh my darling girl,' she murmured and then she, too, asked the same questions. 'Are you sure? Have you seen Doctor Miles?'

Miriam clung to her mother, hiccuping miserably, unable to speak.

Kitty said, 'No, madam, she hasn't. She was too afraid in case he told you or – or the master.'

A tiny groan escaped Mrs Franklin's lips. 'Oh yes, the master,' she murmured. She sighed and then seeming to gather her strength she said, 'Doctor Miles would not break a confidence, Miriam. We must be sure. I'll send word.'

Wildly, Miriam pulled herself free of her mother's embrace. 'No, no. Everyone will know – will guess – if he comes here.'

Mrs Franklin took hold of her daughter by the shoulders and gently shook her. 'Now listen, my dear, just calm yourself. Kitty can take the message and ask Doctor Miles to visit me, not you. But we must be sure, first, before we can begin to think what to do.' She paused and then said, 'Miriam, is Guy Harding the father?'

Miriam was still kneeling in front of her mother, so that Kitty could not see her face, but she saw the girl shake her head.

'Then who, Miriam? Who is the father?' Mrs Franklin persisted in a way that Kitty had not been able to do.

The shake of the head was vehement now. 'I can't tell you. I'm sorry, but I can't tell anyone.'

'Can he not marry you?'

The girl's voice was a tragic whisper. 'No. He won't marry me. He – he's not the marrying kind.'

Kitty's whole being stiffened. Those were words she had heard before; words she knew so well.

Oh no, she cried silently inside her head, oh no. Please not that, please not *him*.

Kitty was alone in Miss Miriam's bedroom, folding her freshly washed and ironed underwear and placing it carefully in the huge mahogany chest of drawers. Mechanically, she opened drawers, placed the garments in the depths and closed them again, but her mind was hardly on the task. Along the landing, on the opposite side of the house, she knew that at this very moment the doctor was in Mrs Franklin's bedroom, examining Miss Miriam. Kitty was tense and anxious. Somehow, she had to get the girl to tell her the truth about the father of her child, if there was, indeed, a child. And even if there wasn't, then Miss Miriam must have lain with him, must have . . .

Kneeling on the floor in front of the open bottom drawer, Kitty leaned her forehead against the cool, shiny surface and closed her eyes and groaned. Then, pulling her thoughts back to her duties, she moved a rumpled white cotton chemise and her fingers touched something prickly beneath it. Lifting up the garment, she saw, nestling in the bottom of the drawer, buried beneath the pile of clothes, a tiny, intricately worked corn maiden.

Now Kitty knew for sure just who was the father of Miss Miriam's child.

Twenty

High up, from the window of her room in the pointed eave, Kitty looked down upon the stackyard beyond the wall. It was silent now, all the straw neatly stacked and thatched. Even the ground had been swept of all the wisps of straw and the chaff. It was almost as if the threshermen had never been there.

But they had. Oh yes, they had. And Threshing Jack had left not one, but two young girls in tears. Mrs Grundy, dear, wise, kind-hearted Mrs G., had warned her, but Kitty had been too foolish to listen. Tears blurred her vision. Maybe he would come tonight. Maybe he would stand out there in the cold and draughty yard. Kitty's mouth trembled and then she clenched her jaw, hardening her resolve. He would wait in vain as she had done so many nights just recently.

She stiffened, suddenly realizing that he must have been with Miriam on those nights. Now she saw it. All the times when her young mistress had said she had no need of her, or that she was out for the whole evening, it had been when Jack had never come. How stupid, how blindly naive she had been. She should have known . . .

But how could she? Kitty argued with herself. How could she ever have thought that a young lady like Miriam Franklin, born into the gentry, would allow herself to be ensnared by a man like Jack Thorndyke? And Jack? How could *he* have been so foolish? It was playing with fire, risking his very livelihood if her father found out. He had said as much himself.

No, tonight, Jack, you'll wait in vain. She said the words over and over in her mind for she had no wish to run down the garden and through the gate in the wall to fling herself against him. Not now. Not now she had learned the truth about the man she had loved. Still did, if she were truthful with herself. She hated him; wanted to throw herself at him, clawing and scratching and spitting like any wild she-cat. She felt her jaw clench. 'Maybe I will, one day, Jack Thorndyke, 'cos I aren't finished with you yet. Not by a long way.' She wanted to make him pay for what he had done, for bringing Miss Miriam into disgrace. A young, well-brought-up girl, who had probably been ignorant of what was happening to her.

Kitty sighed, feeling a sympathetic affinity with her young mistress.

They were both victims of Threshing Jack, and yet, foolish though she knew it was, Kitty could not stop herself loving him still.

'Kitty, come in, my dear. Close the door,' Mrs Franklin beckoned. 'I've made all the arrangements for Miriam and you to go away for several months until after the child is born. All anyone else knows is that I have insisted she go away on a Grand Tour before becoming engaged to Guy Harding.' For a moment, there were tears in Mrs Franklin's fine eyes and her voice was no more than a trembling whisper. 'It has always been my dearest wish that she and Guy should unite our families.' She pulled in a deep shuddering breath. 'No one must ever know the real reason you are going away, except the three of us. I'm relying on you, Kitty.'

Knowing she was exceeding her place, nevertheless Kitty said quietly, 'Mr Guy loves Miss Miriam. Perhaps – perhaps he would still want to marry her even if he knew.'

Mrs Franklin shook her head vehemently. 'No, no, Kitty, believe me. Men – and particularly a man of Guy Harding's standing – always want to marry a – a virgin. They want their wife and the mother of their children to be pure and untouched when they marry them and completely faithful to them afterwards. But for men . . .' a bitter, cynical note crept into her voice, 'it is quite acceptable that they should have affairs, be – be experienced. How I just wish sometimes . . .' She passed her hand wearily across her forehead and sighed.

Kitty gulped, feeling suddenly ashamed. What, then, were her chances of marriage to anyone other than with Jack and he, as he said so steadfastly, was not the marrying kind. Perhaps, she comforted herself, it was different in Miss Miriam's case, her being gentry. Maybe it was more important that she should have kept herself pure for her husband. Maybe in Kitty's own class, it didn't matter so much.

But in her heart, Kitty knew that it did, if all the teaching her mother had instilled into her was to be believed. No one else would want her now. Not now she had given herself to Jack Thorndyke. And besides, she thought sadly, she didn't really want even to think of marrying anyone else but Jack. Damn him!

Arrangements moved with astonishing speed and Kitty had scarcely time to pack clothes for her mistress and herself before their trunks were being loaded on to the back of the car for Bemmy to take to the station.

Kitty was obliged to take charge, for Miriam was

red-eyed and morose, speaking to no one, refusing even to say goodbye to her brother. But not one of the staff came close to guessing the truth.

'Poor Miss Miriam,' Mrs Grundy clucked sympathetically. 'Fancy being packed off on a World Tour when all she wants is to stay and be courted and petted by her nice young man.'

'I think she doesn't know how lucky she is,' Milly piped up. 'And as for our Kitty going with her, well, it just ain't fair. I shall want a picture postcard from every place you visit, our Kitty.'

Kitty bit her lip and turned her face away. Oh heck, she thought. That was one thing they hadn't thought about. What was going to happen not only while they were away, but when they got back? How was she to describe all the places they were supposed to have visited when she would not have been near any of them?

But Mrs Grundy, quite unwittingly, came to her rescue. 'Kitty won't have time for gallivanting, Milly, I can tell you. She'll have her hands full just looking after Miss Miriam. She'll be a handful that one, Kitty. Personally, I don't envy you one bit. And as for sending postcards, they'll be ever so expensive. How do you think your sister is going to find the money to be sending you things like that, eh?'

Poor Milly looked so crestfallen that Kitty hugged her and promised impulsively, 'I'll try to bring you back something nice.'

She was rewarded by her sister's face brightening considerably. 'Oh Kitty, will you really?' She flung her arms about her neck and said ecstatically, 'You are the best of sisters and I am going to miss you so much.'

Kitty hugged her in return but her only thought was, How on earth am I going to be able to buy her a present from foreign parts when I'm not even leaving the country? But all she said was, 'Goodbye, Milly. You be a good girl for Mrs Grundy and give me mam and dad and everyone my love when you next go home on your Sunday off.'

Milly, easy tears brimming her eyes, nodded and then added, 'But you'll see Dad at the station, our Kitty. He'll see you off on the train to London.'

Kitty stiffened and a tremor of fear flooded through her again. That was another thing. They were not going to London, but in the opposite direction entirely. Kitty groaned inwardly and her mind began to race. Whatever could she do?

Then she found herself enveloped in Mrs Grundy's ample embrace. 'Tek care of yarsen, lass. I'll look after Milly, dun't you fret.'

'I know you will, Mrs G.' Kitty hugged the plump woman with genuine warmth. 'And take care of yourself.'

'I will, lass, I will. Now off you go. The master and mistress are waiting at the front and Bemmy's brought the car round. Go and fetch Miss Miriam down, else you'll miss ya train.'

As Kitty went into the hall, Miriam was descending the main staircase. Her face was white and there were dark shadows beneath her eyes. She was wearing a close-fitting travelling costume and, to Kitty's knowing eye, the fabric around her waist was already creasing into stretched folds around her thickening body. Inwardly, Kitty sighed. We're leaving not a moment too soon, she thought, and held open the door for Miriam to pass through.

'Come along, girl,' came Mr Franklin's loud voice. 'And for Heaven's sake – cheer up. You're going to have the time of your life and let me tell you, there's a lot of young gels would give their eye teeth to be in your shoes. Going round the world. And a pretty penny it's costing me.'

155

Kitty cast an anxious glance at Miriam and saw the sudden flash of anger in the green eyes, saw her look at her father as if she was about to speak.

Kitty touched her arm and whispered, warningly, 'Miss . . .'

The girl bit her lip and shot a swift, grateful glance at her maid. Now the tiny smile on her mouth was tremulous and she seemed close to tears. Miss Miriam hardly looked as if she was setting off on the trip of a lifetime, Kitty thought wryly.

The family settled themselves in the rear of the vehicle and Kitty climbed into the seat beside the driver. As Bemmy swung the handle and the noisy engine shuddered into life, Kitty glanced up. At a second-floor window, she saw the pale face of Edward.

'Look, miss, Master Edward's waving goodbye to you.'

Kitty twisted her head to look at Miriam, but her young mistress neither spoke nor even looked up and, as the motor car leaped forward, only Kitty waved her hand to the lonely figure at the window.

Twenty-One

'Two first-class tickets to London, my man.' Mr Franklin's voice echoed along the platform as he bent towards the man in the ticket office.

Kitty saw Mrs Franklin and Miriam exchange a glance and guessed that they had not given a thought to the fact of which train they would have to board for the sake of keeping up the pretence. Kitty went to stand beside her mistress. In a low voice she said, 'It's all right, madam. We'll just get off further down the line and travel north from there. No one will know.'

'Thank you, Kitty,' Mrs Franklin murmured, her lips scarcely moving, and Kitty could see the relief on her face.

'Now, how long's this wretched train going to be?' Mr Franklin demanded as he rejoined them. 'I've matters to attend to, you know. I need to find Thorndyke . . .'

Kitty felt her whole body stiffen and, beside her, she heard Miriam give a little gasp, but, blithely unaware, Mr Franklin continued. 'He's still on the estate somewhere and there's a tree needs felling before he leaves the area.'

Kitty felt her heart begin to pound and a flush start in her neck and creep up into her face. Beside her, Miriam stood rigidly still and, stony-faced, stared directly ahead.

'Here, you.' Mr Franklin was beckoning someone standing further down the platform and Kitty saw her father turn and walk towards them. He was a thin, dapper man, with sharp eyes behind steel-rimmed spectacles. A drooping moustache hid his mouth and his nose was a little too bulbous for the size of his face.

'Ah, good morning. Clegg, isn't it?'

'It is, sir. Fancy you remembering.'

Kitty gasped at the undisguised insolence in her father's voice. Her own moment of discomfort forgotten, she watched the two men and to her surprise, it was the master, not her father, who seemed ill at ease.

'What time's the London train due?' he was asking brusquely.

John Clegg made a great play of pulling out a gold watch on the end of a chain from the pocket of his uniform waistcoat. 'Ten minutes – sir.' His glance went to his daughter. 'Kitty, you've time to go and say goodbye to your mother.'

Kitty almost gasped aloud. She would not have dared to ask such a thing, good though her mistress was. She cast an anxious glance towards Mrs Franklin.

'Very well, Kitty,' she said graciously. 'But, please, don't be many minutes.'

'No, madam. Thank you, madam.' She picked up her skirts and ran the length of the platform towards the station house.

'Mam, Mam . . .?' she called, bursting through the back door.

'Why, Kitty, whatever's wrong?'

In a rare moment of weakness, Kitty felt the over-whelming desire to fling herself into her mother's embrace and pour out the whole sorry story of Miss Miriam's disgrace, of her own heartache caused by the same man and the reason for their hasty departure. Instead, she clamped down the feeling and said brightly, 'We're off on a trip, Mam. Me and Miss Miriam.'

'A trip? Where to? How long will you be gone?'

Kitty swallowed. This was the first deliberate lie she was going to have to tell. At the Manor, the rest of the staff, even her own sister, had heard the news of their proposed tour from the mistress. All Kitty had had to do was go along with it. But now it had to come from her mouth. She licked her lips, suddenly dry. With a forced brightness, she said, 'A Grand Tour, no less, but don't ask me exactly where we're going, 'cos I don't know.'

'A Grand Tour? Kitty, how wonderful for you. Oh, the sights you'll see. You are a lucky girl.'

'Aren't I just?' she said and hoped the bitter irony was not noticeable in her voice.

'How long will you be gone?'

Now she could be truthful. 'I'm not sure. Six or seven months at least.'

'Six months! Heavens!' Betsy Clegg threw her arms wide and hugged her eldest child to her. 'I'll miss you, our Kitty.'

'I'll miss you, Mam,' Kitty said, her voice muffled against the woman's shoulder. Oh how much, she thought silently, you'll never know.

'I'll come and see you off.' Linking arms they left the house, but as they stepped on to the platform, Kitty saw Mr Franklin waving and shouting, 'Come along, come along, girl. The train's due.' At her side, she felt her mother stiffen.

Turning to look at her, she saw that Betsy Clegg was staring down the platform towards the Franklin family. 'Oh, I didn't realize . . .' she began and Kitty could not help but notice a tremble in her voice. 'The whole family has come to see you off. I should have thought – should have known. And your father's there – with them. Oh dear.' She pulled her arm away and turned. Swiftly, she hugged Kitty and for a moment held the girl's face between the palms of her hands. 'Take care of yourself, love. I must go.'

'Whatever's the matter, Mam? It's only Mr and Mrs Franklin. Surely . . .?'

'I can't tell you now. Some day, maybe some day, I – I'll explain.'

Kitty saw her mother glance back just once down the platform towards the Franklins. For a moment her gaze was caught and held by something, and when Kitty, too, followed the line of her mother's look, to her surprise she saw that it was the master who was standing perfectly still and silent now, just staring back at them.

'I – must go,' Betsy Clegg said and though Kitty said again, 'Mam . . .?' her mother turned and hurried away.

As the train pulled in and the porter and Bemmy loaded the trunks into the guard's van, the two girls climbed into a first class carriage.

John Clegg, still hovering nearby, stepped forward. 'You don't mean the two girls are travelling alone, Mr Franklin?'

The master turned. 'Yes. They'll be quite safe. They're being met in London . . .' He turned towards his wife. 'At least, I suppose you have arranged all that, Amelia?'

Mrs Franklin inclined her head. 'Everything has been organized.' She smiled at the stationmaster. 'You need have no fear for your daughter's safety, Mr Clegg.'

The little man sniffed his disapproval and Kitty, listening from the carriage window, cringed at her father's pomposity and his daring. 'Well, I should hope not.'

Kitty bit her lip. Her father thought they were merely going to London. If he should hear that it was a supposed Grand Tour, then . . .

The engine gave a great spurt of steam and John Clegg stepped back, checking up and down the platform, his mind now on his duties. There was a sudden flurry of last minute activity. Goodbyes were called, a whistle sounded and the train began to move. As it gathered speed out of the station, Kitty sank back in relief.

'What are we going to do about being on the wrong train?' Miriam said suddenly.

'Simple. We'll get off at the very next station it stops at and catch the first one going north.'

'Will there be a train going north?'

'Oh yes, miss. This London train stops at Harthorpe at eleven twenty and the northbound one comes through there at eleven forty-three. Lucky I've spent me life near the railway, ain't it, miss?'

Miriam's left eyebrow rose slightly. 'Oh absolutely, Clegg. What would we do without your superior knowledge?' Then her scathing tone changed completely as she said, 'How I wish we could stay on the London train.' A look of wistfulness crossed her face and then suddenly her expression brightened. 'Couldn't we, Kitty? Couldn't we stay on this train and go to London?'

'You know we can't, miss.'

'Just for a few weeks, Kitty. No one would know and I could at least have a bit of fun before – before I start to show.'

'No, miss. Your mother has arranged it all. We're going north.'

The girl slumped back against the seat. 'You're a spoil-sport, Clegg. I've a good mind to go anyway. I've got my ticket. You can't make me get off this train.'

Kitty looked at the petulant pout of Miriam's mouth. 'If you do that, miss, you'll go on yar own.' She paused and then added firmly, 'And I – will go straight back to the Manor.'

'You wouldn't dare.'

Quietly, Kitty returned her stare. 'Oh yes, I would, miss.'

Kitty watched as Miriam sat hunched in the corner seat, her pale face turned towards the window and yet her eyes glazed as if she was seeing nothing. She looked such a picture of abject misery that for a moment Kitty felt a real pang of sympathy for the girl. Then a fresh thought suddenly struck her. It could be me running away to hide my shame. It could be me carrying Threshing Jack's child. Maybe it would have been better if it had been, she pondered, recognizing that she was, despite all the problems and the disgrace, the tiniest bit envious of Miriam. I haven't so much to lose as Miss Miriam and maybe, just maybe, Jack would have married one of his own kind. Maybe he *would* have married *me*.

The switch to the correct train, heading north to York, was made quickly and easily and there was no one at that station who would recognise them.

They were silent on the journey and Kitty had plenty of time for her own thoughts. It was very strange, she realised, that she felt no animosity towards Miriam because she was carrying the child of the man she, Kitty, loved. I ought to be hating her, Kitty thought in surprise, but I don't. If she hated anyone, it was Jack Thorndyke. Hated and loved him and still, despite everything, wanted him. Part of her was thankful – oh, so very thankful – that she had not fallen pregnant and yet, deep in her heart, there was a niggling jealousy that it was Miriam who was carrying Jack Thorndyke's child. Kitty sighed inwardly. Her emotions were so mixed up that she didn't quite know what she did feel. All she knew was that, sitting opposite Miriam Franklin, she didn't hate her. She was sorry for her and maybe cross that the girl could have been so stupid. But, Kitty acknowledged wryly, she, too, had been just as foolish.

Oh Jack Thorndyke, you've got summat to answer for an' no mistake. An' one day it'll all catch up with you. You see if it don't, because I'm going to be the one to make sure it does.

'Why do I have to be dressed from head to toe in black and wear this stupid little black veil?' Miriam asked petulantly, standing in front of the long mirror in the hotel bedroom.

They had broken their journey in York and, on dressing the following morning, Kitty had laid out the clothes that Mrs Franklin had insisted Miriam should wear from now on when they went out.

Patiently, she explained. 'Your mother wants you to pretend that you are a young widow whose husband has just been drowned at sea. Oh, I almost forgot . . .' She fished in a tiny pocket inside the handbag Mrs Franklin had given her. 'Here, you must wear these too.'

'What?'

Kitty held out her hand with two rings resting in the palm.

'I can't wear those, Kitty. They're my Grandmother Franklin's engagement and wedding rings.'

Kitty shrugged. 'I don't know nothing about that, miss. All I know is that your mother said you were to have them and wear them.'

'But they're too good, I mean . . .' The girl gulped and faltered. Glancing at her sharply, Kitty was amazed to see tears shimmering in Miriam's eyes. 'Whatever would Grandmother have said if she knew I was wearing her rings and – and wasn't married?'

Kitty was surprised to find the girl did, after all, have

some conscience about the feelings of others. But then, she reminded herself, she had already seen another side of Miriam's nature from the selfish, spoilt girl of indulgent parents. She was truly concerned for her brother. There could never be any mistaking the genuineness of Miriam's love for the invalid Edward.

'I shouldn't worry, miss. It's what your mother wanted you to do.'

'Just so long as my father doesn't find out the reason I am wearing his mother's rings,' the girl murmured, as she slipped first the gold band and then the ring with a cluster of diamonds set with a sapphire in the centre on to the third finger of her left hand.

Perhaps I was wrong, Kitty thought, disappointed. Maybe her fears are more for herself should her father find out the truth than any qualms about wearing her grandmother's rings to hide her shame.

'Come along then, miss,' Kitty said, forcing a bright cheerfulness she did not quite feel. 'The motor taking us to Robin Hood's Bay is waiting outside.'

Miriam stood still. 'Where? Where did you say?'

'Robin Hood's Bay, miss.'

'I've never heard of it. Where is it?'

'On the coast, miss. It's a little village.'

'A village? You're not serious? I'm not going to be buried away in a village.'

'But your mother—'

'My mother!' Miriam flung her arms wide. 'My *mother*. That's all I seem to hear from you, Clegg.'

Kitty stepped closer and said slowly and deliberately, 'Your mother has been wonderful over all this. And you ought to remember it.'

Miriam's green eyes flashed. It was the first spark in them that Kitty had seen during the last few days. Her mouth pouted and she leaned towards Kitty and said slowly, 'Don't preach at me, Clegg.' There was a malicious glint in her eyes as she added, 'I *aren't* in the mood for it.'

Far from being intimidated, Kitty threw back her head and laughed aloud. 'That's better, Miss Miriam. I was beginning to think you'd lost all your spirit. I'm pleased to see you 'aven't. Come on, now. Time we was going.'

'I'm not going to some god-forsaken village, so you can think again. Oh Kitty,' she said, grasping the girl's arm, 'let's stay here. In York. I know it's not London but . . .'

'Your mother said Robin Hood's Bay and that's where we're going. Everything's arranged.'

'But why? Why on earth can't we stay here? Nobody knows us in York, for heaven's sake.'

Kitty stood her ground. 'Yes, they do. Didn't your mother say the Hardings had some friends who live in York?'

'How ridiculous! As if we're likely to meet them in a city this size.'

The argument raged on for another ten minutes, but in the end Miriam followed her maid down the stairs and out to the waiting vehicle. But the look on her young mistress's face would, as Mrs Grundy would have said, turn a milk pudding sour.

At the thought of the motherly cook, even the stout-hearted Kitty suddenly felt a moment's homesickness.

And as for Jack Thorndyke, well, she dare not even think of him at all.

Twenty-Two

'Well, if you think I'm staying here, you – and my mother – have got another think coming.'

'But, miss, it's lovely. Just look at the sea and the cliffs and all the birds and look – oh do look – at all the little houses. It's as if they're sitting on top of each other.'

The tiny village of Robin Hood's Bay nestled in a wide cove between two headlands. The houses, built on the steep incline leading down into the bay itself, did indeed look as if they were tumbling over each other, huddled together on either side of the steep, winding road that led down to the beach.

Kitty gazed about her, her eyes wide with wonder as if she could scarcely believe her own eyes. She had never before travelled any distance from home and the rugged beauty of the Yorkshire coast was so very different from her flat homeland of Lincolnshire. The girl was over-whelmed. She whirled around, clasping her hands together in an excitement she could barely contain. 'And look at the moors, miss.'

Moodily, Miriam said, 'What's there to look at? They just stretch for miles and miles and miles.'

'They're wonderful. So wild and romantic.'

'Huh.' Miriam drew her cloak around her and frowned. 'You've been reading too many novels by the Brontë sisters, Clegg.'

'Eh?' Brought back to earth, Kitty blinked.

Miriam smirked. 'I was almost forgetting. You are, after all, only a servant. Maybe you can't even read.'

The remark was cutting and, intended to be hurtful, sharply reminded Kitty what her station in life was and that the only reason she was here at all was to care for her young mistress. She was not meant to be enjoying herself.

But Kitty Clegg was untouched by such taunts, so she merely smiled and said, 'Well, we're here, miss, and this is where we've to stay, so you'd best get used to it.'

And with that she climbed out of the motor car and stood holding the door open for such an age that, in the end, Miriam was obliged to duck her head and step out.

The cottage where they were to stay was high up overlooking the village. Kitty ran from room to room exclaiming at the magnificent views, while Miriam sat morosely on a chair with her back to the window refusing to look at anything. Black beams ran crookedly across the low, whitewashed ceilings and tiny windows let in shafts of pale sunlight.

'I hope you'll be comfortable here, Mrs Franklin.' The woman who owned and rented out the cottage stood in front of Miriam and smiled kindly down at her, her eyes taking in the black widow's weeds and the sullen face of the young girl.

Kitty, turning round, bit her tongue just in time. It was very strange to hear her nineteen-year-old mistress addressed as 'Mrs', but she had better get used to it quickly if she were to carry on the deception convincingly. 'I'm sure we will, Mrs – er ?'

'Bradshaw.' Getting no response from Miriam, the woman turned, with obvious relief, to talk to Kitty.

'I've arranged for a woman from the village to come up every day to help about the house and my husband keeps

167

the bit of garden front and back tidy. The privy's just outside the back door.'

Miriam raised her head. 'Outside? You mean we have to go outside every time we want to . . .'

The woman looked at her in astonishment. 'I don't know what you're used to, Mrs Franklin, but here . . .' Her voice died away as she saw Miriam's lip curl with disgust.

Hurriedly, Kitty put in, 'We'll be fine, Mrs Bradshaw.'

The woman wriggled her shoulders, obviously put out by what she saw as an insult. 'I do my best to make my visitors comfortable, I'm sure, but if you . . .'

'No, no, really. We'll be fine here. Everything is most comfortable.' Kitty tried to usher the woman towards the door. 'Thank you so much, Mrs Bradshaw. Mi— Mrs Franklin is very tired from the long journey.'

Outside the low front door of the cottage, Kitty whispered confidentially, 'She's expecting a baby and what with the awful news of her husband's death . . . well, she's . . .' She shrugged her shoulders expressively and spread her hands, palms upward, in a plea for understanding.

'Well,' the woman said slowly, softening a little. 'I'm right sorry for the poor lass, of course, but that doesn't mean she can be rude.'

'I know, I know,' Kitty said soothingly, more than a little shocked at how the lies were slipping glibly off her tongue. 'Everything is wonderful. The cottage is lovely. She'll be better when she's rested.'

'I certainly hope so,' the woman bridled again. 'I can't say as I've ever had my little cottage criticized before. It was my mother's. Left it to me when she died and I've kept it just as it was. She wanted it to give me an income, you know, a bit of my own money. And it does.' The woman nodded. 'My husband is a fisherman and it's a hard life, Miss Clegg.'

'I'm sure it is, Mrs Bradshaw. And it is a dear little cottage.'

The woman nodded and smiled and seemed placated and as Kitty closed the door behind their landlady, she leaned against it and breathed a sigh of relief.

When she had unpacked their trunks and hung up Miriam's dresses, she said, 'I'll have to go down to the village and fetch some food. There are some things in the kitchen cupboard but there's no fresh food. You know, milk and meat and bread.'

'All right,' Miriam said listlessly, still sitting in a chair by the window, a book on her lap, though she did not appear to have turned a page within the last half hour. 'How long will you be?'

'I don't really know, miss. I've got to find the shops first.'

'Don't be long. I'm getting hungry. And get me some chocolate, will you?'

'Yes, miss, and I'll be as quick as I can.'

But the Bay was not a place where anyone could hurry. The shops lay on either side of the steep winding road leading from the top of the hill right down to the Bay itself. From where the cottage lay, Kitty first had to go down a steep pathway between the houses to get on to the road and then walk quite a way up the steep hill to find all the shops she wanted. And she was fascinated even by those she did not actually need.

There were several shops that sold pictures, original watercolours and oil paintings of the Bay and the surrounding countryside. It seemed, thought Kitty, to be a place where artists liked to come and paint the scenery. It had everything, she supposed, bending forward to peer at the pictures. The sea, magnificent cliffs, picturesque houses, brooding moors, turbulent skies and deep valleys with trees and waterfalls; everything an artist could possibly want. There were decorated shells, and ornaments and jewellery made from shells, painted and unpainted. And there were old, musty-smelling second-hand bookshops. Kitty would dearly have loved to spend the afternoon delving among the shelves of old books. Perhaps she could persuade Miss Miriam to come down one afternoon. After all, Miriam did like reading and, much to her disgust, there would be little else to do once her pregnancy advanced.

With two loaded baskets, Kitty struggled back up the hill.

'Where on earth have you been, Clegg? You've been ages and I want some tea.'

'I'll make some right away.'

A short time later, she carried the fine china through to the front parlour and set the tray down beside Miriam who was once again seated in front of the window, but at least now she had turned her chair to look out at the scene below.

Kitty stood beside her. 'Will there be anything else, miss?'

When Miriam did not even bother to answer her, Kitty left the room closing the door quietly. There was one thing she was sure of. If Miss Miriam did want something, then Kitty would soon know about it.

'I suppose it's a bit silly, me eating on my own in the front room and you sitting out here in this tiny kitchen when there's only the two of us,' Miriam said, a few days after their arrival at the cottage. She had still not ventured outside and her moods swung erratically between ill-temper when she berated Kitty for anything and every-thing, and dark, silent moroseness.

'If you say so, miss,' Kitty said.

'I do say so. I'm sick of sitting hour after hour in that stuffy little room on my own. Even your company is better than nothing.'

Kitty hid her smile and agreed demurely.

The following morning as Kitty dried the last of the pots after breakfast, Miriam appeared in the doorway dressed in her hat and coat.

'Come along, Clegg. I want to go for a walk. Get your coat.'

They walked down the hill, right to the bottom and stood on the slope of the roadway where it opened out and ran away into the sand.

Miriam shaded her eyes and looked out to sea, but a low, swirling mist covered the water offshore and there was little to see. On a low wall, three old fishermen sat mending their nets.

'Can we walk on the sand, Kitty? Or along one of those rock things.' Miriam pointed to where a long scar of rock ran right out into the water so that the waves lapped on either side of it.

'I should think so, miss.'

As they stepped on to the sand one of the old fishermen lifted his head and shouted, 'Mind ee the tide, 'tis on the flow, young missie, and she comes in fast.'

Miriam pulled a face and did not turn around, but Kitty glanced back over her shoulder, smiled prettily at him until the dimples deepened in her cheeks and said, 'Thank you. We'll be careful.'

'Silly old fool,' Miriam muttered and stalked ahead of her maid.

'Don't walk so fast, miss. These rocks are slippy.'

'Don't fuss so, Clegg. I'm quite capable of— Oh!' Whatever she had been going to say was cut off by a little cry of alarm as Miriam felt her foot slide on a lump of seaweed and her arms flailed the air as she tried to stop herself falling. Kitty, just behind her, grabbed hold and managed to steady her.

Miriam gave a rueful laugh. 'I do see what you mean, Kitty. Sorry – you're right.' She walked on again, but carefully now, watching where she placed her feet. They were walking along the scar where the sea lapped on either side and still Miriam walked further, the water becoming deeper.

Kitty glanced over her shoulder worriedly. 'We're getting an awful long way out. I think we ought to turn back now.' In places the rock surface was uneven, dipping so low that they had to jump across the water that flowed into the hollows.

'I don't want to go back.' Miriam flung her arms wide, throwing back her head to the sky. 'I'm never going back. I'm going to keep on and on and on until the water covers my head. And it'll all be over!'

Kitty stood still. Fear gripped her. In this mood, the silly girl was capable of doing anything. If she were to plunge into the water, Kitty was no swimmer. Miriam could drown them both.

There was only one way, Kitty decided. Call her bluff.

'Oh well, if that's what you mean to do, then you don't need me with you. I'm off back to the beach.'

She turned and took a step back towards the shore, praying fervently that her ruse would work. She held her breath, expecting, fearing, any moment, to hear a splash behind her. Instead she heard her mistress give a brittle laugh. 'Don't worry, Kitty. I'm only being melodramatic.' They both turned at the same instant and stood facing each other, the grey mist swirling around them, the mournful

172

cry of a seagull somewhere overhead and the sea lapping dangerously close to their feet.

'You know,' Miriam said, 'I have to admit it, Kitty, but you really do know how to treat me, don't you? And I want you to know – though I'm only ever likely to say this once and out here where no one can hear me – I do like you. And I'm not saying that now, just because you're standing by me in my, er, predicament.'

Softly Kitty said, 'No. I know you wouldn't do that, miss. And – thank you.'

'Don't mention—' She stopped as her glance went beyond Kitty's shoulder towards the land and her eyes widened. 'Where's the beach? Oh Kitty, Kitty,' Miriam said gripping her arm, 'we're lost. We'll drown. I didn't mean it. I didn't mean I wanted to drown, truly I didn't. What are we going to do?'

'We'll be all right, miss,' Kitty said firmly, sounding calmer than she was feeling inside. 'Take hold of my arm and we'll walk steadily back along the rock to the beach.'

'No, no,' Miriam clung to her. 'You're going the wrong way. It's this way.'

'No, it isn't. You've been twisting and turning about and you've lost your sense of direction. It's this way.'

'Are you sure?'

'Quite sure,' Kitty said, mentally crossing her fingers and praying that she was right.

They moved forward together, holding on to each other and staggering like two drunken old men.

'There's water. I told you we were going the wrong way.'

'It's only where the rock is lower and the water's come in over it. Can't you remember jumping across as we walked out?'

'Yes, but . . .'

173

'Stand there, miss, while I get over to the other side.'

Kitty released the girl's limpet hold on her arm and stepped down into the freezing grey water.

'Don't leave me, Kitty . . .'

'It's all right, miss, I'm only a step away.' The water was deeper than she had imagined and she had taken three steps and then another and still she could not feel the rock jutting up out of the water on the opposite side of the expected hollow. Kitty knew a moment's panic. What if they had turned in the wrong direction? What if they were indeed walking further out to sea?

Then with blessed relief she felt the toe of her shoe stub against something hard and she bent forward and, reaching with her hands outstretched, felt the rough surface of the rock rising above the water.

'*Kitty?*' The wail was terror-stricken now.

'It's all right. I've found the other side.' She gained the rock surface, turned and held out her hands towards Miriam. 'Come on, miss. It's about five steps. You'll have to get your feet wet because it's too wide to jump now. That fisherman was right, I reckon. The tide does come in fast.'

Making little whimpering sounds, Miriam stepped into the water and, arms outstretched, waded towards Kitty. Then they turned and staggered along the scar. They crossed three more hollows before, with tears of relief, they stepped on to the firm sand and saw the old fishermen still calmly mending their nets.

They stood a moment to regain their composure and then, with heads held high, walked past the old men with as much nonchalance as they could muster. They climbed the rough-hewn steps up a narrow passageway and gained the path leading to their cottage.

Once out of sight of the old men, Miriam began to

laugh, and, though there was a little note of relieved hysteria in her mirth, Kitty found herself laughing too. 'Oh Kitty, I fully expected them to say, "We told you so," didn't you?'

Kitty nodded. 'I did, miss. But come along, let's get you out of those wet things. You don't want to catch cold.'

'You do fuss so, Kitty,' Miriam said, but now her tone held affection and a hint of gratitude, as she allowed her maid to bustle her home and strip off her saturated garments, before Kitty dealt with her own cold, wet feet.

'I'm bored.'

They had been at the cottage for three weeks now and Miriam's mood swings were no better. This morning, as Kitty cleared away the breakfast things, her young mistress was moving restlessly about the small room like a caged tigress.

'Shall we go for a walk along the cliff top?' Kitty suggested. 'It's a lovely bright day, a bit windy, maybe, but we'll be all right as long as we don't go too near the edge.'

'No, we won't go for a walk along the cliff.'

'It would do you good. You haven't been out anywhere for the last three days, not even down into the village. You must take a little exercise. You've got to think of the baby . . .'

'The baby? The *baby*? What do I want to think of that for? I don't want it. I hope it's born dead.'

Kitty gasped, her eyes round with horror. 'Oh miss, that's a wicked thing to say.'

'Stop being so sentimental, Clegg. Of course I don't want the brat. I don't even want to see it.'

Kitty was stung to anger. 'Then you should have thought about that afore you took a tumble in the hay with Jack

Thorndyke . . . Oh!' She clapped her hand to her mouth, but it was too late, the words were out.

Miriam moved towards her menacingly. 'How do you know?' She reached out and, with a surprisingly strong grip, took hold of Kitty's arms and shook her so hard that the maid's teeth actually rattled against each other. 'How – do – you – know?' she demanded again, her voice rising almost to a scream.

'I found the corn dolly among your clothes. He – he gave me one too.'

The two girls stared at each other and now Kitty could see the realization of Threshing Jack's true nature dawning on Miriam. She could see it in her face. 'You? *You?* You've been with him too?'

Kitty bit her lip and admitted, 'Yes, miss. But I know what he is, you see. He's a real Jack-the-Lad. He's got a reputation around all the farms he visits.'

'You mean, he's got girls into trouble before? Before me?'

Kitty shrugged. 'I've never actually heard that about him. But everyone knows he's got an eye for the girls . . .'

'And you? You still went with him even knowing that?'

Kitty felt the colour suffuse her face as she whispered, 'Yes. But you see, I love him.'

Miriam's laughter was high-pitched with hysteria. 'Oh yes, oh yes, very fine, I'm sure. I suppose we all think we're in love with him.' Wildly, she swung about and picked up a small glass vase from the mantelshelf.

'No, miss.' Kitty put out her hand as if to fend off what she knew was going to happen next. 'Please, miss, they're not our things . . .'

The vase flew through the air and smashed against the wall. 'How could he? After all the things he said . . .' Miriam screeched as she picked up a hand-painted cup and flung that in Kitty's direction. 'And how could you? Why didn't you tell me? How could you be so disloyal?'

'I didn't know. Not then. How could I?' Kitty said as calmly as she could, though keeping her eyes firmly fixed on Miriam's right hand as it sought and found the next missile.

'You're a slut, Kitty Clegg. Nothing but a common slut.'

Now Kitty was angry too. ''Tain't any good calling me names just to make yasen feel better. You should have kept to your own kind instead of lying down with a bit of rough.'

'Why, you impudent little . . .'

The saucer followed the cup against the wall, shattering into a hundred pieces.

Then Kitty heard a frantic knocking on the outer door of the cottage and the voice of their landlady.

'Mrs Franklin. Miss Clegg. What's going on? Open this door. What's happening?' The pounding on the door came again but now, above Miriam's long-drawn-out screaming, Kitty could not hear Mrs Bradshaw calling. She was too busy trying to avoid the flying ornaments and closing her ears to the obscenities issuing from her young mistress's mouth. Words Kitty had never expected to hear from Miss Miriam Franklin.

'The bastard! I'll kill him for this. I thought he loved me. He said he loved me. And you, Kitty Clegg. You bitch! You little *whore* . . . I'll kill you, too.'

Twenty-Three

'You'll have to go.'

'Oh Mrs Bradshaw, please don't turn us out. We'll pay for all the damage and I'll replace as much as I can.' Kitty's pleas were in vain.

The woman shook her head. 'No. I'm sorry – sorry for you, that is – but you'll have to go. And I'll expect payment for everything that's been broken or damaged. All my mother's pretty things . . .' The poor woman's eyes filled with tears and Kitty felt dreadful. She was silent, unable, this time, to make excuses for her young mistress's unforgivable behaviour.

Since the incident, Miriam had locked herself in her bedroom and had refused to speak to Kitty, emerging only to visit the privy or drink a glass of water.

'You must eat, miss,' Kitty called, bending low to speak through the keyhole. 'You must keep your strength up.'

She jumped back from the door as a thud sounded on the opposite side and, mentally, she added another few shillings to their bill for breakages. Sighing she went into her own bedroom and dragged a box into the centre of the room. Opening drawers and the wardrobe, she began to pack her few belongings.

Later, she went again to stand outside Miriam's door. 'Miss Miriam? Can you hear me? You've got to let me in. I've got to pack your clothes. We've to leave tomorrow. Mrs Bradshaw—'

The door was flung open and Kitty blinked in the sudden light from the far window.

'Leave?' Miriam's eyes were sparkling and there was a smile on her mouth. It was the first sign of real interest the girl had shown for weeks. 'We're leaving? Oh Kitty . . .' She flung her arms around the surprised maid and hugged her. 'I'm sorry for all the horrid things I said. Where are we going? I don't care where it is as long as it's away from here and that horrible witch next door.'

'I don't know where we can go. And besides, your mother . . .'

'Don't worry about Mother. I'll write to her.'

'But how can you?' Kitty argued worriedly. 'When we're supposed to be abroad?'

'Oh yes, I was forgetting that. But never mind, I'll think of something.' Excitement lit her green eyes again. 'Let's go to York, Kitty. There'll be so much more to *do* there.'

Now Kitty had no argument, for leave they must and they had to go somewhere.

'All right,' she said heavily. 'We'll go back to York, but I don't think your mother will be happy about it. We don't want to run into those friends of the Hardings.'

Miriam dismissed Kitty's anxieties with a wave of her slim, elegant hand. 'In a city that size? Talk sense, Kitty. It's hardly likely, now is it?'

'I suppose not, miss,' Kitty said reluctantly. 'But I still don't think your mother will approve.' Or, she thought silently, about what's happened here. But because she was relieved that at least Miriam was in a better mood now, Kitty held her tongue.

*

The hotel they booked into was sumptuous. Miriam demanded a room on the second floor where the long windows overlooked a fine view of the racecourse.

'You're on the next floor up,' Miriam informed Kitty. 'A smaller room. You don't need a room this size.'

'Thank you, miss,' Kitty murmured and turned away to hide her smile. Back in Miss Miriam's world, she was immediately put in her place as maid. There would be no further sharing of meals and cosy chats in front of the fire on lonely evenings. Now Miriam dressed in brighter colours and insisted on taking her meals downstairs in the dining room with the other guests.

'I don't see why I have to wear black all the time. Why can't my supposed husband be away at sea, or somewhere?'

'Because,' Kitty explained patiently, 'if he's not dead, then it would look rather strange that he didn't come home at the time of your confinement.'

'That's ridiculous.' A frown puckered Miriam's smooth forehead. 'We'll just say he's at sea and that he can't get home.'

Kitty sighed. 'As you please, miss.'

'Well, I do please, Clegg. I'm sick of hiding myself away.'

Kitty was silent, but inwardly she sighed. They had been away from home not quite four weeks and already Miriam was bored and longing for company. It would not be possible to hide her condition much longer with voluminous clothing and then it would be considered 'not quite the thing' for a woman to be seen out in polite society. For the moment Kitty said nothing, but she could foresee more storms ahead.

*

Kitty loved the city of York and never tired of wandering through its narrow streets where sometimes the timber-framed houses overhung the street itself almost as if they were leaning towards each other to touch.

On the first full day after they had settled into the hotel, the young maid was eager to witness, first-hand, the sights and sounds and smells of a big city.

'Come on, Miss Miriam, do come into the town with me. It'll do you good.'

'I can't be bothered. And I don't want to be "done good". I just want to lie here and be miserable.'

Kitty argued no more and closed the door softly behind her. If Miss Miriam wants to wallow in self-pity, she thought grimly, then, just for once, today I'm going to let her. Today, Kitty promised herself, I'm going to enjoy myself.

It was a long walk into the centre of the city, but, keeping the Minster as a beacon, Kitty set off at a brisk pace, well wrapped up in her cape and hat. Soon, she found herself in a maze of streets all radiating from the Minster, narrow cobbled streets where shopkeepers' wares encroached on to the pavements. Then suddenly she was in a market place where farmers brought their vegetables in season from the countryside in huge round baskets. One such farmer, dressed incongruously in a black jacket and top hat, sat on a sack of potatoes amid an early harvest of spring cabbages, Brussels sprouts, carrots and broccoli overflowing on to the pavement all around him. Women moved among the produce, questioning and bartering for the best bargain and Kitty paused to listen to the banter. It reminded her of Mrs Grundy and how she haggled over the price of a joint of beef with the butcher in Tresford. Even though the money was not coming from her own pocket, it was a matter of pride for the cook to get the best cut at the keenest price for her mistress.

Kitty moved on to where a woman was perching on the edge of a box surrounded by row upon row of china plates, cups, saucers, bowls, even a pair of spotted china dogs, all spread around her on the cobbles of the square. The woman, her hands folded across her ample stomach, was dressed in a black dress, cape and hat and wore a long white apron. 'Best Staffordshire pottery,' she called out in a loud, raucous voice. 'Not a crack, not a chip nowhere . . .'

A young woman pushed a perambulator close by, the large wheels rattling over the cobbled surface so that the child inside the carriage was shaken and buffeted and began to whimper.

Kitty stood still, suddenly realizing that they had bought nothing in readiness for the child that would surely be born. Not even a blanket to wrap it in, never mind clothes, she thought. She frowned. Miriam flatly refused to talk about the child, so that any preparations would be difficult, if not impossible, to make.

Kitty moved on down another street and was obliged to step smartly out of the way as a bus, drawn by two horses, rattled close by her. The bus had large wooden wheels just like those on a farm wagon, but instead of the vehicle carrying crops, it carried people. The lower deck afforded some shelter for the passengers, having glass windows, but on the top deck, reached by curving steps at the back of the bus, the passengers sat on wooden seats open to the weather and looked not only in a decidedly precarious state, but very cold too.

On she walked and now she saw a tram running on metal rails in the middle of the street, designed in much the same manner as the horse-drawn bus, with a covered lower deck and an open upper deck. Then Kitty found herself standing on the slope of the bridge crossing over the river. She leaned over the parapet looking down into the swirling waters and then up at all the tall warehouses that lined the banks on either side. She turned and walked back again to lose herself in the maze of streets, entranced by so many different shops and all the people hurrying about their business.

She walked past a florist's where the smell of the flowers made her think instantly of home, then on past a tailor's who, incongruously, advertised firewood for sale. Next door was a restaurant with the day's menus chalked on a board propped in the doorway. Kitty paused, feeling suddenly hungry, yet she must not spend their precious money on treats for herself. Cut off from contacting home, except in the case of a real emergency, Kitty knew they must eke out the money Mrs Franklin had given them. Too much already had been spent on reimbursing Mrs Bradshaw for breakages.

Resolutely, Kitty turned away from the restaurant almost catching her head on some tyres hanging up outside a cycle shop next door. 'I wish I could ride a bicycle,' she murmured wistfully. 'Then I could go for long rides out into the country.'

While she loved the new adventure of city life, she yearned for the smells of the countryside, the open roads and the fields of waving corn . . .

And then she thought of Jack.

'Kitty, lay out my best blue silk gown for this evening. I'm having dinner with Mr Radford tonight.'

'We didn't bring your blue gown, miss. And who,' she added, a note of sternness in her tone, 'is Mr Radford?'

The girl spun round and, deliberately ignoring the last

part of Kitty's question, berated her maid. 'Didn't bring it? *We* didn't bring it? You, you mean. You didn't bring it. Why on earth not? You're useless. I've a good mind to dismiss you.'

Calmly, knowing full well that this, at least, was an idle threat for Miriam Franklin could not do without Kitty, certainly not for the next few months, she said, 'I didn't bring it because you're supposed to be a widow and a blue gown is hardly appropriate.'

'I told you to forget all that nonsense now. Well, there's nothing for it, we shall just have to go into the city and buy a gown for tonight. I'm certainly not going out to dine with a gentleman wearing *black*.'

'He can't be a gentleman if he's asking a married lady out to dine,' Kitty said tersely.

'He's not going to know I'm married.' Inclining her head coyly to one side, Miriam made a great show of removing the two rings from her finger and slipping them into her jewellery case. 'He's a very handsome man and . . .'

'So's Jack Thorndyke,' Kitty muttered, but Miriam, lost in her romantic notions, appeared not to hear.

' . . . and I deserve a little fun.'

'Really?' Kitty said tartly. 'And how did you meet this handsome Mr Radford?'

'He was here three evenings ago, dining with some friends in the hotel restaurant. I saw him keep looking across at me all evening and later he spoke to me. Then last night when I came out of the dining room he was waiting in the lounge and we got talking.'

Appalled, Kitty said, 'Do you mean you weren't introduced to him properly by – by . . .' she hesitated and finished lamely, 'someone?'

'And just who around here,' Miriam said with sarcasm,

'is going to make formal introductions for me when I don't know anyone? Talk sense, Kitty.'

'But – but you shouldn't allow anyone to – to just start talking to you like that. It isn't done.'

'Well, I'm not exactly noted for sticking to the rules of polite society,' Miriam said and patted her stomach. 'And as for any reputation I might have had, well, I rather think that's gone now, don't you?' There was bitterness in her tone and Kitty stepped towards her.

'That's why we're here, miss. To try to save your reputation. Please, don't go making things worse.'

Miriam turned her back on her but not before Kitty had seen the tears that sprang into the girl's eyes. Feeling suddenly sorry for her, Kitty put her arm about the girl. 'I'm not trying to stop you having a bit of fun. Just – just worried for you. Honestly.'

The girl's shoulders, beneath Kitty's arm, were stiff and resentful. 'You don't know anything about how I feel. How could you?'

There was a moment's silence and then Kitty felt her relax. Miriam leaned against her and a huge sigh, welling up from deep within, escaped her lips. The two young girls, close in age yet so different in their station in life, looked into each other's eyes.

'I suppose,' Miriam said slowly, 'maybe you do understand. I thought I loved him, you see, and I thought he loved me. He was so handsome, so strong. He was like a magnet drawing me to him and I – I couldn't resist.'

I know, I know, Kitty felt like screaming at her. Do you think I don't know exactly how it feels? But she was silent.

Miriam's mouth twisted with a wry smile. 'There but for the grace of God go you, eh, Kitty? Maybe it wouldn't have been so bad for you. I mean, it often happens in your class, doesn't it?'

Kitty bristled and swallowed a sharp retort, managing to say, 'It's still considered wrong to give yasen to a man before marriage.' And added, with a pointed sarcasm that was completely lost on Miriam, 'Even in our class.'

'I suppose so,' Miriam murmured, her mind still full of her own problems.

'And I'd have been dismissed without a reference and sent home in disgrace.' Kitty gave an involuntary shudder. 'And what me dad would have said then, I don't know.'

Miriam was silent, but she pulled away from Kitty and moved restlessly about the room, picking up a hairbrush and then putting it down again; opening and shutting the wardrobe door.

Suddenly, she whirled around, her eyes shining and her good mood obviously restored. 'Oh Kitty, please, let's go into the town and buy me a gown for this evening?'

Kitty opened her mouth to argue again, but she realized that it would be futile. 'Yes, miss,' she said, with, for once, the submissiveness that was to be expected from a servant.

Anything, she was thinking, to keep Miss Miriam in a good temper.

Twenty-Four

From the guests' lounge, looking through an internal window into the dining room, Kitty watched as her young mistress dined with the young man, Mr Radford. Miriam's face was animated. She laughed and fluttered her eyelashes and allowed her hand to rest every now and again, just for a moment, on the young man's arm.

She's flirting with him, Kitty thought. Openly and outrageously. Was that how she had flirted with Threshing Jack? Or with him, had she remained aloof and seemingly untouchable so that the challenge for a man like Jack Thorndyke had been just too much and he'd crossed the class divide to claim a trophy?

Kitty turned away feeling lost and lonely, as pictures of Jack and Miriam together tortured her imagination. But there would be someone else now, for he would not go long without finding another girl to meet in the shadows of a stackyard, to nestle into the hay . . . She gave a low groan, closed her eyes and shook her head. In spite of her anger, she was missing him. Even the thought of him, the memory of his arms about her and the warmth of his lips upon hers, made her heart quicken. And it was not only Jack she was missing. She missed Mrs Grundy's motherly ways as well as her own family; her mother, father and Milly and all her brothers and sisters.

She gave an involuntary shudder at the sudden thought of what would happen when they went home. Already she felt guilty about all the deceit. Just how were they going to carry it off with tales of their wonderful trip abroad when they hadn't even left England?

Kitty sighed as she took one last glance at Miriam with her head thrown back, laughing gaily and coquettishly at something Mr Radford was saying. She looked as if she had not a care in the world while Kitty felt she bore the whole weight of their trouble on her young shoulders.

Mr Radford, Kitty had to admit, seemed a gentleman. He was courteous, attentive and charming and even polite to Kitty herself, whereas she was quite used to being completely ignored by the so-called gentry.

'Mr Radford is taking me into the city today. We're going to have lunch somewhere. You can take the rest of the day off, Kitty.'

'Thank you, miss,' Kitty replied, her pleasure genuine. She never tired of walking around the beautiful city and today she would have another chance.

'See you later,' Miriam said gaily, waving her now ring-less hand.

Watching her go, Kitty shook her head. You won't have many more weeks of freedom, she thought, maybe you had better make the most of it. When Miriam's condition became obvious, life was going to be very difficult.

The three weeks in the little village on the coast had proved that.

'Oh Kitty, Anthony is wonderful. And he's wealthy. He's got a brand-new motor car. He's taking me for a drive into the country tomorrow.' Miriam clapped her hands together and twirled around the huge bedroom like any girl who has just met a handsome young man and knows herself attractive to him too.

Kitty opened her mouth to remind Miriam of the reason they were here at all, but she closed it again without saying a word. Time enough, she thought with a sigh, to spoil her fun when I must. Instead, all she said was, 'Then you must wrap up warm, miss. Those motor cars are draughty and it's still cold, even though it is spring.'

'Yes, yes, yes, Kitty. Don't fuss so. You're beginning to sound like my mother.'

Yes, me fine lady, Kitty thought grimly. And I feel like it, an' all. But again she said nothing, knowing full well that in the months ahead she would have to be everything to her young mistress. Maid, friend, comforter, mother and maybe even midwife. Thank goodness she had been beside her own mother when she'd given birth to the youngest. At least Kitty knew what lay in store even if Miriam didn't know what awaited her. Caught up in the whirlwind of this new romance, Miriam seemed to have forgotten that she was carrying a child. Or she was deliberately ignoring the fact.

The following day was wet and cold and a strong wind blew across the vale of York.

'It's not quite the weather for our little trip, Miss Franklin.' Kitty watched as Anthony Radford took Miriam's hand in his and raised it to his lips. He was quite a nice-looking young fellow, Kitty thought, eyeing him critically, though she wouldn't have called him handsome. His colouring was too dull for Kitty's liking. Mousy hair and pale grey eyes and a skin that was almost sallow. Compared to the earthy, swarthy features of Jack Thorndyke, poor Anthony Radford looked insipid. Yet he seemed kindly and was undoubtedly a gentleman. And, as Miriam had said, a wealthy one too, if the gleaming new motor car parked in front of the hotel was anything to go by.

'But we'll drive a little way out of the city. I know a quaint little restaurant where we can have lunch. Low beams and a log fire burning. You'll love it . . .' He crooked his arm and with a small laugh of delight, Miriam put her hand on it and allowed herself to be led out to his motor without so much as a backward glance at Kitty.

Kitty was lying on her bed late in the afternoon while the light faded from the window of her small room. She had spent the day inside the Minster, marvelling at the beautiful stained-glass windows, walking on tiptoe across the flag-stones so that her footsteps did not echo in the reverent silence. Now she was tired and she felt herself drifting into sleep when suddenly the door was flung open so violently that it crashed back against the wall and shuddered on its hinges.

'Kitty, Kitty, get up. Get our things packed. We're leaving.' Miriam was grasping her shoulder and shaking her awake.

'Wha—?' Kitty struggled to sit up, blinking the sleep from her eyes. 'Whatever's the matter, miss?' But even as she asked the question she was swinging her legs to the floor, standing up and straightening her uniform. 'What's happened?'

Her question followed Miriam out of the door, for she was hurrying out of Kitty's bedroom, across the landing and down the stairs towards her own room. 'Don't argue, Kitty. Just do as I say.'

So, Kitty followed.

As she entered Miriam's room, her young mistress had already flung wide the wardrobe doors and was scooping armfuls of clothes from their hangers and flinging them on to the bed as if there was not a moment to lose.

'I'll ring for the bellboy to bring our trunks and boxes, miss.'

'Yes, you do that, Kitty, but hurry. We must *go*.'

'But where are we going?' Kitty asked helplessly. 'We can't keep moving about like this. Not for much longer, specially when—'

Miriam whirled around, her green eyes flashing angrily. 'Do as you're told, Kitty, get our things packed.'

Kitty took a deep breath and decided to stand her ground. She liked York, she liked the hotel they were staying in. She didn't want to go. And unless Miriam had a very good reason, she was damned if they were going to move on again like a couple of gypsies.

'Not,' she said with quiet, controlled firmness, 'until you explain to me why we have to go.'

Miriam came towards her and for a split second Kitty thought the girl was about to strike her, but suddenly the fight seemed to drain away. She gave a groan and put her hand to her belly and sank down into a chair near the window. Covering her face with her hands, she said, in a muffled voice, 'We've got to go, Kitty, else we'll be found out.'

Kitty moved closer and knelt in front of her, trying to pull her hands away from her face. 'Why? Is it something to do with Mr Radford?'

'Yes, yes, *yes*.' With sudden impatience, Miriam stood up, flinging Kitty off balance so that she ended up sprawling in an ungainly heap on the floor. Taking not the slightest notice of her maid, Miriam began pacing the room with angry, jerky movements.

'We were talking . . .' she waved her hand expressively. 'You know how it is?' Kitty did not know for she had

191

never been wined and dined in expensive restaurants by a wealthy young gentleman, but she made no comment. 'He was telling me how his family have a large estate just south of York and – and that they have land in other parts of the country. In other counties. He – he asked me where I came from . . .' She leaned on the wide windowsill and rested her forehead against the cool glass. 'Oh Kitty, I wasn't thinking. I told him. And – and then,' her voice dropped to an incredulous whisper, 'I can hardly believe it, he – he said he knew someone from that part of the world. Sir Ralph Harding and, more particularly, his son, Guy.' Flatly, she said again, 'Kitty, he knows Guy. In fact it's worse than that, he's quite friendly with him. Evidently, Guy often c-comes to York . . .' Her voice faltered and fell away.

'Oh miss,' Kitty said, aghast. 'It must be the people your mother meant. That was why she was so adamant that we must not stay long in York.'

'But it's so stupid. To think, out of all the people in York, I have to meet up with *him*.'

'Well yes, it does seem too much of a coincidence to be believed, but there it is. It's happened.'

Miriam glanced at Kitty. 'So, what are we going to do?'

Kitty bit her lip. 'I suppose you're right,' she said slowly at last, her voice heavy with disappointment. 'We had better leave York.'

'What are you waiting for then, girl? Get packing. There's not a moment to lose.'

'There's one thing we must do first, though, miss.'

'What?'

'Check what money we've got.'

Miriam blinked. 'Money? What do you mean, what money we've got?'

'Your mother only gave us a certain amount and this

hotel has been expensive. Then there was your new gown . . .'

Miriam frowned. 'But I thought Mother made arrangements for money to be sent to us?'

Kitty nodded. 'She did. At Robin Hood's Bay.'

'Well, won't the old witch send it on?'

'We haven't told her where we are, have we?'

Miriam pulled a face. 'Then you'd better write and tell her, when we've got settled somewhere.'

Silently, Kitty thought, but how long will we be in the next place? Aloud she said, 'I will, but in the meantime, have we enough money for our fare to – well – wherever we're going and enough to book into a small guesthouse or rooms?'

Miriam looked at her blankly. 'How should I know? I don't know anything about money.'

Kitty, sighing at the helplessness of spoilt little rich girls, said, 'Show me what we've got left.'

Miriam found her purse and tipped out a few coins on to the bed. 'There. Satisfied?'

Kitty counted it swiftly. 'There's not nearly enough here. Is that really all?'

'Well, yes. You see, I thought the hotel would just give us a bill at the end of our stay and that my father . . .' She stared up at Kitty. 'Oh. I hadn't thought.'

'Exactly, miss,' Kitty said grimly. The girl had indeed thought nothing out. 'How can your father possibly settle the bill when he thinks you're in the south of France, or somewhere?'

Miriam stared down at the coins. 'What are we going to do?'

Kitty folded her arms and tapped her toe on the floor. 'Well, in my class, miss, if we need a bit of extra money in a hurry, we pawn summat.'

Miriam looked up at her again and blinked. 'Pawn? What's that?'

Kitty was startled. 'You mean, you don't know what to pawn something means?'

Miriam shook her head.

'Most places have one. We've got one in Tresford.'

'Really? Where?'

'Old Mr Rivers on Main Street.'

'Oh. I always thought that was just a second-hand shop.'

'Well, it is – of sorts. What Mr Rivers does – and I expect it's more or less the same anywhere – is lend you money on an object of some value for a certain length of time, say a week or maybe two.'

'Then what?'

'You redeem it. You pay him back the money he lent you, plus a bit for him having lent you it.'

'Sort of interest, you mean?'

Now it was Kitty's turn not to understand a term, but she was a bit more wily than to admit her ignorance. 'I expect so. And you get the goods back.' She giggled. 'A lot of the farm labourers' wives take their husband's best suit in on a Monday and redeem it on a Saturday ready for Church on Sunday and then, by Monday, it's back in the pawn shop.'

'Really?'

'Yes, really.'

Miriam was quiet for a moment as if thinking. 'But what can we pawn?'

Kitty was amused at the 'we', as if Miriam assumed her maid had anything worth pawning, but she said, 'Well, there's your rings of course, but I don't think you should pawn them, miss, as we might not get back to redeem them and . . .'

Miriam shuddered. 'Oh heavens, no. If my father found out I'd pawned his mother's rings . . .'

She did not continue. She had no need to do so, for Kitty understood only too well. She put her head on one side, eyeing Miriam and knowing she was taking a risk. 'There is that new dress you've bought. You're really not going to have much use for it for a while, now are you?'

She had fully expected an angry outburst, but Miriam merely looked at the dress lying on the bed waiting to be packed and said dolefully, 'No, I suppose you're right. Take it, Kitty, but mind you get a fair price for it.'

An hour later Kitty was walking along a narrow street searching above her head for the pawnbroker's sign. There were various signs bearing shopkeepers' names or advertising the nature of their business, like the huge broom-head that hung above one entrance, but nowhere could she see the well-known trade mark of the pawn-broker. It was not until she had walked up and down the same street three times reading every sign that she realized that the lamp decorated with a leaf design was, in fact, adorning the premises she was looking for.

As she entered the dusty interior, a bell above the door clanged and an elderly man shuffled out from the back of the shop.

'How much could you give me on this gown, please?' Kitty asked holding up the blue satin garment.

'My word, that's a fine gown.'

She felt the old man eyeing the maid's uniform beneath her cape. 'Belong to your mistress, does it?'

Kitty nodded.

'You pinched it?'

Kitty gasped and indignation flooded her face. 'No, I did not.'

The old man grunted and reached out with dirty fingers to touch it. 'Mm, well, I could only give you two pounds.'

'That's not nearly enough.' She made as if to fold up the dress. 'I'll look for another broker.'

'Wait a minute. Now, don't be so hasty.'

They haggled for at least ten minutes until Kitty had driven the man to ten pounds. 'You see, we're leaving and I somehow don't think we'll get back to redeem it,' she told him truthfully, 'so I am sure you'll be able to sell it at a good profit.'

She knew by the gleam in the man's eyes that she was right in her assumption.

Within an hour of Kitty's return to the hotel they were packed and, with the bill settled, on their way out of York in a hired motor car and on the road to Harrogate.

'It's a very nice place, Harrogate. A spa town.'

'Whatever you say, miss,' Kitty murmured, growing increasingly weary of all the moving from one place to another.

They travelled in silence for several miles until Miriam said suddenly, 'What if Guy finds out, Kitty? He won't want to marry me then, will he?'

Appalled, Kitty said, 'Is that what you're planning to do? Go back and marry Mr Guy?' She knew that Mrs Franklin still clung to the hope, but Kitty had thought it a vain one. Surely Miriam – and her mother – would not deceive the poor young man? But it seemed that she was wrong.

Miriam shrugged. 'What else can I do?'

'But do – do you love Mr Guy?'

The girl's face was stony. 'What's the good of loving

someone? I thought – I thought I was in love with – with *him*. And look where that's got me.'

'But you shouldn't marry Mr Guy if you don't love him, miss. It – it's not fair on him, because he loves you. Anyone can see that.'

Miriam sighed and then asked bluntly, 'Do you still love Jack Thorndyke, after all you know about him?'

Now it was Kitty's turn to sigh and say heavily, 'Yes, I do.'

'Then you're a fool, Kitty Clegg.'

'I know. But I can't help myself. I'd do anything – anything to get him to marry me.'

'Really?' Miriam said slowly. 'Would you really?'

Kitty looked away from her mistress to hide the tears that sprang into her eyes. Her glance went out of the car window across the moors stretching into the far distance. 'Yes,' she said, quietly. 'I really think I would.'

With her face averted, Kitty did not see the scheming look in the green eyes of her young mistress.

Twenty-Five

They found lodgings in a guesthouse on the hill leading up from the Spa rooms. The landlady, Mrs Lawrence, was a kindly soul who reminded Kitty of Mrs Grundy. On the journey, Kitty had managed to persuade Miriam to wear the rings once more and to act the part of a recently widowed mother-to-be.

'Your mother was right, you know. It'll be so much easier, when – when your time comes.'

Miriam, still shaken from her recent brush with the possible exposure of her shame, agreed, though Kitty could see that it was with reluctance and the stormy expression in Miriam's fine eyes warned Kitty of more petulance to come.

Kitty was enchanted with the town just as she had been with the city of York, though for different reasons. The old city with its feeling of history, its beautiful Minster and quaint, old streets had fascinated her, but Harrogate seemed elegant and the carriages and motor cars spoke of affluence and a place visited by the wealthy. Even the shops seemed to cater for the rich rather than for a lowly maid. But Kitty was not envious, merely enthralled.

Not so Miriam. As her condition became more obvious and impossible to hide, so she became bored. Her irritability increased and Kitty found herself with no freedom to explore the town. Miriam demanded her maid's presence and attention the whole time now.

'Let's go to the baths, miss – madam,' she suggested, trying hard to remember to address her mistress as if she were indeed a married lady.

'Whatever for?' Miriam frowned.

'It's like a meeting place for the ladies of the town on certain days and – well – soon it won't be seemly for you to go out except for a little walk after dusk.'

'How can I go for walks here?' Miriam asked listlessly. 'It's all hills. I'm out of breath by the time I've walked a few paces.'

'Then it's high time you walked a bit more,' Kitty replied sharply. 'It won't do you nor your baby any good if you neglect your health.'

Coldly, her mouth tight, Miriam said, 'What do I care about Jack Thorndyke's bastard?'

Kitty pulled in a deep breath and before she had stopped to think what she was saying, the words were pouring out of her mouth. 'Well, I care what happens to his child. And I'll tell you summat else. I wish it were me having his child, bastard or not. I'd love it, I'd care for it. Love it and care for it, I would, while there was breath in me body. There now, it's said.' She swung away and marched out of the room before Miriam should see the tears smarting in her eyes.

Left alone in the bedroom, Miriam stared at the door. 'Would you?' she murmured, the calculating look once more in her eyes. 'Would you indeed, Kitty Clegg?'

'It's no good, Kitty, I really can't walk any further.' Miriam leaned against a lamp post and panted heavily. Through the dusk of the August evening, Kitty peered at her.

'You feeling all right?'

'It's this awful backache. I've had it for a while and it seems to be getting worse.'

'Why on earth didn't you say something? Come on,' Kitty said firmly, 'we'd best get you back to the boarding house. Now.'

'Why, what's the matter?' Miriam said, but allowed Kitty to take her arm, turn her round and begin leading her back up the hill towards their lodgings.

'Maybe your time's come. Backache's one of the signs that you might be going into labour.'

'I didn't know that.'

'Well, it is,' Kitty replied shortly, anxious now to get her mistress back into the house.

By the time they reached their rooms, they were both panting with exertion and anxiety.

'I'd better get Mrs Lawrence to send for the midwife. Go and lie down, madam, and I'll be back in a minute . . .'

Five hours later, Miriam Franklin gave birth to a lusty boy. Red-faced with exertion and crying hysterically, Miriam pushed the midwife away as she tried to put the child into her arms. 'Take it away. I don't want it. I don't even want to see it . . .'

Helplessly, the midwife turned to Kitty who held out her arms for the infant. The moment Kitty Clegg held Jack Thorndyke's son in her arms, she loved him. Loved him with a love as fierce and protective as if she was indeed his natural mother. Her eyes devoured the tiny, puckered features, the tuft of black hair. 'Jack's boy,' she murmured with wonder. 'You're Jack Thorndyke's son. I just don't understand,' she whispered, nuzzling the infant's head with her lips. 'How can she turn her back on you?'

*

Physically, Miriam recovered very quickly and, in a few days, she was demanding to be allowed to get up from her bed. But still she took no notice of her son, refusing to feed him herself so that Kitty had the trouble of bottles and teats and suffered sleepless nights until the child took to what was, to her, an unnatural way for a tiny baby to have to feed. Kitty was soon exhausted and pale with dark shadows under her eyes, while Miriam pampered herself and slept soundly through every night. Before many days had passed, to the casual observer it would indeed have seemed that the maid, and not the mistress, was the natural mother of the infant.

'I'm going home,' Miriam announced two weeks after the birth of her child. 'I can't stand it here another minute.'

'I don't think the child can travel yet. I—'

Miriam whirled around on her. 'The child? The *child*? You can't possibly think I'm taking it home, do you?' Miriam never referred to her son as anything but 'it'.

'Well, what are you going to do with *him*?' Kitty asked pointedly.

Miriam shrugged and preened herself in front of her mirror, pulling in her waist so that, even for Kitty, it was difficult to remember that the other girl had given birth only two weeks earlier.

'I know what I'd like to do with it,' Miriam muttered darkly. 'Leave him out on the moors . . .'

'Oh miss . . .' Kitty began, forgetting, in her anguish for the tiny life which seemed already to be in her sole charge, to call her 'madam'. Miriam mocked her in a whining voice. 'Oh miss, oh miss, how wicked you are . . .'

Kitty stood up and laid the boy in his makeshift cradle – the bottom drawer of the chest from her bedroom. Then, turning to face Miriam, she said, 'You can't go home yet. Your mother's arriving tomorrow.'

Miriam gasped. 'How . . .?' Then as realization dawned, she demanded angrily, 'Did you send word to her?'

'Yes,' Kitty said boldly, squaring her shoulders. 'Before we left, she asked me to let her know when – when your child had been born.'

'Oh that's wonderful! What if anyone sees the letter? What if . . .'

'Do you think I'm that stupid?' Kitty snapped, her patience which had been so long held in check giving way at last. 'Of course I was careful how I worded the letter. I said that we had arrived back in England and were staying in Harrogate. I didn't even give her the name of the guest-house but a poste restante address at the local post office.'

'How extremely clever of you, Clegg,' Miriam sneered but she turned away, unable, for once, to think of any further retort.

'So,' Kitty went on, 'your mother will be here tomorrow. She'll decide what's to be done.'

Kitty's voice and demeanour were so much stronger on the surface than she was feeling inside. Her heart was breaking at the thought that tomorrow she might have to part from the baby boy who already had Kitty Clegg wrapped firmly around his tiny little finger.

'So – this is my grandson?' Mrs Franklin stood looking down at the child in the cradle.

'Do – do you want to hold him, madam?' Kitty asked tentatively, unsure what the woman's feelings were towards the child, yet she could not imagine the gentle, kindly Mrs Franklin being as vehement in her dislike of the circumstances of the innocent child's birth as Miriam.

Mrs Franklin glanced up at Kitty and then back to the

baby. 'I would, Kitty, I would indeed like to hold him. But I am so afraid that if I did . . .'

Kitty breathed a sigh of relief. 'You mean, you might not want to part with him? Oh madam, he's a beautiful baby. Are you really going to give him away? I don't know how Miss Miriam can bear to. But – but . . .' She faltered, unwilling to tell tales, yet Mrs Franklin should know of her daughter's attitude towards the child. At her mistress's next words, however, Kitty's heart grew cold.

Mrs Franklin was shaking her head. 'We can't possibly keep him, Kitty. It would ruin Miriam's life.' She looked up and met Kitty's haunted eyes. The girl was shocked. It was as if they were discussing a kitten or a puppy, not a child.

'But madam, even if he's adopted, how can you be sure he'll be loved and cared for properly? Won't you always be wondering where he is and how he is and—?'

'Oh don't, Kitty, please don't,' Mrs Franklin whispered and Kitty saw her own feelings mirrored in the woman's tortured eyes. 'Please don't make this any harder than it already is.'

The door opened and Miriam swept into the room. 'Have you done my packing, Kitty?'

Mrs Franklin and the maid exchanged a glance and Kitty heard the older woman give a small sigh. 'So,' she murmured, her gaze still on the sleeping infant, 'nothing has changed.'

'What?' Miriam demanded. 'What did you say?'

Quietly, her mother said, 'Nothing, my dear. Nothing of importance. Now, we had better all sit down and decide what is to be done.'

'Done? What do you mean what is to be done?' Miriam's voice was high-pitched. 'It's obvious, isn't it? Isn't there an orphanage or somewhere that will take it? Or the workhouse?'

Kitty noticed that Mrs Franklin winced at her daughter's callousness, but calmly she moved across the room and sat down on a small bedroom chair. 'It would be kinder to have the child placed for adoption, Miriam.'

'Do that then. I don't care what you do,' the girl shouted. 'Just get rid of it.' At the sound of her raised voice, a whimper came from the cradle so that Kitty rushed towards it and scooped up the child into her arms. She held him close, crooning softly against his ear, her body swaying in a soothing, rocking motion.

'Look at her, just look at her,' Miriam sneered. 'She ought to have been the mother. It ought to have been her giving birth to Jack Thorndyke's bastard.'

Mrs Franklin gave a gasp, for it was the first time that Miriam had divulged to her the name of the father. But Miriam ignored her mother and, her eyes glittering with malicious calculation, she took a step towards Kitty and said, 'Why don't you take him, Kitty? Why don't you present Jack Thorndyke with his son? After all, you did say you wished it was you having his child, didn't you? And you said you'd do anything – *anything* – to get him to marry you. Maybe this way – you can.'

It was a monstrous idea and yet, once the seed had been planted in her mind, Kitty could not pluck it out. That she loved the child already was without question, but could she – dare she – do such a thing?

Though they all knew that the suggestion had been made with malicious sarcasm, it had not been taken as such. Kitty had taken it seriously – very seriously.

Even Mrs Franklin murmured, 'I suppose it would be a way out.' Then looking straight at her, she added, 'But it must be your decision, of course, Kitty. You must be aware that you would face all sorts of problems. I mean, for instance, what would your family say? How would they treat you?'

But Kitty was only listening with half an ear. Jack's son. She could take Jack's son as if he were her own. All men wanted sons and surely a man like Jack Thorndyke would be bursting with pride to think he had a son. Maybe Miriam was right, maybe he would even marry her if he thought she had borne him a son?

It was dishonest, of course, but not entirely so. The child was indeed Jack's, Miriam had admitted it, even before her mother now. The only dishonesty was that she, Kitty, was not his natural mother. But oh how she loved him, this tiny little human being, the living replica of his father.

She heard Mrs Franklin's voice as if from a great distance. 'We'd make sure you were looked after, Kitty. That you had everything you needed. After all, we could truthfully say that we wanted to look after a valued servant.'

'Yes, madam. Thank you, madam,' Kitty murmured, her mind still reeling with her own thoughts. Then at Mrs Franklin's next words, Kitty was jolted into full attentiveness.

'There is just one thing I must insist upon, Kitty, if you do decide to take this course, and it's this. You must never, ever, divulge the name of the real mother. If you take the boy now, he is your child and yours alone. No matter what happens in the future, you must carry that secret to your grave. You must never tell him, not even when he's grown.' A note of firmness crept into the woman's tone. 'Do you understand me, Kitty?'

Kitty's eyes were wide and through lips that were suddenly dry, she murmured, 'Yes, madam.'

'Very well, then. Now, in those circumstances, do you wish to take the child?'

For a long moment, Kitty stared into Mrs Franklin's lovely face, then her glance went to Miriam standing beside her mother, for once silent and watchful.

The baby moved in Kitty's arms and gave a little whimper. She felt the warmth of him against her breast, breathed in the sweet baby smell of him and looked down into the deep blue eyes that seemed to be looking up at her so trustingly and Kitty Clegg was lost.

'Yes, madam. Oh yes, I'll take him and, whatever happens, even if . . .' she glanced towards Miriam just once, 'even if Jack still won't marry me, I'll love him and care for him as if he were me own.'

Mrs Franklin nodded and said slowly and deliberately, 'From this moment on, Kitty, he is yours.'

Twenty-Six

'A child? You – you've got a child?'

Kitty stood in the kitchen of the stationmaster's house, the baby in her arms, and faced her mother and father across the table.

'I know it's a shock for you, Mam, but . . .'

Her mother was standing rigidly still, her hand to her throat and her eyes wide, almost bulging. It was her father who moved towards her, thrusting his face close to her, his thin, wiry neck jutting out of his stiffly starched white collar. 'A shock? A *shock*? Is that all you think it? You bring shame to our door and you call it a shock? Have you listened to nothing you've been taught in this house? Haven't you always been told . . .?'

Suddenly her mother gasped and reached with trembling fingers for the edge of the table to support herself. 'Oh no—' Her face was white, her lips parted, and in her eyes was such an expression of fear that it was almost terror. 'Oh no, you can't have. It's not – not *his* child?'

Her father glanced back over his shoulder at his wife, just once, with a look so filled with hatred and malice that Kitty reeled. Now it was Kitty who was shocked. She had never seen her father act this way. He had always been a stern man and strict in the upbringing of his children, but she had thought all fathers were like that. Certainly, he had never before displayed rages and tempers like Mr Franklin. Until this moment, she had always thought herself lucky in her parents. She had always thought that whatever happened they would stand by her . . .

Now John Clegg was reaching out and grasping Kitty's shoulder in such a vice-like grip that his fingers dug into her flesh. 'Who is the father?' he demanded through his teeth.

'Whose is it?' came her mother's frantic echoing whisper. 'Who's the father?'

Kitty's puzzled glance went from one face to the other and back again. They were staring at her, hanging on her answer. It was the usual question that was asked in such circumstances, Kitty knew, yet there seemed to be a desperation behind her parents' asking, a fear that was out of all proportion.

'Tell us, girl,' her father's voice came harshly and made her jump. There was a burning anger in his eyes that made even Kitty suddenly afraid.

Her throat constricted so that the words came out in a strangled whisper. 'Jack. Jack Thorndyke. He's the father.'

As soon as the name left her mouth, she saw her mother's shoulders sag with relief and a low groan escaped her lips and even some of the anger went from her father's eyes, though his lips were tight with bitterness.

'What is it?' Her glance was darting between them again. 'Who did you think it might be?'

'I thought . . . maybe . . . he . . .' Betsy began, but again her father glanced at his wife and Betsy Clegg, meeting his eyes, dropped her own gaze and fell silent.

'Well, there's one thing for sure,' her father gave a snort of contempt, 'Jack Thorndyke'll never marry you, girl. If the tales are to be believed, he's got bastards scattered across half the county. You're a fool, Kitty. I'd have thought better of you. Milly, now, when she's grown a bit, I can well imagine she'll be the sort to get herself into trouble because she's a simple, silly girl. But you? I had hopes for you.'

Betsy Clegg's voice came tremulously. 'What are you going to do, John?'

Not what are 'we' to do, Kitty noticed, but 'you'.

'Do?' He turned on his wife so that she blinked and shrank back, seeming suddenly smaller. Defeated, yes, that was it, Kitty thought, her mother seemed defeated. 'Do? I'm going to throw her out of this house. Aye, her and her bastard, that's what I'm going to do.'

Betsy gave a low moan and hung her head as if it were she, and not her daughter, who bore the shame.

But Kitty tossed her head with a show of defiance, although inside, her father's words about Jack had shaken her badly. 'I'll be all right. Don't you worry about me. The mistress – Mrs Franklin – she's been very kind. Ses she'll see I have everything I need.'

Betsy raised her head slowly, a wary look now on her face. Again Kitty saw a glance between her mother and father. 'The mistress? Why should she concern herself with a maid who gets herself into trouble? Turned away without a reference, that's what usually happens unless . . .'

Then her father leaned towards her, demanding harshly, 'Are you telling us the truth, girl? Is it Thorndyke's?'

Fortunately, the question was phrased so that Kitty could answer quickly and truthfully, 'Yes, yes, he is Jack's. I swear it.' But her mind scrabbled around for a plausible reason as to why Mrs Franklin should be taking an interest in a servant's welfare. A servant who, to all outward appearances, had brought shame not only upon her own family but on the household in which she was employed.

Kitty swallowed. 'She – she's a kind lady. She always has been and – and I'm the only one who can handle Miss

Miriam's tantrums,' she added triumphantly and congratulated herself on her quick thinking.

But the questioning was not over yet. 'What? Do you mean she wants you to continue working there?'

Now Kitty hesitated. 'Well, no. At least, I don't expect so. I mean, I'll be married to Jack, won't I? It depends . . .'

'Oh it depends, all right,' her father said sarcastically. 'But if you're going to *depend* on Jack Thorndyke, me girl, you're going to be sadly disappointed. You mark my words.'

'You're wrong, Dad.'

The man's fist was bunched before her face. 'Don't call me "Dad" again. I'm no father of yours. Not any more, I'm not. Get yourself away from this house. I never want to set eyes on you again.'

For a long moment Kitty stared at him, then turned her eyes to her mother. 'Mam . . .?' she began, but Betsy dropped her eyes and remained silent.

Kitty stood there, reeling from the violence of their reaction. Anger, disappointment, bitterness and, finally, total rejection. They were going to cast her out. The thought that her mother and father might do this had never once entered Kitty's mind. She had to admit now that she had not thought things through carefully before agreeing to return home allowing everyone to believe the child was hers.

In her arms the baby moved and began to cry. She felt his warmth, his sturdy little body, already so strong even though so tiny and her heart turned over with love for him. 'He's getting hungry, Mam. Can't I just feed him here? Then – then – I'll go.'

Once again, Betsy cast an appealing look to her husband who uttered an oath and thumped one fist against the palm of his other hand. 'Do what ya like,' he spat, 'but she's to be gone from this house by the time I get back. You hear me?'

'Yes, John,' her mother said in a meek tone the like of which Kitty had never heard from her before. Her father left the house, banging the door behind him with the sound of finality.

Kitty sighed and heaved the bag she was carrying on to the kitchen table. 'I've got everything in here except I'll need some boiling water. Then I'll be on me way.'

'Where will you go?' Betsy faltered.

'To Jack. Where else?'

Her mother's attention was caught as Kitty opened the bag and laid the boat-shaped feeding bottle on the table. 'What on earth's all this?' she began, and then, scandalized, she said, 'Do you mean you're not feeding him yourself?'

Kitty kept her eyes averted from her mother's questioning gaze. 'No, Mam, I – er – couldn't.' Holding the baby in her left arm, she continued to prepare his feed with her right hand. To her relief the baby's crying increased to such a level of noise that any further conversation was quite impossible.

When the baby was sucking contentedly on the teat, her mother stood over her, watching with disapproval in every line of her face. 'You should have tried harder, our Kitty, 'tain't natural, 'tain't good for the bairn. A mother's milk is the best.'

Now her father was no longer present, her mother was acting more like Kitty had imagined she would.

Kitty felt hysterical laughter welling up inside her, the picture of herself trying to breast-feed the child comical and yet hurtful at the same time. Her tone was sharper than she intended as she answered, 'Well, I couldn't do it, Mam, and that's all there is to it.' She bent her head and said, truthfully, 'No one was more disappointed than me that I couldn't.'

She felt her mother's hand rest lightly on her bowed head. 'Aw well, dun't fret, lass. He'll do nicely, I'm sure.' But her tone lacked conviction.

Kitty did not look up but silently breathed a sigh of thankfulness that her mother had let the matter drop.

After a few moments, while the only sound in the tiny kitchen was the sucking noise the baby made and the gentle hissing of the kettle on the hob, Kitty asked quietly, 'Mam, do you know where Jack Thorndyke is?'

When her mother did not answer at once, Kitty looked up.

'At the Manor, lass,' Betsy Clegg said slowly. 'You've been away a long time, Kitty.' She paused, believing that she now knew the real reason for her daughter's prolonged absence. 'Harvest's over, but he's there to do a bit of threshing and waiting while Ben does his thatching work.'

Kitty stared at her mother, thankful that the other woman could not read her thoughts. For at that moment her mind was not on Jack, or his son, or even on her own uncertain future.

It had been last year's harvest when all this had begun, when Miriam, playing the part of his Harvest Queen, had first met Jack.

How would Miriam feel, Kitty was wondering, if she looked out of the windows of the Manor House now and saw the handsome Jack Thorndyke in the stackyard beyond the wall?

Twenty-Seven

Mrs Grundy wept with disappointment.

'After everything I've telled you, girl. You should've known better. And him! Jack Thorndyke. Didn't I tell you? Didn't I warn you time and again, but oh no, you knew it all didn't you? And now ya've brought shame on ya mam and dad and to this house too. I thought it funny when the mistress and Miss Miriam returned without you. Bin hiding yasen away 'til it was over, 'ave ya? I 'spect you never even went abroad with Miss Miriam, did ya?'

Kitty shook her head. At least she didn't need to lie about that now.

'Huh. I thought as much. Well, that's put paid to ya grand ideas of bein' a lady's maid good an' proper, ain't it? And after all I've done for you, this is how you repay me.' The woman lifted the corner of her apron and dabbed at her eyes though whether her tears were for Kitty or for her own disappointment, the girl could not be sure.

'Oh please, Mrs G.,' Kitty moved towards her and made to put her arm about her shoulders, but the woman shrugged her off.

'Don't you touch me, miss. And don't you go seeking out Master Edward, neither. He's too young to know about you and your bad ways. Too young to be tainted with the likes of you.'

'Tainted!' Kitty was stung to retort. 'Is that how you

213

think of me now, Mrs Grundy? That I'll defile those I touch?'

The cook did not answer at once but delved deep in the pocket of her apron, drew out her handkerchief and blew her nose loudly into it. She moved towards the range and dropped heavily into the wooden chair set to one side. 'I'm disappointed in you, Kitty Clegg. I looked upon you like me own daughter and now look what you've done?'

Kitty came and squatted down in front of her, feeling the heat from the fire in the range on the side of her face. 'But if you'd had a daughter, you'd have stuck by her, wouldn't you? You'd have been shocked and angry, yes, I can see that, but you wouldn't have turned her off, would you?'

Mrs Grundy sniffed noisily. 'Well, mebbe not. But I'll have to get used to it. Have to come to terms with it.' Her eyes, still full of bitterness, bored into Kitty's. 'What's ya mam and dad to say, then?'

Kitty sighed and stood up. 'I think me mam would have stood by me but – but me dad's turned me out. And – and she's going along with it.'

'Aye well, I can't say I can blame 'im. He's been through it afore and through no fault of his own. It must bring it all back to him. You might have thought of ya poor dad, Kitty, and what he's had to bear.'

Kitty put her head on one side. 'What are you talking about, Mrs G.? Brought what back?'

Mrs Grundy flapped her hand. 'Oh never you mind. I've said too much already. I'm lettin' me mouth run away with itself and saying things I shouldn't, 'cos I'm that upset. Forget I ever said owt.'

Kitty said no more, but she would not forget. And in that moment she realized something else too. Through the long years that stretched ahead, never for one second must she let her 'mouth run away with itself'.

'Well then,' she said, picking up the plaited rush cradle her mother had found for her, 'I'd best go and introduce Jack Thorndyke to his son.'

Leaving the kitchen, she went out into the back yard, up the steps and walked the full length of the path through the garden. Near the door in the wall at the end she paused and looked back at the house. In the first-floor window of Master Edward's room, she saw the shadow of a person standing, not close to the glass, but a little way back, as if not wanting to be seen and yet unable to stop himself watching. She was tempted to wave, yet did not. Mrs Grundy had left her in no doubt that her friendship with Master Edward must now be at an end, disgraced as she was. Kitty sighed heavily. The thought that she would never be allowed to sit and talk to the lonely young boy actually hurt her. She really liked Master Edward – Teddy. As she remembered the nickname he had insisted she call him when they were alone together, a wistful smile played on her mouth and tears prickled her eyelids.

Then, resolutely, she turned her back on the house and opened the garden door leading into the stackyard beyond.

'And what have we got here then?' Jack bent over the tiny bundle wrapped in a shawl against the autumn wind and touched the baby's cheek with his rough fingertip. 'Yours, is it, Kitty Clegg?'

Neatly avoiding answering his question directly, she said softly, 'He's your son, Jack Thorndyke.'

Jack straightened up and looked down into her face. 'Oh aye?' he said guardedly. There was a pause before he added harshly, 'Think I ain't had that one thrown at me afore now, young Kitty?'

The girl gasped and her eyes widened. 'But he is, Jack. He is your son. Why, he even looks like you. See . . .' She pulled open the shawl and the baby screwed up his tiny features, opened his mouth and bawled, resentful at his cosy nest in the cradle being disturbed. 'See his black hair and his nose. He's got your nose, Jack. You can't deny that. You've got to believe me. He is yours.'

The huge shoulders lifted in a shrug. 'I aren't saying he isn't. But if you think you're going to tether me to you 'cos of a bairn, you've got another think coming.'

'But we could be a family, Jack. I'd look after you. You and the baby. I'll do anything you want, if you'll only—'

'I aren't the marrying kind, Kitty. I've told you that afore.'

'But don't you want to give your son a name? Surely you don't want him to grow up a – a . . .' She hesitated and Jack threw back his head in a loud guffaw as she shrank from saying the word.

' . . . a bastard. Can't bring yourself to say it, eh Kitty?' He bent his dark head towards her, thrusting his face close to hers. 'Well, you ain't catching me with that one 'cos you're not the first to try it and,' he added cruelly, 'you probably won't be the last.'

'Jack . . .' Kitty almost sobbed in her frustration and was on the point of dropping to her knees, of begging him, but some spark of pride deep within her flared and shone brightly. Instead she raised her chin and straightened her shoulders.

'Very well, Jack Thorndyke, if that's all you have to say, I'll be on me way. We'll manage on our own. Me and *your son*. Though where we're to sleep tonight, I don't know, 'cos me own dad's turned me out.'

'Now, now, young Kitty, hang on a minute. Don't go getting all uppity on me. I haven't said I won't stand by you, only that I won't *marry* you. I won't marry anyone, Kitty. I've always told you that. You can't deny it.'

Kitty's lower lip threatened to tremble. No, she couldn't deny it. That was exactly what he had always said. But carried away by her own overwhelming passion for him, she had not believed him. Like countless young girls blinded by love, she had thought she could change him.

In that moment, as she stared into Jack's undeniably handsome face, Kitty Clegg grew up. He would not change – not for her, not for anyone. She could either take what he offered – whatever that was – or turn her back on him, walk away and make her life without him.

'Jack . . .' she tried, just once more. She stepped forward and held out the child towards him. 'Would you like to hold your son – just for a moment?'

He took the little bundle into his great arms and bent his head, looking down into the tiny features nestling in the shawl. The baby screwed up his face, wriggling and stretching.

'Strong, ain't he, for such a little chap?'

'Yes, yes, he is,' Kitty said eagerly, desperate to hear a change of heart, a slight weakness in his resolve. 'He's a fine, healthy boy. A son to be proud of, Jack.'

With a sudden movement he thrust the bundle back into her arms and stepped away. 'Now then, none of your woman's wheedling, Kitty Clegg. I've work to do.' He turned and strode away from her.

Though she called again, 'Jack. Jack . . .' he did not look back.

Twenty-Eight

'I've got to see the mistress.'

Mrs Grundy straightened up from where she had been bending over the range and turned to face Kitty, standing once more in the kitchen of the Manor House. Setting the cradle on the table, Kitty moved towards the door leading to the upper part of the house.

'By heck, girl, you've got a cheek and no mistake.' The cook's face was bright red, though whether from bending over the heat, or from anger and embarrassment caused by her former kitchen maid, even she could not have said. 'And why do you think the mistress will want to concern herself with the likes of you?' She paused and added, pointedly, 'Now?'

Kitty thrust her chin out determinedly. 'She will. That's all.'

'Well, she ain't here. She's gone to visit Sir Ralph.' Mrs Grundy nodded her head knowingly and the smirk on her mouth held a look of triumph. 'There'll be a wedding afore long, if I'm not much mistaken. At least Miss Miriam does things properly. But then, she's a lady.'

Kitty stared at the cook and realized in that moment the enormity of her rash decision to take Miriam's child as her own. She, Kitty Clegg, was now the outcast, while Miriam sailed on blithely deceiving everyone.

Through clenched teeth, Kitty said, 'Then I'll see Miss Miriam.'

'Oh no, you won't . . .' Mrs Grundy began, but before the stout cook could make a move towards her, Kitty had whirled about and was through the door and down the three steps into the hall. There she hesitated, poised on her toes, listening. She had no wish to run into the master, and yet at this moment she would face even him. This family had a duty to help her, she told herself.

Then she was running up the twisting stairs towards Miss Miriam's bedroom. She rapped on the door and, without waiting for a reply, flung it open and marched into the room.

Miriam was sitting at the dressing table, brushing her hair and still in her nightgown although the morning was half over.

'What on earth . . .?' she began, obviously startled by Kitty's sudden appearance. But her surprise was soon replaced by anger. 'What are you doing here? How dare you burst into my room like this?' The girl turned from the mirror and stood up. 'You have no right even to be in this house. Get out.'

Kitty stood her ground. 'I wanted to see your mother, but she's not here.'

'No,' the girl smiled and smoothed her long hair. 'No. She's gone to see my future father-in-law to discuss the terms of the marriage settlement.' The smile became smug. 'After Christmas, we shall go to London. I'm to have a Season next year, be presented at court and then my engagement to Guy Harding will be announced.' Miriam tilted her head to one side and her eyes glittered with malice as she said, 'You could have been a part of all that, Kitty, as my personal maid. You could have come to London with me. Oh I'm going to have such a wonderful time and you could have been there too, if . . .' she paused with deliberate intention, 'if you hadn't been so foolish as to get yourself pregnant by Jack Thorndyke.'

Kitty gasped and knew she turned pale. She felt suddenly dizzy and swayed slightly. So that was it. Miriam intended to play the part to the hilt, even pretending that Kitty had really given birth to Jack Thorndyke's son. She was going to deny her own involvement completely.

'But I need your help.'

'Help? From me? Why should I help a maid who has brought shame on herself and all of us?'

Kitty, recovering swiftly from the shock, said, 'Your mother would help me, if she were here. She promised.'

Miriam moved closer, thrusting her face close to Kitty's. 'And you made certain promises too. Promises you're breaking already. You shouldn't even be here.'

'Jack won't marry me,' Kitty blurted out.

Miriam's smirk broadened. 'I never thought for one moment that he would,' she drawled. 'You're a fool, Kitty Clegg, if you harboured such hopes.' She turned away and sat at the dressing table once more, picked up the hairbrush and began to brush her hair with long, languid strokes.

'Of course,' she drawled, her glance catching and holding Kitty's gaze in the mirror, 'I don't know the man concerned, but I can imagine that his sort cannot be relied upon.'

Kitty could not believe what she was hearing. Miriam was playing her part so well that it seemed she believed she had never lain with Jack Thorndyke, had not borne his child. Now, she was denying even knowing him.

Kitty's mouth tightened. 'So, that's how it's going to be, is it?' She added grimly, 'Well, so be it then. I'll not look to you or your family for any help. I'll grant you one thing though, Miss Miriam. You're a good actress. You should go on the stage.'

Kitty spun around and pulled open the door.

'Oh Kitty,' Miriam said and the girl paused momentarily in the doorway, glancing back over her shoulder.

'What?' she said curtly, without any of the deference she had once shown her young mistress.

'If you've nowhere to go,' Miriam drawled, 'I believe there's a place called the workhouse that takes in the homeless of the parish, including fallen women.'

Kitty stared at the beautiful face in the mirror and wondered how such loveliness could be so spiteful, almost to the point of wickedness.

'I wish you joy, Miss Miriam. I just hope Mr Guy knows what he's taking on.'

As she began to turn away, she saw Miriam swivel on the stool, saw her raise her arm and heard her screech of rage. Before she could duck, the hairbrush came flying through the air to hit Kitty smartly on the forehead. The pain jolted her and she reached up to touch her head, expecting to feel the stickiness of blood, but instead she found the tenderness of a bruise that would swell very quickly. Slowly she reached down and picked up the brush and then, taking deliberate aim, she flung it towards the startled Miriam. Her aim was poor and the brush flew past Miriam's head and hit the mirror behind it, shattering the glass into a thousand pieces and making such a noise that surely the whole household must hear.

'Temper, temper, Kitty,' Miriam mocked. 'Now you've brought seven years' bad luck on yourself.'

'My bad luck started the day I got mesen tangled up with you, miss.'

Miriam shook her head. 'Oh no, Kitty Clegg, your bad luck began when you got tangled up with Jack Thorndyke. He's *your* bad luck.' Her emphasis on the word 'your' did not go unnoticed by Kitty. Miriam was cleverly passing the whole burden of guilt – her own guilt – on to Kitty, and she, foolish girl that she was and rendered helpless by her love for Jack and now the baby too, was taking it on to her own shoulders.

There was nothing left to say between them, nothing that could be said, so Kitty turned away, sick at heart. Quietly, in the silence that followed the tumult, she closed the door with the feeling of finality lying heavy in her breast.

She was moving away towards the stairs, when she heard her name called softly. She half-turned to see Master Edward's face peering round his bedroom door. He beckoned her and when she hesitated, he hissed, 'Kitty, come here. Just a moment.'

Glancing back towards Miriam's door, Kitty bit her lip but then, thinking that she had little else to lose now, moved towards him and slipped into the room. Softly Edward closed the door and they stood staring at each other.

Despite her own problems, Kitty smiled at him. 'Why, Master Edward, I do believe you've grown. You're taller than me now.' And, as she took in the fact that he was fully dressed, added, 'And you're up and about. I do hope that means you're better.'

The boy – a young man now for in three months' time, in January, he would reach his sixteenth birthday – smiled at her. She noticed that he had put on a little weight, that his fair hair shone with health and his eyes sparkled with vitality. Gone, too, was the pallid complexion of an invalid. 'I'm much better than I used to be, Kitty,' he was saying. 'I still get asthma attacks, but they're not so severe. I'm even going away to boarding school now. I started at the beginning of September and I'm going back tomorrow. I've just been home for the weekend.'

'Really? And do you like it?'

'It's great. Forget all those horror stories you hear about boarding school. I've made friends with several other chaps, two especially . . .' He stopped suddenly as his gaze roamed over her face and he registered the bruise now swelling on her forehead.

'Oh Kitty, did my sister do that? I heard the commotion.'

Kitty put her fingers up to touch the lump and winced. 'Yes, I didn't duck quick enough.'

'Come, let me bathe it for you.' He touched her arm and, although she protested, Edward drew her across the room towards the washstand and made her stand meekly while he wetted the corner of a towel with cold water and held it on the bruise.

With his face solemn now and so close to hers, he said, 'I'm sorry to hear about your trouble, Kitty. If there's anything I can do . . .'

Anger welled within her and Kitty felt a sharp retort spring to her lips. She was about to say, Oh yes, Master Edward, your family are great at making offers of help and fine promises, but when it comes to carrying them out then it's quite another story, but she held her tongue. This boy, probably more than any other member of the Franklin family, even Mrs Franklin, would, she knew, always keep his word. So close to him, she looked into his eyes and read there his concern for her and his sadness. And there was something else too. Was it disappointment? Disappointment that she had so disgraced herself by bearing an illegitimate child.

With a shock, Kitty realized that Edward Franklin's disappointment in her hurt more deeply than either Mrs Grundy's or even her own family's rejection.

She let her glance fall away from his steady gaze and

stammered. 'I-it's very kind of you, Master Edward, but I'll manage. I'll be all right.'

'It's Teddy when we're alone, Kitty Clegg,' he reminded her gently. 'Have you forgotten?'

He paused until she whispered, 'No, no, I hadn't forgotten. But – but things are very different now.'

Of all the people in the world, she wanted to confide in him, wanted him to know the truth. But she could not break her solemn promise. She would never break the promises she had made, no matter what others did.

Softly, he was asking, 'Won't the – the father – marry you?'

She shook her head, not trusting herself to speak.

'It's him, isn't it?' Edward's voice was low and shaking with anger. 'Threshing Jack?'

Miserably, Kitty nodded. If only, she thought, I could tell him the truth. But how could she? Not only had she made a faithful promise, but she would be shattering the boy's illusions about his own sister, whom she knew he loved dearly and admired for her strength. How could she hurt and disillusion Edward in such a way? So Kitty held her tongue, but it was with a heavy heart that she left his room and went back downstairs to the kitchen.

Only when she picked up the cradle and gently opened the shawl to look upon the face of the sleeping child, did determination flood through her again. When she held the baby in her arms, all her doubts and fears vanished. Whatever the future held for them both, she had not one moment's regret when she held the child close and nuzzled her cheek against his dark, downy head.

'But you'll not get away so easily, Jack Thorndyke,' she vowed. 'Not from me and your son, you won't.'

Twenty-Nine

'You can feed him, Kitty, I'll not be that cruel to the little chap, but then you must be on your way.'

Mrs Grundy watched as Kitty went through the performance of bottle, teats and warmed milk again.

'Can't you feed him yarsen, lass? It'd have been a lot less bother, wouldn't it?'

'No, I couldn't.' Desperately, Kitty searched her mind for a reasonable excuse. 'I hadn't enough milk.' She hid a wry smile thinking how very true that was and remembering also how appalled she had been to see Miriam's ripe and overflowing breasts and yet the girl had still refused to suckle her child.

She heard Mrs Grundy's sniff of disapproval. ''Spect you didn't try hard enough. It teks time and patience and you never did have much of that.'

Kitty was tempted to retort, 'How would you know?' but she held her tongue. Further argument might lead her into saying far too much.

It was as she was finishing feeding the baby that they heard the sound of the front door being opened and voices in the hall.

'That's the mistress back and it sounds like the master's with her. You'd best be on your way, Kitty. Go out the back way, will ya?'

Kitty laid the baby in the cradle and packed the feeding

equipment into her bag. Then she faced Mrs Grundy again. 'I'll see the mistress, now she's back.'

'Oh no, you won't, Kitty Clegg. You've caused enough trouble here this morning. I 'eard all that ruckus upstairs.'

But once more, Kitty was through the door into the hall and up the stairs towards Mrs Franklin's sitting room. When she knocked on the door, the bark that bade her enter was unmistakably the voice of Mr Franklin. Kitty took a deep breath, pushed open the door and stepped into the room.

Standing with his back to the fire, the master glared at her. 'What the devil do you want? I thought you'd been dismissed. Come to beg for reinstatement, eh? Well, my wife must have had a good reason to dispense with your services, so you'd best be on your way.' He paused and then shook his head. 'I'm disappointed in you. Very disappointed. I'd have thought better of you, of all people. Got yourself into trouble, I'll be bound. But if that is the case, I'll not have you in this house, not anywhere near *my* daughter.'

Kitty was sorely tempted to blurt out the truth. Instead she said calmly, 'I need to see the mistress, sir. She's been very kind to me. She understands.'

He gave a grunt of annoyance. 'Huh, a soft touch is my dear wife. A pushover for all the waifs and strays and fallen women of the town. But I won't have it.' He took a step towards her and raised his arm, pointing at the door. 'Get out, girl. Go.'

It was like a scene out of a play she had once seen at the theatre. She almost expected him to add the words, 'And never darken my doorstep again.'

Kitty held her ground and stared back at him, standing very quiet and still. He let his arm fall to his side and he shook his head. 'You've got courage, girl. I'll give you that.

But then . . .' He was turning away from her now and moving back to take up his former stance in front of the blazing fire. 'I suppose,' he turned to look at her again, 'you're like your mother. She had courage . . .' His voice dropped. 'A splendid courage, far more than I ever possessed.' The words were spoken so softly now, more to himself than to her. Kitty said, 'I beg your pardon, sir. You know my mother?'

'Eh? What? Oh – er, well yes, a long time ago. She worked in this house, you know. Of course I knew her.' This much Kitty knew, but surely the son of the house would not have known a maid *that* well. There was a defensive note in Mr Franklin's voice as he recovered his composure. 'Is that what this is all about? A little bit of blackmail, eh? Even after all this time.'

Kitty shook her head. 'I really don't understand what you mean, sir.' She opened her mouth to say more, to ask questions, but at that moment the communicating door, which led directly into Mrs Franklin's bedroom from her sitting room, opened and she came into the room.

Kitty saw at once that the woman was startled to see her there. Mrs Franklin's anxious glance went immediately to her husband and then back to Kitty.

Before she could speak, Mr Franklin's voice boomed again. 'The girl's come to try a little bit of blackmail. Be damned if I'll give her a penny piece and I'll be obliged if you'd take the same attitude, Amelia.'

Mrs Franklin's eyes widened and her hand fluttered to her mouth. 'Oh Kitty, no, you haven't—'

Before Mrs Franklin could say anything further, could say something that would let out the secret, Kitty put out her hand towards her and said urgently, 'No, madam, I haven't. The master's misunderstood me. He thinks it's because me mam used to work here.'

She noticed the glance that passed at once between husband and wife and the sudden tightening of Mrs Franklin's lips, and yet at the same time there was relief in her eyes. She seemed to understand at once, yet Kitty herself was still mystified.

'I only wanted to see you, madam,' Kitty said in a small voice. 'That's all. I'm not trying to cause trouble,' and she added pointedly, knowing that her mistress would understand, 'not for *anyone*.'

'No, no.' Mrs Franklin moved to her side, patted her arm and said in a low tone, 'I know you wouldn't do that.' And in a whisper added, 'I trust you, Kitty. I know I – we – can rely on you.'

'Eh? What's that? What are you whispering about? Send the girl packing, Amelia. I won't have her dredging up the past and . . .'

Mrs Franklin turned and moved across the room to sit on her sofa. 'She's doing nothing of the sort, Henry. She knows nothing about any of that. She has enough problems of her own and that is what this is about.'

'Eh? What?' His startled glance went from one to the other. 'Oh, have I got it wrong?'

'More than likely,' Mrs Franklin said drily. 'So, if you'd be kind enough to leave me with the girl, I will sort it out.'

His manner seemed to change suddenly, to soften almost, Kitty thought. His eyes went from her to his wife and back again. 'What problems? Your family? Something wrong in your family. Your mother . . .?'

'Henry . . .' Now there was a warning note in his wife's voice and her clear eyes caught and held his gaze. 'I will talk to you later.'

To Kitty's surprise, Mr Franklin's glance fell away and he muttered, 'Oh very well then.' He marched past Kitty and out of the room, slamming the door behind him so violently that the delicate china in Mrs Franklin's glass cabinet gave a shiver of fear.

'Come and sit down, my dear.' When Kitty did so, Mrs Franklin continued. 'Now, I don't mean to be harsh and I'll do what I can to help you this time, but it really would be better if you did not come here again. As you can see, your presence can soon make things very – well – awkward. Questions start to be asked and so on.'

'What did he mean about me trying to blackmail you?'

Mrs Franklin dismissed her question with a wave of her hand. 'Oh never mind all that. It has nothing to do with you or with our present problems.' She lowered her voice. 'Kitty, I have some money here for you. Five pounds, but that is all I can do for you, I'm afraid. I – I dare not do more.'

'That's very generous, madam. I didn't expect that.'

'I know you didn't.' There was a pause before she added, a little uncertainty creeping into her tone, 'Is everything all right? You haven't any regrets about taking . . .' Her voice faltered and died away.

'No, madam.' Kitty's face shone as she spoke of the baby boy. 'I love him dearly, every bit as much as if – well, you know.'

'Yes,' Mrs Franklin's voice was a whisper. 'I do know.' She paused then asked, 'And – and the child's father. Will he marry you?'

Kitty's eyes flashed. 'He ses not, but I aren't finished with him yet.'

A small smile played at the corner of Mrs Franklin's mouth, but the sadness did not leave her eyes. 'But your family will stand by you, won't they?'

Kitty's glance dropped and she plucked nervously at her skirt with fingers that trembled slightly. Their reaction, more than anything else, had been a shock to her. If she were honest, Jack's response had not been entirely unexpected, but her father's outrage had stunned her. She had fully expected their anger and disappointment, but the thought that her own father would cast her off had never once entered her head.

She shook her head. 'No, madam. I don't think they will. At least, me dad won't.'

'I'm sorry, Kitty, I don't know what else I can do.'

'I'll manage now, madam, with the money. It's very good of you.'

'I wish it could be more.'

At least, Kitty thought, Mrs Franklin is not forgetting her promise as quickly as her daughter has done.

Now there was a quaver in the woman's voice as she asked, 'And how – is my grandson?'

Dusk was closing in when Kitty stepped out of the back door of the Manor House and it was shut firmly behind her by Mrs Grundy. She sighed. She hated deceiving Mrs Grundy, yet she had made her promise and she must keep it. And besides, deep in her heart, she rather feared that even if Mrs Grundy did know the whole truth, the cook would still view what she had done as even more foolish than becoming pregnant by the man she loved.

Kitty hitched the baby up and planted a swift kiss on the tiny forehead. 'I don't care, my little man, as long as I have you.' She sighed. I really must decide on a name, she thought, but I did so want Jack to have a say in the naming of his son.

Jack. She lifted her head and listened, but the deepening dusk was silent. No sound was coming from the stackyard beyond the garden wall. And now, a light drizzle was beginning to fall.

Coming to a decision, Kitty walked purposefully down the garden path to the wall at the end and through the door into the stackyard. Maybe Jack was still there, cleaning and polishing his beloved *Sylvie*. But the yard was deserted of workmen, the huge engine silent and only the wind scurried along the ground blowing bits of straw in little flurries. Kitty sighed. She would wait a while to see if he came back. The baby, sleeping peacefully, was warmly wrapped and would take no harm even in the cold night air. She lifted him out of the cradle and nestled him inside her cloak, close to her breast so that the warmth of her body would keep him warm too. Then she burrowed a nest for them both in the side of a straw stack. The child stirred at the movement but as she settled herself, Kitty began to croon a lullaby to him and soon he was asleep again.

Kitty dozed fitfully, waking every few minutes to listen for any sound that meant Jack was returning to the yard, but only night sounds filled the air. The baby slept on and soon Kitty, too, fell into a deeper sleep.

She awoke with a start to feel the child stirring in her arms and whimpering. The night was pitch black now and the rain was falling heavily, soaking through the straw to reach them. Kitty was stiff with cold and at once concerned that the baby, too, must be chilled. He must be hungry too and not for the first time Kitty bemoaned the fact that she could not feed him from her own breast.

She could not stay here. She certainly dare not knock upon the back door of the Manor again. There was only one thing she could do; walk the mile through the darkness and the rain to her parents' house at the station. Surely even her father would not turn her out again into the night. Surely even he, in his anger, could not do that to a tiny baby.

'Oh I'm sorry, my little love. I should not have kept you

here in the dark and the cold waiting for him. Shush, shush,' she crooned. 'Someone will hear you.'

She was beginning to lever herself up out of the cocoon of straw when a sudden light shone in her face. Blinking, she gasped thankfully, 'Jack, oh Jack – thank goodness you've come.'

'It's not Thorndyke,' said a voice and there was no hiding the bitterness in its tone. 'It's me.'

'Oh – oh Master Edward . . .' Now she was standing and shaking the straw from her skirts and trying to move away. 'I'm sorry. I'm – we're just going.'

'And where on earth do you think you're going at this time of night, for heaven's sake?' His concern for her was making him speak sharply and, hearing it from the gentle young man, for a moment Kitty's usual determination deserted her and tears sprang to her eyes. 'We're g-going,' she stammered, 'to my p-parents.'

'Don't be ridiculous, Kitty. That's at least a mile away. You can't possibly walk all that way now – at this time of night. It's gone midnight. And carrying the child. Come back into the house.'

'Oh no, Master Edward. I couldn't. I daresunt. Really.'

'Nonsense, Kitty. Do as I say. Think of your child, if not of yourself.'

That, more than anything else could have done, swayed her. 'Well,' she said, though still reluctant, 'just into the kitchen for a moment or two. Maybe I could just feed him. I think he's hungry.'

'Whatever, but do come into the warm. Come along.' She felt his grasp on her elbow, surprisingly firm and determined and, despite the incongruity of her situation, in the darkness Kitty found herself smiling. How Master Edward was indeed growing up!

The kitchen was deserted. Settling her into the chair at

the side of the range, Edward bent and roused the fire, setting the kettle on the hob. 'A hot drink's what you need.' She felt him looking at her and she looked up to meet his gaze. 'Is there anything you need for the baby?'

As Kitty told him what was required to prepare a feed, Edward reached out and gently eased back the shawl around the child's face. The baby stared up at him with round, dark blue eyes.

'Isn't he tiny? I've never seen such a small baby before.' He continued to stare down at the child as if drinking in the sight of him. Watching Edward, Kitty saw a tender smile curve his mouth, then his gaze moved slowly to meet her own. They stared at each other for a long moment until a log shifted in the fire, sending sparks up the flue and breaking their reverie. Edward cleared his throat and turned away to sit down on the opposite side of the fire-place to watch Kitty feed her child.

At least, she thought wryly, as at last she held the teat to the tiny mouth, Master Edward isn't asking why I'm not feeding the baby myself like everyone else is doing.

'You can stay here the rest of the night, Kitty.'

She looked up, startled. 'Oh I couldn't, Master Edward. I'd be in awful trouble – and so would you.'

He grinned and it warmed Kitty's heart to see mischief in his eyes, a boyish mischief that she had never seen before when he was an invalid. But he was no invalid now and she was so thankful for it. Now Edward had the chance of living a proper life and with it, she could already see a strength and determination that before had been blotted out by his sickness and suffering.

'But I'm going back to school tomorrow,' he told her, arching his left eyebrow. 'And you can be gone in the morning. Who's to know? And even if they did, well . . .'

he spread his hands. 'We'll soon be away from any recriminations, won't we? Both of us.'

'Well,' she wavered, torn by the desire to keep the child warm and fed and the fear of causing more trouble for herself and for Edward. But the young man was insistent. 'You can sleep in my room and no one need know. You can leave before anyone gets up in the morning.'

'But what if the baby cries in the night? I can't be sure to keep him quiet, you know.'

Edward shrugged and grinned again. 'Well, we'll worry about that if it happens, shall we?'

But the little boy behaved perfectly, and, before it was light, Edward roused Kitty and together they crept down into the kitchen once more. When the baby had been fed, Edward opened the back door and Kitty stepped out in the pale mist of dawn. Turning, she whispered, 'I don't know how to thank you, Master Edward.'

'Teddy,' he reminded her. 'Remember your promise?'

Kitty smiled tremulously. So many promises, she thought briefly. But this one was easy to keep, for in her heart she always thought of him as 'Teddy'.

'Thank you, Teddy,' she said simply. 'For everything.' And her words encompassed not only his help of the previous night, but his lack of censure, of judgement. She was so grateful for his unquestioning concern for her welfare.

Briefly, he nodded but seemed unable to speak. Then he touched her arm and gave it a comforting squeeze before he turned away and closed the door between them.

Thirty

Kitty stood at the side of the stackyard watching the men work until one of them should notice her. Noise filled the air and it was impossible to shout above it and she knew better than to move in among the workers. They worked as a team and a sudden disruption was not only a nuisance, but it could be dangerous.

It was Jack himself who saw her as he stood on the footplate of the threshing engine. He waved and smiled, but gestured that he could not leave the machinery for a few moments. Kitty nodded and settled herself on a pile of straw to wait. The early mist was clearing now and it would be a bright morning, but the chill of winter was in the air and Kitty knew that while in the height of summer she and the child might have survived by sleeping in a barn, in this weather the tiny baby would not.

She sighed. She must not look to the Manor House and the Franklin family again, or to her own family. Jack Thorndyke was her only hope. Only he stood between her and the workhouse.

And then she remembered the money hidden in the deep pocket of her coat. The money Mrs Franklin had given her. It was a generous sum, but even that would not last for ever and then . . .

In the shelter of the wall and burrowed into the straw, she must have dozed, for suddenly she heard his voice and blinked herself fully awake to see him standing over her, wiping his oily fingers on a rag. 'Now then, young Kitty. What brings you here?'

'I should have thought,' she said tartly, levering herself up from the straw, 'that would be obvious, even for you, Jack Thorndyke.'

He raised his eyebrows and then threw back his head in a guffaw of laughter. 'You're getting a sharp tongue on you, Kitty Clegg. I hope becoming a mother hasn't turned you into a shrew of a woman.'

'If it has, then you're to blame.' She stopped, quelling her anger with him. This was not what she had intended and the meeting would turn into a quarrel if she was not careful. So instead she moved closer to him, put her hand on his arm and looked up into his eyes. 'Jack, I don't want us to fight. I came to ask you what you wanted your son to be named. I – I thought you've a right to be involved. I *want* you to be involved with him. Please, Jack?'

For a moment, the big man's eyes softened, but there was a wariness still in their depths, a wariness that told her he was still neatly avoiding any traps. 'Well, that's nice of you, Kitty. Had you any name in mind?'

She shook her head. 'Do you want me to call him Jack?'

He laughed. 'That's not my given name. The name on my birth certificate is John.'

'That's my father's name, too,' Kitty murmured.

'How about you name him John, then, but we call him Johnnie?'

Kitty smiled. Perhaps it would be a way of appeasing her father too. 'Yes, yes, that's fine. I like that.'

There was a slight pause as they stood looking at each other.

'So, where are you living?'

She shrugged. 'Nowhere. I've nowhere to go, Jack.'

He looked at her keenly. 'Where did you stay last night, then?'

Kitty swallowed, not wanting to give away the fact that she had stayed in Edward's bedroom. 'Here – at the Manor. I stayed here.' She held her breath but he pursued the matter no further. He seemed to be thinking.

'Well,' he said slowly, 'I've got a bit of news for you. Rather funny, really, considering.' He paused and then went on, 'Mr Franklin came into the yard this morning when I was oiling up and offered me a cottage on the edge of Sir Ralph's estate that's empty at the moment.' Jack put his head on one side. 'Said he'd heard as how you had a bairn now and that he understood it was mine. "I don't think her father will help her," he said.' Jack smiled oddly and there was sarcasm in his tone as he said, 'Now, I wonder why he would know that? And why should a man like him be concerning himself with a kitchen maid who's got 'ersen into trouble? Eh Kitty?'

Kitty shook her head, 'I don't know.' That was the truth, but somewhere in the recess of her memory she seemed to have heard similar words spoken before. At this moment, however, her thoughts were on something else. Quite unwittingly, Mr Franklin was providing a home for his own grandson.

'No,' Jack said slowly, watching her. 'I don't believe you do understand why he's doing it, do you?' He paused a moment and then went on, 'But we'll take up the master's most kind offer. At least, while I'm still working in this area. He's given me the key and I'll be going there tonight. Bring the boy and we'll talk things over, Kitty. But don't . . .' Gently he tapped her nose with his forefinger but he was smiling as he added, 'Don't go getting your hopes up that I'll be going down on one knee to make an honest woman of you.'

Kitty managed a tremulous smile, but inside her heart was thudding.

An honest woman? she thought wryly. Oh Jack Thorndyke, if only you knew!

She waited for over an hour outside the low, whitewashed cottage, the baby in one arm, his feeding equipment in a bag at her feet. Impatiently, she tapped her foot. Again she tried the cottage door, but it was locked. She went round to the back to see if there was any way into the cottage, even through a window. But everything was securely locked and bolted.

The child began to whimper and though she rocked him, trying to soothe him, the whimpers grew into wails as hunger gnawed at his tiny stomach. By the time Kitty heard Jack's jaunty whistling through the gathering dusk, the child's crying echoed through the shadows to greet his father.

'By heck,' came Jack's chuckle. 'He's a good pair of lungs on him, ain't he?'

'He's hungry and probably cold too. We've been waiting over an hour.'

Unlocking the door, Jack glanced at her in surprise. 'You could've fed him. There's no one around to see.'

'No, I couldn't,' she told him shortly. 'He needs a bottle.'

'What? Ya not feeding him yasen?'

'No,' Kitty said and volunteered no further information. 'Come on, let's get inside and get him fed, for heaven's sake.'

An hour later the child was satisfied and had fallen into an exhausted sleep. Kitty looked about her. The cottage was nice. Or rather it could be, given a woman's touch.

The range was grey with dirt instead of a shining black and the peg rug on the hearth needed a good beating in the fresh air. Every surface had a layer of dust and in the back scullery the sink was stained brown.

'So, what do you think, Kitty?'

'It could be a nice little place,' Kitty murmured and then looked straight at him. 'But it depends on you, Jack. What are you offering me?'

He put up his hands, palms outward, as if to fend her off. 'Now, now, I've told you . . .'

'I know, I know. You're not the marrying kind.' She smiled ruefully and sighed. 'Well, Jack, I accept that now.'

There was silence for a moment as they stared at each other and then he said, surprise in his tone, 'You mean, you'd come and live with me and not be married? What about your reputation?'

Kitty shrugged. 'Me reputation, as you call it, is in tatters now, isn't it?'

Jack gave a long, low whistle through his teeth. 'Well, I have to admit you've shocked even me, Kitty Clegg.' He tilted his head to one side and regarded her thoughtfully. 'I just hope you're not banking on being able to change me mind, though.' He shook his head slowly and said, almost with a note of sadness, 'Because I'm sorry, Kitty, for some things I am truly sorry, but I won't change me mind about marrying you.'

Kitty folded her arms across her bosom as she asked quietly, 'Just tell me one thing, Jack. Is it just me you don't want to marry – or anyone?'

'I won't marry at all,' he replied bluntly. 'But I have to say,' he added, seeming to mellow a little, 'of all the women I've known, I reckon I could live with you, Kitty.'

It was on the tip of her tongue to say, But you wouldn't be faithful, would you, Jack? You wouldn't know how to be faithful to one woman, married to her or not. You've already proved that. But the words lay unspoken for she knew that she was treading on dangerous ground if she made any reference, however vague, to Miriam Franklin.

All she did say was, 'But you don't love me, Jack, do you?'

He took a stride and reached for her, pulling her into his strong arms. Resting his cheek against her hair, he said, 'Oh Kitty, I love you for giving me a son. No one's ever given me a *son* before.'

She tilted her head back and looked up into his face. 'And yet, you still won't marry me?'

He looked down at her, an unusually tender look in his eyes. Slowly, he shook his head, then said, 'So? What is it to be? Bring the child up on your own or come and live with me?'

Kitty's mind was in a turmoil. She loved this man with all her being, loved him with a love that had driven her, who had been brought up to be good and honest, to take actions of which she would never have believed herself capable only a year or so ago. And yet she was not completely blinded by her love for him. She knew him for what he was and, she had to admit, he had his own brand of honesty. He was a rogue, at least where the ladies were concerned, yet he freely admitted it and he made no false promises either. She knew he would never marry her, yet he was offering her a life with him, but only on his terms. Knowing all this, she loved him still. Thoughts of him filled her every waking moment, and, away from him, she yearned to be near him.

And now there was another love in her life too; a tiny, helpless child whom she already loved devotedly. He was

Jack's flesh and blood and he deserved to be brought up by his father.

'I – will come and live with you, Jack.' Even as she said the words aloud, she felt as if she were stepping into a void, into the unknown and a sudden tremor of fear shook her. Resolutely, she lifted her head. This was as much for Johnnie as for herself. 'Your son,' she said softly, 'should have a father.'

Thirty-One

It was difficult now for Kitty to see her mother. Because their house was attached to the station, there was hardly ever a time when her father was unlikely to come through the door. But once a month, the stationmaster took the train to head office and was gone all day. Luckily for Kitty, the following day was one such occasion. So, when Jack disappeared off to work the following morning, she fed Johnnie, wrapped him warmly in a shawl and carried him to her old home.

As she walked, she thought again how surprised she had been when Jack had made no attempt to make love to her the previous night. She felt disappointed. During the months away from him, she had longed for him, for the feel of his arms about her, for his loving. And she had hoped he had missed her too. Now, she was hurt that, although he had got into the double bed beside her, he had merely kissed her cheek, turned on his side and fallen asleep immediately, while she had lain awake into the early hours, her young body burning for his touch.

As Kitty opened the door, her mother turned from the range, her tired eyes lighting up at the sight of her daughter. 'Kitty, I'm so glad you've come.' She bustled forward and drew Kitty and the child into the warmth, pushing her gently into a chair and taking the shawl-wrapped bundle into her arms. 'There, there now, me little bairn,' Betsy crooned.

'Me dad's not here, is he?' Kitty said.

'No, no, we're quite safe today,' her mother said with only half her attention for she was unwrapping the shawl and inspecting the sturdy limbs of the little boy she believed to be her first grandchild. Kitty felt a sudden stab of guilt at the thought but pushed it resolutely away.

'Mam, I'd better tell you straight away. I – I'm going to move in with Jack.'

Her mother raised her gaze and her eyes were deep pools of anxiety. 'Aw lass, aw me lass,' was all Betsy could say. 'Are ya sure? He's no good. Cut loose, girl, while there's still time. Mebbe I could talk ya dad around. Mebbe you could come back here.'

Kitty shook her head. 'No, Mam. You know me dad. I must say I never expected him to be quite so hard, but . . .' She shrugged and sighed. 'If that's how he feels, I know he'll never change his mind.'

Betsy shook her head. 'No, you're right. I know that if I'm honest.' She was silent a moment, seeming to struggle with herself, then the words burst from her, tumbling from her mouth as if she could not get them out quickly enough. 'It's not all your fault. It's the past. It's raked all that up again. It's my fault an' all.'

Kitty stared at her mother. 'Raked all what up, Mam? What are you talking about?'

Betsy bit her lip and sat down in the chair on the opposite side of the range. 'Mebbe it's time I told you about it, lass. Mebbe you've a right to know, and – and if nothing else, it'll help you to see why your dad is acting the way he is. Being so hard on you, like.'

Kitty was silent as Betsy Clegg's head came up very slowly until her eyes met her daughter's questioning gaze. Gently she rocked the child in her arms until the infant's eyes closed and he slept while Betsy stared straight ahead, seeming to see, not the cluttered kitchen of the house she had shared with her husband for over eighteen years, but images from the past. A past in which Kitty had no part.

'If I . . .' Betsy began slowly, 'if I tell you something, Kitty, do you promise me that you will never mention it to ya dad that I've told you, nor tell any of your brothers and sisters about it?'

Kitty stared at her mother. Not more secrets and more promises, she thought, but aloud she said quietly, 'Yes, I promise.'

Again there was a long silence as if Betsy were struggling to say out loud things that had lain hidden and unspoken of for years.

'I worked at the Manor once. Years ago . . .'

'I know that. Mrs Grundy told me.'

'Oh aye, and what else did Mrs Grundy have to tell you?' There was a trace of resentment in her tone, but gradually she relaxed again when Kitty wrinkled her brow, trying to remember.

'Nothing really,' Kitty said, 'though there were times when she would say summat I couldn't quite understand. But whenever I asked her what she meant, she'd just clam up.'

'Aye well, she were a good friend to me all them years ago and I ain't ever had cause to think her otherwise.'

Kitty waited and her mother paused again.

'It's all so long ago now. Not that you ever forget, you know, but – well – you sort of bury it. When I worked at The Manor, I was only your age and Henry Franklin – the man you call "the master" now – he was about twenty-two. A right young rogue, he was . . .' Yet the term was used fondly and, even as Kitty watched, her mother's face seemed to soften and her eyes glazed over at the memory.

'He was a fine figure of a man, tall and with such a

beautiful head of chestnut hair I always thought it was wasted on a man. Mind you, you couldn't have called him handsome.' She giggled, almost girlishly. 'His nose was too big. But he had this kind of – of air about him. Dashing that's it. He was dashing.' Betsy Clegg was savouring her memories. 'He was what they call "an eligible young bachelor" and though his family weren't aristocracy, his father had a good job as Sir Ralph Harding's farm bailiff and they were much respected and comfortably off. Mind you, his mother came from a bit better class than the Franklins and always tried to make out her family were out the same drawer as the Hardings at the Hall, but they weren't. They still aren't, even though they farm in their own right now.'

Patiently, Kitty waited, knowing that eventually her mother would come to the point.

'He had an eye for a pretty girl and – well – I suppose I was young and giddy and took his flirting and his flattery far too serious.'

Again she stopped and glanced down at the sleeping child in her arms. Then she raised her gaze again, looking straight at her daughter. 'I – I fell for him, Kitty, just like I 'spect you've fallen for Jack Thorndyke. That's why I can't blame you and, though I'm disappointed and worried what will come of it all, I do understand what it – it's like to love a man that much that you'd do anything for him.' Her voice fell to a whisper. 'Anything he asked of you.'

'Oh Mam,' Kitty breathed. 'What happened?'

Flatly, Betsy said, 'I got pregnant. That's what happened.'

Kitty gasped, staring at her mother in horrified disbelief. Then as her jumbled thoughts began to make more sense, she said hesitantly, 'Oh Mam, you don't mean that I'm – that he's my . . .'

Swiftly, even before Kitty had finished voicing the

question, her mother reached out and patted her daughter's hand. 'No, no, lass, you're your dad's child. I mean, John Clegg's your real dad.'

'So . . .?' Kitty had to know, but now she hesitated, her mind reeling with all the possibilities. Had her mother, all those years ago, given birth to a child and given it up to someone else just as Miriam Franklin had done? Had Kitty a half-brother or half-sister somewhere? The questions whirled around her mind, but her mother was speaking again and even now, after all the intervening years, there was still sadness in her voice. 'Of course, his family were horrified. His mother sent me packing. In her eyes it was all my fault and I'd caused trouble, you see, by naming him as the father.'

'Oh Mam,' Kitty breathed, knowing what her mother must have suffered.

'But I was lucky, Kitty, more lucky than I deserved to be. My parents stood by me and would have let me keep the baby and helped me bring it up, but – but the baby – a little boy—' again she glanced down at the baby boy in her arms and there were tears in her voice as she whispered, 'was stillborn.'

Kitty reached across and clasped her mother's hands tightly in her own, but could think of no words to say.

There was a long silence in the room before Kitty asked hesitantly. 'And me dad?'

'He was a groom at the Franklins' and of course he knew all about it. But about a year after – after it had all happened, he started coming to see me and – and said he'd marry me.'

'Did he love you? Did you love *him*?'

'In a way, I've come to love him. I'm grateful to him and he's been a good husband to me and a good father, but . . .' She stopped and her silence said more than her words.

'But you have never forgotten Henry Franklin, have you, Mam?'

There were tears in her mother's eyes as she pressed her lips together and shook her head, not trusting herself to speak now.

'And me dad, did he love you?' Kitty urged.

Betsy lifted her shoulders in a slight shrug. 'I really don't know, Kitty. I – I always had the feeling that he made the offer thinking that in some way Mr Henry would be grateful to him, would see him all right. But after we was wed, well, it sort of backfired on him and he was sacked over something quite trivial. I even forget exactly what it was about now.'

'Was that how he came to get a job on the railway then?'

Betsy nodded. 'He started as a porter and he hated it. He's hated it all these years, even when he got to be stationmaster, a position with some status to it. All he ever wanted, he said, was to work with horses. That's why he's so bitter at the bottom of him.'

'And deep down he blames you and now I have, as you say, raked it all up again.'

Her mother nodded but Kitty was thinking now that this was what the hints and half-remarks up at the Manor had been about. And why Mr Franklin thought she had been trying to drag up the past again. That's what he had meant about 'a little blackmail'. It had nothing to do with the secrets of the present, but with the scandal from the past.

'So after you left, Mam, Mr Franklin married his wife, did he?'

'Oh aye,' Betsy said bitterly. 'His mother couldn't get him safely married off quick enough. Almost the first suitable girl that came along was snapped up and he was married to her.' Betsy sighed. 'I feel sorry for her, really. I always have done, she's a lovely lady and she hasn't had a happy marriage, or much happiness with her children to my way of thinking. Miss Miriam's a spoilt little madam and her boy, well, if he makes old bones, it'll be a miracle.'

Kitty said nothing about Miriam Franklin, knowing, more than anyone else, just what trouble her wilfulness had led her into and the heartbreak she had indeed caused her gentle mother. But of Edward she said, 'He's much better now, Mam. He's going to boarding school and he's grown and filled out. Why, he's taller than me now.'

'Really? Well, I am pleased to hear that. Really I am. But Kitty, promise me you'll keep this to yourself. It's not that your dad doesn't know all there is to know, but I don't want him reminded any more. And please, please don't tell young Milly, or the others.'

'Of course not, Mam. I promise.' She gave her promise gladly, but in that moment Kitty was sorely tempted to spill out the details of the other secret, but her promise was sacrosanct and must, in Kitty Clegg's mind, be kept.

Thirty-Two

'I just hope you know what you're doing, Kitty, that's all.'
Betsy's eyes were worried as she helped her daughter pack
her few belongings to move to the cottage with Jack. 'He'll
never marry you, you know, not even to give his son a
name.'

'I know, Mam, I know,' Kitty said quietly.

Betsy sighed and then, more brightly, said, 'I've found
you some baby things I had packed away upstairs. Tek
'em, lass, because I don't reckon I'll be having any more
bairns mesen.' She smiled down at the baby. 'I'll just have
to enjoy me grand-bairns now, at least when I can get the
chance.' For a moment, mischief sparkled in Betsy Clegg's
eyes and despite the sadness and hardship life had brought
her, Kitty knew that it was from her mother that she had
inherited her strength of character.

Again she felt a pang of conscience that the child Betsy
believed to be her flesh and blood had no connection to
her. And yet, Kitty thought now, there was a connection,
one she had not known about, could not have known
about until today. The child might not be Betsy's own
grandchild, but he was certainly the grandson of the man
she had loved all those years ago, and, if Kitty was right,
had continued to love down the years.

'Oh Mam.' She moved across the space between them
and put her arms about Betsy's thickening waist, feeling

tears spring to her eyes. 'I'll bring him to see you whenever I can. When me dad's away. It'll be our little secret.'

'Yes, yes, love,' her mother said patting her back. 'And don't tell our Milly. Though I ses it as shouldn't about me own, that girl's got a spiteful streak in her.'

Kitty leaned back and looked into her mother's face. 'I haven't seen her since I came home. Is she still at the Manor?'

'Oh yes. Ses she's going to take over as cook when Mrs Grundy finally retires. Though when that'll be, your guess is as good as mine.'

'She's ambitious, then, I'll say that for her. I would never have thought it of Milly.'

'She's changed a lot while you've been away. Put on a bit of weight and it suits her. Her skin's a better colour. She's not bad looking now, but she'll still have to make her own way in the world.' Betsy sighed. 'Same as you, Kitty love, though I can't say I'm happy about the way you've chosen. Not happy at all.'

Kitty forced a bright smile on to her mouth and hugged her mother once again. 'I'll be fine, Mam. As long as I've got little Johnnie. And no one – *no one*,' she repeated as if saying it aloud would make it so, 'can ever take him away from me.'

While Jack worked, Kitty moved her belongings and the clothes her mother had given her for the baby into the cottage. Between caring for little Johnnie's needs, Kitty scrubbed and cleaned the little home and prepared a tempting meal in readiness for Jack's return that evening. As he stepped through the door, ducking his head beneath the low doorframe, Jack sniffed the air appreciatively. 'By, that's a fine greeting for a chap after a hard day.' He chuckled and smacked Kitty's backside playfully. 'But you should be careful not to tire yourself. It's not that many weeks since ya birthing, is it?'

Kitty felt a tremor of fear pass through her. In her anxiety to please Jack, she had not stopped to think that she must play the part of a woman who had recently given birth. Hiding her face, she bent over the pan of soup bubbling on the range, stirring the liquid and trying to regain her composure, while attempting to visualize how a young mother would be feeling.

She had stayed with Miriam just over six weeks. And besides, Miriam Franklin had seemed to make a remarkably quick recovery, no doubt because she had not had the drain on her energy of caring for the child. Desperately, Kitty searched in her mind for the memory of how her mother had been when she had given birth to her youngest child. Kitty had been a young girl and had helped her mother, not only at the birth itself, but during the weeks following her confinement. But how long had it been, Kitty asked herself, how long before Betsy had been up and about and doing her own housework?

She straightened up, pressing the palm of her hand into the small of her back as if weary. 'Oh we're tough, us country girls,' she laughed and, composing her features, turned to face him. 'No lying abed for our sort, ya know.'

Thankfully, Jack seemed to lose interest in the topic as he attacked the mound of steaming beef and potato pie she placed before him. Silently, Kitty sighed with relief.

In the lumpy feather bed Kitty snuggled close to Jack, laying her head against his chest and listening to the deep thud of his heart. His hand touched her shoulder and his fingers tugged at the tiny buttons on the front of her cotton nightdress and then his hands were caressing the roundness of her breast. She put her arm across him and lifted her face up, searching for his mouth as he raised himself on one elbow and leaned over her, pushing her on to her back. She lay unresisting, opening her arms invitingly, her body already beginning to respond to his touch. So long she had been denied his loving that she craved him with a passion that almost frightened her in its intensity.

His mouth was gentle on her lips, his hand stroking her breast and then she felt him move down, running his palm across her stomach, down, down until he touched her private place. She gave a low moan of pleasure and began to arch herself towards him, welcoming, beseeching . . . Then his hand moved away, up again, over the flatness of her belly. His mouth moved from hers and he buried his face in her breasts, his mouth searching for the nipple, his lips sucking it, his tongue encircling it. She gave a cry as a spasm of ecstasy that was almost a pain gripped her groin and she drove her fingers deep into the thickness of his hair, pulling him against her and increasing his ardour so that he opened his lips wider and her breast filled his mouth, his tongue sucking hard now.

Then suddenly he pulled himself up from her and straddled her, sitting on her groin so that his weight crushed her and she gasped out. 'Jack, you're too heavy, don't . . .' she began to protest, but then his fingers dug into her shoulder and, in the darkness, she felt his breath upon her face as he leaned down over her.

'You bitch! You've no more given birth to a bairn in the last few weeks than I have.'

'Jack . . .' she began, but his fingers dug deeper.

'You thought you'd trap me, didn't you? But you hadn't reckoned on me knowing what it feels like to lie with a woman who's bin with child. Aye, an' my child at that.

Well, I know, Kitty, oh yes, I know the feel of a woman who's given birth and I tell you, you haven't. Ya've no milk . . .' His anger was vicious now and cruelly he gripped her breast and squeezed it till tears smarted her eyes and she cried out not in pleasure but in pain.

'The truth, Kitty, I want the truth. Where did you find a bastard to try to trick me with, eh? Some gyppo's?'

'No, no, Jack, I swear,' she gasped. 'The boy is yours. He is your son. You've got to believe me . . .'

'Why should I, 'cos he's not yours, is he?' His grip was vicious again. 'Is he?'

'No, no,' she cried in pain. 'But he is your son.'

'Then whose . . .?' he began and then suddenly, in the darkness, he was still, with a stillness that was far more ominous than his anger.

'It's hers, ain't it?'

Kitty said nothing, but a heaviness filled her that had nothing to do with Jack's weight pressing her down.

'It's Miss Miriam Franklin's bastard.'

'Oh Jack, Jack,' she was babbling now, crying and clinging to him, oblivious to the pain he was inflicting upon her. 'She was going to give him away, to strangers, have him adopted. Jack, I couldn't bear to think of your son being brought up by strangers. The moment I held him, I loved him. I know I shouldn't have tried to deceive you and I'm sorry, but she – they made me swear to keep it secret. No one must ever know, Jack. But they were going to give him away and I – I couldn't bear that.'

'So,' he spat, 'you want my child, do you? You want my bastard so bad that you'd take another woman's to try to trick me, eh?'

'Listen, Jack, please listen to me . . .' she begged.

'I've heard enough – more than enough. But let me tell

you something, Kitty Clegg. I'll mind you never – ever – bear a child of mine. You hear me? Never!'

Then he was astride her, thrusting into her, using her body to take his revenge upon her. At the moment of his climax, in a final act of punishment, he withdrew from her, leaving her empty and bereft.

He raised himself from her now and rolled over on to his back. Lying beside her in the darkness, he neither spoke to her nor touched her again.

Kitty curled herself into a ball of misery and sobbed into her pillow.

Thirty-Three

'I'm leaving on Saturday and giving up this cottage. The work's finished round here.'

Kitty stared at him. 'Where are we going?'

His eyes glittered. 'Who said anything about "we"?'

'I see, so that's it. I've been good enough to clean your house and cook for you and care for your son for the past three months – and warm ya bed . . .'

She hesitated, thinking back again to the night Jack had found out that she was not Johnnie's natural mother and, worse still, had guessed at once just who had given birth to his son. That fact – that Johnnie was indeed his son – he had never since questioned, but his anger at her deception, which he saw as her way of trying to force him to marry her, was devastating. The following morning he had risen and left the cottage without speaking to her. On his return in the evening, she had placed a meal in front of him and he had eaten it in total silence without even looking at her.

As he had finished, mopping the gravy with a piece of bread until the plate was so clean it scarcely needed washing, she had stood in front of him. 'I suppose you want me to leave?' she said quietly.

He had looked up at her then, a hard, calculating expression in his eyes. 'You can do what you like, Kitty Clegg, but my son stays with me.'

She had gripped the edge of the table, her face white, and leaned towards him. 'Never. I'll never leave him.'

He had shrugged. 'As far as I'm concerned then, you can stay. He needs looking after, at least while he's so small, and . . .' A lascivious, leering look had come into his face. 'And so do I. There's a surprising lack of pretty girls around here,' and then he had added cruelly, 'now that Miss Miriam Franklin is no longer – available.'

Kitty turned away swiftly to hide the tears in her eyes. She was angry with herself for being so stupid, yet she could not, would not, leave the baby, and, to her chagrin, she had to admit that she did not want to leave Jack either.

Why, oh why, was she so besotted with him? She could see him for exactly what he was and yet he held her heart in the palm of his hand and she would grasp at whatever he offered if only she could stay with him.

They had settled into an uneasy life together, but over the weeks that followed Kitty was determined to win him back and to make him forget her deception. Though, at first, he used her roughly in their bed at night, little by little her tenderness had drawn from him a kinder response.

Yet now here he was callously telling her he was moving on and not even asking her to go with him.

'So, you're leaving us after all, then?'

He shook his head. 'You, mebbe, but not the boy. My son comes with me.'

'Don't be daft, Jack. How can you look after a tiny baby?'

The huge shoulders shrugged. 'I'll manage. He's not that small now. Six months old and growing fast. Besides, what was good enough for me is good enough for my son.'

'What do you mean?'

'I travelled round with my dad and my uncle. They ran the threshing set afore me.'

Slowly Kitty moved forward and sat down at the table,

staring at him across it. 'You mean – you mean, you didn't have a mother?'

'Must have had at some point, but I don't remember her.'

'Did she die?'

'I reckon.'

'You mean, you don't know?' Kitty, with mother, father, brothers and sisters, could not imagine what his life must have been like.

'She was never mentioned.'

'Never?' Kitty was scandalized. 'Your father never told you anything about your own mother?'

'No. All I can remember is travelling around with them – me dad and his brother, that is – staying here and there. Sometimes sleeping rough, sometimes finding lodgings. It's all I've ever known. And it ain't done me no harm.'

Kitty was silent, just staring at him. For the first time, she felt real pity for this man who had never known a mother's love. 'Were they – your dad and your uncle – good to you?'

Again, his shoulders lifted. 'It was a tough life, I suppose, and I had to work hard, right from being a bairn. But it meks a man of you, Kitty. I've never been ashamed of me background, or bitter about it.'

'And that's the sort of life you want for your son, is it?'

'Never done me no harm,' he repeated.

'Then what about me? Are you telling me you don't want me to come, because if that's the case, then . . .?'

He did not wait for her to finish her sentence, did not wait to hear her vow, yet again, that she would never, ever, let him take Johnnie away from her. Instead he said, 'You can come along if that's what you want. But I warn you, Kitty, you take me as I am, 'cos I aren't going to change.'

'What about Ben Holden and his family? Do they come along too?'

'Oh Ben . . .' There was a sneer in his tone. 'He's the perfect husband and father. No, his family live here, in Tresford, and they stay put. He comes back home whenever he can, but we're often away weeks at a time.'

But he's the faithful type, Kitty said to herself. Ben Holden won't be taking up with other women all over the county when he's away from his wife.

She pulled in a deep breath and for a long moment, she stared at him. She knew what to expect: a gypsy's life, following Jack wherever his search for work took him. Living in tumbledown shacks or even beneath a haystack. But if she put up with the hardships, cared for him and his son, maybe she could win him back. Maybe she could wipe out the bitterness in his heart and make him love her. In spite of everything, she could not stop herself from loving him. And now, she understood him better.

Resolutely, she lifted her chin and said quietly, 'I'll come with you, Jack. I still love you.'

For a moment, he returned her steady gaze, but then he glanced away, gave a grunt, rose from his chair and left the cottage without another word. Kitty stared after him, seeing her life stretching before her down the years, trailing in Jack's wake, following him wherever he went, having to be content with the crumbs of his brusque affection. Yet, still, she could not bring herself to break free from him.

'Kitty.'

She straightened up from where she had been bending over the flowerbed, a trowel in her hand, and was surprised to see who was standing at the gate leading into the garden of the cottage.

They were back in Tresford, in time to help with another harvest. They were earlier this year for it was only July but Kitty welcomed the respite from their nomadic existence and was looking forward to several weeks, even months, in the area. Soon there would be plenty of work here for Jack and they had been lucky that the little cottage was still available. It had not been easy following Jack from village to village with a young child.

'You ought to stay put in one place, Kitty,' Jack had said irritably. 'Like Ben's wife.'

'Oh aye, you'd like that, wouldn't you, Jack? Playing the bachelor again while I stay safely tucked away somewhere.'

'I am a bachelor, Kitty,' he had said cruelly. 'And don't you forget it.'

'I'm hardly likely too, am I,' she had snapped back, 'when everywhere I go the finger points at me for the fallen women I appear to be.'

He shrugged, completely uncaring. 'It was your choice.'

Kitty had been silent, knowing he spoke only the truth. But Jack's next words, 'I don't know why you don't stay in Tresford,' had stayed with her, and now that they were back once more in the place she called home, she felt she never wanted to leave it again.

There was only one tiny fear in Kitty's heart. At any moment they might run into Miss Miriam and she would see her son.

She smiled a genuine welcome at her unexpected visitor. 'Why, Master Edward, what are you doing here?' She dropped the trowel on to the earth and rubbed her dirty fingers on the hessian apron she wore for gardening. She glanced at the child who, walking strongly now on his sturdy plump legs, was pushing a wooden horse on wheels that Jack had made for him. The toddler had stopped in his play and his dark blue eyes were upon the stranger.

Edward was coming forward, smiling down at the boy. He dropped to his haunches to bring his eyes on a level with the child's. 'My word, there's no mistaking whose boy he is.'

Kitty's heart seemed to jump inside her chest. No, no, it wasn't possible. Surely Edward hadn't seen a likeness to his sister? So much so that . . . But his next words dispelled her panic.

'He's his father's double, isn't he?'

Kitty breathed again and managed to smile, but her voice came out a little high-pitched as she said, 'In looks, yes.'

Edward looked up at her then and slowly rose to his feet. His gentle eyes searched her face and he gave the briefest of nods as if he understood without the words even passing between them.

Suddenly shy, she said, 'Can I offer you something? Tea or lemonade on this hot day?'

'Lemonade, Kitty, would be very nice. Thank you.'

'Perhaps you'd like to sit on the bench under the apple tree,' she gestured behind her. 'And I'll bring it out.'

When she returned carrying a small tray with a jug and two glasses, he was not sitting down but pretending to feed Johnnie's toy horse with a handful of grass. The child was chuckling with delight and plucking at the ground to pull a handful for himself to copy him.

Straightening up, Edward smiled. 'He's a grand little chap, Kitty. You must be very proud of him.'

Her answering smile trembled a little on her mouth and she swallowed quickly, realizing that, although of course he had no idea of the fact, Edward was little Johnnie's uncle.

She set the tray down on the grass and bent her head over it to pour the lemonade. 'I am, Master Edward. He's a lovely little boy.'

'Teddy,' his voice came gently. 'There's no one to hear, is there?'

Looking up and holding out a glass to him, Kitty shook her head. 'No, there's no one else here.'

Edward seemed to relax visibly and patted the wooden bench beside him. 'Come and sit down, Kitty. I've a favour to ask of you.'

Startled, Kitty said, 'A favour? Of me?'

A little hesitantly, she sat beside him, still unable to see him in any light other than as the son of her former employers. But he was smiling at her, as friendly as ever and as if she was his equal. She found herself smiling in return. It had always been easy to smile at Master Edward – Teddy – especially when he had been so ill, a virtual prisoner in his sickroom. Looking at him now, she marvelled at the change in him during the last three years. He had grown, filled out and lost that terrible sickroom pallor. Now he looked the young man of seventeen that he was.

He was twirling the glass in his hand, looking down at the liquid in it as if he were suddenly nervous. 'Are you happy, Kitty?' The words tumbled out suddenly. 'Is he – good to you?'

Kitty watched him for a moment before she replied. Now, faced with Edward's question, she was able to say, quite truthfully, 'We get along very well together and he's very proud of his son.'

Edward nodded and glanced away again. For a moment he did not speak and then, clearing his throat, he began. 'It's about Miriam. She – she's in London and has got in with a very wild crowd. Mother . . .' He looked straight at

261

Kitty then. 'Mother can't handle her. None of us can – except you.'

Kitty could not hide her surprise. 'I thought she'd have been married by now to Mr Guy. She told me . . .' She hesitated a moment, about to say 'when we came back from Harrogate'. But that was a memory best forgotten. 'They were going to be married.'

Edward's mouth tightened. 'They were, or rather, they are, but Miriam keeps putting off the day with first one excuse and then another.' He smiled at Kitty. 'Poor Mother's at her wits' end to know how to deal with her. I tried to find you once before, to ask you to talk some sense into her, but we didn't know where you were living. I even went to the station house, but your mother said you were always on the move and even she had no address for you.'

Kitty bit her lip. Edward was the last person she wanted to know what her life had been like over the last eighteen months or so. Sleeping under stacks, the child pressed close to her to keep him warm; cooking in the open air over a fire; washing in a cold stream and always, moving on, moving on, from one place to another to find a day's work here, another there.

But for the next few weeks at least, she had a roof over her head and a settled life, so now she lifted her chin and smiled at Edward. 'But what can I do?'

Edward took a deep breath. 'Kitty, would you go to London?'

Kitty's mouth dropped open but he hurried on, giving her no chance to protest. 'Miriam is staying at Sir Ralph's house in the city and you could go there too. I'll pay all your fares, of course, that goes without saying and I'll pay you for going too.'

'But how can I go? I – can't take Johnnie . . .' she hesitated, not wanting to say she could not take the boy near Miriam, 'to London. And I certainly can't leave him.'

'Couldn't you leave him with your mother? I mean, he's almost two now, isn't he?'

Kitty nodded. 'Yes. He's two next month. August.' She smiled fondly. 'But he's a real handful now. Into everything.'

She was silent for a moment. She could safely leave him with her mother. July was a quiet time of the year for a thresherman and Jack had already told her that the following week he and Ben were going to a farm several miles away to cut wood and that they would not be coming home each night.

'We'll get lodgings somewhere in the week and come home on a Sunday,' he'd said. So, she thought now, as long as she was back by the Saturday, he need never know she'd even been away.

But there was one other stumbling block. Would her father agree? He had mellowed a little – but not completely – towards Kitty. She was now allowed to visit her mother openly and to take the child to the stationmaster's house, but John Clegg himself neither spoke to Kitty nor took any notice of Johnnie. He made a point of leaving the house the moment they arrived and did not return until they had left. Kitty doubted very much that he would allow his wife to care for the child for several days.

Kitty took a deep breath. 'If my mother would have him, then I could go next Monday. But I must be back by the Saturday.'

Edward nodded. 'Good. Bemmy can drive us to the station on Monday and we can go down by train and back later in the week, no later than the Friday.'

As he rose to go, Kitty looked up at him. 'Us?'

He looked down at her and said firmly, 'Oh yes, Kitty. I'm not letting you go all that way on your own. I'm coming with you.'

Thirty-Four

'I don't know, Kitty, really I don't.' Betsy plucked at her apron in a nervous gesture that was totally unlike her. 'Your dad's been so difficult since – since – well . . .' She stopped and bit her lip.

Kitty said sadly, 'Since I shamed the family, you mean?'

Her mother nodded. 'It's not just you. It brought back all his bitter memories and made him realize that he's been stuck all his life in a job he hates, just 'cos of me.'

Kitty was silent. There was nothing she could say. She was sorry that she had brought fresh sorrow to her mother, yet the mistakes of a generation ago were not her fault.

Suddenly, Betsy smiled, showing some of the spirit Kitty knew so well, the same spirit that was in her. 'Oh bring the little chap here. I shall love to have him. I miss a tiny bairn about the house. Ne'er mind what your father says.' She laughed. 'He's not likely to turn me out into the street, now is he? He likes me cooking too much.'

'Mam, are you sure? I don't want to make more trouble, but – but I would like to help the Franklins.'

'Aye, I'm sure. But it's a rare how-do-ya-do when a little maid can manage Miss Miriam better than anyone else. Better than her own parents or her intended.'

Kitty grinned. 'I know. But you see, I stand up to her and no one else does. Though I think Edward might, in time.'

*

Kitty did not tell Jack that she would be away from the cottage for most of the week. Because it involved Miriam, she found it difficult to say anything. She thought, too, that he would forbid her to go. Harder even than that was parting from little Johnnie. She hated being away from him for even an hour, never mind almost a week and when she handed him into her mother's arms, it was like tearing the heart out of her. Yet part of her – like any young woman – was excited at the prospect of a trip to the city.

There had been one awkward moment when she was standing on the platform beside Master Edward waiting for the London train.

'That's your father, isn't it?' Edward touched her arm and pointed. 'I don't think he's seen us. Do you want to go and speak to him?'

Kitty glanced along the platform to where her father was standing with his back to them. He was rigidly stiff, almost as if standing to attention, staring down the track in the direction from which the train would appear. 'He's seen us, Master Edward – Teddy – but he's not speaking to me.'

'What?' There was a silence and then Edward said flatly, 'Oh, I see. I'm sorry, Kitty.'

She sighed. 'I'm not bothered for myself.' And to her surprise, she was not. 'It's me mam I feel sorry for.'

'Mm. But she agreed to have Johnnie for you?'

'Oh yes. She loves him.'

Edward smiled. 'Well, I suppose she'll love having her grandchild around the place for a few days.'

Luckily, Kitty was saved from having to answer by the whistle of the approaching train.

*

London terrified her and as she stepped from the train on to the bustling platform, she clung to Edward's arm, completely forgetting the gulf of class between them.

He laughed and patted her hand. 'Come along, Kitty. We'll find a cab to take us to Beresford House.'

Once safely inside the horse-drawn cab, Kitty's fears subsided a little and she peered out of the window, fascinated by the shop-lined streets, the pedestrians, the buses and the fine horse-drawn carriages.

'Is that the King?' she asked in awed tones as a carriage with a coat of arms emblazoned on the doors swept past them.

'I shouldn't think so, but you never know. Maybe you've set eyes on the King of England, Kitty,' he teased her gently, but she was still gawping out of the window, determined to miss nothing of the sights and the sounds and the smells of the capital.

Newspaper boys, with placards about their necks, stood on the corners of the streets, shouting the latest headlines.

'Suffragettes burn church . . .'

Beside her in the cab, Edward sighed. 'That's what Miriam has got herself mixed up in. All this Votes for Women campaigning.'

She looked at him. 'I remember arguments between her and the master over the dinner table.'

Edward grinned, remembering. 'How I admired her then. She was the only one who could stand up to Father.'

'Oh, I don't know. Your mother did too. In her own quiet way.' Feeling his gaze upon her, she turned to look into his eyes.

'You know a lot about our family, Kitty, don't you?'

Quickly, Kitty looked away lest he should see far more in her eyes than he ought. With a forced brightness, she laughed. 'You'd be surprised, Master Edward, just how much servants do know about their betters.'

And you'd be really shocked, she thought silently, if you knew what I know about your dear sister.

To change the subject from what was becoming dangerous ground, Kitty said, 'And what do you think about this Votes for Women then?'

'Me?' Edward wrinkled his brow. 'Well, I think women should be given the vote, but I don't agree with the way they're going about it. Burning churches, causing riots. One woman even threw herself in front of the King's horse at the Derby last month. I just think there ought to be a better way than becoming a martyr for the Cause. Any cause.'

'What better way?'

He smiled wryly. 'That's just the trouble, Kitty, I don't know. I don't know what the alternative is. Women need something whereby they can prove themselves worthy of being given the vote. Unfortunately, I don't know what that is. But I'm sure *this* is not the way.'

'Maybe,' Kitty murmured, 'maybe one day we'll get the chance to prove ourselves.'

After a ride through what seemed a maze of streets, the cab drew up outside a tall Georgian mansion in a terrace of such buildings.

'Is – is this it?' she asked, wide eyed.

Edward leaped from the cab and held out his hand to help her down. While he settled with the driver and collected her one piece of luggage, Kitty stood on the pavement gazing up at the tall, imposing edifice above her. As if by magic, the front door swung smoothly open and she found herself gazing at a liveried footman, thin faced

and solemn, who hurried down the steps to take her bag
from Edward's hand. 'Allow me, sir.'

'We are expected?' Edward began.

The footman inclined his head graciously. 'Most certainly, sir. If you will follow me, I will show you to your
rooms.'

Kitty found it hard to stifle her giggles at the plummy,
exaggerated tones of the high-class servant, but, anxious
not to give offence, she straightened her features and followed the man while he conducted them up the stairs to
the front part of the house and ushered Edward into a
guest room.

'If you will follow me, miss, your room is on the next
floor.'

The servants' quarters, Kitty thought, but any resentment she might have felt was dispelled in an instant when
she stepped into the pretty room where a fire burned wel-
comingly in the grate even on this summer's day. She ran
to the window and to her joy found that it looked out
over the street.

She turned back to the man, her eyes large with wonder.
'It's lovely. Thank you.'

The man nodded but still no smile curved his lips.
'You'll eat with the servants, miss, of course, but I'll show
you Miss Franklin's room now if you wish.'

'Thank you,' she said again and followed him back
down the stairs to the second floor where he knocked on
one of the doors. On hearing a 'Come in,' the man opened
the door, but stood aside for Kitty to enter. Giving him a
quick smile of thanks Kitty stepped past him and into the
room. As the door closed quietly behind her, she found
herself staring into the surprised gaze of Miriam Franklin
reflected in the mirror of the dressing table where she was
seated.

'What on earth are you doing here?' she demanded without preamble, but before Kitty could even form an answer, Miriam held up her hand. 'Don't tell me. Mother's sent you to "look after me".'

'Not exactly,' Kitty said carefully.

'Ah. Then it was Edward.'

Kitty could not deny it. She waited a moment, returning Miriam's wilful look with a steady gaze. Then she asked quietly, 'Aren't you going to ask after Johnnie?'

Not even the merest flicker of emotion passed across Miriam's face as she said idly, 'I haven't the faintest idea who you're talking about.'

With deliberate emphasis Kitty said, '*My* son. I thought at least you would want to know if he was well and thriving.'

Miriam picked up a silver-backed hairbrush and drawled languidly, 'And what makes you think that I would be interested in the bastard child of a silly servant girl?'

Kitty didn't even flinch as she stepped closer and bent down to stare into the mirror, their reflected faces close together. 'Of course not, miss,' she said, her tone laced with sarcasm. 'How could I, for one moment, have imagined that you would have a thought for anyone else in this world except yourself?'

Miriam's face was dark with rage. 'How dare you!'

Kitty straightened up, but kept her eyes on the array of glass jars and bottles on the dressing-table top, knowing that at any moment one might come hurtling in her direction. 'Oh I dare, miss. I dare right enough.'

'Don't think you have any kind of hold over me, Kitty Clegg, because if you ever – *ever* breathe a word I'll have you arrested for slander.'

'I gave you my word and I'll keep it, miss, to my dying breath.'

Kitty bit her lip. She was on the point of telling Miriam that Jack had guessed the truth, but then she stopped herself. It was better that Miriam did not know that they were now both at the mercy of Jack's volatile temper.

But Miriam's thoughts, too, had turned to Jack. 'I hear you're living with – *him*.' Watching her, Kitty saw a brief flicker of jealousy in the girl's eyes as she asked, 'Is he going to marry you?'

So Miriam did have feelings after all and Kitty marvelled, not for the first time, at the hold Jack Thorndyke seemed to exert over women.

'I don't think he'll ever marry anyone,' she said slowly, remembering how Miriam herself had once said that the father of her child was 'not the marrying kind'. By the look on her face, Kitty could see that Miriam was remembering it too.

'But we have,' Kitty went on, trying to blot from her mind those first difficult months, 'settled down quite nicely together. And he – he is very proud of his son.'

'Is he? Is he really?' Miriam's voice was a tremulous whisper and, as she raised her fine, green eyes, Kitty was startled to see the glimmer of tears in them.

Kitty was unsure exactly what she had come here for or what she was supposed to do. Automatically she began to help Miriam with her clothes, without being asked to do so, and when she picked up the dress lying on the bed and scurried away down the back stairs to press the creases from it, Miriam made no demur.

'It's the latest fashion, Kitty,' Miriam told her, preening herself before the long mirror. Then she pulled a moue at her reflection. 'Mind you, the women at the meeting I'm going to this afternoon take little interest in clothes or their appearances.' She laughed suddenly. 'One or two of them look like scarecrows. But I don't see why I can't have a little fun. Surely one can look one's best and still be a campaigner for the Cause.'

Meeting? Campaign? Cause? The new words rang in Kitty's mind, indeed they sounded alarm bells. She opened her mouth to warn her young mistress, for despite what had happened, she still thought of Miriam Franklin as precisely that. But then Kitty clamped her lips closed. Instead she said, deliberately casual, 'May I come with you, miss? I know I'm not in me maid's uniform, but I've got me good black coat with me and—'

But further wheedling was unnecessary. 'Of course you can come, Kitty. We're all sisters in the Cause. There's no class distinction.' She glanced at her gold watch. 'But look sharp if you're coming, because we've a good way to walk.'

Walk! Kitty's amazement was complete. She had never known her mistress to walk anywhere. Not back home. Ride, yes, on horseback, but failing that she had always demanded that Bemmy should drive her or that the pony and trap should be made ready for her. But walk? Never!

Miriam was waiting in the hallway for Kitty, tapping her foot impatiently. In her hand she carried what looked suspiciously like a broom handle with a cloth wrapped around it.

'Come along, Kitty. I don't want to be late.'

Another surprise. Miriam had never been on time for anything in her life, yet now she walked swiftly along the city pavements turning up one street and down another, obviously knowing exactly where she was going. And she was walking so fast that Kitty had to take little running steps to keep up with her. The day was grey and a light drizzle was beginning to fall, wetting the pavements so that they reflected the shapes of the buildings above them.

'Where – where are we going, miss?' Kitty panted.

'You'll see,' was all Miriam would say.

The meeting was in a tumbledown warehouse in a dingy street. Kitty, wide-eyed, looked about her. The whole assembly was made up of women. Not one man was present. On a makeshift platform of crates at one end of the building, three women sat together. As one of them rose, the chattering fell silent and all eyes turned towards her. Above Kitty's head a loose board rattled, punctuating the speaker's words. The rain, heavier now, clattered on the tin roof and a steady drip came through a hole and fell on to Kitty's neck, running down and making her shiver.

The woman was dressed in a wide-brimmed hat, a long dark skirt and a matching, close-fitting short jacket trimmed with braid. The white blouse beneath it had soft, white ruffles at the neck. Well, she doesn't look like a scarecrow, Kitty thought, but then her musings were brought abruptly to a halt by the commanding presence of the slight figure of the woman on the platform. Her voice, though a little strident, was nonetheless compelling and Kitty found herself beginning to be swept along on the tide of fervour emanating from the audience. Then she shook herself and muttered, 'Politics! What do I know about politics? Or want to?' Then she glanced at Miriam. The girl's face was a study of rapt attention. Her green eyes were bright with excitement, her lips slightly parted as if in breathless wonder.

Kitty pulled at her sleeve. 'Miss, miss. We should go. This is no place for you. What would your mother say? And Sir Ralph? You're a guest in his house, don't forget. You really shouldn't be getting involved—'

'Shut up, Kitty,' Miriam hissed. 'I wouldn't have

brought you if I'd thought you were going to turn all good-goody on me.'

Close by, one or two heads turned and whispered, 'Ssh.'

Briefly, as if aware of the slight disturbance, the speaker glanced in their direction and Kitty felt her face redden. She had no wish to make a scene, but this was no place for her young mistress. And now she realized just why Edward had asked her to come to London. This was the 'wild crowd' he had meant. These were the suffragettes.

The speaker's voice was rising to a crescendo and all around the room banners were being unfurled and held aloft. Miriam was unwrapping the fabric from the pole she held and then Kitty saw the writing on it: 'Votes for Women'. And the assembly took up the cry until it became a chant. The three women on the platform now each wore a sash crosswise over their bosoms. They stepped down and marched into the centre of the throng, through the rickety double doors and out into the narrow, grimy street. With one accord the gathering fell in behind them, marching along with their banners held high and their chant echoing through the damp streets.

Kitty caught hold of Miriam's arm, determined not to be separated from her as she was jostled along with the mass. 'We shouldn't be here, miss,' she began again, desperate to separate Miriam from this gathering which she could visualize becoming an unruly mob. A shiver of fear ran through her as she remembered the master ranting about these women chaining themselves to railings and Edward telling her about the one who had thrown herself beneath the King's horse. There was no knowing what might happen and, with Miriam's erratic temperament, there was certainly no guarantee that she would not allow herself to be swept along into all sorts of madcap schemes.

Kitty, in strange surroundings and among people with

whom she had no affinity, wished fervently that Edward, or even Mr Guy, was with them. She was out of her depth and could handle neither Miss Miriam nor this situation.

Then she remembered how she had pleaded to become Miss Miriam's personal maid, how she had vowed that whatever happened, she could handle the wilful girl. She recalled the difficult times they had had in York and Harrogate and how firm she had had to be then.

It was the same silly girl she was dealing with. Despite the trouble she had got into, Miriam Franklin had still learned no common sense. Perhaps, Kitty thought wryly, common sense was not something you could learn. Maybe you were born either with it or without it. Strength flooded back into her. It was up to her, Kitty Clegg, yet again.

With a sudden movement, she reached across and wrenched the pole carrying the banner from Miriam's grasp. Caught unawares, Miriam let go and though she made a futile grab at it, she was too slow and Kitty had flung it to the ground where it was quickly trampled upon by those following them.

'What do you think you're doing?' Miriam began, but already Kitty had clamped her hand firmly on the girl's arm and was pulling her to the side of the band of marching women. 'Let go of me this minute.' But Kitty clung on and while Miriam was no weakling, she was no match for Kitty whose years as a kitchen maid, and, more recently, working in the fields alongside Jack, had strengthened her arms and her grasp. So Miriam resorted to kicking and Kitty felt the toe of Miriam's boot strike her shin. She gave a yell of pain. Then, thrusting her face close to the other girl's, she said, 'Stop that, miss, else I'll kick you back.'

For a moment, their faces close together, they glared at each other but then, as if remembering the time that Kitty had pulled her hair in retaliation, Miriam made no further attempt to kick. Instead she continued to wriggle, vainly trying to twist herself free of Kitty's hold.

A woman passing close by, her banner still held aloft, shouted, 'Wait till we get there, girls, then you can start a riot.'

At once Miriam stopped her struggling and Kitty saw her eyes widen. 'A riot?' Miriam said, looking at Kitty. 'That's not what they're going to do, is it?'

Grimly, Kitty said, 'I shouldn't be at all surprised, miss. Come on, let's get away from here. You've been to your meeting, now let's go home.'

'But Kitty, I . . .' Miriam's protests were half-hearted now and, beneath her grasp, Kitty felt the girl's resistance slacken. She allowed herself to be led along the street in the opposite direction, away from the march.

Once, Miriam glanced back over her shoulder with a little regret, Kitty thought, but then, as they walked along, she said, 'Kitty, you – you won't tell Guy or – or Sir Ralph about this, will you?'

'Of course not, miss. There's no harm done, thank goodness, so there's no need.'

They walked the rest of the way back to Sir Ralph's house in silence, but Kitty was thinking, How many more secrets must I carry for this silly, headstrong girl?

Thirty-Five

At breakfast the following morning, it was splashed across the headlines of the newspaper.

'Just listen to this.' Sir Ralph, sitting at the head of the table, shook his paper. ' "Violent scenes broke out today between suffragettes and the police as the latter sought to re-arrest Sylvia Pankhurst whose appearance is in direct defiance of her current licensed release from a three-year prison sentence . . ." '

Kitty, helping to serve breakfast, held her breath. Any moment she expected an outburst. At the Manor, she could well imagine Mr Franklin's voice raised in outrage. 'Silly women! A pity they haven't something better to do. They should be caring for their husbands and families, not involving themselves in matters that don't concern them.'

She glanced at Miss Miriam sitting demurely to one side. The girl was calmly eating her kipper, but, Kitty noticed, she kept her eyes fixed upon her plate. Only the slight trembling of the fork she held betrayed her feelings. Kitty turned away to hide her smile, knowing how sorely tempted Miriam must be to make some sharp retort to Sir Ralph. She was relieved that the girl was actually refraining from doing so and only Kitty knew what a supreme effort that must be costing her.

To Kitty's surprise, Sir Ralph was shaking his head sadly. 'What a pity they feel obliged to take such action. I'm sure it does their cause no good. No good at all, and yet, because of the blinkered view of our "House of Men", what else can they do.' It was a statement rather than a question, but at his words Miriam lifted her eyes.

'You sound as if you have some sympathy – or at least understanding – for these women, Sir Ralph?'

The man was an older edition of his son. His fair hair was now silver, but the eyes were just as gentle as Guy's, though there was a trace of sadness in their depths that never quite disappeared even when he smiled. He was tall and thin, and carried himself with an air of distinction. He smiled now at Miriam. 'I do indeed. And in my own quiet way I have been trying to further their cause in the House, but . . .' his smile broadened, 'I don't go in for riots. I'm getting a little old for that kind of action.'

Kitty felt her heart sink as she saw the sparkle of triumph in Miriam's eyes.

Back in her room, Kitty watched as her young mistress marched excitedly up and down its length. 'I can hardly believe it. To think that someone like Sir Ralph, a Member of Parliament, is actually on our side. I was so sure he'd be like my father. Old-fashioned and arrogant, thinking all women are good for is to look after the home and bear children. Oh Kitty, you mark my words, our day will come. And if we've people like Sir Ralph on our side, it will come all the sooner.'

Kitty moved forward and began to make the bed. 'Yours might, miss, but I doubt very much whether the likes of me will ever get the vote.'

Miriam swung round. 'Whyever not? That's defeatist talk, Kitty. Why shouldn't you have the vote? You've as much right to vote for the way your country – and your life – is governed as anyone else.'

Kitty bent and smoothed the sheet with the palm of her

hand. 'How can I vote for summat I don't know owt about, miss?'

A puzzled frown wrinkled Miriam's forehead. 'What do you mean, you don't know anything about it? Don't you read the papers? Don't you talk about politics?'

Kitty shrugged. 'I've heard your father talking at the table sometimes and me own dad, well, him and his mates talk about things like that in the pub, I reckon. But never at home. Never . . .' she glanced over her shoulder at Miriam and added pointedly, 'in front of women.'

Miriam sat down at the dressing table and asked, curiously now, 'You mean, your mother and father never talk about such things?'

'No, miss.' Kitty plumped the pillows and pulled the counterpane up to cover them.

'How strange,' the other girl murmured.

And the thought ran through Kitty's mind, though she did not voice it aloud, We're too busy trying to survive in our little world to be thinking about such lofty matters as how the country should be run.

'How very strange,' Miriam said again and turned away to admire her reflection in the mirror.

'Where is she? Where's Miriam?' Edward, standing at the head of the stairs, his face creased with anxiety, looked down at Kitty who was carrying clean laundry up from the kitchen below.

She smiled up at him. 'She's gone out with Mr Guy. She's quite safe.'

'Oh no, she isn't. Guy came back half an hour ago. *Without her.*'

Now Kitty stared at him. 'But – how – how come? I mean, where is she?'

Edward ran his hand distractedly through his hair and pulled in a deep, unsteady breath. Kitty was sure she heard a hint of the tell-tale rasp. Without stopping to think, concerned only for him, she put her hand on his arm. 'Go and sit down, Teddy. I'll see Mr Guy and then I'll go and look for her.'

Edward covered her hand with his own. 'I'm all right, honestly, Kitty. I can't let you go out alone in London.' He smiled at her, though the worry over his wayward sister never left his eyes. 'You'd get lost.'

Kitty gave a snort. 'I've a tongue in me head. I can ask, can't I? Go on, do as I say,' and then, fearing she had been too forceful, she added, 'please?'

'Just for a while then, but if – if you don't find her quickly, then – then I must . . .'

'I'll find her. I promise.'

She turned away, feeling guilty at making a promise that she was not sure she would be able to keep. 'I'm going home tomorrow,' she vowed as she picked up her skirts and hurried downstairs again to find Guy Harding. 'I've been away from my little man long enough.'

At the thought of the boy who had wound his way into her heart and taken possession of it, Kitty felt a sob build in her throat. How she missed Johnnie, how she longed to hold him in her arms.

She knocked on the door of Guy's study and his voice bade her enter. He was sitting behind the wide expanse of his polished desk. Managing to make her voice sound casual, she asked, 'I was just wondering where you left Miss Miriam, sir. She's not back yet and me and T— Master Edward were a little anxious. I mean, she doesn't know the city all that well, and . . .' She was beginning to babble.

Guy, knowing nothing of the real cause for their

concern, said cheerfully, 'Oh I shouldn't worry, Kitty. She said she was meeting a friend for afternoon tea in one of the big stores.' His smile widened indulgently. 'I'm sure there's no need to worry, they're probably spending a small fortune in Oxford Street and have completely lost track of the time.'

Friend? Miriam had no friends in London that she knew of – except the women in the suffragette movement. She swallowed her fear and smiled brightly. 'Right you are, then, sir. Thank you.' She bobbed a slight curtsy and backed out of the room. Closing the door quietly, she ran then, on light feet, up the stairs to her room to fetch her hat and coat. She was determined to sneak out of the house by the back stairs before Edward realized she had gone. What a nice man Mr Guy is, Kitty thought, Miss Miriam really doesn't deserve someone like him.

Minutes later she was walking quickly down the road. At the corner she paused and then asked a road sweeper for directions, but when she arrived in Oxford Street, to her dismay it stretched as far as she could see into the distance. She couldn't hope to find Miriam even if she was somewhere here, which Kitty rather doubted. It was more likely that the 'afternoon tea' was just a story for Guy's benefit and that Miriam had gone to the old warehouse again.

'I've no hope of finding that either,' Kitty muttered aloud. She could not even remember the name of the street. She bit her lip, aware now of just how foolish she had been to venture out alone into the big city. But she had wanted to prevent Edward becoming involved.

For more than an hour she wandered the streets, realizing eventually that she was completely lost.

She heard the noise even before she turned the last corner into a square and gave a gasp of alarm when she saw what was happening. Policemen with flailing truncheons were advancing in a line towards a band of women standing with placards and banners and chanting, 'Votes for Women, Votes for Women.' Then three mounted policemen appeared and galloped straight at the group of women who scattered in fear. It was at that moment that Kitty saw Miriam and before she could stop herself a cry had escaped her lips. 'Miss Miriam, no, oh no.'

Miriam was standing directly in the path of one of the oncoming horses, boldly facing the creature. She had no fear of horses, Kitty knew, but this was not the country, not her own home-bred horse who would obey her every command. But she stood with the stillness of a statue and, at the last moment, the animal veered to the left. Its rider brought it to a halt with such a vicious tug on its bit that the animal reared. Close by, women screamed, terrifying the horse even more. The officer lost his stirrup, slipped sideways from the saddle and fell to the ground. Kitty watched in horror then as Miriam moved suddenly to grasp hold of the horse's bridle, but she was not in time to save the policeman from being trampled by the animal's restless, frightened hooves. She held on to the bridle and patted the horse's head, though the crowd of women, bent on continuing their demonstration or saving themselves, did nothing to help the young man on the ground.

Kitty thrust herself through the mass, elbowing, shoving and pushing until she reached Miriam.

'Hold him still, miss, while I get to the copper.'

The horse stood relatively quietly now, though his eyes were still bulging and he breathed and snorted noisily. Kitty, confident of her young mistress's way with horses, ducked beneath the animal's neck and bent over the young man lying motionless on the ground.

'Give us a bit of room,' she shouted angrily. 'Can't you

see he's hurt?' But the women, still chanting and screaming, took no notice. Kitty knelt on the pavement and cradled the young man's head in her lap, bending her body over him to protect him from the crowd which seemed to her to have lost all sense of reason.

Then one of the other mounted officers came towards them and the women scattered in alarm, leaving a clear pathway for the rider. He flung himself from his horse.

'You're under arrest, the pair of you. I saw it all. You grabbed at his horse and made it rear.'

'I did no such thing. I was trying to calm it,' Miriam retorted hotly, while Kitty felt fear twist her stomach. Arrested? Her? Why, she had done nothing.

Other officers were arriving now and Kitty looked up to see one or two women being led away, obviously under arrest, yet the majority seemed to have disappeared, fleeing down the side streets, dispersing swiftly to stay free to fight another day.

Someone brought a stretcher and the young policeman was lifted on to it. Kitty then found herself grasped firmly by the arms and hauled to her feet. But instead of being thanked, both she and Miriam felt the cold ring of steel around their wrists as handcuffs were clamped on them and they were marched towards the black, square-shaped contraption drawn by two impatient horses parked at the edge of the square.

Thirty-Six

They appeared in court the following morning, standing side by side in the dock like common criminals. Kitty, her face flaming red, saw Edward and Guy sitting together in the gallery. Edward's face was contorted with anxiety, Guy's grim with anger.

Kitty glanced towards Miriam but she was staring steadfastly straight ahead, refusing to look towards her fiancé or her brother.

The constable who had arrested them gave his evidence and Kitty's heart sank. It looked very bleak for them and every limb in her body trembled as she thought of having to spend even one more night in that cold cell with its dark stone walls and dank smell.

What if they were sent to prison? What would happen to little Johnnie and to Jack? Fear rose in her throat, threatening to choke her. What if . . .?

Another constable was being called forward by the defence lawyer Guy had hurriedly summoned from the firm of solicitors in the city who acted for Sir Ralph. The policeman mounted the steps into the witness box and was sworn in. A request was made to the judge.

'My Lord, I know this is somewhat unusual but, as you may know, the officer who would be able to give the clearest evidence of the particular incident involving these two women is lying injured in hospital. With your indulgence, my Lord . . .' the barrister gave a little bow towards

the bench, 'the officer now called has taken a sworn statement from his injured colleague and, with your permission,
my Lord, will now read it to the court.'

The judge seemed to deliberate, then he leaned forward
and there was a few moments' whispered conversation
between him and the Clerk of the Court before he straightened up and nodded. 'Very well, then.'

Kitty's knees felt weak. She clung on to the edge of the
dock, afraid that at any moment she would collapse with
fear. Beside her, Miriam stood tall and erect.

The officer in the witness box opened his notebook and
cleared his throat. He seemed like an actor on stage making
the most of his big moment. After giving his colleague's
name and number he began to relate what had happened.

' "As I rode through the crowd, I could sense that
my mount was becoming very unsettled by the
screams and shouting of the women around us. I
then noticed a woman who was standing very still
and although she was wearing a banner across her
chest and was obviously one of the gathering, she
was not at that moment taking an active part in the
riot. She was obviously watching my horse, and,
although at first I thought she intended to make more
trouble of some kind, I now realize that in fact the
opposite was the case. As my mount reared in fright,
this woman caught hold of the bridle, I believe in an
attempt to steady the animal. I was unfortunately
unseated and fell to the ground, the horse's hooves
catching me a number of times. As I fell, I hit my
head on the ground and sustained a mild concussion.
I remember being vaguely aware, however, that the
woman had brought the horse under control and
that another woman was kneeling beside me and

appeared to be trying to protect me from further harm either from the horse or from the surging crowd. Whether or not these two women had been involved in the riot earlier I cannot say, but I do know that at this point they were certainly taking no further part in the commotion and were, in fact, assisting me. I respectfully request that this evidence should be presented to the court in mitigation should charges be brought against the two women concerned." '

A whisper like a light breeze ran around the room as the constable snapped his notebook shut and stood to attention, awaiting either further questioning or dismissal. He received the latter and stepped down.

The judge consulted further with the clerk and then, frowning, looked solemnly towards the dock.

'It seems that, although you were involved in the fracas, you did not intend injury to the constable and, indeed, came to his aid. With this in mind I bind you both over to keep the peace for a period of six months.' He cleared his throat and Kitty saw him glance meaningly towards the gallery. 'I suggest you should return home and leave such distasteful matters to those women who have nothing better to do.'

Kitty felt weak with relief but then, with a shaft of horror, she felt Miriam tense and saw a look of anger cross her face. Miriam opened her mouth and Kitty knew at once she was about to make some sharp retort to the judge.

Immediately, Kitty raised her voice and said clearly, 'Thank you, my Lord.' At the same moment she gripped Miriam's arm fiercely and muttered beneath her breath, 'Don't you dare say a word, miss. Get yarsen into trouble if you must, but not me.' And with a strength born of anger, she pushed Miriam from the dock and down the stairs away from the glowering face of the judge who could, she knew, at any moment change his mind and commit them both to that awful prison.

'Kitty, I don't know how to thank you.' Guy Harding was smiling down at her. 'I can see now that Edward was right. You are the only one who can handle her.' He shook his head and sighed. It was obvious he loved Miriam devotedly, yet he was overwhelmed by her rebelliousness.

'Take her home, Mr Guy, out of harm's way,' Kitty said. 'Even if she agitates a bit in the country, she won't get herself into such bother there as she does here in the city.'

He gave a short laugh. 'I wouldn't bank on it, Kitty.'

Kitty sniffed. 'It'd be better if she were to have another—' She bit her tongue and felt the colour rise in her cheeks. For one dreadful, unguarded moment, she had been about to say, 'Have another child'. Swiftly, hoping he had not noticed her hesitation, she hurried on. 'Another interest. Something a bit less, well, dangerous.'

'What she really needs,' Guy murmured, almost as if he had been reading her mind, 'is to be a wife and mother.'

Kitty forced a smile but said nothing. So close were his musings to her own thoughts that she did not trust herself to speak.

'Well, Kitty,' he said, his smile broadening. 'The first I can do something about straight away. With her parents' approval, I think we should be married as soon as possible, don't you? As for the second, I hope it won't be too long, once we're married, before we're blessed with children.' There was a wistful note in his voice as he added, 'I'd love a big family. I've missed having brothers and sisters.'

Kitty swallowed. Latching on to the first suggestion, she said, 'That's a wonderful idea, Mr Guy. Miss Miriam will make a beautiful bride.'

'Yes, yes.' The young man's eyes softened. 'She will, won't she?'

'If – if you'll excuse me, Mr Guy, I must be getting ready. Mr Edward and I are leaving.'

'Oh yes, yes, of course. You must be wanting to get home to your little boy. I'm sorry you're already a day later than you intended, but thank you again.'

'I-it's all right, Mr Guy,' she murmured. She knew in her heart that it was anything but "all right". Just what Jack would say, or do, when he returned home to the empty cottage, she dare not think.

'Where the hell have you been?'

Jack caught hold of her shoulders and slammed her roughly against the wall as she stepped through the door of the cottage. Kitty let out a cry of pain as her head banged against the wall and his strong fingers dug deeply into the flesh on her upper arms.

'Jack—'

'You've been with some man. You whore! Is this what you do when I'm away all week?'

'Jack!' Now she gasped his name. 'How can you say such a thing?' Then as rightful indignation brought courage, she lifted her arms and thrust him away from her, anger lending her extra strength. Caught unawares, he released his hold and stepped backwards.

'How dare you even think such a thing about me?' she shouted at him. 'Judge everyone else by yar own standards, d'ya? I shouldn't think you go to bed every night on yar own when you're away from me in the week, d'ya?'

It was what she had thought for several months, but she had kept the fear pressed down, pushed to the back of her mind. Now, in her rage, the accusation hung in the air between them.

'A man's got his needs.'

'Aye, and you've got more "needs" than most, Jack Thorndyke,' she cried bitterly.

He thrust his face, dark with anger, close to hers. 'It's him, ain't it?'

Genuinely puzzled, Kitty stared up into his face. 'Him? Who are you talking about?'

Again he gripped her arm, but not so fiercely this time. 'You know very well. Master Edward Franklin. Don't think I don't know he comes here when I'm away. There's nothing you can do, girl, that I won't get to hear about, so don't you forget it. And he's not to come here again. You hear?'

'He came here the once,' she retorted. 'To ask me to go to London to help with—'

'London?' His voice was an enraged roar. 'You've been to London?'

Kitty bit her lip, realizing her mistake.

'You left my son to go gadding off to London?'

'It wasn't "gadding off",' she retorted hotly, thinking of the cold, damp cell where she might very well have ended up for weeks, even months, but for the honesty of the police constable.

'Johnnie's with my mother. He's quite safe.'

'He'd better be, or else . . .' The threat hung between them.

Then suddenly Jack laughed and folded his arms, leaning back against the wall. 'I suppose you'll be trying to tell me next that he came to see his nephew?'

Kitty's lips parted in a gasp. 'No, no. He doesn't know. He mustn't know. He must never know.'

'Mustn't he?' Jack's eyes were glinting now with malicious delight. 'Mustn't he indeed? Then you'll just have to be a good girl and behave yourself, won't you, Kitty Clegg?'

He turned and dragged open the back door and walked away across the small yard towards the shed while Kitty stared after him.

'What a fool,' she murmured. 'What a fool I have been.'

But now, with his final threat still echoing in her ears, she knew she was trapped, tied to Jack Thorndyke whether she wanted to be or not.

Thirty-Seven

Jack was in a black mood.

'Madam . . .' the word was heavy with sarcasm, and for a moment Kitty was unsure whether he was speaking about Mrs Franklin or Miss Miriam, 'sent word out to the yard this morning that she wants to see you up at the Manor.' He glowered. 'I don't want you seeing any of the Franklin family, but there's not a lot I can do about it, seeing as me work's there for the next few weeks.' He paused and then said grudgingly, 'Ya'd better go an' see what the Mrs wants.'

Kitty bent over the range and made no reply. She did not tell him that she had every intention of going to the Manor whether he gave her his divine permission or not. She ladled stew on to a plate and placed it before him. As she made to turn away, Jack grasped her wrist in his strong grip forcing her to look at him.

'I don't want you to have owt to do with *her* . . .' now she knew he was referring to Miriam, 'or any of them. I don't want her suddenly deciding to claim her son back.'

Kitty stared at him. 'She'll not do that. That I do know. She's more frightened of anyone finding out she *is* his mother.'

Jack's expression became devious. 'Is she now? And I wonder how much my silence is worth?'

Kitty was shocked. She twisted her wrist out of his grasp and then leaned close to him. 'Don't you dare try it,

291

Jack, 'cos it's only your word against mine – and *hers*. And her family's a mite more powerful than a thresherman, big though he thinks he is.'

He, too, thrust his face close to hers. 'Aye, but it'd sow seeds of doubt in everyone's mind, especially in that fancy – wealthy – fiancé of hers.'

Kitty shook her head. 'Don't, Jack, don't even think about it, 'cos you'll be sorry if you do.'

'You threatening me, Kitty Clegg?' He never lost an opportunity to use her full name, accenting the surname and taunting her that she was still a single woman and likely to remain so, emphasizing each time he used it that she would never bear the name of Thorndyke.

'No,' she said levelly. 'But you would be sorry. Not for anything I might do, but for what it'd cost you. The influence of the Franklins, and the Hardings too don't forget, reaches far. Throughout the county, I shouldn't wonder and if you—'

'Yes, yes, I know all that. D'ya think I'm stupid enough to cut off me own living?'

Kitty raised her left eyebrow but said nothing. She would have liked to answer him back, to say, 'you didn't think of that when you tumbled Miss Miriam in the hay, did you?' but it didn't do to argue with Jack in this mood. It was not that she was afraid of him, but she had a favour to ask. Aloud she said, 'Will you look after Johnnie this afternoon, then, while I go?'

'I ain't no nursemaid. That's women's work. 'Sides, a stackyard's no place for a bairn. Another couple of years and I'll have him doing little jobs, but not yet.' His grin was sly as he suggested, 'Tek him with you. I'm sure Mrs Franklin would like to see her grandson, and as for Miss Miriam, well, any mother must long to see her own child.'

Kitty almost snorted aloud and retorted, not Miss Miriam, but she managed to hold the words in check.

'Now you stay with Mrs Grundy while I go upstairs and see the mistress. Be a good boy, Johnnie. Maybe Mrs G.'ll give you a scone and butter, if you're very good,' she added in a whisper that was deliberately loud so that the cook should hear.

Mrs Grundy stood before him, arms akimbo, looking down at the boy, whose mischievous eyes twinkled back at her.

'So this is your boy, then, Kitty?'

Careful as ever in her choice of words, Kitty said, 'This is Johnnie. He'll be no trouble, but just keep your eye on him, Mrs G. He'll do anything to get out into the yard and to his dad, if he can.'

The boy pointed towards the back door. 'Dad, engine, puff-puff. Me go.'

'No, no, you stay here.'

'He'll be all right, Kitty. Me an' him'll have a nice little chat, eh, now won't we, an' I'll see what I've got in me pantry.'

Kitty ran up the stairs and knocked on Mrs Franklin's sitting-room door. Moments later she was sitting with the mistress on her window seat and it seemed, for an instant, as if the years fell away and she was once again the little kitchen maid begging to become a lady's maid.

Oh what trouble she might have saved herself, she thought suddenly, if only she had not been sitting here all that time ago.

'Kitty, my dear. How are you?'

'Very well, madam, thank you,' Kitty said, careful not to let any sign of emotion creep into her tone. There was so much she could have said, could have told Mrs Franklin, yet she did not.

'Kitty, I need your help over the wedding. Miriam is being . . .' she paused, sighed and then added, 'difficult.'

So nothing had changed, Kitty thought with wry amusement, but she kept her face straight.

'One moment she's on top of the world, excited and planning her wedding, the next she's in floods of tears saying she doesn't want to marry Guy, that she doesn't want to marry anyone. Kitty, will you talk to her?'

'Of course, madam, but I can't promise that it will do any good.'

Mrs Franklin sighed. 'I know, my dear, but there's only you, apart from me, who understands – fully.' The slightest hesitation before the final word spoke volumes.

Kitty rose. 'Is she upstairs now, madam?'

'Yes.'

'Then I'll go up.'

'Thank you, Kitty.' Her voice dropped as she murmured, 'I really don't know what we'd do without you, my dear.'

As she closed the door behind her and mounted the stairs, Kitty thought, What you'd have done without me is you'd have given that darling little boy away to strangers. A gentle smile curved Kitty's mouth. Whatever happened in her life, whatever cruelties she had to suffer under Jack's threats, she would never regret having taken Johnnie.

As long as she had him, then nothing and no one else mattered.

Miriam's bedroom door was ajar and even before she reached it she heard the girl's voice. 'Get out, you stupid girl . . .'

So, Kitty thought, the latest lady's maid is getting just

294

the same treatment. As she reached the door it was flung wide and a girl in maid's uniform marched out, her face red, her mouth pressed into a grim line. At least she's not in floods of tears, Kitty thought as she stood aside to let her pass. The maid strode straight past her without a word and ran downstairs. Kitty shrugged her shoulders, tapped on the half-open door and stepped into the room.

'May I come in, miss?'

Miriam was standing in the middle of the bedroom, still in her nightgown, her auburn hair in a tangle of wild curls. Her face was tear-streaked, her green eyes flashing with rage. 'That stupid girl can't dress my hair properly,' she said, as if for Kitty Clegg to step unannounced into her bedroom was the most natural thing in the word. She moved towards the dressing table and sat down on the stool. 'Just see what you can do with it, Clegg.'

Kitty hid her smile, picked up the hairbrush and with quick, strong strokes began to bring some shape and style back into the disarray.

'Oh Kitty...' the girl began and Kitty glanced at Miriam's reflection in the mirror. Suddenly her face crumpled and her lower lip trembled. 'Kitty, what am I to do?'

'Do, miss?' Kitty said, feigning surprise. 'What about?'

'About Guy and – and getting married.' Her voice dropped to a whisper. 'I can't marry Guy. I don't love him.'

Through the glass the two girls stared at each other.

Softly Kitty asked, 'Are you still in love with – *him*?'

Miriam shook her head vehemently – too vehemently, Kitty thought shrewdly. 'No – no. I *hate* him.'

Kitty sighed and with a sudden insight and wisdom beyond her years, she said, 'Hate isn't the opposite of love, you know. That just means you still feel a strong emotion for him.'

'I don't – I don't.' The tears were starting again.

Kitty patted her shoulder. 'All right, miss. All right. Now listen.' She bent down, putting her face above the girl's shoulder so that they looked at each other in the mirror. 'You're fond of Mr Guy, aren't you?'

Miriam nodded.

'Well then, in your class lots of marriages start with no more than that when they've been arranged by the parents, now don't they?'

'I suppose so.'

'And you can't deny that Mr Guy loves you.'

'I know, but . . .'

'No, "buts", miss,' Kitty said firmly, straightening up and resuming her brushing. 'Just you enjoy all the planning and the day itself. You'll be the most beautiful bride this town's seen in a long time.'

'Oh Kitty, but what if . . .?'

Kitty raised the hairbrush and shook it in admonishment. 'No more doubts. It's the right thing. And in time, well, I think you'll come to love Mr Guy, 'cos he's a lovely man.'

'Oh he is, he is,' Miriam agreed, 'but . . .'

She fell silent and stared at Kitty for a few moments, then she gave a huge sigh and began to smile. 'You're right, Kitty. I will marry Mr Guy and become Mistress of Nunsthorpe Hall and forget all about – well – everything else.'

'That's right, miss. That's what you ought to do,' Kitty said firmly, and silently she prayed, *And forget all about your son too. He's mine.*

The wedding, as Kitty had foreseen, was a grand affair and all the town turned out to watch Miss Miriam ride to the church in the open carriage. Even the late October day was kind. A light breeze ruffled the bride's veil, but the sun shone and the autumn weather was surprisingly warm.

Kitty slipped into the church to listen to the service, for, right at the back, she could see very little. But when Guy and Miriam came out of the door and walked between guests lining their pathway towards the waiting carriage, she thought she had never in her life seen such a beautiful bride. She inched closer, smiling to see Guy tenderly handing Miriam into the carriage and then climbing in beside her. Oh, how he loves her, Kitty thought enviously. He can hardly take his eyes off her. And today, Kitty was relieved to see that Miriam looked happy too. She was laughing gaily and waving to all their relatives and friends, enjoying being the centre of attention. She will love him in time, I know she will, Kitty prayed.

She saw Guy about to give the order to the driver to move off, back to the Hall and no doubt to a sumptuous reception that awaited them and their guests, when Miriam touched his arm and said something to him. Then Kitty saw him smile and nod and Miriam stood up in the carriage holding the beautiful bouquet in her hand and looked around her, seeing the upturned, smiling faces. Her glance roamed over the throng. She appeared to be looking for someone. Then her gaze met Kitty's and for a long moment they stared at each other. Suddenly Miriam's smile broadened and Kitty heard her laugh aloud and say, 'There you are, Kitty Clegg . . .'

Before Kitty realized what was happening she heard Miriam call out, 'Catch!' and saw her throw the bouquet high into the air towards her. The crowd cheered and clapped with delight as Kitty put up her hands and caught the flowers, petals and leaves showering about her.

'Another wedding,' a voice called somewhere. 'Now there'll be another wedding.'

Kitty's eyes filled with tears as she smiled tremulously towards Miriam and waved her hand in thanks, but now Mrs Guy Harding had turned away, back to her new husband and the carriage was moving off, the crowd surging forward, following it as far as they could.

Kitty was left standing alone at the church gate staring after them, feeling strangely lost and suddenly very lonely.

It had been a kind gesture on Miriam's part, Kitty thought, and so much more lay behind it than the other watchers – even Mr Guy – could ever know. Kitty thought that it was Miriam's way of wishing her well, perhaps even a way of saying that she hoped Jack would, one day, marry her.

But that, thought Kitty sadly, bridal bouquet or not, would never happen.

Thirty-Eight

In the small kitchen of their cottage, Kitty was sitting near the warm range, Johnnie fast asleep in her lap, his head against her breast, his thumb in his mouth, when the door flew open and the February wind lifted the rug on the tiled hearth.

'It's all right for some with time to sit near the fire all day. Come on, rouse yarsen. I need help. The lad's not turned in. And get that boy's thumb out of his mouth. He's not a babby any more.'

Johnnie stirred and whimpered as he woke and Kitty saw Jack's lip curl. 'He's becoming a mother's boy. Soon be time I took him in hand and made a man of him.'

Kitty lifted the boy to his feet and got up herself. 'You'll do no such thing yet, Jack Thorndyke. Time enough. Now, what is it you want me to do?'

'The chaff hole. You'll have to mind the chaff hole. It's a mucky job, but I've no one else.'

Kitty shrugged. 'I've done muckier jobs in me time, but what about Johnnie? Do you want me to take him to me mam's.'

'No, it'll take too much time. He'll have to come with you. I'll put some straw in a barrel and he can stand in that and watch. That way your precious little boy will be safe from the rats.'

Kitty did not answer. She knew Jack was fond of his son, but he was the kind of man who expected a boy to

299

be rough and tough. But Johnnie was only two and a half, Kitty told herself again, time enough.

She wrapped Johnnie warmly against the blustery day and, leading him by the hand, they walked from the cottage to the Manor and entered the stackyard. For a moment, Kitty and the child stood watching, both fascinated by the scene before them. For the child, it was the first time he had been allowed close to such excitement and for Kitty, although she had often come into the yard during threshing days, she had never before taken the trouble to try to understand how things worked. Until this moment, she had always come to see Jack. Now the atmosphere of the yard enveloped her and drew her in. The air was filled with noise: the steady throb of the engine, the whirring wheels and belts, the rattle of bright metal rods and the hum of the thresher.

Jack stood on *Sylvie*'s footplate, his glance ever watchful of the water gauge, his ears listening to the rhythmic chug-chug of his engine, attuned to the slightest change. A young boy, with two buckets suspended from a yoke, carried water across the yard to the engine, while Jack himself jumped down to stoke the fire box with coal from a heap a few yards from the machine.

On top of the corn stack to be threshed, men swung loaded pitchforks to a man on the top of the drum. He cut the band and passed the sheaf to Ben, who, standing over the hole, laid the corn on his left arm and fed it steadily and evenly into the jaws of the rotating drum.

And already another stack was being formed by the straw falling from one end of the thresher on to the teeth of an elevator that carried it high and dropped it to the men waiting below who, skilled in their work, built a new stack with as much precision and care as a bricklayer would build a house.

'You going to stand there gawping all day?' Jack's voice made her jump. 'That chaff hole'll be choked if you don't keep it clear . . .'

Kitty moved forward to become part of the operation of manpower and machinery that worked in unison, each with their own part to play.

It was indeed the worst job on the threshing team. The chaff hole was where the chaff poured out of the drum just behind the small front wheels. Kitty spread the chaff sheet – a hessian sack cut open and tied at each corner with bands to pull it by – on the ground at the side of the machine. The dust and chaff flew everywhere, hazing the air. It clung to her hair, her clothes; it blocked her nostrils, tickled her throat and made her cough. It even stung her eyes and made them run, but doggedly Kitty stayed, raking the chaff on to the sheet and dragging it across the yard to the small chaff shed at the side of the barn.

She leaned against a post and pressed the palm of her hand to the small of her back, trying to ease the ache. She closed her eyes for a moment.

'Not quite the lady's maid now, are we?'

Kitty opened her eyes and turned to see Milly standing a few feet away. In the last three years Milly had grown and blossomed. Gone was the scrawny, lank-haired, rather pathetic, young girl. Now she was plump, but it was a roundness that was voluptuous. Her face was no longer pasty and her cheeks were smooth and pink with health. Even her hair, once so lank and colourless, was clean and shining. It was skilfully plaited and wound into a coil on the top of her head beneath her kitchen maid's cap.

A sharp retort sprang to Kitty's lips. 'Well, I see you aren't a lady's maid yet either?'

Milly laughed. 'I don't want to be, not to the likes of

the new Mrs Harding at the Hall anyway. No, I'm quite happy where I am, thank you very much. Mrs Grundy can't last for ever. She's getting on a bit and some days 'er legs are that bad, she can hardly stand.' The girl's smile widened slyly. 'I don't reckon it'll be long afore she gets thrown out because she can't do the job.'

There was not an ounce of pity in the girl's tone for a woman who had given a life of service.

'Mrs Franklin wouldn't throw her out.'

Milly shrugged uninterestedly. 'I expect she'll get a little cottage on the estate somewhere to see out her days. That's what usually happens, isn't it?'

'Selfish, that's what you are, Milly Clegg. Can't wait to step into the poor old dear's shoes, can you? Anyway, I can't stand here talking to you all day. Some of us have got work to do.'

As she moved away, she heard Milly say, 'I wouldn't swap jobs with you now, our Kitty, for all your fancy notions of being me lady's maid. Look where it's got you!'

Kitty did not look back but marched towards the chaff hole under the huge threshing drum.

They were getting near the last of the stack and the rats started to run from it as the forks drove deeper and deeper. Kitty glanced towards the barrel, checking that Johnnie was safe. The boy was watching with wide eyes and pointing at the scurrying vermin.

Jack climbed down from his engine. 'Ben, Ben, where's that useless mongrel of yours?'

Ben's rumbling laugh came from the top of the thresher where he stood to feed the drum. 'He'll be cowering at the back of the barn, I shouldn't wonder. Afeard of rats, he is, Jack.'

'Is he, begum? We'll soon see about that.'

He turned and walked towards the barn, whistling and

calling, 'Here, boy.' Then Kitty saw him glance towards Milly and nod and she saw her sister dip her head and slant her eyes coyly at Jack.

He can't stop it, can he? she thought bitterly. It's as if he can't even help it. Any girl and he has to flirt with them. Even me own sister.

At that moment, four huge rats scuttled out of the straw and ran wildly about the yard, one making a bee-line towards Milly. The girl screamed and clutched at her skirts. Holding them high, she ran towards Jack. He caught her up in his arms, lifting her feet high off the ground and swinging her round, laughing. Milly, safe now, laughed up into his face and though Kitty watched, her mouth tight, she neither spoke nor moved from her place by the chaff hole as she saw Jack carry Milly round the corner of the barn.

He was back in a few moments, however, carrying Ben's black and white terrier. He brought the dog to the diminishing stack and set it down. Rats of all sizes still appeared from the heap, but the minute Jack released his hold on the dog, it fled back to the deep shadows of the barn.

'Why, the little beggar!' Jack said and Ben's laugh could be heard again.

'I told ya, Jack, didn't I?'

Jack strode after the terrier, anger in every long stride. 'I'll teach you, you little runt.'

He came back carrying the struggling dog and went towards the barrel where Johnnie stood. Kitty threw down her rake and crawled out from the chaff hole, wiping away the dust and wisps of straw with the back of her hand.

Still keeping hold of the terrier in one hand, Jack lifted his son out of the barrel and set him on the ground. Then he reached down into the barrel and pulled out all the straw he had placed there for the boy to stand on.

'What doin'?' Kitty heard Johnnie ask as she drew near and put her hands on his shoulders.

'You'll see, lad,' Jack said grimly. Then he dropped the terrier into the depths of the now empty barrel, turned and strode towards the mound of wheat, still moving with vermin that had yet to escape. Kitty and the boy watched as Jack plodded into the last remnants of the stack, stamping with his feet. Then he was suddenly still and they saw him bend down to part the straw near his foot. They heard the squealing then and, a moment later, Jack held a rat aloft by its tail. He turned and came back towards the barrel.

Instinctively, Kitty drew Johnnie back, but the child pressed forward, crying, 'See, see, me see.'

She bent and picked him up in her arms, unsure what it was exactly that Jack meant to do. In a second, she knew. He stood by the barrel, holding the wriggling rat suspended in midair above the petrified terrier below. And then, with a grin that was almost evil, he dropped the rodent into the barrel.

There followed such a scuffling, yelping and squealing that Kitty drew back even further. 'Jack, no, oh no. Stop it at once. That's cruel.'

But Jack only laughed while in her arms Johnnie struggled, leaning towards the barrel and shouting. 'See, see.'

'Ben . . .' Kitty turned, yelling above the noise of the engine to the owner of the little dog. But Ben Holden, still on top of the drum, merely shrugged his huge shoulders and shook his head, making no effort to stop what Jack was doing.

The yelps of pain from the terrier were more than Kitty could bear. Holding the boy fast in one arm, she reached out with her other hand to tip over the barrel and free the poor trapped creature.

'Oh no, you don't, Kitty.' Jack, seeing her intention, grasped her wrist and held her back.

She glared up at him. 'You're a bastard, Jack Thorndyke.'

'Language, Kitty,' he remonstrated, laughing all the while. 'And in front of the boy too. Tut-tut.'

But Kitty was too incensed to care. 'A cruel bastard.'

'So I've always been led to believe, Kitty, because me father weren't the marrying kind either.'

'Oh.' Kitty pulled herself free. 'You!' was all she could say.

From the barrel came a yelp and then, suddenly, a growl, a low ferocious growl followed by a high-pitched squeal and then there was silence. The three of them looked at each other, Jack with a wide grin on his face, Kitty with puzzlement and the child reaching out with one arm, still crying, 'See, me see.'

Jack looked down into the barrel and then he tipped it over on to its side and the terrier trotted out carrying the dead rat in its jaws.

'Well, I'll be . . .' Kitty began as the dog laid the rat at Jack's feet and looked up at him, panting. There were patches of blood on the dog's coat and one paw was oozing, but in the animal's eyes there was triumph.

From the team of threshermen, who, though taking no part, had been fully aware of what was happening, there came a cheer. Jack reached down and patted the dog's head. 'Good dog.' Then, straightening, he raised his arm and gestured towards the stack. 'Go on then, boy. Fetch.'

To Kitty's amazement the dog now raced towards the depleted stack and burrowed beneath the straw. He emerged a moment later shaking a rat in his mouth. A quick nip and the rodent was dead. The dog dropped it and was back beneath the straw again.

'If I hadn't seen that with my own eyes, I'd never have believed it,' Kitty said.

Jack only laughed and began to move back towards the engine. 'It's a tough life, Kitty. Sometimes you have to be cruel to be kind. You can take the boy home now. We can manage.' He glanced back at her just once. 'You've done a good job today. Thanks.'

Kitty raised her voice and said, 'I thought for a minute you were going to pat me on the head and say "Good dog". Come on, Johnnie. I've had enough for one day.' She held out her hand to the boy. 'Let's go home.'

Though the boy walked alongside her, he was craning round to watch the dog and the rats until the last possible moment.

Thirty-Nine

'I'm sorry, Mr Guy, I really can't go to London again.'

'I don't like having to ask you, Kitty, but . . .' Guy Harding's deep voice, gentle smile and kind eyes melted Kitty's heart and, with it, her determination to refuse what he was asking her to do yet again.

'Please, Kitty,' Edward said. They were both here this time, standing in the small living room of the cottage, filling it with their presence.

'You see, it's because she's so involved with these women,' Guy went on, twirling his hat round and round between agitated fingers. 'She's gone to London to join in a big rally and I'm afraid for her safety.'

'They ban men from their meetings, you see,' Edward put in. 'Guy and I can't get anywhere near them. We need a woman, Kitty. We need *you*. You're the only one she might take notice of . . .'

His voice died, but the pleading in his eyes made Kitty say, 'Well, I would go, and gladly, but there's not only little Johnnie to think of.' She spread her hands in a helpless gesture. 'My mother usually takes care of him, but she's not well just now and I don't like to ask her. And there's something else too – Jack's short-handed with the threshing team. He's behind with the work now and I'm having to help out.'

'I could send another couple of men, if that would help,' Guy offered. 'And your son could come to the Hall. I'd make sure he was well cared for and that Mrs Bembridge understands.'

His mouth twitched and Kitty stared at him. It sounded almost as if Mr Guy was in awe of Mrs Bembridge too. Kitty shuddered. The Hall was the last place she wanted Johnnie to go and yet perhaps, because Miriam was away, it wouldn't matter. But what if awkward questions were asked? What if someone should remark on a likeness to his mother? No, no, Kitty reassured herself silently. That wasn't possible. The boy was the image of his father. There was no mistaking who the boy's father was and because of that, it helped to hide the identity of the mother.

But inwardly Kitty trembled. She didn't like the involvement. What if Jack should take it into his head to tell? Stop being silly, she told herself sternly. Jack Thorndyke had as much to lose as anyone if he revealed the secret. He'd be hounded out of the county most likely and never be able to work again in these parts.

She smiled a little uncertainly, and said, 'Well, if we can make arrangements, sir, I will come.'

'Thank you, Kitty,' Guy said and Edward smiled and nodded his thanks.

As she watched them walk away from the cottage, Kitty was overwhelmed with anger against Miriam. Why on earth can't she settle down and behave herself now? she thought crossly. She's got a lovely husband and a marvellous home and still she's not satisfied. The wayward girl was still disrupting all their lives with her rebellious spirit – even Kitty Clegg's.

Jack was surprisingly sanguine about Kitty going to London again, but it seemed that Mr Guy had 'made it worth his while' to agree. 'He's sending two of his own men over to help out and he says I can go up to the Hall for me tea while you're away and I can collect the boy and bring him home then.'

'Oh, I thought Johnnie was to stay there, I mean, sleep there. I don't think . . .'

Jack's face darkened. 'Think I can't look after me own son, Kitty?'

'No, no, Jack, I wasn't meaning that. Only that – only that it'd be a bother to you.'

The man shrugged his broad shoulders. 'No, he's growing into a real lad now. It's babies I can't abide.' He grinned and arched an eyebrow at her. 'And I've got to make sure he grows up into a real chip of the old block, now, ain't I?'

'Perish the thought,' Kitty retorted, but she was smiling as she said it.

'Where is this rally then?'

The three of them were hurrying along the platform towards the exit from the railway station.

'Trafalgar Square.' Guy glanced at Kitty. 'We'll go straight there, Kitty, if you're not too tired?'

Kitty smiled. 'Me, Mr Guy? No, I'm fine, thank you.' She was touched by his thoughtfulness, but was inwardly amused to think that he knew so little about the daily life of a servant, who scrubbed and washed and cooked from early morning until late at night without a moment's respite, that he thought a mere journey could exhaust her. To her, sitting on a train watching the countryside flashing past the window was like a holiday.

Guy hailed a cab and, as he gave their destination, the driver said, 'I don't think I'll be able to get close to the square today, sir. There's a big rally. These suffragette

309

women, you know. Hundreds of 'em, there's going to be, but I'll do my best . . .'

'We'll never find her, will we?' Kitty whispered as the cab jolted round corners and weaved among the other traffic.

'We must,' was all Guy said, grimly determined.

Edward was silent.

They alighted a street away from the square.

'Sorry, sir, that's as near as I can get.'

Around them as they walked were groups of women, all moving in the same direction. Some were smartly dressed, with white frilled blouses and trim, fitted jackets and broad-brimmed hats perched upon their heads. Others pulled shawls around their shoulders and their heads were bare, the shoes on their feet worn. There were young girls, linking arms and chanting the war cry of the suffragette movement, 'Votes for Women, Votes for Women', looking for all the world as if they had come to the city on a charabanc outing.

Perhaps they had at that, Kitty thought.

There were older women too, but all marched along side by side, united in their cause.

Kitty felt their fervour, recognized that if she had not been here on a mission of her own, she could very well have found herself swept along by their enthusiasm. She could understand how Miss Miriam could be caught up in it, especially, she thought sadly, if there was something lacking in her marriage and she was not entirely happy.

'I think Kitty's right,' Edward's voice broke into her thoughts. 'We'll never find her in this lot.'

She glanced at Guy's face. It was strained with anxiety. 'Edward, keep Kitty between us. I don't want her getting separated from us.'

'Right.' Kitty felt Edward take her arm and tuck it

firmly through his own. She glanced at him and he was looking down into her face, his expression serious. 'Ready for the fray?' he asked softly and she nodded. Women were arriving in the square from every road that converged on it. Ranks of police began to form lines across the roads as if to contain the gathering within Trafalgar Square and prevent more from joining in. But determined women still pushed their way through to join their colleagues. Now young girls climbed on to the lions at the four corners of the fountain and festooned the stone animals with banners. 'Votes for Women, Votes for Women.'

There was a murmur among a group of women near them, then voices were raised. 'Sylvia. Sylvia's been arrested... on her way here... they've arrested Sylvia Pankhurst... Sylvia... Sylvia... Sylvia...' The news spread and the murmuring grew to a crescendo until they were shouting and chanting with a burning anger. Banners and placards were held aloft and the women formed ranks and surged forward in a swelling wave of furious indignation.

'There she is,' Guy cried. 'There's Miriam. I saw her. Oh damn – I've lost her again.'

His glance raked the crowd and stretching up on tiptoe, Kitty too stared about her. 'There. There she is.' She pointed excitedly and pulled away from Edward's hold, thrusting her way through the throng, using her strength to forge a path.

'We're right behind you, Kitty,' she heard Guy's voice but did not look back. She just kept her eyes on the direction in which she'd seen Miriam and pushed ahead.

Now there were police among the crowd, trying to break up the gathering, trying to calm the growing agitation.

'Free Sylvia Pankhurst,' the chant began somewhere at

the edge of the square, spreading like wildfire. 'Free Sylvia Pankhurst.'

Kitty was about two yards away from Miriam, already reaching out to her, when she saw a policeman grasp Miriam's shoulders from behind. She saw her young mistress turn her head to look back and upwards to see who it was who held her and then, to Kitty's horror, she saw Miriam purse her lips and spit into the officer's face.

'Miss Miriam . . .' But Kitty's shocked cry came too late and the policeman with an expression of disgust tightened his hold upon the girl's shoulders and began to haul her, none too gently, through the crowd. As she screamed in protest, the women around her turned on the officer and began to claw at him and try to pluck Miriam from his grasp. The chaos spread and Kitty felt strong arms about her waist, but, turning, was thankful to see that it was Edward who held her fast. 'Keep out of it, Kitty,' he shouted, close to her ear. 'Let Guy deal with Miriam now. Look, he's almost there.'

Kitty gave up striving to reach her mistress and leaned back against Edward, thankful to leave everything to Mr Guy. They saw him reach his wife and stretch out his hand towards her, but the crowd, obviously thinking that he, a man, had come to the aid of the police constable, grabbed Guy and wrenched him backwards. Briefly, Kitty and Edward saw his arms flail helplessly. For a moment he seemed to rise in the air, as if he had been lifted off his feet, and then he plunged from their sight beneath the seething mass.

'Oh no,' Kitty cried out. 'Edward, we must reach him. He'll be trampled.'

Again she pushed her way forward, all the time aware of Edward holding fast to the back of her jacket, determined with all the strength of his being that she should not be torn from his grasp.

The shouting had lessened and the crowd were pulling back from the place where they had seen Guy fall to the ground. Even the policeman had stopped trying to effect the arrest on Miriam, and she, with a loud shriek of anguish, pulled herself from his hold and lunged forward, elbowing her way through the women to reach the man on the ground.

They reached him at the same moment, and Miriam fell to her knees. 'Oh Guy, Guy, no.' He was lying in the roadway, his body twisted and his head at an unnatural angle. There was a gash on his forehead oozing with blood. His eyes were wide open and staring and Kitty, as she looked down at him, knew with awful certainty that Mr Guy was dead.

She stood and watched as a weeping Miriam cradled her husband in her arms and rocked him. 'Oh Guy, I'm sorry. Forgive me. Oh God – Oh God – forgive me.'

Forty

'You know, Sir Ralph's a wonderful man, to forgive Miss Miriam like he has done. To think, through her thoughtlessness, he's lost his only son and heir and yet he's forgiven her and wants her to stay as mistress at the Hall.' Mrs Grundy shook her grey head and said again, 'He's a wonderful, Christian man.'

Kitty, sitting in the Manor House kitchen, leaned her arms on the table and sighed wearily. The previous two weeks had been the worst in Kitty's young life. After the inquest, Guy's body had been brought home for burial and it seemed as if the whole of the community of Tresford and the surrounding district had attended the funeral in the tiny church on the estate of Nunsthorpe Hall.

Miriam could not have been unaware of the whisper that ran through the congregation like a breeze as she entered the church following the coffin and leaning on her father-in-law's arm. The gossip would run riot through the county in the weeks that followed and though in time other events would push it from the forefront of people's minds, Kitty knew it would never be forgotten by the locals. It would become part of the Harding family's history, and an incident that had no pride, only shame, attached to it.

Even Mrs Grundy was giving vent to her feelings, she who usually would not hear a word against the family for whom she worked.

'It's changed her, Mrs G.,' Kitty said quietly in Miriam's defence. 'If you could have seen her when it happened, and after. She looked like a ghost.'

But Mrs Grundy was not convinced. 'It's all show if you ask me, to get sympathy. She's lucky not to have landed 'ersen in prison. The court was very lenient with her, dropping all charges in the circumstances. It's more than she deserves.'

Kitty stared at the cook in surprise. 'That's not like you, Mrs G., to be so hard.'

The woman wriggled her shoulders. 'Well, she's been a very silly girl and through her a lovely young man's lost his life.'

'But if you could see her,' Kitty persisted. 'She's going about in a dream.'

'A nightmare, more like,' Mrs Grundy muttered.

'Well, I think it serves her right,' Milly put in, banging a pile of plates on the table so hard that they rattled.

'Who asked you . . .? Kitty began.

Mrs Grundy twisted round with surprising agility. 'You mind your business, Milly, and watch what you're doing with them plates. Break just one and I'll have it stopped out of your wages.'

'Oh pardon me for breathing.' Milly tossed her head and flounced out of the kitchen.

Mrs Grundy shook her head. 'Eh dear, that girl. 'Ow she comes to be your sister, Kitty, beats me. She's a spiteful tongue in her head, that one.' She paused, deep in thought for a moment, and then, as if Milly's malicious tongue had made her think again, she sighed and said, 'Ah well, I suppose if Sir Ralph, of all people, can forgive her, then we should too.'

'I think so, Mrs G.,' Kitty said softly.

'Mebbe it isn't all her fault, at that.' Already the

kind-hearted cook was beginning to make excuses. 'She's been that indulged as a child, always had her own way . . .' she glanced up again and nodded at Kitty, 'until she came up against you, that is.'

Kitty gave a small, sad smile, but was thankful that it wouldn't be long before Mrs Grundy was once more defending Miriam fiercely.

'I must get back outside,' Kitty said. 'No peace for the wicked, eh?'

'There's going to be a war.'

Kitty paused in pounding clothes in the tub of soapy water and leaned on the long handle of the posser, smoothing the damp hair back from her forehead. 'So, all the rumours were true then?'

'Seems like it. All the young fellers are falling over themselves to join up.' Jack's mouth tightened. 'Even Ben's got caught up in the fever. And if he goes . . .'

Kitty made no answer. She knew Jack relied heavily on Ben Holden. They had worked together as a team for years, knew each other's ways. If Ben went, it would be very difficult for Jack to find anyone to replace him. She resumed her work, splashing the posser up and down. Above the noise, Jack said with a sly note creeping into his voice, 'I hear Master Edward was first in the queue to volunteer.'

The shock was so sudden and unexpected that, for once, Kitty could not hide her feelings. She paused again in her work and stared at him.

'Aye, I thought that'd mek you stare. Your precious Master Edward off to play the hero.'

Kitty said nothing and lowered her eyes. Poor Edward. Her heart twisted at the thought of him being maimed or even killed. She knew why he was doing it, of course. He was trying to prove to his father that he was not the weakling, the disappointment that Mr Franklin had always believed him to be. Edward meant to prove himself.

Keeping her voice calm, Kitty said, 'And what about you, Jack? Are you going to be a hero?'

His laugh was loud. 'Not me. I've a job to do here. Agricultural workers won't have to go. Not unless they want to, I reckon. Ben and all the rest of 'em are fools.'

But the day Edward came to say goodbye, Kitty thought her heart would break. He came upon her suddenly, so quietly that she did not hear him approach.

It was a Sunday afternoon and Kitty had taken Johnnie into the garden to play, keeping the boisterous little boy away from his father who was sleeping off his dinner and several pints of beer.

The child was laughing as Kitty chased him round the thick trunk of a tree. He darted first one way and then the other, avoiding capture and laughing louder each time he evaded her. 'Can't catch me. Can't catch me.'

'That's a pretty picture for me to remember, Kitty,' Edward said softly, unable to hide the catch in his voice and the longing. 'A happy picture of you and your son.'

They both looked up to see him standing there, so tall and resplendent in his uniform that Kitty caught her breath and Johnnie's eyes shone to see a real, live soldier.

'You got a gun?' Fascinated, the child moved closer, with no hint of shyness.

'Not yet, Johnnie.' Edward reached out and ruffled the boy's black hair. Johnnie grinned up at him.

Kitty bit her lip. She had never wanted anything more than to spill out the truth to him at this moment. It seemed cruel that Edward was saying goodbye to his own nephew and yet was completely unaware of the fact.

She blinked back the tears that threatened and said, 'Do you have to go, Master . . . Teddy?'

He was looking at her and smiling gently. 'Do you know, Kitty, I think that's the first time you've called me "Teddy" without having to be reminded.'

But Kitty was not going to allow him to make light of the moment. 'You once told me that you didn't think any cause was worth being a martyr for,' she persisted. 'But isn't that exactly what you're doing by volunteering for this war?'

'It's a bit different when one's country is threatened to whether women have the vote or not. Don't you think?'

Kitty smiled, a hint of mischief in her tone, yet she was still very serious. 'Perhaps the women who fight for the vote think that our country – and it is ours just as much as yours – is threatened when it's governed totally by men!'

'Why, you cheeky wench, Kitty Clegg. I do believe underneath you're as much a suffragette as Miriam.'

Their faces sobered as they remembered just what sacrifice Miriam's involvement in the movement had cost her.

Softly, he said, 'I think you, of all people, understand why I have to go, don't you, Kitty?'

She nodded. 'Yes.' Her voice was no more than a whisper. 'Yes, I do understand. But – but I don't want you to get hurt or – or . . .' She could not bring herself to name the dreadful fear that was in her heart.

He forced a cheerful laugh. 'Don't you worry about me, Kitty. Just – just take care of yourself and – and little Johnnie. Promise me, now?'

Her throat was so constricted by threatening tears that she could only nod dumbly.

'And,' he added softly, coming to stand very close to her and take her hands into his. She felt the gentle pressure

318

and suddenly she gripped his hands in return. 'Keep an eye on Miriam for me, won't you?'

'Yes, yes, I will.' There was a quaver in her voice as she tried to blink back the tears. She put her arms about him and he leaned his cheek against her hair. He was much taller than she was now and whenever she looked at him, she never failed to marvel at the straight-backed, handsome young man he had become. The pale, vulnerable invalid was now a distant memory, a shadow.

'Oh Teddy, Teddy, take care of yourself,' she whispered, overwhelmed with love for him. The realization shuddered through her. She loved this man deeply. Maybe she always had done, a true and steady love that was nothing like the infatuation she had felt for Jack Thorndyke. This was real love, when you loved someone more than you loved yourself. Like the love she felt for little Johnnie, yet different, oh so very different. She felt longing sweep through her and involuntarily her arms tightened about him. The strength of her feeling consumed her, overwhelmed her and almost frightened her. If she could have kept him here, safely with her, if she had been able to stop him marching away to war, she would have done so. She couldn't bear to let him go, yet she must, for she had no hold on him, could have no hold on him.

Not while she was bound to Jack.

It was as if he read her thoughts for, against her hair, he whispered softly so that the boy should not hear, 'Oh Kitty, Kitty, why are you so foolish over Thorndyke, when you're so strong, so positive, so – so sensible about everything else?'

Kitty pressed her lips together to still their trembling and tears welled in her eyes. Against his shoulder, she shook her head, not trusting herself to speak. If she were to say one word, just one word, then she was so afraid that the floodgates might open and she would spill out everything, all the hurt and misery that loving Jack had brought her. Her girlish infatuation had trapped her, shackled her for life, it seemed, to a man for whom she not only now had no love, but could not respect either.

If only . . .

She felt a tremor run through Edward and he released her suddenly and stepped away, but his eyes were still on her as he gave them both a smart salute, turned and walked away.

Only now, as he marched away from her, his back straight, did Kitty realize exactly how she felt about Edward Franklin.

She bent and scooped the child into her arms, clutching him with such a fierceness of love and longing that the boy struggled.

'Oh Johnnie, Johnnie, what a fool I've been.'

Forty-One

Even after the death of her husband, Miriam continued to live at the Hall, keeping house for Sir Ralph and helping to run the vast Nunsthorpe estate.

'She's thrown herself into it,' Edward had told Kitty just before that final visit when he had come to say goodbye. 'It's as if – as if – she's trying to make amends.'

'I think she is,' Kitty had said quietly. 'I haven't seen much of her since – since it happened, but she seems changed. Very subdued. Not at all like we think of Miss Miriam.'

Despite her married, or rather widowed status, Kitty could never think of her as anything but 'Miss Miriam'.

And now with Edward gone to war, there was nothing to prevent Kitty taking Johnnie to the Manor when she went to help Jack with the threshing, though she was careful to keep him in the stackyard or the kitchen area so that there was no chance of Mr and Mrs Franklin seeing him. Lately, Mrs Grundy had mellowed in her attitude and quite enjoyed spoiling the little chap with scones and butter and raspberry jam, although she was still disapproving of Kitty 'living in sin' with Jack.

'I know it's his bairn, Kitty, and I know you're besotted with the fellow, but . . .'

Kitty lowered her eyes and bit her lip, hiding the fact that over the months she had seen a new side to Jack Thorndyke, a side of him she did not like. In fact . . .

321

Mrs Grundy's voice intruded on her thoughts. 'Eh dearie me, these men have got a lot to answer for. Look at 'em now. Rushing to join up as if they're going on a picnic. It'll be no picnic, let me tell you. My nephew was in the Boer War and even though he wasn't injured, he came back that unsettled, he didn't work for two years.' She shook her wise head sadly. 'No, the young fellers don't know what they're letting themselves in for. Look at Master Edward now. We all know why he's joined up. Just to make his father proud of him. But what good's a dead hero to a mother, eh? You answer me that, Kitty. How would you feel if it was your little lad there they was taking for cannon fodder?'

Kitty shuddered and her fingers, resting on Johnnie's shoulder, tightened involuntarily.

'Oh, and talking about your bairn, that reminds me. Madam asked to see the little lad next time you came over.'

'Madam?' Kitty's head jerked up. 'Mrs Franklin wants to – to see Johnnie?'

Mrs Grundy nodded. 'Sarah, run up and ask madam if it's convenient.'

'Oh, but I don't know if I ought to take him up there . . .' Kitty began, scrabbling around for a plausible excuse. Any excuse. But the maid had gone.

'But she's asked to see him, Kitty,' Mrs Grundy insisted. 'You'll have to take him.'

When the parlourmaid, resplendent in a smart black dress and crisp white apron with a fancy bib, returned to say that madam was waiting for them, Kitty wondered, for a brief moment, what her life would have been like if she had not become embroiled, not only with Jack, but with Miriam and her son. A safe, yet dull existence, she supposed. As she scooped the boy up into her arms, she thought, but then there would be no little Johnnie. She hugged him to her and felt his chubby little arms creep about her neck and his soft cheek rub against her own. He was her life now and nothing and no one would part them.

As she followed Sarah, Kitty felt a tremor of fear. The boy was about to meet his real grandmother and Mrs Franklin was a sweet-natured woman. What if, after all, she fell for the little boy's charms and wanted to acknowledge his existence? Perhaps she *could* take him away from her.

The door was opening in front of her and she was stepping into her former mistress's sitting room. Mrs Franklin looked up from her needlework and at once Kitty saw the expression in her eyes soften as she looked upon her grandson, her only grandchild. Her voice was not quite steady as she patted the place beside her on the sofa and said, 'Come and sit down, Kitty.' But her gaze never left the boy's face. Johnnie, standing beside Kitty and leaning against her knee, smiled up at the strange lady without a trace of shyness.

'He's a handsome little chap,' Mrs Franklin murmured, still staring at him.

'Yes, madam,' Kitty began. 'He's like . . .' She had been about to say 'like his father' but then, thinking that the mention of Jack Thorndyke would bring back unhappy memories to this woman, Kitty said instead, 'He's got a lovely, sunny nature too, ma'am. He's a bit mischievous and a mite too adventurous for my peace of mind – but then he's a real boy,' she added indulgently and there was a note of pride in her voice. 'He loves to get out into the fields to be with the men. He even tries to help them and his dad . . .' She hesitated, but there was no avoiding mention of the child's father. 'He's made him a set of wooden tools.'

323

Mrs Franklin was smiling down at him. 'How wonderful it must be,' she murmured, 'to have such a healthy, sturdy little boy, even if he is a handful for you, Kitty.' She cast an amused glance at her.

'Yes, madam.' There was a pause and then Kitty said, 'I'm sorry but I must go. There's work . . .'

'Of course, I'm sorry. But if you want to leave Johnnie with me for an hour or so . . .?'

Kitty's heart froze. Was this it? Was this the beginning of Mrs Franklin's change of heart? Did she want her grandson?

Her sudden fear made her speak sharply. 'No, no, madam. I'd best take him with me. Keep him with me.' She couldn't help the slight emphasis on the word keep. When she saw the sudden pain in the older woman's eyes, she knew that Mrs Franklin had noticed it and recognized its meaning too.

But with her usual serenity, Mrs Franklin said, 'Of course, Kitty, I do understand.'

And in her words, too, there was unmistakable meaning.

'So, it's not going to be over by Christmas like they all said,' Jack said with a sneer in his voice. 'Here we are in January and, by all accounts, both sides are digging in. Silly fools! Throwing up their jobs and rushing off to volunteer to be heroes. How am I supposed to cope with young boys and women in me threshing team?'

They were working at the Manor, and while Kitty always made sure she left Johnnie with either her own mother or Mrs Grundy, she was nevertheless obliged to come to help Jack. Daily, it seemed, more and more of the men were volunteering. She said nothing in reply to Jack's statement, but smiled inwardly. Already women were beginning to take over many of the jobs that the men had left behind. Perhaps this was the way they could prove themselves. Perhaps this was what they needed, as Edward had once suggested, to show themselves worthy of being given the vote. Maybe this way . . .

Jack's voice broke into her thoughts again. 'What about Milly? Would she help out, d'ya reckon? Or is she a lady's maid now?'

Kitty glanced down at her hands. For the brief time she had been Miss Miriam's maid, her hands had been well cared for. Now they were as rough and chapped and calloused as when she had been a lowly scullery maid at thirteen.

She looked up and met Jack's eyes. 'I doubt it,' she said shortly. 'Our Milly's got her eye on takin' over the cook's job.'

She saw Jack's glance go beyond her, over her shoulder. 'Talk of the devil,' he murmured and the smile on his mouth widened.

Kitty turned and saw Milly coming across the yard towards them carrying a basket covered with a checked cloth.

As she drew closer, she glanced at Kitty and nodded briefly, but it was to Jack that she aimed her sly smile. 'I've been baking and I thought you'd like a hot scone straight out the oven.'

'Plenty of butter, I hope, young Milly.'

'Lashings of it, Jack. Just the way you like it.' Provocatively, Milly ran her tongue round her lips.

Jack reached out and tickled Milly under her chin. 'Oh you know what I like, don't you, Milly?'

The girl bridled coyly but did not pull back. Kitty waited for the shaft of jealousy to strike through her but, to her amazement, it did not come. The only emotion she felt was a strange kind of pity. Pity for Jack that he still could not resist flirting with any girl he met, and for Milly too, as she, like so many before her, began to fall under Threshing Jack's spell.

'Thanks, our Milly.' Kitty dropped her rake and moved deliberately forward. 'I've been wanting to see what a famous cook you're becoming.'

Milly blinked and said, 'Oh, I ain't brought one for you, Kitty. 'Tain't good for that skinny figure of yourn. Besides,' she added, as if quickly trying to think up an excuse, 'Mrs Harding wants to see you.'

'Mrs . . .? Oh, you mean Miss Miriam?' She kept her gaze steadfastly on her sister and did not even glance at Jack. 'Me? Why does she want to see me?'

Milly shrugged. 'How should I know? She don't confide in the kitchen staff. She's here visiting her mother and saw you from the window.' There was a pause, but Milly made no move to take her there. 'Well, are you going or not? She's waiting.'

'I can't go into the house like this. I'm covered in chaff.'

Milly shrugged. 'Please yourself. I'll tell her I've given you the message.'

'Oh, all right then.'

Kitty leaned the rake against the side of the drum, dusted herself down as best she could and let herself through the gate in the wall leading to the house.

Moments later, in Mrs Franklin's sitting room, Miriam was saying, 'Ah Kitty. I was wondering when I might have a chance to see you.'

So, thought Kitty shrewdly, she had not asked specifically for her at this moment. That had been Milly's devious ploy. She wondered why and what lay behind it.

Miriam was moving towards the chair where her coat

lay and feeling in the pockets. 'I have a letter for you here somewhere. Now where did I put it?'

'A letter, miss? For me?'

'Mm. From Teddy – Master Edward,' Miriam corrected herself, knowing nothing of the fact that Teddy was the name he insisted Kitty should call him when no one else could hear.

'Ah – here we are. It's a week old, I'm afraid. I am sorry. I meant to get it to you earlier, but I've been so busy, so caught up in plans.'

She held the folded letter out to Kitty. 'He sent it in one to me. He didn't want to cause embarrassment to you by sending it to you direct.'

Kitty took the single sheet of paper between her fingers. 'Thank you, miss.'

'If you want to write back, Kitty, and I hope you will for it's dreadful out there for all our boys, I can send it with my next letter, though after that I don't expect to be here.'

Kitty's eyes widened. 'Not here, miss? But where are you going? Oh no,' she breathed, suddenly afraid. 'Oh no, miss, not back to London. You wouldn't. . . .?'

Miriam was shaking her head, her lips pressed together as if to stop them trembling. 'No, Kitty. I wouldn't be so foolish as to get caught up in all that again, even though I still have great sympathy for the Cause. Besides . . .' She moved about the room, touching an ornament, a book lying open on a small table. There was an air of restlessness about her, a tension. Kitty watched her. 'Besides, the suffragettes are suspending all their activities while the war's on, you know.'

'No, miss. I didn't know. I – I don't really follow what's happening with – with all that.'

'No,' Miriam glanced at her and then away again. 'No,

I don't suppose you do.' There was a pause and then she added, her voice slightly higher pitched, 'Miss Pankhurst, Miss Sylvia Pankhurst sent me such a kind letter of condolence, you know.'

'Did she, miss?'

'Yes, yes, she did. But it didn't help. It – it couldn't bring him back, could it?'

Quietly, Kitty said, 'No, miss.'

Miriam was moving around the room again, her hands clasped in front of her. 'Kitty, I've got to do something. I can't stay here just playing at being the mistress of the Hall. I've volunteered to become a VAD nurse. That's why I've come today. To tell my mother that I'm going to train as a nurse and go out to the Front. Oh Kitty . . .' She whirled around and now her eyes were shining with some of their old fire. 'Why don't you come with me?' She rushed across the room and grabbed Kitty's hands in her own. 'Oh please, Kitty, come with me. Think of all the good we could do, the two of us.'

'I can't, miss. For some things I wish I could, but I really can't. I can't leave him . . .'

Miriam released Kitty's hands as if they had stung her. 'Him?' Now her voice was almost hysterical. 'Him? Jack Thorndyke? You won't leave him?'

But Kitty was shaking her head and her answer shocked even her as the words left her lips. 'No, miss. I don't mean Jack. It's Johnnie I can't leave. Little Johnnie.'

Miriam stared at her for a long moment, her eyes wide, her mouth slightly open. Suddenly a fleeting pain showed deep in her eyes and then she swallowed as if there was a great lump in her throat. 'Of course.' Her voice was husky. 'I was forgetting. Of course you can't leave – your son.'

Forty-Two

The letter from Edward was friendly and said nothing that could not be shown to anyone. Nevertheless, Kitty kept its arrival a secret from Jack. And to do so, it was necessary for her to destroy it, for there was no place where he might not, some day, find it.

But it didn't matter, she told herself, for by the time she dropped it into the glowing coals of the range, she knew the letter by heart.

My dear Kitty,

There's not much I can tell you really for, because I am an officer and have to censor the soldiers' letters home, I know too, what I must not put myself. Enough to say I am homesick and miss everyone, but the comradeship and the spirit out here are magnificent. I hope you are well. My regards to your son, and tell him the soldier now has his gun, though, Kitty, I wish with all my heart now, that I did not have it. I didn't know what it would be like. I just didn't know. I wish I were fourteen again and back in my room at home . . .

His words had escaped the censor's pencil for in themselves they said nothing, but to Kitty, who knew exactly what those last few words really meant, they told her everything. At fourteen, poor Master Edward had been suffering the life of an invalid and he was telling her that even that life would be preferable to the one he was now leading.

He was telling her that where he was at this moment was hell on earth.

'Oh Teddy, Teddy,' she whispered into the flickering flame. 'Come home safely.'

And now, too, there was Miss Miriam to worry about.

'What will that silly girl do next?' Mrs Grundy ranted, slamming down the rolling pin so hard on the pastry she was rolling out that, sitting at the opposite end of the table, Kitty felt the vibration. 'Madam's sick with fear. First Master Edward, who she's convinced will never come back, and now Miss Miriam fancies herself soothing the fevered brow and bandaging handsome soldiers.'

'I don't think Miss Miriam has any illusions, Mrs G.,' Kitty said quietly. 'I think she's heard enough from T— ... Master Edward's letters to realize what it must be like out there.'

The back door was flung open and crashed back against the wall, then they heard his stride and he was standing in the kitchen doorway. Kitty rose quickly to her feet. 'I'm coming, Jack. I was just—'

'Do you know who's responsible for this?' His voice boomed and his face was thunderous.

'Responsible? For – for what?'

'You.' He jabbed his finger towards the cook. 'Is it you, or one of your silly kitchen maids?'

Mrs Grundy puffed out her chest in indignation. 'Ya can stop ya ranting in my kitchen, Jack Thorndyke. Sit down and have a cup of tea and tell us what's biting ya.'

'Sit down? Sit down, you say? I've a good mind never

to set foot in this place again. Aye, an' I've a mind to tek me threshing tackle and leave his stacks to rot.'

Mrs Grundy and Kitty exchanged a stricken glance. 'Jack, what—?' Kitty began but Jack took a step towards her and opened his clenched fist. On his palm, curling innocently, lay a white feather.

'This. This was on me engine.'

Mrs Grundy gasped and Kitty stared at the pretty thing lying in his strong hand. But its meaning was not pretty.

'Who,' he thundered, 'put it there?'

'Jack, maybe no one put it there,' Kitty tried to calm him. 'There's feathers blowing all around the yard. Mebbe it just blew on to your engine.'

Jack spoke slowly and deliberately through clenched teeth. 'It was fastened to the wheel. Tied on with a bit of straw. That's no accident.'

To this Kitty could make no reply.

Mrs Grundy seemed to recover first. 'Tek no notice, Jack.'

'I bet it's one of the farmhands,' he growled. 'They're leaving in droves. I'll have no one left except Ben and women and bairns to work the tackle soon.' He flung the feather to the floor, turned and strode outside again.

'I'd better go and help, Mrs G.'

'Aye, lass, you go. Bring the lad in here, I'll keep an eye on him. Looks like you're going to have ya hands full with 'im.' She nodded her head towards the departing figure of Jack striding away down the garden path.

He worked himself like a maniac and, like a tyrant, he drove the few workers left until they were almost dropping with exhaustion.

Kitty, still with the worst job of all at the chaff hole, worked doggedly until her hair was clogged with dust, her throat parched and her eyes stinging and watering from the dust and with tiredness too. But still she worked on, uttering no word of complaint. Jack was like a man possessed, flinging coal into the fire box, pouring gallons of water into the tender. Poor *Sylvie* had never worked so hard in her life.

'Ya'll have yon belt breaking,' Ben nodded towards the governor belt, 'if you drive 'er too hard.'

Jack, climbing to the top of the drum to help feed in the crop, merely glowered at his workmate. Shaking his head, Ben calmly carried on working at his own pace, steadfastly refusing to have his rhythm disturbed by Jack's temper.

But in the end it was Ben, big, quiet Ben Holden, who at last threw down his pitchfork and climbed down from the top of the drum. 'I'm doing no more work today, Jack. I'm fair done in and if I work another minute, I'll be toppling into yon drum along o' the sheaves. Call it a day, man. We're all fit to drop and as for young Kitty there, why, I don't know how that lass is still standing upright.'

'You mind ya own business, Ben,' Jack growled, 'where she's concerned and leave me to mind mine.'

The two men glared at each other, standing only a foot apart, yet Ben thrust his face even closer. He was perhaps the only one there who could match Jack Thorndyke in physical strength. 'Well, if that's ya attitude, Jack, I'll be away to me home and me family and come the morning, I'll be going into the town to volunteer.'

'What? Don't be a fool, man. There's no need for you to go.'

'No, there's no need. I know that, Jack. But there's a need within me. I've been feeling it. Me, a big strong chap, staying safely at home while others not 'alf as strong have gone to fight for their country. And I've no wish to find a white feather tied to me pitchfork one morning.'

There was silence around them now, for all the workers had downed their tools and were listening to the exchange between the two men.

Jack reached out and grasped the front of Ben's jacket, but the big man caught hold of Jack's wrist and they stood, locked together, neither giving way, just glaring at each other.

'Did you – put that – that *thing* on my wheel?'

'No, Jack, I didn't. You should know me better than that after all the years we've worked together. Nor do I know who did. But the way you're so upset about it, it must have struck a chord of guilt somewhere in you, now mun't it?'

Jack let out an angry curse and flung the man away from him. 'Go then. Go, and good riddance. I don't need you.' He flung his arm out to encompass all of them standing around. 'I don't need any of you.'

He turned and strode away, disappearing into the gathering dusk while the other workers dispersed, muttering among themselves.

'I'm sorry, lass,' Ben said. 'I didn't mean it to happen like this. I was going to tell him, all quiet like, get him to see how I feel, but with this feather business . . .'

Kitty laid her hand on the big man's arm. 'I know, Ben, I know. But I wish you weren't going.'

'Aye well,' he said, his big shoulders drooping suddenly. 'I feel it's me duty.'

Kitty smoothed back the hair from her damp forehead. 'I must go and get Johnnie and go home. Take care of yourself, Ben.'

*

It seemed as if they were the words she was saying far too often these days. First to Edward, then to Ben, and now here she was standing awkwardly beside Miss Miriam on the station platform, waiting for the train that would take her to London to become a VAD nurse.

'Do take care of yourself, Miss Miriam.'

Miriam smiled thinly and her voice was husky as she said, 'I only wish you were coming with me, Kitty . . .' adding so softly that Kitty hardly heard the words, 'this time.'

They were both remembering the last time they had stood on this platform.

More strongly, Miriam said, 'And you take care of yourself. You're looking dreadfully tired these days, Kitty. And I'm sure you've lost weight.'

'It's just the work, miss. With all the fellers going off to the war . . .' She did not need to say any more for Miriam nodded.

'I know. But look after yourself and – and Johnnie.'

It was the first time Kitty could remember Miriam saying her son's name, actually voicing his name aloud.

There was a whistle from down the line and a sudden flurry of activity cut off any further conversation. When the train drew in, the porter loaded Miriam's luggage into the guard's van and then she was on the train and leaning out of the window and waving. 'Thank you for coming to see me off. I didn't want Mother to come. She's upset enough.' She pulled a face. 'And as for Father, well, I'm not exactly in favour at the moment. I'll write, Kitty, and you must write back and tell me all the news about – about everyone.'

Kitty nodded and tears prickled her eyelids as she waved her hand in farewell. When the train was a distant speck,

Kitty was still standing on the edge of the platform staring down the line.

Miriam had said his name. For the first time ever she had spoken of her son. But instead of bringing joy to Kitty, it was like a knife in her heart.

Forty-Three

In the month that the war entered its third year, Johnnie was five years old. When threshing started in the winter of that year, Jack decided that his son was old enough to help. 'He can carry the water to the barrel near the engine and release an older boy for other work.'

'Don't be daft, Jack. He's too little,' Kitty argued.

Jack glared at her. 'I worked alongside me father and me uncle for as long as I can remember. It never hurt me.'

Kitty returned his glare placidly. Quietly, she said, 'Have you really no memory at all of your mother? Or – or of any woman? Didn't anyone try to stop you being put to work so young?'

The frown on his handsome face deepened and the shadow that Kitty had once before seen in his eyes was there again. His voice was full of harsh bitterness. 'I've told you before, I don't know owt about me mother, at least . . .' His voice dropped as he added, 'At least not much.'

Sudden realization flooded through Kitty. She stepped forward and put her hand on his arm, moved to deep compassion for this man. 'But – you knew her name, didn't you, Jack?'

His eyes were dark as he looked down into hers. Slowly he nodded and his voice was no more than a hoarse whisper. 'Aye, that's all I did know. All I ever knew about her was her name.'

Very softly, Kitty murmured, 'Sylvie.'

And now, all Jack could do in reply was to nod, for in that moment he could not speak.

Kitty put her arms about him and laid her head against his chest. 'Johnnie can help in the yard, Jack, just so long as you don't expect him to do more than he can manage. And I'll be there to keep me eye on him.' She leaned back now to look up at him, and smiled, trying to lighten the anguish the man had relived for a brief moment. 'Because I'm Queen of the Chaff Hole now, aren't I?'

She was relieved to see a smile curve his mouth. 'It's not the best of jobs, Kitty. But at least it's safe. I can't risk you disappearing down into the drum, if I was to let you go up on top.'

For an instant his arms were tightly about her and he bent his head and kissed her hard on the mouth. He rubbed his face against her hair and then sighing said, 'I must go. I've got the boiler tubes to clean out and steam to get up before the men arrive. Sir Ralph's sending some of his lads over this morning.'

She smiled too. 'Right you are. We'll be there by the time you're ready to start.'

When Kitty told Johnnie what had been decided, he jumped up and down and clapped his hands. Kitty had to laugh. 'Anyone would think I'd just told you it was Christmas tomorrow.'

The boy grinned up at her. 'It's better than Christmas. I won't have to go to school, will I?'

'Oh yes, you will, me lad. You're not getting out of that.'

The boy's face fell. 'Aw Mam . . .' he began.

She ruffled his head and promised, 'But you can help after school and at weekends.'

They arrived in the yard to find four young boys she

had not seen before standing about looking as if they didn't know what to do. Jack was not quite ready to begin. He was still oiling up and, every so often, stoking the fire. 'Ten minutes, Kitty, and she'll be up to pressure,' he called. 'Can you explain what they have to do?'

Kitty nodded and raised her hand in acknowledgement. Then she turned to the young men. For a moment she glanced around at their boyish faces. 'Nathaniel should be here in a minute,' she said, referring to the elderly man who now helped Jack in Ben Holden's place. 'Between them, he and Jack run the engine and feed the drum on the top. One of you can go up there with Jack as band cutter for him – that's to cut the twine round the sheaves as they're passed down to you from the stack.' She paused, calculating. There were not nearly enough of them to do all the jobs. Sighing, she went on, 'We'll have to manage with one on the stack being threshed and only one instead of two on the straw stack.' She pointed with her finger towards the elevator positioned at the end of the drum. That was where the straw was thrown out by the beaters and fell on to the tines, to be carried up and dropped over the end to build another stack. 'You . . .' She put her hand on the shoulder of the fourth boy, not yet assigned to a job. Of the four, he looked the strongest. She smiled ruefully. 'You and me will have to cope with everything else. I'll mind the chaff hole and, in between, carry the coal across. Can you manage the bag end where the grain comes out? It's heavy work 'cos you have to barrow the full sacks into the barn yonder.'

'Yes, missis. I'll manage.'

'Good . . .' Kitty stopped. She had been about to say 'boy', but these lads were to do men's work and deserved the title. 'Good man,' she said.

The boys glanced at each other, grinned and shuffled

their feet, but Kitty had the feeling that one little word would have them working for Jack Thorndyke until they dropped.

'What am I to do, Mam?' She turned to see Johnnie standing close by, listening wide-eyed to everything she was saying.

She held out her hand to him but the boy ignored it. She let it fall to her side, feeling a pang of regret that already he was growing up. So soon, she mourned in her heart. But she forced a smile and said, 'I've just had a good idea. Mrs G.'s got some smaller buckets in her kitchen. I'm sure she'd let us use them. Come on.'

'I can manage the big one,' Johnnie frowned, his glower so like Jack's that Kitty's heart constricted.

She bent towards him. 'I know you *could* manage it, of course,' she agreed tactfully. 'But this way, you'll be able to carry two, one in each hand to balance the load. Just like your dad does.'

The boy grinned, his fierce pride appeased, and followed her towards the house. Moments later they were standing in Mrs Grundy's kitchen.

'Why, Kitty lass, and little Johnnie too. Come to keep me company for the morning, 'ave you?' She leaned towards him. 'I've a fresh batch of scones'll be out of the oven in five minutes.'

The boy licked his lips, but said firmly, 'I'm working today. I'm helping me dad.'

Mrs Grundy straightened up. 'Oho, a working man, is it? Ah well then, you'll be wanting a man's breakfast along with the rest, eh?' She chuckled and then glanced up at Kitty. 'An' you could do with feeding up a bit, lass. I reckon you get thinner every time I see you.'

'Mrs G., you're sharper than a drawer full of knives,' Kitty smiled, but did not contradict the cook. Then her face sobered. 'It's been difficult for Jack, you know, with all the best men going off to the war. Ben joining up was the last straw.' She gave a quick laugh. 'Hark at me mekin' jokes and it's no laughing matter.'

The cook shook her grey head. 'No, I know it isn't. And last week, when there was several local lads' names in the casualty lists, well, I'm sorry to say it, but the feeling against Jack for not going is getting stronger.'

'Is it? Oh no,' Kitty groaned. 'I just hope he doesn't get to hear about it.'

Milly, coming in from the scullery, said, 'Even Bemmy was ranting on about him yesterday.'

Mrs Grundy's mouth tightened. 'You listening at doors again?'

The girl shrugged. 'I can't help hearing what's said in here when I'm in the scullery. You've got a very loud voice, Mrs Grundy,' she smirked. 'Didn't you know?'

'Mebbe so, but I need it to keep you in line,' the cook snapped.

Milly turned to her sister. 'You want to tell that man of yours to watch himself on a dark night.'

'Whatever do you mean?'

'Haven't you heard?' The girl's face was alight with malicious glee. 'There was a feller over Nunsthorpe way walking home from the pub three nights ago. He's another who ought to be fighting for his country. Well, he was set on by some lads. They poured whisky down his throat till he was just about senseless, then they dragged him to the recruiting office and made him sign up.' Milly was laughing now. 'When he sobered up, he was on a train to an army camp.'

'And you think that's funny, our Milly?'

'Serves 'im right for being a coward.'

340

'I don't believe you. They couldn't do that. What about the recruiting officer? He wouldn't have acted that way.'

'They broke into the office and filled out the papers themselves.'

'But it wasn't legal then.'

Milly shrugged. 'It's what I heard.'

'It couldn't happen,' Kitty insisted and added drily, 'I wouldn't put it past you to make it up, Milly.'

'Suit yourself,' the girl shrugged. 'I ain't bothered if you believe me or not.'

'There's a lot of funny things happening nowadays,' Mrs Grundy sighed. 'Not very nice things either. Anyway, Kitty, what was it you wanted?'

'Eh? Oh yes,' Kitty dragged her thoughts back to the reason she had come into the kitchen. 'You used to have some small buckets under the sink, Mrs G. Jack wants Johnnie to carry water from the pump in the yard to the water barrel near the engine. I was wondering if . . .?'

'Of course you can 'ave them, and welcome.' Already Mrs Grundy was waddling towards the sink and bending down. 'Here they are.'

The day went surprisingly well. The young boys worked harder and longer than Kitty would have believed possible and even little Johnnie, following a nap after dinner, managed to carry as much water across to the barrel as Jack needed to run the engine for the whole day.

But the evening found the boy, and Kitty too, quite exhausted and they were both in bed before the sun had set. The following morning, however, Johnnie was up and trotting after his father as he left to complete all the necessary jobs before the rest of the workers arrived.

'You don't need to go yet, Johnnie.'

'I want to,' the boy called back over his shoulder, trying to match his father's huge strides. Jack turned too, winked broadly, and raised his arm in a wave.

Kitty stood in the doorway of the cottage, watching them walk across the field towards the Manor. Two dark heads glinting in the early morning sunlight streaming across the flat fields. The man marched with long, easy strides, his arms swinging while his son skipped and hopped alongside him, glancing up every so often towards his father, his piping little voice echoing back to her. 'Are you going to show me how to start *Sylvie*, Dad? I know how to stop her because I saw how you did it yesterday . . .'

Now she could no longer hear him but she knew he was still talking, still asking questions and she shook her head, smiling fondly.

It was a happy picture; a picture that Kitty was to keep in her heart and remember. It was an image to treasure and down the years Kitty was to wish, countless times, that she could turn the clock back to that last moment of contentment.

Forty-Four

'Mam, Mam. Come quick!'

Johnnie was back before she had finished her early morning chores ready to join them in the yard. She stood up from banking down the fire in the range and ran to the back door.

The boy was breathless, leaning against the wall outside the door. 'You must come. Me dad—'

Kitty clutched at him. 'What is it? What's happened? Is he hurt?'

Panting, Johnnie shook his head. 'Just come and see.'

She hurried after him, her heart thumping painfully, fear rising in her throat and threatening to choke her. Oh Jack, Jack, what now?

As she turned the corner of the stables and saw the machinery she stopped suddenly. 'No, oh no,' she breathed.

The threshing engine was daubed with some thick black stuff and over it all had been flung a bag of white feathers. Most clung to the sticky substance, but some fluttered freely, blown about the engine and the yard.

Jack was standing, his arms akimbo, just looking at his beloved engine.

She moved towards him and put her hand on his arm. She could feel his anger in every muscle. 'Oh Jack. Poor *Sylvie*. It's not – not tar they've used, is it?' She'd heard tales about tarring and feathering a person. But this . . .

He didn't answer but moved closer and ran his finger

along one of the rods, picking up some of the stuff. Then he put his finger to his nose and sniffed it. 'No,' he said. Then she saw him lick his finger. 'It's treacle. Black treacle.'

'Treacle!' she repeated. She blinked at him. 'Treacle,' she whispered again. Treacle came from a kitchen.

With a sudden, jerky movement she turned about, picked up her skirts and ran towards the house. Past the stables and through the gate in the side wall, she rushed in front of the windows of the master's room, not even caring if he saw her.

Crashing open the kitchen door, she cried, 'Where is she? Where's that spiteful sister of mine?'

Mrs Grundy turned startled eyes to her. 'Milly? She's upstairs in Master Edward's old room, giving it a good going over . . . Hey, where do you think you're going?'

But Kitty had dodged around the table and was through the door and down the steps leading into the hall. She took the servants' stairs two at a time and then, twisting and turning through the passageways, came to Edward's bedroom. The door was slightly ajar and she could hear Milly singing as she worked, shaking the feather bed and banging the dust from it.

Kitty pushed the door wider. 'You might well sing, our Milly.'

'Oh! It's you, Kitty. You made me jump. What are you doing up here? Shouldn't you be—?'

Kitty marched into the room and round the bed. She reached out and grabbed her sister by the hair.

'Kitty – ouch! Whatever's got into you?'

'Come here. Look.' She pulled the girl towards the window. 'Down there. Did you do that? Did you take a tin of Mrs Grundy's treacle and daub it all over *Sylvie* and then chuck an old feather pillow over it? 'Cos if you did . . .'

The girl's eyes widened as, above the wall, she saw the outline of the engine, saw the feathers, like snow, upon its surface. 'No, no, Kitty. I didn't . . . I wouldn't. Honest.'

Kitty tightened her grip on Milly's hair and twisted her wrist. The younger girl cried out. 'Honest, Kitty. I didn't. I admit I put that one on his steering wheel a while back, but no, I wouldn't do that. Not all that. I like Jack. You've got to believe me. Please, Kitty.'

Kitty released her as suddenly as she had taken hold of her and Milly, losing her balance, fell to the floor. Kitty bent over her. 'Do you know who did do it? Have you any idea? Was it them same lads you were on about setting on that poor feller?'

'I don't know. Could 'ave been,' the girl muttered morosely and as Kitty reached out again, she said, 'I don't know, honest, Kitty. But there are one or two folks in the town who's lost their boys and they don't take kindly to Jack still being safely here.'

'Who?'

'I don't know,' she insisted again. 'Honest. I just heard Bemmy telling Mrs G.'

'Bemmy? You don't mean that Bemmy . . .?'

Milly was shaking her head violently so that two hairpins dislodged themselves and hung down over her ear. 'No, no, he wouldn't do summat like that. He'd tell Jack to his face exactly what he thinks about him.'

She was right about that, Kitty thought. Bemmy might be a grumpy old man but he was not the sort who would skulk around in the night smearing treacle and feathers over machinery. She sighed. It must have been someone from the town. Perhaps some poor soul who had lost a loved one and it had affected their mind. Perhaps, she thought, her anger dying, the perpetrators were more to be pitied than blamed.

'I'm sorry if I misjudged you, Milly.' She wagged her finger at her. 'But you can hardly blame me, seein' how you were talking the other day and now you've admitted you did put that other feather on his wheel. How could you do such a thing, Milly? It was wicked.'

Milly coloured. 'I know, our Kitty. And I'm real sorry now I did it. Don't ever tell him, will you? Please?'

'All right,' she nodded. 'But you shouldn't have done it, because it did upset him at the time.'

'But this is worse,' Milly said in a small voice.

'Oh aye,' Kitty said wryly. 'This is much worse. Goodness only knows what this'll do to him.'

Kitty left Milly and ran downstairs again. She filled a bucket with hot, soapy water while she explained briefly to the startled cook what had happened.

'Never!' Mrs Grundy exclaimed indignantly.

'It's a blessing it's only treacle, Mrs G.,' was Kitty's philosophical remark now. 'I thought at first it was tar and that surely would have ruined poor *Sylvie*.'

'I bet Jack's in a right tekin', ain't he?'

Kitty's answer was to cast her eyes to the ceiling, pick up the bucket and some clean cloths and step out into the yard.

They missed a whole day's threshing because of the incident and the following day it rained heavily and work was impossible.

Jack was quiet and morose and paced about the small cottage in a foul temper.

'I'll not be forced into throwing me life away by a lot of patriotic nonsense,' he burst out at last, beating one clenched fist against the palm of his other hand. 'But I expect you agree with them, if truth be told, don't ya?'

346

'No, Jack,' Kitty said wearily. She was still tired from all her efforts to clean every last bit of the sticky treacle from the engine. 'I really don't have a lot of thought on the subject one way or t'other to tell you the truth. And besides, it's not up to me, is it?'

'Ah, but your fine friend, Master Edward, he volunteered straight away, didn't he? Even before he was properly old enough. And he's the hero now, ain't he? Got a medal to show off on his chest an' all.'

Patiently, as if explaining to a child, she said, 'Master Edward only joined up to try to prove to his father that he was, well, something. The master had belittled him all his young life. Specially when he was so ill all that time. I saw it with me own eyes, so I know . . .'

'Oh aye, you know all right, don't you, Kitty Clegg? You and the Franklins. I'm sick of hearing about them. You hear me?'

'You can talk,' she muttered as she turned away from him and bent to take out a rabbit pie from the oven in the range.

'What did you say?' he roared.

She was straightening up and turning towards the table, when Jack grasped her roughly by the shoulder, spinning her round so that she lost her balance and fell over. The scalding gravy splashed on to her hand and she dropped the dish. It smashed on the tiles and the pie spilled out over the floor.

Tears of pain filled her eyes as she clutched at her hand, the skin burning and reddening already.

She clenched her teeth against the pain, but faced him. 'I said, *you* can talk about being involved with the Franklins.'

The air was thick with unspoken accusation and recrimination. His mouth twisted cruelly. 'Well, at least I had m'lady. Oh, she was begging for it, I can tell you. Threw hersen at me, she did.'

Kitty closed her eyes, but she could not close her ears to his bragging.

'If only she hadn't fallen for the kid, she'd have been with me still, I reckon.'

To that, Kitty had no answer, for even she did not know what might have happened if Miss Miriam had not found herself with child.

Yet despite everything, Kitty did not for one moment regret her decision to take the boy as her own. And the decision had cost her a great deal. Her face was gaunt, her cheeks thin and her complexion worn and dry from working outdoors in all weathers and the constant dust that attacked it. Her hair, drawn back into a bun at the back of her head, was dull and badly needed washing. Exhaustion filled her every waking moment and the days of her carefree girlhood were gone for ever.

Jack's lip curled. 'Just look at you. You look what you really are. A dirty scullery maid. You're certainly no lady, not even a lady's maid. Never were. And you're always too tired, ain't you, nowadays to be any use to me?' He thrust his face close to her. 'If you don't pretty yarsen up a bit and be a bit more lovin', like, when I come home at night, you'll be out, Kitty Clegg. D'you hear me? Out on your ear. But . . .' menacingly, he wagged his forefinger in her face and said slowly and deliberately, 'but the boy stays with me.'

Despite her weariness, anger flooded through her, giving her back some of her old strength and vitality. In turn she thrust her face towards him, her dark eyes flashing. 'Never. Never in a million years.'

He laughed, a wry, mirthless laugh. 'But he's my son, Kitty Clegg, which is more than you can say.'

Rage made her reckless. 'Prove it, Jack Thorndyke, prove it in a court of law.'

He raised his left eyebrow in sarcasm. 'What, and drag your precious Miriam through the witness box and tell the world she's had a bastard?'

Kitty trembled at the very thought and knew herself beaten, trapped by the promise she had made years earlier.

There was no way out for Kitty and no escape from Jack for as long as he wanted to keep her bound to him.

But she would never, ever, allow him to take Johnnie from her. Never.

Forty-Five

'Madam wants to see you. She's got some news.'

'Oh Mrs G., I can't stay. Jack needs me in the yard. We've missed two days' threshing, what with that feather business and then it raining. And he's short-handed enough without . . .' Her eyes widened as the meaning behind Mrs Grundy's words struck her. 'News? Oh no, not about Master Edward or – or Miss Miriam?'

She knew that Miriam had been nursing in a field hospital for the past year, the nearest one to the Front. Of course, Miriam hadn't been able to say as much in her letters, but Mrs Franklin had told Kitty, 'She's near the thick of the fighting, at least that's what Mr Franklin thinks.' Mrs Franklin had held the thin sheet of writing paper between her hands. 'She doesn't say, of course. She can't, any more than Edward can tell us where he is, but . . .' The woman had raised her fine eyes to Kitty, eyes that were now clouded with constant anxiety. It was bad enough that her son should be a soldier, but her daughter was out there too. She could lose both her children.

Now Mrs Grundy was shaking her head. 'No, nothing dreadful, well, not the way you mean. But you'd best go up. You needn't stay long, but she asked particularly to see you when you got here. Leave the lad with me.'

'I'll go out to me dad,' Johnnie said.

Kitty nodded. 'Keep well back,' she said quietly. 'Don't

get in his way.' She could well have added 'and make him worse tempered than he is already' but she held her tongue.

The boy grinned as he headed for the door. 'No, Mam. I know what to do.'

'Spitting image of his dad, ain't he?' Mrs Grundy grinned. ''Spect he teks after him for the work an' all. And he'll break a few hearts in time.'

'I hope not, Mrs G., oh I do hope not.' Kitty was shaking her head but nevertheless smiling fondly after him. 'You're right about one thing though. He does love the outdoor life and he's quite a help even though he's so young.'

Mrs Grundy sniffed. 'Farmers' lads, and their men's bairns if it comes to that, have always had to help from being young. Why, me brother and me used to be tatie picking nearly as soon as we could walk, following our mam . . .'

Kitty turned and said, 'I'd best go up then.' She didn't want Mrs Grundy getting launched into her reminiscences. She'd be here all morning.

'Oh Kitty, come in, come in.' The door was wide open when she reached the top of the stairs and Mrs Franklin was beckoning her into her sitting room. 'They're home. They're back. Both of them.'

For a moment Kitty was puzzled. 'Back, madam?'

It was the most animated Kitty had ever seen the usually serene Mrs Franklin. There was an excitement about her and her lovely eyes were shining with relief and happiness.

'Edward *and* Miriam. They're at the Hall. They arrived yesterday. Miriam had special leave to bring him home. He's been wounded in the leg.'

351

'Wounded?' Kitty gave a little cry of horror. 'Oh no . . .' But Mrs Franklin reached out and took hold of her hands.

'But it's all right, Kitty, don't you see? He's hurt, yes, but not badly, not life-threateningly and it will keep him out of the war for good.'

Kitty's face cleared. 'Oh I see now, madam.' She smiled a little tremulously, recovering swiftly from the shock. 'I couldn't understand why you were so happy if he'd been wounded.'

Mrs Franklin laughed, girlishly, light-headed with relief. 'No, I suppose it must have seemed a little strange.'

'And – and Miss Miriam? Is she going back again?'

'Not yet. She has a lot of leave due to her. As you know, she's never been home since she first went out there more than a year ago. So she'll be at home for a while anyway.'

'Oh madam, I am so pleased for you, so thankful that your son is safe.'

There was a commotion on the stairs and then suddenly, without warning or even a knock, the door was flung wide and a flustered and distressed Mrs Grundy stood there, clutching the corner of her apron. 'Oh ma'am – I'm sorry, but there's been an accident. A dreadful accident – in the yard . . .'

Both Mrs Franklin and Kitty turned to stare at the cook with wide frightened eyes. 'Oh no, no, not Johnnie,' Kitty whispered, but then she heard his high-pitched cry from the hallway below.

'Mam, mam, come quick. Dad's fallen in the drum . . .'

She heard Jack yelling as she ran down the garden path and as she came through the door in the wall and into the yard, the terrifying scene made her stop and press her hands to her ribs as panic threatened to engulf her. Then she was running again towards the huge red threshing drum.

Nathaniel had climbed up on to the top and was leaning over, looking down into the drum. The rest of the workers, boys too young for war, stood around helplessly, wincing at the cries of agony coming from above them. From the ground, she could not see Jack. But she could hear him, oh how she could hear him and they were sounds she had never thought to hear from a man like Jack Thorndyke.

Then suddenly, as loud as the screams had been, there was silence, an eerie, heart-stopping silence.

'Jack,' she breathed as she began to climb up the ladder and scramble on to the top of the thresher. 'Oh no, Jack.'

'I stopped it working, Mam. Me an' Billy closed the regulator, just like Dad showed me.' Johnnie's face was upturned and she glanced down at him briefly and nodded. Her mind, for once, was not on the boy but on the man.

The old man straightened and turned to face her, wiping the back of his hand across his mouth. 'Reckon he's passed out, poor sod. He'll be lucky if he survives this, missis.' Then he sniffed and glanced down again. 'If ya'd call it lucky,' he muttered.

Jack was lying head downwards in the opening, the trunk of his body and his legs twisted as if he had been struggling to free himself from the drum which had caught hold of his right arm and tried to drag him into the machinery. Kitty swallowed and moved forward, dropping on to her knees beside Jack's inert figure.

'Oh – my – God,' came her strangulated whisper, then suddenly she was on her feet and shouting down to those below, gaping up with fearful eyes.

'Find the master – Mr Franklin. Hurry. And you, Billy, get up top here.' This to the biggest, strongest lad there. To the smallest and wiriest, she shouted, 'You, run into the town for the doctor. Tell him it's – it's a very bad accident. Life or death. Mek him realize . . . Johnnie, fetch towels and water from the house. Tell Mrs Grundy to come.'

They were scurrying now in all directions, anxious to do her bidding and fearful lest their inactivity would bring about a dreadful fate for poor Jack.

'Now,' she turned back to Jack and knelt beside him once more. Thank the good Lord he was still unconscious. At least he was out of pain while they tried to free him.

Though the three of them – old Nathaniel, Billy and Kitty – pulled and tugged, they still could not turn the drum to release its hold on him.

'We need summat to lever it round. What . . .?'

There was the sound of running and Kitty glanced round to see Mr Franklin climbing the ladder to the top of the drum. Then he was standing beside her and looking down at Jack. 'My God,' he muttered. 'We must get him out.'

'We've tried, sir, but we can't move the drum with our hands.'

'You'll not do it from up here. We need to pull on the belt – gently. You stay here and as we turn it, get him out.'

Kitty licked her dry lips and pushed her hands, wet with sweat, down her skirt. She nodded. She was trembling in every limb, but she would do it. She'd do whatever she had to.

Mr Franklin stripped off his jacket, carelessly flinging it aside. Then he climbed down the ladder, bellowing to the two lads as he went. 'You two, help me with the belt.'

For the first time in her life, Kitty was thankful for the master's roar of authority, his strong presence and positive action in a crisis.

Moments later he was shouting up to her. 'Right, we're going to start. Get ready . . .'

Kitty and Nathaniel knelt by Jack, Kitty nearest to the

drum, her hands reaching to ease out Jack's arm, Nathaniel by his legs to help lift him clear.

The machinery gave a jerk and Kitty winced as Jack groaned. 'Oh please don't come round now,' she mouthed a prayer.

Then slowly the drum began to turn backwards, while all the time Mr Franklin's voice floated up to her. 'Steady, hold it, keep an even pressure or we'll cause him more damage.'

Kitty swallowed hard and for a moment her head swam. She mustn't faint now, she told herself fiercely, but the sight unfolding before her was enough to make even the stout-hearted quail. His arm was a mess of mangled flesh and white, splintered bone as far up as his elbow. Yet, strangely, as the injured limb came free, there was not as much bleeding as Kitty had expected.

'By heck, lass,' Kitty heard Nathaniel mutter, 'it's all but hanging off. He'll lose it. They'll never be able to save that, I know.'

Kitty was silent as she looked down at Jack's ashen face. The shock of losing his arm would kill him, she thought, even if the accident itself didn't. Old Nathaniel, who had probably seen several such incidents in his long life, was right. From the elbow down, the limb was crushed beyond recognition as the strong right arm it had once been.

Swallowing the bile that rose in her throat, Kitty stood up, lifted her skirt and tore her petticoat into strips to bind his arm roughly to his chest while they carried him down to the ground. They managed it, but how, Kitty could never remember afterwards for the big, inert man was a dead weight.

'Oh Kitty – lass.' Mrs Grundy was standing there, her

arms full of towels and old sheets, Milly carrying a bowl of steaming water. 'Is he – is he . . .?'

Mr Franklin, who was kneeling down beside Jack, said, 'Not yet, but he's bad. Have you sent for the doctor?'

Kitty nodded. 'I sent one of the lads.'

'Then I don't think we should move him again till the doctor's seen him. Blankets, Cook. We need blankets to keep him warm.'

In her turn, Mrs Grundy sent Milly scurrying back to the house just as pounding feet heralded the return of the boy sent to fetch the doctor.

'He's out, mester,' he panted. 'On t'other side of town.'

'Damnation,' Mr Franklin muttered between his teeth. He stood up, appeared to think for a moment and then said, 'Have him carried into the kitchen. As carefully as you can, mind. On to the table. I'll fetch Miriam. She'll be used to sights like these after what she's seen. Maybe she'll be able to do something until the doctor gets here.' He raised his voice and bellowed, 'Bemmy, start the car.'

Kitty opened her mouth, stung, in a moment's thoughtlessness, to protest. But she closed it without uttering a word.

This was out of her hands now.

Forty-Six

Within half an hour the car returned, swerving into the driveway and skidding to a halt and Miriam was jumping out even before the vehicle had come to a halt. Momentarily, she paused in the doorway of the kitchen as she took in the scene. Her glance went, just once, to Kitty and then her whole attention was on the man lying on the table.

Gently but skilfully, Miriam set to work, and Kitty, standing on the opposite side of the table, feeling ignorant and helpless, was filled with admiration for the girl whose deft hands unwound the makeshift bandage as she calmly assessed the appalling injury to the man who had fathered her child, the man in whose arms she had lain . . .

Guiltily, Kitty pushed away her thoughts as Miriam said quietly, 'Kitty, wash your hands thoroughly. You'll have to help me try to clean some of the dirt from the wound.'

Kitty felt sick, but valiantly she fought to carry out Miriam's instructions. A low groan came from Jack and his eyelids seemed to fall open. His legs jerked in an involuntary movement. Then suddenly his left arm came up and he reached out and grabbed at Miriam's skirt, but the young woman seemed not to notice or to care.

'Kitty, he's starting to come round. Hold his shoulder. Mrs Grundy, hold his head. Father . . .' This to Mr Franklin, who was still standing near the doorway. 'Hold his legs please. When the pain hits him, he'll . . .'

At that instant Jack let out a yell that made everyone in the kitchen jump, even though they had been half expecting it. 'Hold him,' Miriam snapped. 'Kitty, lie across his stomach. It's the only way we'll hold him down. Where's that blasted doctor?' she muttered in language that befitted a field hospital rather than the kitchen of her former home. Yet the bloody scene before them resembled a battlefield.

'Mam,' Johnnie shouted from the back door. 'Mam, the doctor's here.'

'And not before time, either,' Miriam murmured, but Kitty could detect the relief in her voice.

'Nasty,' was the doctor's terse verdict after his examination. He was a big man in his late fifties with an abundance of grey hair and a drooping moustache that hid his mouth, but his eyes, a clear blue, twinkled with a mischief that some found disconcerting in a doctor, yet others found reassuring and human. He was one of them, a man who dealt with tragedy in a bluff, no-nonsense manner, yet with a kindly concern, and with the greatest respect for the blunt truth. 'The arm will have to come off at the elbow.'

'Oh no,' Kitty breathed. She had realized that it might happen, yet until the doctor actually voiced the words, she had clung foolishly to a tiny vestige of hope. Now there was none, she was horrified to think what it would mean to Jack. All the bad times fell away and she could think only of the laughing, handsome man who had captured and held her heart so completely that she had been besotted with him, casting aside all caution, all common sense. She thought of his daring eyes that were at once mischievous or dark with passion. She thought now only of the sunlit days when his flirting had swelled her heart with love. Memories of his betrayal, of his threats to keep her chained to his side, all faded before her sorrow at the sight of the lacerated body of the handsome, virile man. A man so proud of that virility and manhood that such a mutilation could ultimately destroy him.

'Is there no other way? No chance that you can save it?' she asked, her voice trembling.

The doctor shook his head. 'He'll lose either his arm or his life. Which is it to be?'

He glanced first at Miriam and then at Kitty, not quite knowing, being very new to the area, who was the closest to the patient.

Briefly the two women exchanged a look. They spoke together and with one accord. 'His arm.'

'Right. I'll need help.' He glanced at Miriam. 'Seems you know what you're doing, young woman. Nurse, are you?'

She nodded. 'A year at the Front.'

'Ha. This is nothing to what you've seen then, I'll be bound. Was there myself until the end of 'fifteen. Right.' He turned away, took off his jacket and rolled up his sleeves and moved towards Mrs Grundy's deep white sink.

'Good job I've learned to carry the tools of the trade with me at all times.' He turned to face those standing watching him, drying his hands on a towel. 'Another thing you learn at the Front,' he added quietly, his glance resting for a moment on Miriam once more. Then he turned to Johnnie hovering in the doorway. 'Fetch the large bag out of the back of the trap, lad, will you?'

'You don't mean you're going to do it here? On me kitchen table?' Mrs Grundy asked, scandalized.

'Certainly am. Move him and there wouldn't be any point in trying to operate.'

'Eh?' Her eyes widened and then came back to the twitching, moaning form on her table, once scrubbed to white cleanliness, now stained with blood and straw and dust. 'Oh.'

'Now . . .' His face grim, the doctor glanced round at them all. 'I'm going to need your help.'

There had been little in the way of an actual amputation for the doctor to do; the thresher had done it all too well.

'A bit rough and ready,' the doctor commented, washing the blood from his hands. 'And I don't know whether he'll live even now.' He glanced again at the two women. 'Need good nursing. Can the two of you manage it? I don't want to risk moving him to the hospital for a day or two, though I'd like him to go then to have a better job made of that stump.'

Again Kitty and Miriam looked at each other. 'Of course,' Miriam said. 'He'll stay here,' she decided without deference to her father. 'We'll carry him up to Teddy's room. Father, can you manage his legs, while Kitty and I . . .?'

'That's all right,' said the doctor, a strong burly man whose size belied the dexterity of his surgeon's hands. He moved to take Kitty's place, near the truncated limb. Laying a hand on her shoulder, he said gently, 'You sit down in that chair near the fire before you fall down, and let someone make you a cup of tea.' The perceptive doctor had at last picked out which of the two women was most affected. He looked kindly at her, adding, 'Else I'll have another patient on my hands.'

She smiled thinly and moved towards the chair, though her gaze never left Jack as they lifted him gently and carried him upstairs, leaving a mesmerized Mrs Grundy staring at her table. 'Well, I never thought I'd see owt like that on here. Never.'

Exhausted, Kitty leaned her head back against the wooden chair and closed her eyes. Oh thank you, God, thank you for Miss Miriam . . .

Kitty jumped as someone touched her hand gently and she opened her eyes to see Johnnie watching her, his eyes large in a round face that was suddenly unusually pale.

A shaft of horror stabbed her. 'I'm so sorry, darling,' she whispered, at once consumed with guilt that she had not prevented the boy from witnessing the mutilation of the father he idolized. 'I shouldn't have let you see . . .'

Kitty had been so caught up with the drama that she had not even thought about Johnnie being there, seeing everything. But the boy's concern was not for himself. 'Is me dad going to be all right?'

Kitty looked into the dark blue eyes, so like Jack's. And yet there was more in these eyes. Despite his youth, there was a concern for others in the boy's expression, a trait missing, Kitty felt, from Jack Thorndyke's nature.

She smiled tremulously and reached out to touch his cheek. The boy's question, asked with a maturity beyond his years, demanded the truth. 'I don't know, Johnnie, but with Miss Miriam's help, we'll pull him through.'

The boy leaned closer. 'Isn't she pretty? Who is she?'

Kitty blinked. It seemed impossible that the boy did not know who she was, and yet how could he when the few who did know had been at such pains to hide the truth from him?

She opened her mouth but was saved from having to answer as Miriam herself came back into the room.

'There now, he's as comfortable as we can make him. Milly's keeping an eye on him for us, Kitty, and Father's taken the doctor into his study for a well-earned wee dram, I shouldn't wonder.'

She came and stood beside the chair where Kitty sat, resting her hand on the back as she looked down into the boy's upturned face.

'And who,' she said slowly, her voice low and husky, 'is this handsome young man?' Beneath her breath, so softly that only Kitty heard, Miriam added, 'As if I didn't know.'

Kitty cleared her throat nervously and said, 'This is Johnnie, Miss Miriam.'

'How do you do, Johnnie Clegg?' And she held out her hand.

The boy frowned slightly, but put his own hand into hers. 'My name's Johnnie Thorndyke, missis,' he corrected her. Then he added politely, 'How do you do?'

It was a natural mistake for Miriam to make and Kitty held her breath, but Miriam only laughed and said, 'Of course it is, what am I thinking of? I can't get used to your mother being Mrs Thorndyke any more than she can bring herself to call me Mrs Harding.'

It was quick thinking and Kitty let out her breath with relief. Then she glanced up at Miriam. Was she imagining it, seeing things in her anxiety that weren't really there, or did Miriam hold on to young Johnnie's hand just a little too long?

Now she was moving forward and putting her arm about the boy's shoulders, turning him round and leading him towards the door. 'At the Hall we have a mare that's just foaled. Would you like to come and see it?'

The boy's face was upturned to look at her. 'Oh yes, please, missis.'

In the doorway, she paused and looked back at Kitty. 'I'll have to go back to the Hall to fetch a few things. I think we'll both have to sleep here for the next few nights, and, of course, Johnnie can stay here too.'

All Kitty could do was nod and watch helplessly as Miriam walked out of the back door, her arm still about her son's shoulders.

Forty-Seven

Side by side, Kitty and Miriam stood looking down at the man in Edward's bed, sleeping now but still not peaceful, for his body twitched and his mouth worked. The two women moved outside the bedroom, away from the sickly sweet smell of blood mingling with the man's sweat of fear and pain.

'You'll never manage him on your own, Kitty. We'll use my old room and take it in turns to sleep there. He mustn't be left for a while, day or night. And I'll dress the stump for you.'

Kitty bit her lip, knowing what she said was true. 'Are you sure, miss?'

Miriam nodded. 'I'm sure.'

Kitty stared at the girl who had been her young mistress, wilful, obstinate and selfish. The young woman who now stood beside her was very different. There was a calmness, a serenity about her now and that was not all. Deep in her eyes there was compassion. The horrors she must have witnessed at the Front had left their abiding mark upon Miriam. She was a different being to the petulant girl who had made such a fuss about a sliver of glass in her foot or had been unable to sit with her sickly brother. Kitty could see and admire a new strength and purpose in Miriam.

She was still beautiful of course, and, Kitty guessed, as passionate as ever about what she believed in. And did that passion still include the man lying, so terribly maimed, in the room behind them?

There was a long silence until Kitty whispered 'Are you still in love with him?'

Miriam's green eyes returned Kitty's gaze steadfastly. 'No, Kitty, I'm not. Though I would never have wished something like this to happen, I do see him now for the man he was – is,' she altered her wording swiftly. There was a silence before she said, pondering, 'A strange mixture, isn't he, our Threshing Jack?'

When Kitty made no answer, Miriam went on, though it was almost as if she were speaking to herself rather than to anyone else. 'I've seen so many men die in so many ways. Some with a silent courage, who slipped away without a word, others stoically bearing the most horrific injuries when we hadn't the means to ease their pain. And the others, the poor young boys screaming piteously for their mother or big, strong ones getting fighting mad, like Jack in there. He was a fine figure of a male, Kitty, and I am sorry to see him brought so low. Very sorry, but you know,' Kitty felt Miriam touch her arm, 'Jack Thorndyke is not a *man* in the way that Edward is, or – or that poor Guy was. Maybe you don't see him as I do now, Kitty. Not yet. But if you ever do, I beg you to have the courage to leave him. For if ever you were to stop loving a man like Jack Thorndyke, then your life with him would be a misery.'

Kitty dropped her head and could not answer. How could she tell this girl, who was now so changed, that it was for her – and her son – that she stayed with Jack? How could she ever explain the hold that the man exerted over her, the threat that bound her to him? The threat that he would reveal Miriam's secret. Better that Miriam should go on believing that Kitty stayed with him because she still loved him.

She felt Miriam pat her arm and move away. 'Now, you go and get some sleep, Kitty. You've had a horrible shock today. I'll see to him tonight.'

The weariness washed over her in waves and all Kitty could do was nod and say, 'Thank you, miss.'

As Kitty moved towards the opposite bedroom, Miriam opened the door into the room where Jack lay and closed it behind her.

In the days that followed, Kitty felt awkward being at the Manor with Jack and, more especially, with Johnnie there so often too. What if, in his delirium, Jack said something about the boy or about Miriam? And what if the master heard? But, ironically, it was Mr Franklin himself who put her mind at ease.

Meeting her in the hall the morning after the accident, he said, 'Kitty, come into my study a moment, will you?'

Kitty swallowed, her mouth suddenly dry as he closed the door and motioned her to a seat while he took up a stance before the blazing fire in the huge iron grate. For several moments he stood just looking at her, as if he were assessing every feature, every line of her face, until Kitty, embarrassed, dropped her glance.

'You're very like your mother was, you know, when she was your age.'

Now Kitty looked up to meet his gaze again. 'Am I, sir?' she whispered.

He nodded. 'And you have her brightness, her – her mischief. At least . . .' he paused, considering, and his voice deepened, 'you used to have. When you first came to work here.' He paused again and then there was a gentleness in his tone that Kitty had never, ever, heard before in the master's voice. 'Until life dealt you some unkind blows too.'

She didn't need to ask what the 'too' meant. She knew he was referring to her mother and his sadness told Kitty that he still carried the burden of guilt for the part he had played in the life of Betsy Clegg.

'Is she . . .' his voice faltered, 'all right? Your mother?'

Kitty felt a rush of sympathy flood through her for this man. His bluff exterior hid emotions she had not thought him capable of. With a sudden tenderness, she smiled at the man who, though he was not, could very well have been her father. 'She's fine.'

'Is she – has she been – happy?'

She returned his gaze steadily. She couldn't lie to this man. It wouldn't be fair. 'I think so, sir. As happy as it was possible for her to be.'

He passed his hand briefly across his forehead and asked, 'He's been good to her, Clegg?'

Now she could answer truthfully, for Betsy Clegg herself would never say any different. 'Oh yes, sir. A good husband and father to us all.'

Kitty saw him relax. 'Good. Good. I'm glad.'

She wanted to say, And you, sir? Have you been happy? But she could not. Even though he was talking to her now as an equal, still Kitty could not quite bring herself to cross the divide between master and servant. Not with Mr Franklin. And besides, there was really no need to ask the question, for, sadly, Kitty felt she knew the answer.

Between them, Kitty and Miriam nursed Jack, taking it in turns to sit with him through the long nights when he lay quite still, though his skin was burning to the touch, or when he threshed about in feverish agony, his sweat soaking the bedclothes.

Kitty mopped his brow and changed his clothes and sheets, held a feeding cup to his lips or spoon-fed him the thin soup and milk puddings that Mrs Grundy sent up. But it was Miriam who changed the dressings on his stump, Miriam who washed him and attended to his intimate bodily functions. And though she stayed to help, all the while Kitty could see that it was upon Miriam that Jack's dark gaze rested.

It was ironic, Kitty could not help thinking, as she sat huddled in a blanket near the window in the cold, early light of dawn, that he had avoided going to war only to be maimed in a far worse way than perhaps he would have been at the battle front.

And there was another irony too; the fact that Jack was now lying in the room where for so many months, years even, the young Edward had remained a virtual prisoner in his sickbed, able to watch the outside world only from this very window. She rubbed away the faint mist her breath had made on the pane and strained her eyes to see down the length of the garden, over the wall to where *Sylvie* still stood in forlorn silence. The stack was half threshed, the drum halted in its work, suspended still in that moment of drama, waiting . . .

Kitty sighed, wondering how they were ever going to cope with the work. Who could she get to finish it? For now there was no Ben to take Jack's place and old Nathaniel could not work the engine. Jack would blame it all on Ben for going, she thought suddenly. He would blame anyone and everyone else for his accident; Ben, for leaving, and whoever had plastered white feathers over his engine so that he was so angry and forgetful of the danger. The insult had eaten away at him. And her. Kitty was sure he would blame her too. The doctor had said as much only the previous day.

'He's over the worst physically, but it's his mind you'll have to deal with now, my dear.' He'd stroked his moustache. 'I do not envy you your task, for the suffering tend to take it out on their nearest and dearest. I can see that a man such as Jack Thorndyke will not take kindly to what he will consider being a cripple. I'll get him moved to the hospital tomorrow. It'll give you a respite and time to get things ready at your home. Mr Franklin has said Bemmy can take him in the motor car and Miriam will go with him . . .' The doctor's eyes twinkled merrily for a moment. 'Just to make sure Bemmy's driving doesn't cause a relapse in our patient, eh?'

Kitty tried to smile, knowing the doctor was deliberately trying to lift her spirits, yet all the while she was thinking, Miriam, Miriam, Miriam. It was always Miriam caring for Jack.

As she told him, hesitantly, of the doctor's plans, Jack lay listlessly, sunk against the pillows, his handsome face gaunt with black shadows beneath his eyes. 'I don't see why they're bothering. They can't sew me arm back on, now can they?'

'The doctor wants the – the . . .' she swallowed painfully, 'the wound treated properly. Then you'll come back home to – to the cottage.'

There was silence, then suddenly Jack said, 'This is his room, ain't it?' and he pulled himself up in the bed for the first time since he had been put there, craning to see out of the window. 'Aye, I thought so. You can see the stackyard from here.' He was silent as he stared through the window at the deserted yard and idle machinery. Then he flopped back against the pillows and lay just looking up at the ceiling.

'I used to see him, you know, watching us. Standing at this window, just watching. I reckon he was watching you.'

She began to say, 'Don't be silly . . .' but Jack twisted his head on the pillow to look at her. 'I thought he was home? Doesn't he want his room back?'

'He's staying at the Hall with – with his sister.'

'You seen him?'

'When have I had time to go visiting, Jack? Talk sense.'

He moved his head again to stare once more at the ceiling above him.

'We'll have to move you home soon, anyway,' she told him.

He didn't speak for a while, then, 'Have they said they want us out?'

'No, no, they've been very good. All – all of them.'

His lip curled. 'Aye, even Florence Nightingale herself.'

'There's no need to take that attitude, Jack. Miriam saved your life.'

'Then it's her I've to blame, is it, for still being alive? Getting her revenge on me, was she?'

Kitty's mouth hardened. 'You've no right to say such things. No right at all. You'll have to manage on your own for a while. I must go to my mother's to fetch Johnnie.' She made to turn from him, but Jack reached out with his one hand and grasped her arm. There was still a surprising strength in his grip. She stood quietly, submitting herself to his hold on her.

'Don't bring him here. I don't want him to see me. Not like this.'

'He'll love you just the same, Jack, and besides, he saw it all. He was there when it happened. In fact, it was him who came running to find me and I believe, though it scarcely seems possible that he managed it, he was the one who stopped the machinery. Nathaniel said when it happened Johnnie and Billy scambled up on to the engine and stopped it.'

His voice was a low growl. 'He'd a done better to leave me be. Best all round if I'd . . .' In his eyes, she saw a sudden fear, a desperation. His voice was a hoarse whisper as he said, 'Kitty, you won't leave me, will you?'

She smiled down at him gently and shook her head. There was a sadness in her heart, but she strove valiantly to hide it from the mutilated man. 'No, Jack,' she said. 'I won't leave you.' He needed her now, more than ever before, and she knew she would stay.

She smoothed the hair back from his forehead. 'Try to rest while I go and fetch Johnnie home.'

He sank back against the pillows with a sigh, but as she reached the door, he murmured, 'They should have let me die. I'd be better off dead. And now, I can't even volunteer to be cannon fodder.'

'Well, I aren't staying if you're going to feel sorry for yasen,' she said, making her tone deliberately sharp, realizing, more by instinct than by rational thought, that with a man like Jack goading him to anger was perhaps the only way to rouse him from depression. She pulled open the door, stepped out of the room and shut it behind her with a resounding bang. Then she stood a moment, shocked at her own actions as she remembered, too late, in whose house they were.

If the master were at home, then . . .

But as she listened, holding her breath, no angry voice was raised against the noise and she fled down the stairs and into the kitchen, breathing hard.

Two pairs of startled eyes turned towards her. 'What is it, lass? Is he worse?'

Kitty stopped and placed her hand over her thudding heart. 'No, no, I just got a bit mad with him feeling sorry

371

for himself and I forgot where I was and banged the bedroom door.' She gave a nervous laugh. 'Then I stood waiting for the master to come raging out of his study to shout at me.'

'Oh he's out – and madam, too,' Milly said. 'So you're safe – this time.'

'I'm just going to fetch Johnnie home.'

'All right,' Milly nodded. 'I'll go up in a bit and take him this jelly.'

Kitty said, 'You are good, Mrs G. You spoil him . . .'

But the cook was shaking her head. 'Ain't nowt to do wi' me. 'Tis all Milly's doin'.' The woman laughed. 'Reckon she's glad of a captive guinea pig for her efforts. Mind you, to be fair, and you know I always try to be, Kitty, she's not shaping up badly. I can see I'll be pensioned off afore me time if I aren't careful.'

'Oh Mrs Grundy, you know we couldn't do without you.' Milly dipped her head, pretending embarrassment, but not before her older sister had seen the look of triumph in the girl's eyes.

Kitty hugged Johnnie to her until he wriggled to be set free. 'Leave off, Mam.'

It seemed an age since she had seen him even though it was only days. He'd stayed the first two nights at the Manor, but Kitty had made the excuse that, with Jack to care for, she could pay little attention to the boy. The truth was that she didn't like him seeing so much of Miriam, nor she of him.

'He can go to my mother's for a few nights,' she said, and when she saw the disappointment on Miriam's face, Kitty knew she had been right to be concerned.

'I do believe you've grown,' she laughed now.

Betsy Clegg nodded and smiled. 'He eats well, dun't he? And . . .' Betsy leaned towards her daughter, 'ya dad's even taken to him. Took him on the train with him yesterday. Now, what do you think of that? I'm that pleased he's coming round a bit. After all, the little chap is our own grandbairn.'

Kitty straightened up, feeling the familiar stab of guilt. 'We'd better be going. Thanks, Mam, for having him. And thank me dad, won't you? Come on, Johnnie, come on home and see your dad.'

'Home?' There was disappointment in his tone. 'D'you mean he's back home?'

'Oh no, no. I mean, to the Manor, but he's being taken to the hospital tomorrow. I thought you'd like to see him before he goes.'

The boy nodded, then his face lit up and his next words brought fresh dread to Kitty's heart. 'We're going to the Manor? Oh good, then I'll see Mrs Harding again, won't I?'

Forty-Eight

'So, Jack Thorndyke, are you going to idle your life away in that bed while your threshing drum rots and poor *Sylvie* rusts away from lack of care?'

He had been home for three weeks now after his short stay in hospital and he had lain in bed for most of that time, despite the doctor, who still called regularly, insisting that he should be up and moving about now.

There was a time to be gentle and caring, Kitty thought, and there was a time to be tough with a man who, though physically recovered as much as was possible, had nonetheless sunk into a dark despair which no amount of cajoling and sympathy seemed able to dispel.

So, though her heart was pounding, she stood at the end of the bed in the low-ceilinged cottage, arms folded across her bosom, and said her piece.

The answer, from the depths of his pillows, was a low growl. 'What good is a one-armed cripple in a threshing team?'

'Ya legs gone an' all, 'ave they?'

'By, you're gettin' a shrewish tongue on ya, woman.' But she noticed that anger made him pull himself up in the bed, instead of slouching beneath the covers, sinking lower and lower as if he would bury himself there for ever.

'I never had you for a coward, Jack. I thought you were this strong, wonderful man, who strode through life taking all its knocks and always with a cheerful grin on your handsome face. Oh, a ladies' man all right. A real Jack-by-name and Jack-the-Lad by nature,' her voice dropped a tone, 'and none knows it better'n me. But I loved that man, Jack, faults an' all. Where's he gone now? You tell me that?'

'Down the bloody drum, that's where,' he said bitterly. 'Threshed limb from limb and spewed out like useless chaff.'

She leaned on the wooden rail at the end of the bed. 'You've people depending on you. You can't just give up.'

Jack gestured with his hand. 'They can get someone else and I'll sell me threshing tackle.'

'What?' Now even Kitty was shocked. 'Everything? Even your beloved *Sylvie*?'

She saw the hesitation then, saw the hurt deep in his eyes as he thought about the traction engine with her name picked out in gleaming gold and the drum with his nameplate on the side. Resolutely, Kitty pushed home her point. 'You'd see someone else running *Sylvie*?' she asked softly.

Angry frustration spurted again. 'Well, I can't, can I? Not like *this*.'

'So,' she said with more resolution in her voice than she was feeling inside, 'it looks like it's up to me.' She turned and made to leave the room.

'What are you going to do?'

She paused and looked back at him, shrugging her shoulders. 'What do you care? You'd rather lie there and play the martyr, wouldn't you, Jack?'

She left the room and though he shouted at the top of his voice, 'Kitty, *Kitty*! Just you come back here, Kitty Clegg,' she took not a scrap of notice. For she had suddenly thought of a way to make him get out of that bed.

*

'So, Mr Edward, do you know how to start this thing?'

Kitty was standing in the stackyard looking up at the lumbering bulk of metal, a mystery of boilers and gauges, levers and wheels and a puffing chimney. Standing beside her, leaning on his walking stick, his injured leg sticking out stiffly to one side, Edward grinned. 'Well, I reckon with my one leg and two arms and Jack's one arm and two legs, we ought to be able to work it.'

Kitty snorted. 'He won't get out of his bed.'

Edward's face sobered for a moment. 'For the first time in my life, I actually feel sorry for the poor chap. For a strong, healthy man like him to be so terribly injured, well, I can understand how he must be feeling.'

'But you've been injured and you're not lying in bed letting others wait on you. And you've more reason to than him. After all, you have been injured in the service of your country, which is more than Jack can say.'

'I shouldn't let him hear you saying that, Kitty. You, of all people. Wasn't that why he had the accident? Because he was raging mad about the white feather business? Maybe that's the very reason he is hiding himself away.'

She sighed. 'It was all part of it, I suppose. And the fact that the best workers have gone to the war and all he's left with are old men, boys – and me.'

Edward was staring at her. 'Yes,' he said, so quietly that she scarcely heard. 'He's still got you, Kitty, though he doesn't deserve such devotion.'

They stood a moment, just looking at each other, until Kitty shook herself and said, 'We'd best make a start. I'll get one of the lads to stoke for you and, if you and old Nathaniel can work out how to get her going, I reckon we ought to get a day's threshing in.'

*

When dusk crept into the stackyard, *Sylvie*'s engine died. Two boys slid from the top of the stack, Nathaniel climbed stiffly down from the top of the drum, Edward from the footplate of the engine and Kitty emerged from the chaff hole, red-eyed with tiredness and covered in dust. The last sack of grain was heaved into the barn.

'We couldn't have managed without you,' Kitty told Edward.

'D'you know, I've quite enjoyed myself,' he grinned at her, his teeth gleaming white from out of his smut-blackened face. 'Goodnight, Kitty,' he added softly, 'I hope your little ruse works.'

'So do I,' she said, smiling in return. 'Oh so do I.'

When she reached the cottage, it was to find Milly perched on the end of Jack's bed, while Johnnie played on the floor of the bedroom with six brightly coloured marbles.

'Fancy leaving the poor man on his own when he can't even get out of bed,' Milly said and smiled coyly at Jack. 'You don't know how to treat a man, our Kitty. It's a good job I came across with a basket of pastries.'

Kitty, bone weary, ignored her barb but thought, Aye, and I expect you saw me from the kitchen window and knew I was in the stackyard all day and that Jack was on his own, except for Johnnie. As Mrs G. would say, I'm not as green as I'm cabbage-looking. Aloud, all she said was, 'Come on, Johnnie, downstairs and get yarsen washed for bed.'

'I came with a message, actually,' Milly went on. 'Mrs Harding came to the Manor today but she could see how busy you all were so she asked me to tell you. She's leaving at the end of the week. Going back to the Front, I think. Well, back to nursing anyway. She said to say goodbye to you all for her.'

Kitty watched Jack's face, but he was lying on his back just staring up at the ceiling, almost as if he hadn't taken in what Milly was saying. Then from behind her came a scuffle and she turned to see Johnnie scrambling up from the floor, gathering his marbles together and stuffing them into his pocket. He rushed from the room, his small booted feet clomping down the stairs.

Milly, unaware, prattled on, but Kitty had seen the expression on the young boy's face as he had hurried past her.

He had looked as if his whole world was about to come crashing down around him.

'And I saw Mr Edward working that big traction engine,' Milly was saying. 'Who would have thought he would ever be well enough to—'

'What?' Jack hauled himself upright. 'What did you say?'

Milly turned wide, innocent eyes upon Jack, though Kitty had the shrewd notion that young Milly was not as naive as she would have everyone believe. 'Mr Edward Franklin. He was helping Kitty with the threshing. He was running the traction engine . . .'

'He was *what*?' Jack thundered, so that even Kitty quailed momentarily under his rage.

Trying to keep calm, Kitty said, 'We've done a day's threshing with Mr Edward's help.'

'You got that milksop to help you with my *Sylvie*?'

'What would you have me do? Let it all go to rack and ruin?'

'Huh! I'm surprised he didn't blow it up. I bet the rough stuff's all mixed up with the good grain.'

Patiently, Kitty said, 'No, it isn't. I remembered to set the drum up with the spirit levels at the front and on the side.'

'And the water? Did you keep an eye on the water gauge? If the levels go down, you could melt the lead plug in the fire box, then you'll have trouble.'

'One of the lads kept the water coming all day. There was no danger of that happening, I promise you.'

Ignoring Milly's presence, she sat on the bed then, close to him, and took his hand in hers. 'But you know, there's no need to let someone else take charge of *Sylvie*. You could supervise, Jack. You could teach another man to work her and be on hand all the time. There's no need to let go of the business that your dad and uncle, and then you, have built up over the years.' She paused and then added, so that the decision must come from him, 'Is there?'

She could see the conflict on his face, see the spark in his dark blue eyes once more and her heart was gladdened by it.

He stared at her for a long moment. Then the smile that had so long been absent curved his mouth and there was a glimpse of the old Jack. He reached up and, with the fingers of his one hand, he traced the line of her face. 'D'you know, Kitty Clegg, you're some woman now. Yes, you're really some woman.'

Milly bounced off the end of the bed. 'Oh well, if you two are going to get all lovey-dovey, I'm going.'

'Bye, Milly,' Kitty said, but her gaze was on Jack. If he could get back to work, if he could feel useful once more, a real man again, maybe things would be better.

He needed her now, he really needed her more than ever before. Kitty knew she no longer loved Jack with the passion she had once felt for him. But now she pitied the strong, virile man brought so low by a cruel accident.

She would stay with him but now it was not just because she was trapped, bound to him by the secret they shared. Perhaps there was still a chance that they could become a real family. Jack, his son – and her.

Forty-Nine

From that day, Jack started to recover his spirits. The following morning he got out of bed and, though it was a struggle and he lost his temper, he dressed himself, even before Kitty had left the house.

'Now, don't try to do too much . . .' she began.

'You wanted me out of yon bed. Now ya've managed it, so don't try to be puttin' me back into it, woman,' he snapped, trying to pull up his trousers with his one hand. Though Kitty itched to help him, she stood where she was, keeping her hands firmly by her sides.

He was panting by the time he reached the bottom of the stairs and fell into the wooden chair at the side of the range. His face was pale as he rested his head against the back of the chair, but there was triumph in his eyes.

'Keep an eye on Johnnie, won't you, Jack, now you're downstairs? He'll be no trouble, but I don't want to take him with me today.'

'All right, all right,' he muttered testily, still trying to regain his breath and angry to find how much the accident and the weeks in bed had robbed him of his strength.

In the whole of his life Jack Thorndyke had never before felt so weak and useless.

'Right then, I'll be off. Anything you want before I go?'

'No, no. You go. And just mind what your fancy Mister Edward's doing with my *Sylvie*. Mind he cleans out the boiler tubes and oils up properly. Keep an eye on things. Please, Kitty.'

Kitty laughed, came to him and planted a kiss on his forehead. 'I will. She's in safe hands, I promise you.'

'She'd better be,' he growled. 'I hope he knows what he's doing. I don't want him blowing her up.' Kitty opened her mouth to say, Oh I don't think he'll do that, but the words never passed her lips. Perhaps, she thought deviously, this was what would get Jack back on his feet and out into the stackyard once more. Her eyes narrowed as she watched him. She could see he was deep in thought.

Avoiding her gaze, he said gruffly, 'Mebbe I'll tek a walk over tomorrow.' He sniffed. 'Just see what you are all getting up to.'

'See how you feel.' Kitty turned away so that he should not see the smile of triumph on her face. 'It's our last week at the Manor,' she said, trying to keep her tone casual. 'Next Monday, we'll have to move to Sir Ralph's Home Farm and that's a bit far for your very first walk.'

'Huh, he'll never manage *Sylvie* on the road and towing the drum. I'll have to be there.'

Jack did not manage to walk to the Manor House for three days, although Kitty knew he had tried the very next day after their conversation. She arrived home to find Johnnie standing at the doorway of the cottage, watching the lane.

'Mam, Mam,' he cried, running towards her when he saw her shape looming up out of the dusk. 'Dad tried to walk to the Manor today, but he got tired. I made him sit down and then we came home.'

She rested her hand on the boy's shoulder. 'Where is he now?'

'In the kitchen. Ses he can't make the stairs yet.'

But the following day Jack walked a little further and on the third day he made it to the stackyard behind the Manor House.

All the morning as she had bent almost double to rake the chaff on to the sheet, keeping the hole clear, Kitty had watched for Jack and his son to appear, but it was not until late afternoon that she saw him walking slowly towards the stackyard. He was alone. Calling to one of the young boys to take her place for a moment, she stepped towards Jack, brushing the dust from her clothes.

'Where's Johnnie?' She was very surprised the boy was not with Jack for she knew he loved to be with the threshing. His passion for the threshing set and its work was nearly as great as his father's. And that morning he had grumbled because she had asked him to stay at home once more to be with Jack.

'Oh Mam, why can't I come with you? He's a lot better. He'll be all right on his own now.'

'You stay here, Johnnie, and do as I say.'

For the first time ever she saw a brief flash of a likeness to his mother in the disappointed pout of his mouth.

Now, facing Jack, Kitty said again, 'Where is he?' but Jack did not answer. His gaze was roaming over the lines of his engine. He was drinking in the sight of her as a lover who has been separated from his sweetheart.

Kitty grasped his hand and opened her mouth to shout above the noise of the throbbing engine, but at that moment a loud bang shuddered the air and a hiss of steam blew from a point above *Sylvie*'s fire box.

Jack leaped forward. 'The bloody fool. He's let the water level drop. I warned you, Kitty . . .'

Helplessly, Kitty stood and watched as Edward jumped down from the footplate, away from the scalding steam.

Above the commotion, she could not hear what was said, but she saw Jack bunch his fist into Edward's face and then, turning away, he climbed up on to the manstand.

The jet of steam was dying now as the fire was doused. As Jack operated the lever, the engine stopped. The team threw down their forks and came to see what had happened. Edward stood beside Kitty, a worried frown creasing his forehead.

'I don't know what's gone wrong. Everything seemed all right . . .'

'Melted the lead plug, that's what's happened.' Nathaniel, the most knowledgeable one there other than Jack, sniffed. ''S'what an engine man dreads 'appening. You must have let the water levels drop, mester,' he added, glancing accusingly at Edward. Then the old man turned away. 'Well, I'll be getting mesen home. There'll be no more threshing for a day or two till Jack gets it replaced.'

Even amid the furore, Kitty marvelled that Jack had resumed his rightful place so easily, so swiftly in the minds of the men.

She touched Edward's arm. 'Don't worry,' she said softly, as Nathaniel moved out of earshot. 'Maybe it's a blessing in disguise. Just look at him. Just look at Jack.'

It was not quite what she would have planned to happen, but there was no denying that her object had been achieved.

Jack Thorndyke was back, back where he belonged. Standing on the footplate, Kitty and Edward saw him reach out to touch the well-known levers. His hand was trembling, but when he turned to look at them, all the momentary anger was gone and in its place there was triumph and happiness.

Relief showed on Edward's face and he moved towards the engine. Looking up at the man above him, Kitty heard him say, 'I'm sorry, Thorndyke, for what's happened. Is there much damage, because whatever it is, I'll . . .?'

'No, no,' Jack said and he was actually smiling now. 'She'll just want cleaning out thoroughly and a new lead plug fitted, then she'll be as good as new.' With a proprietorial gesture, he patted the engine's steering wheel.

Jack Thorndyke had taken charge once more, the gesture said.

'If you'll show me what needs doing . . .?' Edward was saying as Jack jumped down and stood facing him. 'And about the plug? Where can we get another? Just say the word.'

For the first time since before his accident, no, even long before that, Kitty saw the wide grin spread across Jack's face. He leaned towards Edward as if sharing a secret. 'I allus carry a spare, Master Edward.' He tapped the side of his nose with his forefinger. 'Just in case, y'know.'

It was then that Kitty moved forward and said again, 'Jack, where is Johnnie?'

'Eh?' He looked down at her now, his annoyance at being bothered by what he considered a trivial matter showing plainly on his face. 'What? Oh, him. I haven't seen him since this morning. 'Spect he's wandered off somewhere.'

Kitty pulled in a shocked breath. 'Wandered off? Jack, he never wanders off. He never goes anywhere without telling me.'

The man shrugged. 'He'll come back when he's hungry.'

'How can you be so – so callous?' she accused through gritted teeth, but he was turning away from her again, Johnnie forgotten. All that mattered to Jack was his beloved, injured *Sylvie*.

'Oh you – *you*!' she muttered and then she turned and

ran towards the wall and through the rickety door into the garden of the Manor. Panting, she ran along the straight path leading to the back door of the house. 'Mrs Grundy, oh Mrs Grundy.' She pounded on the back door, almost falling in as it was opened.

'What on earth's all the racket about? Why, Kitty . . .' The homely figure of the cook was holding her arms wide to embrace her. 'Whatever's the matter?'

Kitty clutched at her. 'Is he here?'

'Who, lass? Is who here?'

'Johnnie. Is he here with you and Milly?' There was just the faint hope that the boy had got bored at home with his father and had come to the yard as usual, and had called in at the kitchen of the Manor to sample Mrs Grundy's scones and strawberry jam again.

But the cook was shaking her head and Kitty groaned. 'Jack was supposed to be looking after him . . .' she was babbling incoherently now in her anguish. 'But he's let him wander off somewhere. He's not seen him since morning. He must have been gone hours.'

Edward, overhearing her brief exchange with Jack, had followed her from the yard and was now standing in the doorway of the kitchen. 'What's the matter, Kitty?'

'It's Johnnie. I don't know where he is. He's been gone since this morning. I know he didn't really want to stay at home. He wanted to come here. He loves being at the threshing, but – but I told him to stay with Jack just – just . . . I mean, I wasn't sure if Jack was really strong enough to be left for the whole day without anyone there if he needed help. Seems I needn't have bothered.' A note of bitterness crept into her tone. 'He's fit enough when it comes to anything wrong with *Sylvie*.'

Edward stepped towards her and, ignoring Mrs

Grundy's watchful presence, took Kitty's hand in his grimy ones.

'Don't worry, Kitty. I expect he got bored at home and he wouldn't dare come to the yard if you'd told him not to. I'll organize a search party. Most of the team are still clearing up. I'll catch them before they leave.'

Back in the yard, Edward called the workers together. 'Have any of you seen the boy today? Young Johnnie?'

They looked at each another, murmuring, and then all shook their heads. At once Edward was issuing orders, sending the boys running in all directions to fetch more help and to begin a proper, organized search party. And all the while Jack Thorndyke remained with the engine, his hand resting possessively upon *Sylvie*'s steering wheel, taking not the slightest interest in the search for his missing son.

Fifty

As dusk fell there was still no sign of the boy and by now the whole neighbourhood had been alerted. Men from Sir Ralph's estate had joined in the search and Kitty knew that by now Miriam, who was due to leave the very next day, would know too. What would she be feeling, Kitty wondered, hearing that her son was missing?

She knew already how Mrs Franklin felt. On returning to the Manor Mrs Grundy had said, 'Madam ses I'm to lay on food for all the searchers, Kitty. Tell 'em all to come back here for a bite. Isn't she good?'

Kitty nodded, unable to speak. Of course she was good, but the cook, bless her, had no idea that it was Mrs Franklin's own grandson who was missing.

They searched the stackyard, the fields, the woods and along the banks of the meandering streams around Tresford. All in vain.

'Where can he be?' Kitty whispered, twisting her fingers.

They were standing in the small back yard at the Manor, taking a respite while Mrs Grundy and Milly bustled in and out of the back door with tea and sandwiches and glasses of homemade beer. Kitty could not hide her desperation. If anything had happened to Johnnie . . . He was her life, she realized suddenly. Even though she had not borne him, from that very first moment when she had taken him into her arms the little chap had wound himself around her heart. If she were to lose him . . . A small sob escaped her and, hearing it, Edward put his arm about her shoulders and gave her a comforting squeeze. 'We'll look again.' Then he was moving away but not before Kitty had seen Jack's glowering face. He had noticed Edward's gesture and a sneer twisted his mouth.

The search continued as dusk fell and then storm lanterns were lit. Kitty watched as the line of flickering lights moved across the fields, the men's voices, calling the boy's name, echoing through the night air. As the darkness deepened, there was still no sign of Johnnie.

'You must go home and rest, Kitty, you're worn out,' Edward tried to insist. Jack had already gone home, but Kitty was no longer angry with him. What he had accomplished this day was little short of a miracle and, had it not been for her anxiety for Johnnie, she would have rejoiced wholeheartedly.

Kitty shook her head. 'I can't leave. I can't rest. Not until he's found.'

Edward sighed, but argued no more. 'Is there anywhere you can think of where he might go? Would he go into the town, do you think? It was market day today – well – yesterday now,' he added, for midnight had come and gone. 'Is there anything he's particularly interested in, like animals or motor cars, anything like that?'

Kitty's voice was little more than a strangled whisper. 'Nothing that I can think of . . . Oh!' She clapped her hand to her mouth and her eyes widened. The words almost spurted out but she held her fingers firmly over her lips until she could formulate the words properly.

'What? What is it? Have you thought of something?'

Indeed she had thought of something, but she could not tell him what was in her mind. All she could say was, 'He – he might have – have gone to the Hall.'

Edward was puzzled. 'The Hall? Whatever for?'

'To – to say goodbye to Miss Miriam.'

'Miriam?' His puzzlement deepened, as well it might, Kitty thought. She swallowed and haltingly tried to find a plausible explanation that would cover the truth. 'During the last few weeks while – while Miss Miriam has been coming to dress Jack's wound, well, the boy has become fascinated by her. He – he thinks she's a pretty lady. And . . .' Kitty smiled, but the smile held a sadness that Edward could not have understood. 'And she's been very sweet . . .' she swallowed the lump in her throat, 'to him.'

'You do surprise me,' Edward said drily. 'I wouldn't have thought my dear sister would have had time for young children. Mind you, she was always quite good to me when I was ill.' He grasped Kitty's hand. 'Come on, we're wasting time.'

He helped her into the pony and trap and in minutes they were bowling through the dark lanes towards the Hall. Edward had his arm about her waist and she leaned against him, drawing comfort from him.

Through the huge gates and up the long curving driveway and then Kitty said, 'Don't let's wake anyone, if – if we can help it.'

'I should think most of the household is still up. They're all out looking for the young scallywag. Even Miriam. For all her faults, she is very fond of you, you know. I'm sure she'd do anything to help you find your son.'

Oh Edward, she cried silently, if only you knew the truth. Of course Miriam's out searching. Kitty hated deceiving this boy who had grown into such a wonderful man.

They had pulled into the yard at the back of the house. Edward climbed down and then turned to help Kitty.

'Now, where shall we begin? Shall we knock at the back door and . . .?'

'No, no.' She clutched at his arm, still anxious not to wake any of the household who might have gone to bed. 'Let's look around the outbuildings first, at least.'

'Right, we'll start with the stables.'

'Miss Miriam brought him here a while back to show him a foal. Maybe . . .'

The horses, disturbed from their night's repose, whinnied a soft greeting and nuzzled their shoulders as they crept down the length of the stalls.

'What about the hayloft above?' Kitty whispered and Edward patted her hand. 'Good idea.'

Kitty was close on his heels as he climbed the ladder and poked his head through the trap door. 'I can't see . . . Wait a minute.'

With a grunt, Edward heaved himself up and disappeared from her view.

'Can you see him? Is he there?'

There was a pause and a scuffle and Edward's voice floated down to her. 'Yes, he's here. Safe and sound and fast asleep.'

Then Kitty wept, leaning her head against the rough wood of the ladder. 'Oh thank God, thank God,' she whispered.

A moment later, the sleepy form of the young boy was gently lowered into her outstretched arms. 'Oh Johnnie, my darling boy.'

Then she had him in her arms and Edward was climbing back down the ladder to stand beside her while she buried her face against the boy, raining kisses on his soft cheek.

'Come along,' Edward said gently. 'We'll take him home. Then I must call off the search party and let everyone get some sleep.'

Johnnie stirred and murmured, 'Mam? I came to see the pretty lady. Mrs Harding. She's going away tomorrow,

391

but they wouldn't let me in.' Then he snuggled into her shoulder and slept once more.

Kitty tightened her arms around him, thankful to be carrying him away from the Hall.

'So, the devoted Edward found him, eh?' Jack sneered. 'Seems a shame he dun't know he was looking for his own nephew.'

'Jack, you promised . . .'

He threw back his head and laughed. Then he stepped closer and with his one hand, he gripped her arm. 'Aye, an' I'll keep it, just so long as you behave yourself, Kitty, and don't get any fancy ideas about young Franklin.'

'He's only a boy. At least, that's how I think of him,' she stammered, but now she knew that her tone was not as convincing now as it had once been. And she was so afraid that Jack would hear it in her voice. If the truth be known, she no longer thought of Edward Franklin as a sickly young boy. Now, he was a man.

Jack's grip tightened. 'Just you mind that's the way you go on thinking about him.'

He released her and walked away and, as she watched him go, Kitty knew for certain that she was no longer obsessed by him. In a way she was saddened by the realization that nothing was going to change. Jack was never going to change. As she had fought to save his life and then to drag him out of the depths of self-pity, she had still hoped that they could build a good life together. But in the days that had followed, as Jack struggled to hold a place in the threshing team once more and to prove that he could still do a man's work despite his injury, Kitty had begun to realize the truth. He was still the old Jack Thorndyke, yet with an added bitterness to his nature now that robbed him of his roguish charm. With a heavy heart, Kitty watched her hopes and dreams blown away like chaff upon the wind. She saw the man now for what he had always been, and still was. Yet there was no escape for her, for she was trapped, bound to Jack Thorndyke by the secrets of others and the solemn promises she had made.

To reveal the truth would hurt so many people; people she loved dearly. Her own family, Miriam and the gentle-natured Mrs Franklin and Johnnie – especially Johnnie. Oh no, she could not hurt Johnnie. And there was someone else now; someone for whom she also cared deeply and could not hurt. It was a love that had been there all the time, had lain dormant, unrecognized by herself for so long. A true, unselfish love that had been buried beneath the blinding obsession that she had carried for Jack. Deep in her heart she knew that she was loved in return and yet there was nothing she could do about it. It must remain locked within her, another secret, and one that held the key to her happiness and yet it could never be used.

Oh no, she could never, ever tell Edward how very much she loved him.

Fifty-One

Resolutely, Kitty determined to rebuild her life with Jack and his son. She would care for them both and perhaps, in time, Jack's bitterness would mellow and they could be happy as a family. Her hopes were short-lived. As daily his strength returned, so did his arrogance and his need of her lessened. Yet, perversely, he took delight now in belittling her, in using her body with deliberate callousness, without even a pretence of affection or tenderness. And always he kept his bitter promise.

She would never bear a child of Jack's yet he delighted in keeping her cruelly bound to him by his threat to expose her secret. And now, worst of all, he was not above lashing out at her in his rage.

In the year that followed the accident, they continued to live in the cottage on the Nunsthorpe estate and Kitty was aware that both Mr Franklin and Sir Ralph ensured that there was work always available that Jack was able to do.

'They owe me that much,' was all Jack would say. 'After all, I was working short-handed for them when it happened.'

Edward no longer walked with a stick, but he would, as he had predicted, always have a limp. Although he was invalided out of the army and home for good, the Franklin family were still anxious for Miriam's safety. Kitty had mixed, almost guilty feelings. While she prayed for

Miriam's safety, her absence from the neighbourhood meant that Kitty could live without the fear that she would get to know and become attached to Johnnie.

But as another harvest came and went and autumn gave way to winter, Edward came with the news. 'The war's over, Kitty. Have you heard?'

'Thank goodness,' she said with genuine relief, but she had to force sincerity into her next question. 'Then Miss Miriam won't need to stay in France, will she?'

He shrugged. 'There'll be all the wounded to care for and bring home. But at least she won't be in so much danger as if the fighting was still going on, thank God.'

Kitty smoothed her palms down the side of her skirt. She glanced up at him and gave a quick, shy smile. Now that she had realized just what she felt for Edward, she could not help feeling a constraint between them.

He was watching her, his gaze upon her so intently that she felt the colour creeping up her neck and into her face. 'What is it, Kitty?' he asked gently. 'More problems?'

'No, no,' she said swiftly, too swiftly. She took in a deep breath, raised her head and faced him squarely. He must not guess, she told herself, he must never guess. Everything would come out, if he did. Everything. And she could not bear that to happen.

She had been in the wash-house when he arrived and now she began to pull down the sleeves of her blouse from where they were rolled up above her elbows. Edward's glance followed her action and suddenly he reached out and caught hold of her hand, staying it. 'Wait. What's that mark on your arm, Kitty? A bruise?' Slowly, he lifted his head to look at her and now there was anger in the depths of his gentle eyes. 'How did you get that?'

She tried to laugh, attempting to hide the truth. 'I don't know. I must have banged mesen.'

Edward moved close to her, so close she could feel his breath on her face. 'Kitty, oh Kitty.' He was shaking his head as if disappointed in her. 'You don't get a bruise like that by knocking yourself. That bruise has the imprint of fingermarks.' He paused and then said, slowly, 'It can't go on, you know. You're a shadow of that lovely, merry girl who used to dance into my sickroom and brighten the day.' He sighed deeply. 'Do you know, Kitty, I wish we could turn the clock back. I'd go through all that suffering again if I could see you once more as you were then.'

Tears smarted in her eyes and a lump came into her throat. Huskily, she said, 'No, Teddy, don't say that. I hated to see you wheezing and so ill. I wouldn't want to see you like it again. Not ever.'

Annoyed with herself for having allowed her own low spirits to show, she brushed away the threatening tears with an impatient gesture and forced herself to smile brightly. 'Don't you worry about me. Whatever happens, I've only mesen to blame. I've brought it all on myself. I've made me bed, as me dad would say, now I've to lie in it.'

His gaze never left her face as he said, 'You can't still love the man, can you, if he treats you like this?'

He took her hands, red from scrubbing Jack's shirts in the hot water in the tub. 'Look at me, Kitty, and tell me you love him, really love him, and – and I'll go away and leave you alone.'

She was shaking her head, not answering his question directly. 'I have to stay. For – for Johnnie's sake.'

'I – see,' he said slowly.

No, you don't see, she wanted to shout. You don't see at all. But Kitty bit her lip and her eyes were downcast. How she wanted at this moment to tell him everything.

His fingertips touched her chin gently, raising it so that she was obliged to look up at him.

'Then – take care of yourself, Kitty Clegg. You and your little boy. And if ever – *ever* – you need help, you know just where I am. I'm only a step away.'

Wordlessly, Kitty nodded.

He turned then and walked away from her and Kitty felt as if her heart was breaking.

Jack's strength had increased steadily and when the threshing season began again in earnest, he was putting in a full day's work running his engine, with only a little help from one of the young lads when two hands were needed. Kitty had to admire his determination and, it seemed, she was not the only one who did.

'Isn't he wonderful?' Milly said, standing at the edge of the stackyard beside Kitty, who was taking a well-earned respite from her place at the chaff hole. 'He's every bit as courageous as them soldiers now.'

Kitty stared at her sister. Wrapped up in her own life, Kitty had not noticed that her young sister had grown up. With a shock, she realized that the girl was now twenty-two, a young woman and an attractive one.

Yet she could not forget that Milly had admitted putting that first white feather on Jack's engine. Outwardly, her appearance might have changed dramatically from the pasty-faced, thirteen-year-old kitchen maid, but Milly was the same person inside, Kitty thought, still capable of being devious and spiteful.

'And in time everyone will forget how he got his injury,' Milly was saying. 'They'll think he got it in the war. He'll be a hero, too.'

'So that's why you tied the white feather on to his engine, is it? To try to goad him into volunteering?'

The girl's lip curled. 'Well, you don't like to think of your man as a coward, do you?'

Kitty pulled in a sharp breath. 'A man – a real man – dun't have to go and get himself killed or maimed to make me proud of him.'

Milly turned to face her, a smirk on her face. A smile that had nothing to do with humour or with friendliness. There was malice and something else there too. Triumph. That was it, there was triumph in Milly's smile.

'I wasn't talking about *your* man, Kitty.' Then Milly turned and walked quickly through the gate and the garden towards the kitchen door of the Manor, while, puzzled, Kitty stared after her.

'You goin' to stand there gossiping all day?' came Jack's roar above the noise. 'That chaff hole'll be choked in a minute.'

'Coming,' Kitty answered automatically and began to move back towards her place, but her thoughts were still on her sister.

'Where's Dad?' Johnnie sat at the table, shovelling meat and potato pie into his mouth.

'Eat slowly, Johnnie,' Kitty remonstrated. 'No one's going to take it from your plate.'

The boy grinned, his dark blue eyes dancing with mischief. 'Sorry, Mam. But where is Dad?'

'I haven't the foggiest idea.' Kitty turned her back on the boy to put Jack's plate of food back in the oven. 'If he doesn't come home soon, this dinner'll be ruined.'

'Maybe he's gone to the Hall. The pretty lady's back, ain't she?'

Kitty stood up and twisted round sharply to stare at him and as she did so the plate slipped from her grasp, spilling meat, potato and gravy over the peg rug and soaking into its thickness. 'Oh, now look what you've made me do,' she cried in her vexation, but even as she said the words, she knew her accusation was unfair.

It was the thought that Miss Miriam was once more close by and already Johnnie knew it and was again intrigued by her.

As she fetched a bucket of water and a floor cloth and knelt on the hearth, she said, as casually as she could, 'Have you seen her? Is she all right?'

'No, I've not seen her. One of the lads working for Dad on the threshing team told me. Said there was to be a big party up at the Hall for her homecoming. The whole neighbourhood's going to be invited. Will we be invited, Mam?'

Kitty opened her mouth to give a wry laugh and say, 'Of course not. We're not gentry,' but the words stuck in her throat.

Maybe she did not have the right, but Johnnie did. Probably more than any of the other guests, little Johnnie Thorndyke had every right to be at the party to welcome his mother home.

Thank God he doesn't know it, she thought.

Fifty-Two

As the early months of 1919 turned towards summer and the threshing work lessened, to Kitty's surprise Jack started arriving home later and later. She was puzzled. At this time of year Jack had always undertaken other work, hedging and ditching, fencing, even building. But, with only one arm, much of this work was now impossible for him. She had expected that, when forced into an idleness he hated, he would become even more quick-tempered and moody. The local estate owners and farmers would try to put work his way that they knew he could manage. Knowing that he lived on their charity would not help Jack's temper either, Kitty thought.

Instead, he was suddenly much kinder to her. He never once raised his hand to her now and he never took her roughly in their shared bed at night, using her body to ease his needs with a savage bitterness. But neither, she thought, did he make love to her as he once had in those early days that seemed so far off now. He was more thoughtful towards her, though his temper still sparked if something annoyed him.

'I'll get one of the lads to look after the chaff hole when we start the threshing again next winter, Kitty. You do a grand job there, but it's the muckiest there is. Think you could manage on top of the drum instead?'

Kitty laughed, touched by his sudden concern. She

400

flexed her muscles. 'I reckon I could. Strong as a carthorse, me.'

He turned away and over his shoulder, with a deliberate casualness that was not lost on Kitty, said, 'I may not be back tonight. I've got to go further afield looking for a bit of work to tide me over until harvest time.'

As he walked away from her without looking back, Kitty stared after him. Then suddenly, she knew. Jack had another woman.

'How could I have been so blind?' she murmured. 'Of course, that's it. That explains his odd behaviour. Nice as pie one minute and shouting his head off the next if summat dun't suit him.'

Then another thought came into her head. A thought that made her gasp and put trembling fingers to her mouth. 'Oh no, she wouldn't. She couldn't be so stupid. Not again. Don't, oh please don't, let it be Miss Miriam.'

Jack did not return that night. In the early morning light, he walked through the fields, the dew dampening his boots and the bottom of his trousers, to find an angry Kitty waiting for him. She flung open the back door and stood on the threshold, barring his way into the cottage. Her arms folded across her bosom, she tapped the toe of her foot on the step. 'You've got another woman, ain't you, Jack Thorndyke? Who is it?'

He thrust his face close to hers. 'Why should you care? You've not been a good wife to me.'

'I aren't your wife,' she reminded him.

'No, and ya never will be neither. All you care about is that lad.' His mouth twisted into a sneer as he added cruelly, 'Anybody would think he was yours.'

Without thinking, Kitty raised her hand to strike him,

401

to shut his foul mouth, but he caught hold of her wrist. 'Oh no you don't, miss. Strike a cripple, would you?'

'You're no cripple, but if it hadn't been for me, you might still be languishing up there in that bed. It was me got you out of it, me got you back to work and made you a man again. I gave you back your pride, Jack Thorndyke, and don't you forget it.'

He laughed, flinging her away from him. 'You think what you like, but it weren't you. Not even then. Oh, I know you like to think so. I know you like to think you were the heroine, looking after me and the boy and working in the team to keep things going. But while you were so busy, there was someone else there for me. Someone who came every day to see me, who nursed me and fed me. She, not you, made me feel the man again.'

The shock was like a physical blow. She felt it in the pit of her stomach and automatically her hand clutched her midriff. Her legs trembled and felt as if they would let her down. 'Oh no! Not – not . . .'

She had to stop it. She had to stop Miriam throwing her life away. Her whole family would disown her. Even the kindly Sir Ralph would have no pity for her. She mustn't, just mustn't, be so foolish. She, Kitty, could stop it. She could make her see sense, could tell her what life would be like with Jack Thorndyke.

Or did Miriam hope to raise him up? To take him and Johnnie to live with her and . . .

The thought was like a knife in Kitty's heart and a little cry escaped her lips.

Johnnie! Oh no! They could take him from her. His real parents – both his parents – they really could take him away from her.

With a sudden jolt, Kitty realized that in all of her

thinking not once had she bewailed the fact that she was losing Jack.

It was not Jack Thorndyke who filled her mind and her heart now; it was a dark-haired, mischievous little boy called Johnnie.

Jack was nodding. 'Aye, that's right. Someone who's proud of me just the way I am.'

Kitty pulled in a deep, shuddering breath and with it, her determination flooded through her again. 'I won't let it happen, Jack. I won't let you ruin her life or take Johnnie from me. I'll fight you every step of the way. I mean it.'

'He's my son. You say so yourself.'

'Yes, I'll not deny that. He has a right to know his father—'

'He has a right to be *with* his father.'

And his mother, Kitty's heart jerked. His real mother. She held her breath, waiting for the dreadful words to come from Jack's lips.

'Besides,' he was saying, 'you'll still be able to see him. I'm sure your sister won't mind.'

'What?' A tumult of emotions was tearing her apart. First hope, then swiftly followed by another fear. 'What are you saying? You don't mean – you can't mean – that it's *Milly*?'

He was staring at her. 'Of course it's Milly. I'd've thought you'd've guessed. You knew how much time she spent with me at the cottage when I was laid up. You knew . . .'

Now Kitty's legs did give way and she crumpled to the ground.

He was staring down at her but made no effort to help her.

'Who on earth did you think it was?' he began and

then, suddenly, he laughed out loud. 'You thought it was her ladyship, didn't you? Miriam. You thought it was her?'

Kitty was rocking backwards and forwards, not knowing whether to laugh or cry, and she found she was doing both; with relief that it was not Miriam and shock that Milly, her own sister, could be so stupid.

Jack was watching her, rather put out by her reaction. A frown creased his forehead and his eyes were dark with anger. 'What's so funny?'

Kitty was shaking her head. 'Of all people, Milly! And she . . .' She stopped suddenly and pressed her lips together. She had been about to say 'and she was the one who gave you that first white feather' but she bit back the words.

And there was another reason too. A reason that made her feel light-headed; a wonderful, glorious reason. If Jack and Milly were together then she would be free. She could leave and take Johnnie with her.

Then as quickly as it had come, the thought died. How could she let Milly wreck her life as she had done? Despite everything, Milly was still her sister, and Kitty, better than anyone else, knew just what Jack Thorndyke was really like.

Oh no, she couldn't let it happen.

The door to freedom which, miraculously, had just begun to open, was suddenly slammed in her face. She was still trapped. Their lives were as tightly entwined as the tiny plaits woven by Jack's clever fingers to make the corn maidens. And just as cleverly had he bound her to him.

She was shaking her head slowly. 'It's not going to happen, Jack. I won't let it happen.'

He threw back his head and let out a great roar of laughter. He stepped close to her then and gripped her chin with his fingers, so hard that it left tiny bruise marks on her jawline. 'You jealous, Kitty?'

Anger flashed briefly in her eyes, but she quelled it. This was not the way. Now she had to put on an act. And she was quite capable of it, for hadn't she fooled everyone – except Jack – about Johnnie? Her own family, even Edward. No, no, she must not think of him. Not now, not at this moment, she must not allow herself to think of Edward or her resolve would crumble. Now she must make Jack think she still wanted *him*, still loved *him*.

'And how,' he was saying slowly, 'do you think you're going to stop it?'

'I'll tell our dad. He'll stop it – and Mrs Grundy. Milly wants to be a cook, more than anything. She . . .' Kitty's voice faltered as Jack shook his head.

'Oh no, that's where you're wrong, Kitty. Milly wants – more than anything else in this whole wide world – to be with me.' With deliberately measured cruelty, he added, 'To – be – my – wife.'

The shock was complete. 'You're – you're going to *marry* her?'

'That's right. She'll make a good wife and – a good mother for Johnnie.'

Kitty felt as if her blood had turned to ice. There was a moment's stillness as if they were both frozen in time and then she wrenched herself free and screamed, so loudly and so suddenly, that even Jack was startled and stepped backwards.

'No, no, never. I'll never let you do that.'

He had regained his composure, his sureness. 'How are you going to stop me?' he said again. 'A boy should be with his father or, of course, his *real* mother. You're nothing to him, Kitty Clegg. Nothing!'

'I'm the only mother he's ever known. He – he's everything to me.'

'Oh aye,' he laughed wryly. 'I used to be everything to you once upon a time.'

She shook her head. 'You changed, Jack, even before your accident. You were so bitter and twisted, you . . .'

'Oh aye, and hadn't I good reason. You tried to deceive me, Kitty. Tried to use that child to force me to marry you. If you'd only been honest with me from the start then maybe we'd've had a chance, but as it was . . .' He left the accusation hanging between them.

'It wasn't my secret, Jack, that's why I couldn't tell you. It was wrong, I know that now. But what I did I didn't do for myself. I did it for Johnnie. He would have been given away, handed over to complete strangers. I couldn't let that happen. The minute I held him, I loved him. Partly because he was yours and I – I loved you, but for his own sake too. I loved *Johnnie* – for himself. I still do and I always will.' Blind rage filled her and she shook her fist at him. 'You won't take him away from me. I won't let you.' She was beyond caring now. This was the one thing that would make her break her years of silence. 'Whatever it costs, you won't take Johnnie.'

Fifty-Three

'He won't marry you, Milly,' Kitty said bluntly, facing her sister across the table in the kitchen at the Manor, the same table on which the doctor had cut off Jack's arm.

'Yes, he will. He's asked me.'

'What's this?' Mrs Grundy, bad on her legs now, waddled from the range to stand at the end of the table between them, glancing first at one and then at the other.

'You getting married, Milly? Who to? You might 'ave said you'd be leaving, 'cos the mistress won't let you stay if you're married.'

'Now look what you've started,' Milly hissed at Kitty.

'And there was me teaching you all me secrets, an' all,' Mrs Grundy was in full, indignant, flood. 'You deceitful, ungrateful girl . . .'

'Oh shut up, you silly old woman. What do I care—?'

The cook's mouth dropped open and her eyes bulged. 'Well, I—'

'How dare you speak to Mrs Grundy like that? Apologize this minute.'

'I'll do no such thing,' Milly snapped. 'How I've put up with her whining on at me these last few years, about how wonderful *you* were and how you'd thrown yourself away on a useless, good-for-nothing Jack-the-Lad. Oh, I've had it all and now I've had enough.'

'She was right. I did. The only good thing in my life is little Johnnie. And let me tell you, our Milly . . .' she wagged her forefinger in her sister's face, 'and I've told Jack an' all. You're not having him. Not Johnnie.'

The girl shrugged. 'Suits me. I don't want the little brat. I only agreed because Jack wants his son. But I reckon a child should stay with his mother, anyway. So you're welcome.'

Kitty stared, surprised that Jack had not told Milly the truth. But he would, she knew he would. Now.

The fight drained from her. 'Oh Milly, Milly . . .' She sank down into a chair at the table and rested her arms on its surface. 'Think what you're doing. Please. You've seen what's happened to me. Look at me. I look an old woman before me time. Worn out. He'll never change, can't you see? He'll always be a Jack-the-Lad. Once he's tired of you, he'll . . .'

'No, he won't. I've told you, he's going to *marry* me.'

'I'll believe it when I see it.'

She had never seen such spite in her sister's face as Milly said, 'You will, Kitty, you will.'

Kitty dragged herself wearily to her feet, turned and left the kitchen. As she went out of the back door she heard Mrs Grundy's voice raised once more. 'You can pack your bags and leave this minute. And I don't care what the mistress says, *I'm* dismissing you. I won't have you in my kitchen a moment longer.'

'Jack, Milly doesn't want Johnnie. She said so herself.'

When she got back to the cottage, Jack was cutting wood, wielding the huge axe with his one arm. Johnnie was there, helping. He placed each log on the chopping block and then stood back, well out of the way, while Jack swung the axe. He had perfect aim each time, and the log split into two. Johnnie ran forward and repositioned the wood, then stepped back as the man cut it once more.

Jack paused and looked up at her, the axe resting on the block. Kitty was aware too that Johnnie was looking at her, an unspoken question in his eyes. She turned to him. 'Johnnie, go into the house and collect your belongings. We're leaving.'

'Leaving?' His startled gaze went from one to the other, between the two people he believed to be his parents. Both his parents. 'But we can't. I'm helping Dad.'

'That's right, son,' Jack's voice came, deceptively soft, but Kitty could hear the underlying menace. 'You're staying with your dad. She can go if she wants, can't she? But you're staying here.'

'No, Dad. Don't let her go.' He turned wide, perplexed eyes on her. 'Don't go, Mam.' He couldn't understand what was happening. All he knew was that he didn't want anyone to go anywhere. He wanted them to stay together, the three of them.

Kitty squatted down and held out her hand to him. 'Come here, Johnnie.'

Reluctantly the boy moved towards her, all the time glancing back towards his father. 'What?' he muttered morosely.

She caught hold of his hands and pulled him to her. 'Your father is going to marry Milly. My sister, Milly.'

'No, no,' the boy shouted, pulling his hands away and turning back to face his father. 'You aren't, Dad, are you? Say you aren't.'

Ignoring his son, Jack picked up the axe and took a step towards Kitty. 'I'm warning you,' he said. 'You stop trying to turn that boy against me, else I'll . . .'

Kitty stood up, caught hold of Johnnie and pushed him behind her. 'Go, Johnnie, run. Run, I tell you.'

And he went, on flying feet through the gate and into the lane. As they stood facing each other, they could hear his feet pounding on the hard surface of the lane, the sound growing fainter and fainter.

Kitty breathed more easily. Johnnie was safe.

'Now, Kitty Clegg, it's just you and me, then.'

Squarely she faced him, but the anger had drained out of her now to be replaced by a terrible sadness. How had it all come to this, that she was facing the man she had once loved so passionately and he was brandishing an axe?

'Remember the dog and the rat in the barrel, Jack? Well, I'm like that little dog you put in there that day. I'm turning, Jack. It's taking me a mite longer than that terrier, but now I'm biting back. I'm biting back at long last. I loved you, then. I really did, I'll never say otherwise, but slowly over the years you've killed that love and now I feel nothing for you. I don't even hate you, Jack,' she added sadly, ''cos even that's a – a feeling. And I don't have any feelings left for you. None at all. And that . . .' There was a lump in her throat and a catch in her voice. 'And that, to me, is very sad.'

'You do what you like, but he's going nowhere. He's staying here. He's *my* son.' Jack stepped towards her, lifting up the axe as he came. Kitty put out her hand as if to fend him off when they both heard a voice behind them, a voice that made them stop.

Jack held the axe suspended in midair, and Kitty closed her eyes and breathed, 'No, oh no. Not now.'

'Thorndyke,' Edward's voice came again. 'Step back. Away from her. This instant. Do you hear me?'

Jack held the axe higher, gripping it firmly, but now he was facing the approaching Edward.

'Don't be a fool, man. Drop it.'

'Don't come any nearer, mester. This is nowt to do wi' you.'

'That's where you're wrong, Thorndyke. Very wrong. Kitty is not staying with you a moment longer.' Though his gaze never left Jack or the axe in his hand, Edward spoke to Kitty. 'Get your things, and the boy's. You're coming with me.'

'Edward, I – I can't . . .'

The axe came even higher. 'You've no business here, mester. Be on ya way afore I . . .'

'Before you what, Mr Thorndyke? Knock Kitty senseless again? Kill her? Do you really think,' Edward's voice dropped to a low, controlled, yet menacing growl, 'do you really think I am going to leave her one second longer with you?'

Jack took a step towards Edward. 'Oh yeah? And what are ya going to do about it, *Mester* Franklin? Knock me down, eh?'

Jack stood a good three inches taller than Edward. Despite the loss of one arm, his shoulders were still broad and he wielded the axe as if it were as light as a feather.

'If I have to, yes,' Edward said quietly. 'And don't think I'd have any compunction in hitting a one-armed man, Thorndyke, because I wouldn't. Not after what you've done to Kitty. You're a very brave man, aren't you, Thorndyke, with an axe in your hand against a defenceless woman?'

A low growl came from Jack. 'Just 'cos you've been in the war, Mester High 'n' Mighty, it dun't mean—'

'I said nothing about the war, man. That has nothing to do with this. Put the axe down and let her go.'

Jack hesitated for a moment longer, then he flung it away from him. It clattered against the chopping block

411

and lay there at a drunken angle. 'What makes you think she'll come with you?'

Kitty saw a flicker of sadness in Edward's eyes but he said firmly, 'She'll come, if only for the sake of the boy.'

'Ah yes.' Jack's tone was suddenly as smooth. 'The boy.'

There was silence as the two men challenged each other like two fighting cocks.

'The boy,' Jack said slowly and with deliberate menace, 'stays with me.'

Edward shook his head. 'Oh no. A boy of his age should be with his mother.'

Jack's sudden bellow of laughter startled both Kitty and Edward.

'His mother? His *mother*?'

Kitty moved swiftly and caught hold of his arm. 'No, Jack, no. Please – don't . . .'

He flung her away, knocking her to the ground. She fell awkwardly on her arm and winced in pain.

Jack pushed his face close to Edward's, bending slightly so that their eyes were on a level. Slowly and deliberately, he said, 'She is not his mother.'

For a long moment Edward stared at him. 'Don't be stupid . . .' he began and then his glance slid past Jack to where Kitty, still sitting on the ground, gave a low moan. She closed her eyes and, bowing her head, buried her face in her hands. Her shoulders shook as sobs convulsed her. She rocked backwards and forwards, the tears coursing down her face and sobs choking her throat. 'No, no, oh no.'

Above her the two men faced each other, Edward's gaze now meeting Jack's malicious eyes. 'Then who . . .?'

Enjoying every moment, the triumph evident in his

voice, Jack said, 'Your dearly beloved sister, Miriam Franklin, is Johnnie's real mother.'

Kitty, daring to look up, saw Edward's face turn deathly pale. He continued to stare at Jack for what seemed an eternity, a moment suspended in time, and then very slowly his gaze came down to rest upon Kitty's upturned, tear-streaked face.

'Edward,' she began. 'Please – I . . .'

With a sudden movement he turned and walked away.

'Edward,' she cried out with hollow desperation. 'Edward, please . . .'

But Edward Franklin continued to walk away from her and though she watched him until he passed through the small gate and into the lane, not once did he look back.

Jack turned and looked down at her. 'There now, that's how much ya fancy man thinks of you. Can't take the truth, can he?'

Anger surged through her, a red, uncontrollable rage that made her scramble to her feet and clench her fists. She raised her arms and beat his chest. 'You fool! You stupid, stupid fool.'

He caught hold of her, pinioning both wrists easily in the broad grasp of his one hand. 'Don't you call me a fool.'

'You promised, Jack. You . . .'

'I never promised any such thing.'

'Let – me – go,' she cried, wrenching herself free. Standing back, a little way from him, she shook her fist. 'I'm done with you, Jack Thorndyke. The only thing that's held me here these last few years has been the truth about Johnnie. And now that's out, there's nothing to keep me here.'

His lip curled. 'The boy stays with me. He is *my* son.'

'Prove it,' she spat back at him. 'Your name's not on

his birth certificate, because I registered him. I am his mother in the eyes of the law.'

He stepped closer, menacing, trying to intimidate her, but Kitty was too angry now to be afraid. 'In the eyes of the law, then, you've committed a criminal act if you've registered yourself as his mother.'

'Prove it,' she said again boldly. 'Who's to prove it?'

For a moment he looked nonplussed then the devious smile curved his mouth again, a mouth, Kitty noticed now, that had a cruel twist to it. 'There must have been people who knew when he was born just who did give birth to him. There must have been a midwife or a doctor present.'

Now it was Kitty's turn to smile deviously. 'Oh aye, and where was he born then? Only me and Miss Miriam know that and we aren't going to tell.'

His face was thunderous, but he was not beaten yet. Not quite. He shook his fist in her face. 'I'll report you for giving false information on his birth certificate. That's a criminal offence.'

Kitty realized he was probably right, but she had one final card to play and it was as if her whole future depended upon it. 'Go on, then. Report it. But just think – before you do – what it would do to Johnnie. You make out you care for him so much. Let's see if you really do. You know full well that you are his father, but is it the action of a loving, concerned father to drag such a scandal through the courts? And how would you come out of it? When you seduced Miss Miriam, she was a young, genteel girl who, for all her fiery temper, was very naive and probably didn't know much about how babies were made. But you did, Jack Thorndyke. How will that look, eh, splashed across all the local papers?' She paused, seeing the glimmer of uncertainty creeping into his eyes now. Then she made her final thrust. 'Go on then, Jack, report the whole sorry story. You can't hurt me any more than you already have done. But there's others you will hurt and badly. Miss Miriam and her family – and that includes Sir Ralph now, because despite the way his son died, he's stuck by her and he's very fond of her. Treats her like a daughter, he does, even though she mebbe doesn't deserve it. And you – who do you think is going to employ Threshing Jack around here after that? Because Sir Ralph and Mr Franklin will see to it that no one does.'

'By, you're spiteful, Kitty Clegg, when it comes to it, ain't you?'

Kitty shook her head and said, with infinite sadness in her tone, 'There's no spite in what I'm saying. I'm just stating the simple truth. But I'm finished with you, Jack, 'cos there's no more you can do to hurt me now. I loved you once, oh how very much I loved you. I'd have done anything for you . . .' she nodded, 'and I did. But slowly you've killed that love and now I feel nothing for you, except perhaps a great sadness for what might have been.'

'I suppose you think your genteel lover, Master Edward, is going to rescue you, eh?'

She shook her head. 'No, not now,' she said hoarsely. 'Not after what he's learned this day.'

'No, turned his back on you, hasn't he, now he's found you out for the scheming little hussy you really are.'

They glared at each other, but no more was said. Everything had been said, and that had been a mite too much. How true it was, Kitty thought, that you could never undo something once said.

Jack's outburst could never be undone and oh, what tragedy might yet unfold because of his few vengeful words.

Fifty-Four

'Good morning, Mrs Clegg. Are Kitty and – and young Johnnie staying with you?'

She heard his voice at the door and, straightening up from where she had been bending over to black-lead the range in her mother's kitchen, Kitty's heart began to pound.

'Teddy,' she breathed, the pet name of their youth coming to her lips. She half-turned, looking towards the door, absent-mindedly rubbing her hands down her apron, leaving grubby streaks. A smudge on the end of her nose gave her a vulnerable, girlish look and this was how Edward saw her when he came into the room at her mother's invitation. They stood staring at each other while behind Edward, Mrs Clegg quietly closed the door and tiptoed out of the house.

On the day her world had finally fallen apart, Kitty had spent three hours searching the fields and woods for Johnnie. At last she had found him, once more huddled in the hayloft in the stables at the Hall.

She had climbed up and sat down in the warm dry hay beside him. For a long time they had not spoken. Then he had moved in the hay beside her and she felt his warmth as he snuggled against her side. 'I met Mister Edward in the lane and he – he asked me if anything was the matter. I – I . . .' The boy hesitated, as if ashamed to admit it. 'I was crying.' Her arm went about him and in the dusk, she smiled sadly. It seemed to her infinitely sad that a boy as young as Johnnie should feel shame at shedding tears.

'I didn't tell him anything, but he must have just come to see what was happening.'

'It's all right. It – it doesn't matter,' she tried to reassure him though it was hard to keep the tremble from her voice. If only, oh if only, Teddy hadn't come at that moment.

Beside her, the boy shifted again and the hay rustled. His voice was muffled against her as he said, 'I don't want to stay with Dad if that Milly's going to come. I don't like her. Why does he want her when he's got you?'

Now Kitty did smile. 'It's all very complicated. Maybe some day I will explain it all to you. It's grown-up silliness. But your dad isn't happy with me any more and he thinks he can be with Milly.' She sighed. 'Maybe he can. I don't know.'

She was tired of it all. Tired of all the secrets and the lies. In a way she was glad it was out, glad that the ties that bound her so tightly to Jack had been severed just as if he had cut them with the axe he had been wielding.

'Then I want to come with you. I don't want to stay with him – and her.' His arms tightened about Kitty and happiness and relief flooded through her. His voice was muffled as he buried his face against her breast. 'I love you, Mam. Whatever happens, I'll stay with you.'

They had climbed down from the loft then, hand in hand, and made their way back through the darkness to the cottage. Jack was gone and Kitty neither knew nor cared where. But she packed their few belongings and left, anxious to be out before he should return. She was not sure what he intended to do about Johnnie. She feared that he would still, if he could, try to take the boy from her.

In the early hours of the morning they were knocking on the door of the stationmaster's house.

'It won't be for long, Mam, I promise,' she told a startled and bleary-eyed Betsy Clegg. 'Just until I can sort out what I'm going to do. We ought to get away, right away from here, but I can't go yet. Not just yet.'

Something had held her here. Was it a vain hope that, even yet, all was not lost?

And now here he was standing in the centre of the cramped and crowded kitchen, the only sound the singing of the kettle on the hearth. She rubbed her hands down her apron again, feeling them damp with nervousness.

'Master Edward.' Aloud the courtesy title still came automatically. 'Won't you – sit down?' Her voice was hoarse.

But he continued to stand, just looking at her. 'Oh Kitty,' he said at last and a small, sad smile touched his mouth. 'Still not "Teddy"?'

She glanced down, awkward and unsure. Then she lifted her head and looked at him again as she felt the tears prickle her eyelids. 'Oh Teddy,' she burst out, no longer able to contain the words. 'I'm so sorry, so terribly sorry. How you must hate me, despise me . . .'

He covered the space between them in two strides and put his hands gently on her shoulders. 'How could you even think that of me? Don't you know how very much I love you, adore you. I always have. All I have ever wanted was your happiness. And now I find that your life has been wretched and all because of my selfish sister. And my mother, if it comes to that. Yesterday, when Thorndyke blurted it out, it was a shock naturally, but when I'd – well – calmed down, I realized that it wasn't so much of a surprise after all. Everything fell into place at once. Even though I was only a boy at the time – and a sick one at that – I remember being concerned about Miriam. I used to see her riding off across the fields, but I thought she was going to the Hall to see Guy. And I knew he would never have done anything to harm her. When you both went away so suddenly, I was puzzled for a while but I believed my mother's explanation that she wanted Miriam to see a bit of the world before she settled down as Guy's wife. And then, when you came back, all I could think of was that I'd lost you for ever to Jack because you'd had his child.' He paused and wrinkled his forehead and there was a note of surprise in his tone now. 'But do you know, even then, it didn't ring quite true that my selfish sister would have been so thoughtful and caring about her maid that she'd have taken her away and looked after her. Now I see that it was much more likely to be the other way about. And it was, wasn't it?'

Kitty nodded wordlessly.

His tone hardened. 'I am not proud of how my sister and my mother have used you, Kitty.'

She was shaking her head. 'No, no, it wasn't like that. I am as much to blame. But they were going to place Johnnie for adoption. They were going to give him away and I couldn't bear it. And that part of it, I've never regretted. Not for a moment. But I was wrong when I – I tried to deceive Jack.'

'Ah yes, Jack Thorndyke.' Edward's hands fell away and his mouth was tight. 'He's at the centre of everything, isn't he?' He ran his hand through his hair. 'Kitty, do you, despite everything, still love him?'

'No, no, I don't.' Briefly, she covered her face with her hands and then she felt him gently pulling them away and taking them, dirty as they were, into his own and holding them tightly. 'Kitty? Kitty, look at me.'

Slowly she raised her eyes to look into his. Never in the whole of her life had she seen such love and devotion in

419

anyone's eyes. And it was for her, all for her. Suddenly, she felt very humble. 'Oh Teddy, I've been such a stupid fool.'

'Hush, my love . . .' and then his lips touched hers in a kiss so gentle it was almost reverent.

She clung to him then, burying her face against his neck and as his arms went about her, holding her close, she sobbed out all the unhappiness, all the burden of the guilty secret she had borne so long.

'I'm sorry, so sorry . . .'

'Hush now, hush, my dearest,' he murmured and when at last she drew back and took the handkerchief he offered, he coaxed her to sit down in the old leather chair at the side of the range that was her father's place. He dropped to one knee on the pegged rug and once more took her hands into his. 'Kitty Clegg,' he said, and though his tone was light-hearted, almost teasing, the expression in his eyes was never more serious. 'Will you do me the great honour of becoming my wife?'

Kitty gasped. 'Oh Teddy, I couldn't – I mean . . . It wouldn't be right.'

The tone was still gentle though now she could see the hurt in his face. 'Why, Kitty? I thought you said you didn't love him any more. I know you can never love me, but I'd take care of you, you and your son. All I want is to make you happy.'

She noticed that he said, with slight emphasis, 'your son', and she loved him all the more for that.

'Oh Teddy, you're wrong . . .' Suddenly she was over-come with shyness and stammered, 'I d-do love you. Truly I do. That's what's so awful – what's been so awful.'

'Kitty,' he said, touching her face with the tips of his fingers. 'Do you mean it? Do you really mean it?'

'Yes, oh yes. I've loved you for so long now, ever since before you went away to the war, I think.'

'Then why? Whyever did you stay with him if . . .?'

She was shaking her head. 'Don't you see? I couldn't leave him, because he threatened to tell the truth if I did. About Johnnie being Miriam's. And – and he threatened to take Johnnie away from me.'

'So you stayed with him, all this time, just to keep the secret? My sister's secret?'

She nodded. 'Yes, but it was for Johnnie too. I love him dearly, Teddy, every bit as much as if he really were my own son. And after all, Jack was his father.'

'I see.' He was silent a moment and then probed gently, 'And now? Are things different now that the secret's out? Well, out as far as me, that is, because I don't plan to let it go any further. But surely Thorndyke has no hold over you now?'

She shuddered. 'I'm afraid he'll tell Johnnie to try to turn him against me.'

'But the boy's too young. He couldn't grasp the full meaning of it. Thorndyke wouldn't stoop so low, surely?'

Kitty shrugged helplessly. 'I really don't know what he might do. He's like a stranger now. I feel as if I hardly know him any more.'

'I suppose he could still demand the boy,' Edward said slowly.

'He could try,' Kitty said, with a renewed surge of determination. 'He did try, but I called his bluff . . .' And she related the events that had followed Edward's quarrel with Jack, but ended, with infinite sadness in her tone, 'So you see, although I do – do love you, I can't bring trouble on you. If he reports me to the authorities like he's threatened . . .'

In answer, Edward raised her hands to his lips and

kissed each work-worn finger, slowly and deliberately. 'Do you really think I care about that? Whatever happens, I'll be there for you. We'll face it together. Just marry me, Kitty. Marry me. Please?'

Fifty-Five

'Over my dead body! She'll marry into that family over my dead body.' John Clegg wagged his forefinger only inches from his wife's face, while Kitty stood staring helplessly as the quarrel – the worst quarrel she had ever witnessed between her parents – vibrated through the house.

'It was bad enough,' he ranted on, 'that she went to work for them. But you – *you* . . .' he almost spat the word, 'you wanted her there. I reckon you wanted her with him. Close to the master.' He thrust his face near his wife's and the bitterness of years was in every line, in the twist of his mouth and the flash of his eyes. 'Did you want the same thing to happen to her, eh, as happened to you?'

For a moment, Betsy wilted under his rage. 'John, how can you say such a thing? How can you even think it?'

He had the grace to look a little ashamed but, belligerently, he muttered, 'Well, how am I to know what to think? I'd've thought you'd have wanted to cut loose from that family altogether, not keep clinging to them. Instead, you send your daughter – two of your daughters – to work for them. How am I supposed to know what to think?' he repeated and then added, with one last shaft of malice, 'Besides, there's bad blood in them girls.' He flung out his hand towards Kitty. 'Your bad blood, bringing disgrace to our door. As if it weren't bad enough what happened years ago, I have to go through it all again. And now Milly an' all.'

'Now just you look here, John Clegg.' As his anger died away into maudlin self-pity, Betsy's indignation flared.

Kitty tried to interpose. 'Mam, don't. I didn't want to cause trouble between you . . .'

But Betsy flapped her away. 'It's not about you, Kitty, this. There's things need to be said. Should've been said years ago.' She faced her husband again. 'You talk as if I'd betrayed you, been unfaithful to you, but you courted me and married me *after* all that business.'

John Clegg glanced uncomfortably at Kitty, but Betsy had an answer ready. 'Oh aye, I've told her all about it. She knows. Your attitude over her bit of trouble wasn't that of a loving father, was it now? I had to make her see it wasn't all her fault.'

Kitty swallowed, feeling fresh guilt sweep over her. 'Mam . . .' But Betsy was in full flow now.

'Just answer me one thing, John. Did you ever love me? Did you marry me because you were genuinely fond of me or . . .?' Now it was her turn to lean towards him and say, 'Or did you think you could worm your way into the Franklins' good books by removing an "embarrassment" for them, eh? Maybe,' she went on, slowly and with calculated deliberation, 'maybe you even thought that Henry Franklin would be so grateful to you that he'd set you up for life in a nice little job and slip you a few extra quid now and then, eh? Well, maybe he didn't keep you on in the job you wanted, but I'll tell you summat that you don't know. He got you the job here, on the railway.'

The man frowned. 'How do you know that?'

Quietly now, she said, 'Because he told me.'

'Well, I've no cause to be thankful for that. A job on the railway when all I wanted was to be with me 'osses.'

Betsy sighed and shook her head. 'But you've a position as stationmaster, some standing in the town, and just remember how fast you got that promotion.'

He stared at her. 'You telling me he was behind that an' all? That it wasn't on me own merit?'

Betsy shrugged but said nothing and Kitty marvelled at her mother's new-found strength. But no, it wasn't new-found. It had always been there, and it was Kitty's strength too.

'You talk about my bad blood, John,' Betsy was saying now, 'but I know you and your devious little ways. I've seen 'em over the years.' Now she prodded her forefinger towards him. 'And it's *you* our Milly takes after, if it's anyone.'

Angrily, he turned away from her and wrenched open the back door of the house. 'Oh you do what you like. But I won't be going to no wedding at the Manor and that's final.'

The door slammed and the two women looked at each other.

'Oh Mam, I'm so sorry.'

To her surprise, Betsy was smiling. 'I've wanted to get that off me chest for years, lass. You've done me a favour.' She took hold of Kitty's hands and looked deep into her eyes. 'Just remember, Kitty, that we're each responsible for what we do in life. Not anyone else. What I did all those years ago was my own doing, my choice. Henry didn't force himself on me, or seduce me. I knew what I was doing. I loved him, and, though I'm sorry that it caused such trouble, I'm not sorry for loving the man. What you did with Jack Thorndyke, you did because you loved him. Yes, you've had a child out of wedlock, but you've borne what others call shame with pride and stood tall. It isn't your fault that Jack's the way he is, that he won't marry you. But now you have a second chance. Take it, Kitty, and be happy, because if ever I saw a man in love with a girl, then that's Edward Franklin with you.'

'I know.' Kitty's voice was choked. 'I know, Mam. But what about me dad?'

'He'll calm down. We'll rub along together just as we always have done. I'm very fond of him, you know, and I think he is of me.'

'Very fond', Kitty thought sadly, wasn't the description she would want to use for the foundation of a marriage. Not when, each day, she found she loved Edward more and more.

'So, will you,' she asked her mother hesitantly, 'come to the wedding?'

'Try keeping me away,' Betsy laughed and hugged her daughter.

It had been a surprise to Kitty that the only objection to their marriage had come from her family and not from the Franklins or Sir Ralph.

'You really mean,' she asked Edward for the tenth time, 'that your mother *and* your father really – well – approve?'

'If this war's done nothing else,' Edward said, 'it has helped to sweep away the – what shall we call it – the gulf between the classes?' His smile widened. 'Besides, Mother's very fond of you, you know. And not only because she has good reason to be grateful to you.'

'Yes, but that still doesn't explain . . .'

'Well,' he said, feigning a modesty he was obviously not feeling, 'maybe I had a little to do with it. I told them all, quite plainly, that I was marrying you whether they liked it or not, so there!'

She put her arms around his neck and kissed his cheek. He, of all of them, had never, ever treated her as a servant.

'Teddy, oh Teddy,' she whispered against his ear. 'I do love you so.'

They were married quietly in the small church on Sir Ralph's estate with only their immediate families present. Sir Ralph generously held a reception at the Hall where no one seemed entirely at ease. Kitty's family stood awkwardly, almost afraid to touch the delicate china as guests, yet as servants in such a house they would not have thought twice about serving their betters with it. Sir Ralph moved among his guests with courteous ease and Miriam too, smiling, handed round the plates of sandwiches and cakes herself while the dreaded Mrs Bembridge stood beside the butler near the door, her mouth tight with disapproval.

Kitty saw Sir Ralph at last come to stand before Mrs Franklin. She saw the tilt of his head towards her and saw the way Amelia Franklin looked up into his eyes. If ever there were two people who should have been married to each other, Kitty thought suddenly, it was Sir Ralph and Amelia Franklin.

'Penny for them,' a voice said softly at her side and, startled, Kitty gave a swift, almost guilty laugh.

'I was just being foolish.' She looked into the eyes of the man who had been her husband for just over an hour and said, 'I'm so happy today, Teddy, that I suppose I want everyone else to be too.'

His glance went across the room. 'My mother, you mean,' he murmured. 'And Sir Ralph.'

'Oh no,' she began quickly, confused and embarrassed. 'I didn't mean . . .'

Edward took her hand in his. 'My darling, it's no secret. It's been the talk of the county for years. In circles where, years ago, suitable marriages were arranged by parents, such liaisons, once a son and heir had been produced, were quite acceptable.'

Kitty gasped. 'You don't mean that she – he – they . . .?'

Edward shrugged. 'I've never been quite sure. If there has been anything more than a close friendship, then they have been very discreet.'

Kitty sighed. 'It's sad, isn't it? And for your father too. I mean . . .' she hesitated and then whispered, 'do – do you know, about when my mother worked at the Manor?'

He nodded. 'I knew a little, but recently I had to find out more.' He squeezed her hand and leaned towards her to whisper impishly, 'I couldn't risk us being brother and sister, now could I?'

Kitty gave a low chuckle and blushed. 'No, oh no.'

She looked around the room but could see neither her own mother nor Henry Franklin. As if reading her thoughts, Edward said, 'I think they've slipped away to the library, just to talk and catch up on all the years, you know. Don't begrudge them a little time together.'

'I don't. Oh I don't,' she said swiftly. 'It's just that I've been feeling so guilty about my mother – believing Johnnie is her grandson.'

'Don't tell her yet, especially not today. Maybe when we have presented her with a child of our own, a child who will be truly her grandchild, perhaps then, eh?'

Kitty nodded, feeling a lump in her throat. 'You're right.'

'Of course I am.' He kissed her and she drew back.

'People will see . . .'

'I want them to see, Mrs Edward Franklin, just how very much I love you. Come . . .' He took the plate she was holding and set it down on a small side table and then tucked her hand through his arm. 'It's time we were on our way to start our honeymoon.'

They moved through the guests saying goodbye, until they came to Miriam.

By her side, carefully carrying a plate piled high with sandwiches, was Johnnie.

'Johnnie . . .' Kitty bent towards him, 'we're leaving now. You go home with Grannie Clegg and be a good boy. We won't be away long and then . . .'

'I'll be fine, Mam.' His piping voice carried clearly around the room. 'Mrs Harding says I may stay here, with her, if you'll let me. She says she'll teach me to ride a pony. Do say you'll let me, Mam.'

Miriam rested her hands lightly on the boy's shoulders. Kitty felt Miriam watching her face. Softly, she said, 'Please say yes, Kitty. It would mean a great deal to me.'

There was nothing Kitty could do, today of all days, except nod her agreement but the look of adoration on Johnnie's young face as he gazed up at Miriam turned Kitty's blood to ice.

Fifty-Six

She was happy, Kitty told herself a dozen times a day. She had a wonderful husband who adored her. They lived in a small house on Sir Ralph's estate and Edward was now his estate manager. And wonder of wonders, she even had a small staff of servants so that if she wished she could be idle from morning till night and not feel guilty about it. Johnnie was growing into a fine young man. Edward treated him as his own son and, in turn, Johnnie now seemed to think of him as his father.

They never spoke of his real father, for Jack Thorndyke had disappeared from the district taking his threshing set and Milly Clegg with him.

Her father, John Clegg, had struck the entry of Milly's birth from the frontispiece in the family Bible and had decreed that her name should never again be mentioned in his hearing. Kitty, it seemed, had been forgiven. Now that she was Mrs Edward Franklin, her father strutted about his station platform, his chest puffed out like a pouter pigeon, telling anyone who would listen about his daughter who was married into the Franklin family and connected to Sir Ralph at Nunsthorpe Hall.

Two years after their marriage, Kitty presented Edward with a son, Joe. The following year their daughter, Amy, arrived and then another son, whom they named Harry after Edward's father.

She had wondered, a little fearfully, whether when she

held her own child in her arms, she would feel any differently towards Johnnie. She need not have worried. Her love for the boy was deep-rooted and he could not be supplanted by any new arrival, not even her own flesh and blood.

Kitty had everything she had ever dreamed of, so why did she still not dare to let herself be completely happy?

She knew why. She knew very well why. There was still a niggling doubt, a tiny cloud that refused to go away. For every time Miriam visited their house, or Johnnie went to the Hall to ride the pony, which Kitty suspected was kept entirely for him, the cloud grew darker and more ominous.

It was on Johnnie's fifteenth birthday that Edward came into the sitting room and closed the door so that no one else might overhear their conversation. As he came slowly towards her, his face sombre and his eyes troubled, Kitty knew that the storm had broken and the heavens were about to open and sweep her away.

'My darling . . .' He took her hands in his. 'Miriam has asked me to talk to you.'

She pulled away from him and stepped back, putting her hands over her ears. 'No, no,' she cried. 'I don't want to hear it. I won't listen. She's not having him. Not after all these years. He's mine. Just because we've children of our own now, nothing has changed. He's still my boy. He still doesn't know. Think what it could do to him.'

Edward put his arms about her, but she resisted, keeping herself stiff and unyielding in his embrace.

'Dearest, just listen. He will have to be told some day and the longer we leave it, the harder it becomes. Besides, Miriam doesn't want to take him away from you. At least . . .' Here even Edward hesitated, for the truth was that Miriam wanted to acknowledge the boy as her son and openly take him to live with her at the Hall. He had known how desperately hurt Kitty would be, for he now knew, better than anyone else other than Jack Thorndyke and Kitty herself, just how much she had suffered all these years right from the moment she had first taken Miriam's newborn baby into her arms. Whatever mistakes she had made, his darling Kitty had paid a thousandfold since. And through it all, her love for the boy had been the bedrock of all her actions.

And now Johnnie's real mother wanted to claim him.

'Come and sit down, Kitty.'

'No, no,' she struggled against him. 'No, I don't want to listen.'

But at last he calmed her enough to have her sit beside him. With his arm about her and her head resting against his shoulder, Edward talked quietly to her, all the while feeling her whole body trembling against him.

'Miriam has changed. Guy's death – and her part in it – affected her deeply. She wants to do something with her life. She found some sort of solace in her efforts during the war, but that was over long ago. She cannot,' he gave a wry smile, 'even return to her Votes for Women campaign for it seems that particular war is won too. She's very lonely and feels there's no purpose to her life.'

Kitty hiccuped miserably, but said nothing. Edward's arm tightened about her. 'She has told Sir Ralph everything and he . . .' Here Edward paused momentarily and his voice dropped a tone as if becoming deeper with emotion. 'He being the wonderful man he is, has been very understanding and has said that he's willing to treat the boy as his own grandson – the grandson he can never have now.'

Slowly Kitty raised her swollen face to look into Edward's eyes. After a long silence she said flatly, 'That's it, then.' And she added with bitterness, 'I can't fight Sir Ralph and all his money.'

'Kitty, Kitty,' Edward remonstrated gently, 'that's not like you. Besides,' he said, forcing a lighter, teasing note into his voice, 'money doesn't come into it, for don't you know that I intend to be a millionaire one day and dress you in diamonds from head to toe?'

Kitty tried to smile. She knew Edward would do just that, if he could. She knew that he would do anything in the world to make her happy and yet here he was, asking her to do the very thing that would bring her utter desolation.

She sniffed and a sob welled in her throat. He held out a clean white handkerchief.

'Johnnie will hate me, despise me for what I did. He'll think – like Jack did – that I used him, a tiny baby, to make Jack marry me. And I didn't, I didn't.' Fresh tears spurted, then she added with supreme honesty, 'Well, not entirely.'

'Of course you didn't,' Edward soothed and secretly cursed the very name of Jack Thorndyke yet again.

'We'll have to explain everything very carefully to Johnnie. Will you entrust that to me, my dearest, because I think . . .' Even as he spoke, a noise sounded outside and they heard Johnnie's voice.

'Please come in. She'll be in the sitting room. She won't mind, honest . . .'

The door opened and the youth, who was almost a young man now, stood there. 'Mam, Mrs Harding's here. We've been riding – right up through the woods and . . .' He stopped as he became aware of the scene before his eyes, of Edward's arm about his mother's shoulder, of her swollen and red-eyed face. 'Why, Mam, what's the matter? Whatever's wrong? It's not one of the young 'uns, is it?'

His immediate concern for his younger brothers and sister touched her and she put out a trembling hand towards him. He covered the space between them and dropped to his knees in front of her, his guest forgotten. But Kitty glanced beyond him to see Miriam standing there in the doorway. Their eyes met and all that had happened since the day that Kitty had become Miss Miriam Franklin's maid was between them in that instant.

'I . . .' Miriam began and made as if to turn away. 'I won't stay. I – I'll go . . .'

Edward stood up. 'No, Miriam, come in. Perhaps it would be better if you were here.'

He turned to look down at Kitty, the question obvious in his eyes, seeking her permission to tell the boy here and now while they were all present.

It had come so fast, this moment she had dreaded, and she wasn't ready. She needed more time. Desperately she scrabbled through her mind for some excuse, any excuse to put off the awful moment.

Yet there was none. She had known, deep in her heart, that this day would come. She could no longer hold back the inevitable.

She nodded and bent her head, twisting the white handkerchief in her hands. A little embarrassed now, Johnnie was patting her hand, not knowing quite what to say, while Edward ushered Miriam to a chair beside the fire and called for the little parlourmaid to bring some tea for them all.

When they were all seated, Edward began with great gentleness. 'Johnnie, you are on the threshold of manhood and there are things you should know before – before perhaps you hear something from the wrong people. Country folk have long memories . . .' He paused and cleared his throat, while Johnnie stared at him with his dark blue eyes, eyes that were so like Jack Thorndyke's. And yet the boy was not like his father in character. There was a gentleness and a maturity about him that had never been evident in Threshing Jack's fickle nature.

'I don't want to speak ill of anyone, Johnnie, for as you grow you will learn that love, infatuation – call it what you will – in the young can bring both great pleasure and, sometimes, enormous heartache. Your father . . .' They all heard the hesitation and Kitty, and no doubt Miriam too, knew just how much Edward struggled to be fair in his telling of the story. 'In his youth your father was a very handsome chap and, before his accident, a fun-loving man who – whom the girls all loved.'

Johnnie, seeing how Edward was having difficulty, smiled and said, 'Oh I know. A lad at school once told me that his older sister was probably my half-sister. "I suppose," he said, "she's half-sister to both of us ain't she, 'cos my dad's not her real dad, yours is." '

The three adults in the room glanced at each other, and Kitty whispered, 'When was this, Johnnie? You never told me.'

'Oh years ago, Mam, not long after you got married. You know what kids are, and of course I didn't tell you. I didn't want you to be hurt.'

Kitty felt tears prickle her eyelids yet again and she brushed them aside. Really, she thought, impatient with herself, I don't seem to be able to do anything but cry.

Johnnie was looking towards Edward again, waiting.

'Well, you see, your mother – um . . .' Here the story was getting very difficult, very delicate. Edward gestured with his hand towards Kitty, for at this moment, to Johnnie, she was his mother. 'Fell in love with Jack Thorndyke, but . . . but she was not the only one.' His glance went across the small space to his sister. 'You see, Johnnie, so did Miriam – Mrs Harding.'

There was silence in the room and Kitty watched as the

boy's glance went from first one to the other. 'I don't understand,' he said at last. 'What are you trying to tell me?'

Miriam leaned forward and said softly, 'Johnnie – I'm your mother – your real mother.'

The boy's eyes widened and his lips parted a little.

'I too thought I was in love with Jack Thorndyke and I – I became pregnant by him. I was sent away. No one knew, not my father, not even Edward then. Only my own mother and – and my maid, Kitty, knew. We – Kitty and I, that is – stayed away until after you were born and then, when we returned, everyone thought you were Kitty's.'

They could all see that the boy was struggling to understand, to take in and to come to terms with what he was being told.

Gently, trying to make it less painful, Edward said, 'Try to imagine how it was for a young girl like Miriam. Our father – you know what he's like . . .'

The boy nodded.

'Then you can guess how he would have – well – I don't quite know what he would have done.' Here brother and sister exchanged an understanding look.

'I do,' Miriam said quietly. 'I was the apple of his eye. He would probably have killed me, and most certainly he would have cast me off. And besides . . .' Now it was Miriam's turn to twist her fingers together. 'I am trying to be honest with you, Johnnie. It's important that we should all be honest. I – I have to admit that when you were born, I didn't want you. Didn't want to have anything to do with you. I would have put you up for adoption, given you away, anything, just to be able to return to my girlhood and forget that your birth had ever happened. And, but for Kitty, that would have happened.'

Now the boy's glance came slowly round to look at her

and Kitty trembled afresh, fearing to see censure in his eyes. But there was only a surprisingly detached kind of curiosity. 'Why? Why did you take me then?'

'I loved Jack,' she said simply. 'I couldn't bear to think of his son being given away to complete strangers. But then, when I held you, it was as much for you as for Jack or myself. More really, for I loved you from that very first moment you slipped into the world. It was as if you *were* mine.' She swallowed painfully, knowing that now she must take up the story. 'When we came back my family were very upset, believing that it was me who had given birth out of wedlock. For a long time my father would have nothing to do with me, although my mother was more understanding.' She paused a moment wondering whether to explain why, but decided not. Time enough another day for that particular skeleton.

'And my father? Jack Thorndyke? What about him?'

Kitty blushed at the telling, knowing how it must hurt Edward too, but it had to be said. 'I told him you were his son, though I never, ever actually said you were mine, only – only led him – and everyone else – to believe that to be the case by – by, oh what's the word . . .?'

'By implication,' Edward said softly.

She glanced at him gratefully and went on, 'Yes, that's it. By implication. But – but when he – he touched me, he knew I hadn't given birth. He said . . .' Her voice faded and she lowered her head almost in shame. 'He said he'd lain with plenty of women who'd had bairns, some of them his and he – he just knew.' There was silence and then she added more strongly, 'And then he guessed just whose child you were.'

Kitty heard a gasp and looked up to see Miriam's startled face. 'He knew? Even then?' Astonishment was in her tone.

Kitty nodded. 'He said if I stayed with him, kept house for him and worked for him, he'd keep the secret. I lived in terror for years, thinking that if I did the slightest thing wrong he'd – he'd tell.'

'My God!' Miriam let out a most unladylike oath. 'He's blackmailed you all these years, Kitty, and you let him?'

'What could I do? At first I still – you know, felt something for him – but slowly, the way he treated me killed any love I had for him. Then I only stayed because of Johnnie. I thought he should be with his father. And when Jack had his accident, well, I couldn't leave him then, could I? He really did need me for a while.'

'Huh, not for long,' Miriam said scathingly. 'From what I hear he played the part of the wounded hero to all the women between here and Timbuktu. Even making out to some who didn't know him, that he'd been wounded in the war.'

Kitty sighed. 'I guessed as much.'

They had been talking almost between themselves, forgetting that Johnnie and Edward were in the room. But then, together, they looked at the boy.

'So, Johnnie, what now?' Miriam said with some of the vigour and directness that Kitty remembered so well from her youth. She allowed herself a wistful smile. Miss Miriam had not changed so completely. She still liked her own way and she wanted her own way now. She wanted her son.

The boy was looking puzzled. 'I don't understand?'

'I want you to come and live with me at the Hall. Sir Ralph knows everything and . . .'

Johnnie was shaking his head. 'It's very kind of you, Mrs Harding, but—'

'But nothing,' she said quite sharply. 'Johnnie, I'm your mother.'

'I understand that, Mrs Harding – Mother.' The word

came awkwardly to his lips and hearing it, Kitty's heart contracted. But at his next words, words she could hardly believe she was hearing, tears filled her eyes.

'I don't mean to be ungrateful, or to hurt you in any way, because to tell you the truth, I've been fascinated by you for a long time. Even from being quite a little boy.' He glanced towards Kitty and Edward and smiled mischievously. 'I seem to remember being found in the hayloft at the Hall once, because I'd gone to see the pretty lady. And now . . .' His gaze was again turned to feast upon Miriam's lovely face as he added softly, 'And now I find that you're my mother.'

There was a long pause and, in the silence, Kitty held her breath. Then Johnnie cleared his throat and said, 'Of course I'd like us to be close, really I would, but . . .' Now he took Kitty's hand into his own and, with an old-fashioned gesture of courtesy and love, he held it to his cheek. 'But this is me mam. She's the one who's always loved me, the one who's brought me up and, by the sound of it, suffered a lot because of me. So, I hope you'll understand if I say that I want to stay with her and . . .' he looked directly at Edward, 'the man I really think of now as me dad.'

Kitty saw the conflicting emotions on Miriam's face, could see – and understand – her struggle. She found she was holding her breath, waiting for the inevitable outburst, the red rage that she had witnessed so often.

But Miriam swallowed hard and her voice was husky as she said, 'I understand. Truly I do. And though I'm – I'm desperately disappointed, I – admire your strength and your loyalty.' She looked towards Kitty and caught and held her gaze. 'It's no more than your mother richly deserves for her devotion to you.'

Kitty's lips parted in a little gasp. 'Oh Miriam,' she

whispered. 'Miriam.' It was all she could say, for in those few words Miriam had acknowledged Kitty's sacrifice and put another's feelings before her own desires.

But for Kitty, even through the hardest times, it had never been a sacrifice. It had all been for the love of the tiny baby boy.

Kitty leaned her head against Johnnie's shoulder and wept again, but now her tears were tears of joy and thankfulness. He was still hers, this boy whom she had loved with such devotion.

Then a comical look came on to Johnnie's face as he stared at Edward. 'Oh heck, I've just realized. You're my uncle. What on earth am I going to call you?'

Edward put his hand on the boy's shoulder and there was a catch in his voice as he said, 'Dad will do just fine – *son*.'

Suddenly the four of them were all laughing together.

Epilogue

'Gran? Grannie Franklin?'

The bedroom door opened and Clare's merry face appeared around it. '*There* you are.'

The girl, sixteen years and one day old, came into the room, closing the door softly behind her. She tiptoed across the thick, fitted carpet just in case the old lady might be dozing. But Kitty Franklin smiled up into the blue eyes. Clare smiled back and flopped down on to the floor, resting her arms on her grandmother's lap. 'What are you doing, hiding away up here? The party's about to start. Mother and Auntie Amy are flapping in the kitchen, worrying that the potatoes are overdone, or that the sprouts aren't done enough, and Dad's struggling to open the champagne.' She paused and then searched the lined face. 'You are all right, aren't you, Gran?'

The wrinkled hand rested briefly upon the girl's springy black curls, but the voice was vigorous, still youthful even. 'Of course I am. I just came up to have a few moments to myself.' Her eyes hazed. 'Just to remember, you know.'

The girl said gently, 'Of course, you must have a lot of memories. Especially on a day like today.'

Kitty nodded. 'Oh yes. A lot of memories, dear.'

As if reading her thoughts, Clare said, 'Grannie Harding's arrived.' She chuckled and leaned forward, sharing a secret. 'I'm surprised you didn't hear the commotion.'

Kitty's smile broadened and she tapped Clare playfully

on the nose. 'Naughty girl,' she murmured, but then she, too, leaned forward, a glint of mischief in her eyes. 'I did. Why do you think I'm up here?'

Clare giggled and their two foreheads touched in a gesture of affection.

'I suppose I'd better come down and welcome her, then,' Kitty said, leaning back again but making not the slightest effort to move.

'I am lucky, you know,' Clare said suddenly.

'Well, yes,' her grandmother agreed, teasing. 'You're spoilt to death by your doting parents and your grandad.' She chuckled. 'And I suppose I'm as guilty as any of them. But why, particularly?'

'Having *three* grannies instead of the usual two.' Impulsively, the girl knelt up and kissed the weathered cheek. 'And they're all such sweet old dears.'

Kitty chuckled. 'We weren't always such "sweet old dears" as you put it. At least, not your Grannie Harding and me. I can't speak for your mother's mother, because I've only known her for a few years.'

'Well,' Clare persisted, 'you're a couple of darlings now, anyway.'

'Why, thank you, dear,' Kitty bowed her head graciously, her eyes twinkling. 'I think your Grannie Harding would be most amused by that description.'

There were no secrets, not now, not in this generation. Clare was Johnnie's daughter, his only child, and the girl knew that her blood grandmother was Miriam Harding, but Kitty and Edward had always been Gran and Grandad.

'I know I shouldn't ask,' the girl began a little hesitantly. 'Not today of all days. Not on your golden wedding day . . .'

She paused until Kitty prompted, 'It's all right, dear. It's all so long ago and I've had such a wonderfully happy life with your grandad . . .' Her face clouded for a moment, 'Except, of course, when your uncle Joe was killed in the war.'

Joe, Kitty and Edward's elder son, had been shot down in 1943 leaving a wife and tiny baby, Eddie.

'You brought Eddie up, didn't you?'

Kitty nodded, smiling fondly. 'Joe's wife, Pearl, was only twenty when he was killed and she came to live here at the Manor with us.'

'She married a GI after the war, didn't she, and emigrated to America?' Clare said, seeking confirmation of the family stories she had been told.

Kitty nodded.

'And left Eddie with you?'

'Yes,' Kitty said simply, remembering how she had felt at the time. Another baby for her to love and to bring up as her own. In a way, she had been grateful to Pearl for leaving him in her care, even though she hadn't wanted to see the child's mother go.

'And now he's all grown up,' Clare grinned. '*And* courting.'

Kitty smiled. 'It looks like it. I'm glad he brought his girlfriend today. Pat seems a nice girl, doesn't she?'

Clare nodded enthusiastically. 'Oh yes. I do hope there's going to be a family wedding soon and maybe you'll be a *great*-grandmother. Wouldn't that be something?'

'It would indeed,' Kitty murmured.

Clare scrambled to her feet and stood by the window. 'Look, they're all down there in the garden. Aren't you going down? Grandad keeps glancing up at this window as if he's looking for you.'

Kitty smiled gently at the thought, but said, 'What was it you wanted to ask me, dear? We seemed to get on to something else.'

'I just wondered – what happened to my real grand-father?'

'To Threshing Jack?'

'Is that what they called him?'

Kitty nodded and explained. Then she shook her head and murmured, 'Poor Milly. Poor, poor Milly.'

'Auntie Milly?' the girl asked. 'But she lives in a cottage near the station, doesn't she? What had she got to do with him?'

Kitty glanced up, surprised. 'Don't you know? Oh, I thought you knew the whole story.'

'I thought I did, but obviously not that bit. What about Auntie Milly?'

'She ran away with him. Full of high hopes that he would marry her . . .' Her voice dropped. 'Just like I'd had once.' She cleared her throat and continued more strongly. 'She came back here years later, nothing but skin and bone and so dreadfully ill. It took us six months' nursing to get her right. And, of course, Jack'd never married her like he promised. Poor Milly,' she said again.

'Didn't she ever get married, then? To anyone, I mean?'

Kitty shook her head. 'No. She stayed with us for a while until she was well again. My father would have nothing to do with her, you see. Then she went back into service. She was at Nunsthorpe Hall at first. Miriam was very kind and gave her a job. Then she went to work in a big house in Derbyshire as a cook. It was only when she retired that she came back to Tresford again.'

'Is she coming today?'

'Oh yes, she'll be here.'

'But what happened to Threshing Jack?'

'Goodness only knows,' she began tartly, but then there was a tiny hint of wistfulness as she added, 'I don't suppose we'll ever know now.' She stared out of the window. 'You know, Clare, you never quite forget your first love. Of course, it's the last love that really counts. The one that endures down the years, the faithfulness, the devotion – that's the one that matters, but you never forget the love of your youth when all the days were warm and golden and the nights . . .' Her voice faded away and the old lady closed her eyes.

Afraid that she had asked too much, Clare moved from the window, bent and kissed her grandmother's forehead again. 'I'm sorry, Gran. I shouldn't have asked you. Not today.'

Kitty opened her eyes and clasped the girl's hand. 'It's all right, really. You run along and tell your grandad I'll be down in a moment.'

'All right.'

The door banged behind her and Kitty heard her feet clattering down the stairs.

Young ones, she thought with indulgent affection. They always seemed so noisy. What would dear old Mrs Grundy have said?

She rested her head against the back of the chair and let her gaze wander through the open window into the garden below.

They were all there now, enjoying the last of the day's sunshine as the shadows lengthened in the walled garden before they came indoors for the dinner party in honour of Edward and her.

Her gaze rested on their second son, Harry. He was talking earnestly to his father, beating one fist against the palm of his other hand as he emphasized every word. He was planning to stand for Parliament at the next election.

Well, if he gets in, Kitty thought, he'll make a good politician. He has a lot of his aunt Miriam in him. Kitty's smile broadened. Her and her Votes for Women. Just look at all the trouble that had caused.

And she'd gone on causing trouble or, at least, always being in the thick of it. Miriam had driven an ambulance in the blitz in London and in the early 'fifties she had gone out to Korea. Even now, she could be relied upon to join a demonstration if she believed the cause to be worthwhile.

Kitty watched her walking down the long path towards Edward, kissing his cheek and then linking her arm through his to stand beside him, listening to Harry holding forth.

Then Kitty's gaze came around to Johnnie. It didn't seem possible that he was in his mid-fifties, with hair as white as Edward's. He was down there now, with all of them, sitting on the seat at the very end of the garden. Contentedly puffing on his pipe, his arms folded across his chest and his long legs stretched out in front of him, he was watching the younger children, Harry's three and Amy's two, playing a lively game of tag.

'Now come on, Dad.' Even from here, she could hear Johnnie's deep voice plainly. 'Come and sit down. When Harry gets on his soap box, it's enough to wear anyone out.'

It still gave Kitty a thrill to hear him call Edward 'Dad' with such ease. She watched Edward move towards the seat and pretend to collapse on to it, breathless, his hand on his chest.

She leaned forward, suddenly concerned, the smile frozen on her lips. And then she saw him catch sight of her at the window of his old room and he raised his fingers to his lips and blew her a kiss.

She waved in return and relaxed once more. He was all right, he was only teasing them.

She half closed her eyes and leaned her head back

against the cushion. Their happy voices came to her and she imagined they came from the stackyard beyond the wall. She heard the sound of a car and in her memory the sound changed to the throbbing of a threshing engine. She could almost smell the dust and the chaff floating in the air, drifting in through her open window. And she remembered the tall, handsome man, his black hair shining in the sunlight and a glint in his eye for a pretty girl . . .

And she was young again.

The Buffer Girls

Putting the shine back into
Sheffield in the aftermath of war

It is 1920 in the Derbyshire Dales. The Ryan family are adjusting to life now that the war is over. Walter has returned home a broken man and so it falls to his son and daughter, Josh and Emily, to keep the family candle-making business going.

The Ryan children grew up with Amy Clark, daughter of the village blacksmith, and Thomas 'Trip' Trippett, whose father owns a cutlery business in Sheffield. Romance blossoms for Josh and Amy while Emily falls in love with Trip, but she is unsure if the feeling is mutual. Martha Ryan is fiercely ambitious for her son and so she uproots her family to Sheffield, but all Josh wants is to continue the family business and marry Amy. As the Ryans do their best to adapt to city life, their friendly neighbour, Lizzie, helps Emily find employment as a Buffer Girl polishing cutlery at a local factory.

It turns out that it is Emily who is best equipped to forge a career but, as time goes on, problems and even dangers arise that the Ryan family could not possibly have foreseen.

FOR MORE ON

MARGARET DICKINSON

sign up to receive our

SAGA NEWSLETTER

Packed with **features, competitions, authors' and readers' letters** and **news of exclusive events,** it's a 'must-read' for every Margaret Dickinson fan!

Simply fill in your details below and tick to confirm that you would like to receive saga-related news and promotions and return to us at **Pan Macmillan, Saga Newsletter, 20 New Wharf Road, London, N1 9RR.**

NAME

ADDRESS

POSTCODE

EMAIL

☐ *I would like to receive saga-related news and promotions (please tick)*

You can unsubscribe at any time in writing or through our website where you can also see our privacy policy which explains how we will store and use your data.

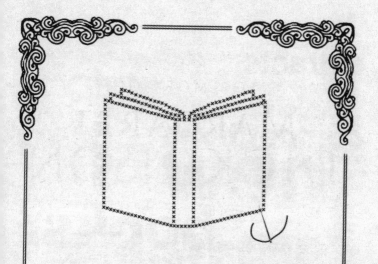

At Bello, we believe in the timeless power of books, and our extensive list of classic fiction has something for everyone. Whether you want to indulge in a heart-warming tale of life in the Hebrides from Lillian Beckwith's *The Hills is Lonely*, read a classic Yorkshire saga from award-winning author Brenda Jagger, or escape to the scandalous world of Renaissance Italy in Sarah Bower's *The Sins of the House of Borgia*, we've got the book for you.

BELL◉

panmacmillan.com/bello

 @bellobooks  bellobooks